These Truths

These Truths
The Greatest Challenge Ever Taken

Lyle Fugleberg

iUniverse LLC
Bloomington

THESE TRUTHS
THE GREATEST CHALLENGE EVER TAKEN

iUniverse books may be ordered through booksellers or by contacting:

iUniverse
1663 Liberty Drive
Bloomington, IN 47403
www.iuniverse.com
1-800-Authors (1-800-288-4677)

ISBN: 978-1-4759-9601-2 (sc)
ISBN: 978-1-4759-9602-9 (hc)
ISBN: 978-1-4759-9603-6 (e)

Library of Congress Control Number: 2013911091

Printed in the United States of America.

iUniverse rev. date: 8/27/2013

PRELUDE

(Summary of EASTER ARMAGEDDON)

John Anderson struggles in a forest of incredible complexity, seeking the source of the babble he hears. He's thirsty with a throat so parched his words are croaked whispers. He's also lost and doesn't know why he is where he is, his last remembrances being contentions at home followed by a hike to his favorite fishing hole.

The situation gets worse as he senses danger all about him. He remembers that Daniel Boone had remarked in his day *the woods are so wild and horrid that it is impossible to behold them without terror.* Then he loses his clothing, leaving him naked and alone in an Eden-like hell far removed from civilization.

Fortunately, John's an Eagle Scout and avid camper. Drawing from those experiences, he survives, aided by recollections that seem to emerge in response to times of need. Those recollections, however, are from another world in time and place, and while helpful, serve to deepen the mystery … It comes to seem as if the memories were more programming than reality. Months pass. Breaking from the shelter where he's been marooned, John finally encounters people—people small in stature like Otzi the Iceman, as well as the *Denas Atjahahni*, a primitive society hidden in the forest.

He becomes acclimated to their simple lifestyle—slow-moving days with little awareness of time.

Then an incident triggers a major recall—a recollection that brings John through college, internship in engineering, environmental

v

awareness, and Annie. But there still isn't a connection, which reinforces the feeling that all of them are some kind of programming. With the riddle remaining unresolved, John comes to believe there must be a reason for his being in this world, a reason that might have to do with ecological preservation. This seems most logical because the people in the world of those recollections, the twenty-first century, had put that world in peril due to its disregard of other elements in nature. The reason, which becomes a mission, is therefore to prevent what happened on Easter Island, and to which the world-at-large appeared to be repeating at that time, for the *Atjahahni* and all other nations that can be found. To do this John needs to establish peace and sustainability in a manner that will be self-perpetrating.

John proceeds in the only way he knows. In the process there's family and challenge and intrigue and tragedy. Twenty years later, progress leads to a special place called Pangaea selected for a Gathering, where assemblies from each of the scattered nations convene.

Unfortunately, before the assemblies can even get settled, there's disaster. The disaster is caused by a maelstrom—the mountain remnants of a category-five hurricane that spirals out of the Gulf of Mexico—combined with superstition and treachery. This combination creates a wild-eyed, armed and chanting mob that moves like a pyroclastic cloud to destroy John, who they feel by being tall must be an evil giant who has violated the gods and caused the storm.

Furthermore, and complicating the situation, an incident just before the mob arrives unlocks the final chapter in John's life in the twenty-first century, and stuns him. This recollection describes Armageddon. It also verifies that John is indeed on a mission—a mission, however, much broader than he had envisioned ... a mission *to start mankind all over again, this time in harmony with all of creation.* In other words ... be resurrected, as in Easter. To have any chance of success in this requires over a dozen others—all, like John, carefully selected for the purpose ... but all, unlike John, or so he thinks, slumbering in incubation after thousands of years in a place deep in the earth somewhere near where he first heard the babble.

John's son Matthew, as pure a prince as ever born, intervenes to save his father, who is still reeling from the latest revelation, and is killed. When the carnage that follows is over, John climbs to the nearest crest to rail at the heavens for what has happened.

Years later it would be written …

After all that had reviled him
and had killed his only son,
had been slain by his hand,
John, the giant of the Americas,
climbed high into the rocks;
Where he railed to the tempest…
What have I done
that this should happen, he cried.
And the heavens rumbled and flashed.
And they spoke thus in anger
until John gave homage;
The Lord then bathed John in thunderbolts
that lighted the sky
and burned the trees
and formed a cloud
that covered over him;
But when the cloud cleared,
John still stood, his hair now white.
And so it went that John
came back down and stood before them.
And as he stood
an arc of rainbow,
the brightest ever seen,
framed about him against the dark of the storm.
And the Atjahahni
who came from the south,
and the Njegleshito from the east,
and the Anlyshendl from the north,
and the Bjarla-shito from the west,
All bowed down before him.

John has succeeded … in a way … but the cost has been awful.

GUIDE TO NAMES IN EASTER ARMAGEDDON

Protagonists

John Anderson ... Civil engineer; selected to be the first of the Chosen to be resurrected at the Cryogenics Center into the new world.

Ann Hollesen ... Ecologist; organizer of the Easter Armageddon Conference; marries John in the world of the twenty-first century.

Gary Edson ... Medical student; hiking companion; John's best friend from early days of scouting.

The Chosen ... Fifteen young adults, including John, Ann and Gary, who are pledged to the Greatest Challenge ever Taken.

John Anderson's family

Robert Alton A. ... Father; Lutheran minister; community leader.

Mark ... Civil engineer; beloved older brother.

Bobby and Sissy ... Mark's children; when the plague nears, they and a number of other tots, are harbored in a food mart in hopes they might survive.

Ann Hollesen's family

Fred and Helen ... Parents

Other key figures in the twenty-first century

Lawrence Smythe ... Creative structural engineer; mentor to John.

Clifton Campbell ... World traveler and investment banker; during a get-away hike, introduces John and Gary to the Easter Armageddon Conference.

Eugene Geoghan ... Engineer friend of Mark; get-away hiker.

Huston Burner ... Billionaire; ecologist; speaker at Conference; creator of the Cryogenics Center.

Reynolds Bascomb ...Greenpeace participant; speaker at Conference; consultant at the Cryogenics Center; Ann becomes his extended family after a tragedy.

Dr. Darby Walker ...Biochemical specialist; medical chief at the Cryogenics Center; nicknamed "Bones"

Atjahahni ... *Nation becoming John's home in the new world, a world thousands of years after the twenty-first century*

Nyaho ...John's first contact in the new world; very perceptive; is thrust into the position of Spirit Man upon the sudden death of Ab Oh jsandata.

Dlahni ... Second contact; strong and steadfast; becomes like a brother to John.

Da-hash-to ... Grand Chieftain; an old and wise leader.

Ab Oh jsandata ...Spirit Man; upon death is succeeded by Nyaho

Braga ...Warrior Chieftain; persuasive and ambitious; kidnaps children, including a young Nshwanji, during a foray north while in his teens.

Ah-ton-jacii ... Sidekick to Braga.

Dresh-na-togl ...Pawn of Braga; John fights to save Nshswanji.

Nshswanji (Willow) ... Becomes wife to John in the new world.

Sara ... First born daughter

Ruth and Naomi ... Twin daughters.

Matthew ... Son; by sixteen year has grown to be almost as tall as John; becomes legendary in his development; is killed at Pangaea.

Mahsja ... Precocious girl; interpreter.

Njegleshito ... *Nation to the east*
Mahacanta ... Grand Chieftain.
Chjenohata ... Young Chieftain; son of Mahacanta; in a lengthy trek with friends, accidently encounters *Atjahahni* girls who are peddling by in canoes; this leads to the first ever interaction between nations, and also to a courtship with Sara, one of the canoers.
Tsjanitca ... Chief; Matthew's killer.

Anlyshendl ... *Nation to the north; birthplace of Nshswanji*
Bren-ta-le-dah ... Grand Chieftain.

Bjarla-shito ... *Nation to the west*

Pangaea ... *At one time all continents of the world were together in a land mass called Pangaea; then they drifted apart to form the world of today. John felt that since the Gathering would bring all nations together, the location of the meeting should be called Pangaea.*

PART ONE

1

Ants

The irregular but generally straight channel, roughly a quarter-inch wide by an equal depth, snaked across the trail, passing beneath John's legs as he sat at the base of a tree atop the beginning spread of its roots. The channel was a busy place, alive with large, red ants, whose legs and antennae were in constant motion.

John bent over, watching the parade as it went by in both directions below him, starting from a series of holes across the far side and disappearing in the humus beyond the tree that served him.

Just look at the little bastards go!

He noted that the heads were about one one-hundredth the size of a human's—about the same proportion of the earth to the sun—yet in that tiny shell was a brain that drove the ant to do all kinds of things. He had seen it all before. When Mark, his older brother, had gotten an ant farm, they had both watched in fascination as the ants—*Pogonomyrmex occidentalis,* the first big word he'd ever memorized, or Western Harvester Ant—tunneled, fed, cleaned and communicated with each other. When Mark wasn't around, he couldn't resist giving the frame a shake and scrambling the whole scene. It was like an early version of EtchASketch.

One thing he noticed then was not only the many different things they could and would do, but that they worked together. He could see that again now. They worked together with the acts of

3

one complementing the acts of another and meeting an objective ... without bickering or fighting!

In contrast the human brain, probably 10,000 times larger in volume, with magnificent capabilities that have led to astounding achievements in a wide variety of interests, can't seem to stop with that. As well as its wonderful workings, the capability also drives men to quarrel, to connive, to be avaricious and jealous, to steal, and even to betray and torture and kill.

John had been well reminded of that the week before. That god-damned storm shouldn't have been such a big deal. He knew of instances in other times and places, that when rains came and calamity resulted—like flooding—people banded together, filled sand-bags and worked to accomplish a common purpose, like ants in the EtchASketch. But that wasn't the case at Pangaea ... and because of the difference a dozen men were returning to dust in the vicinity of the campsites that made up the Gathering. He quickly drove that thought from mind as it was too painful.

*   *   *

When John climbed back down from the heights overlooking the battle site, he'd expected the worst ... after all, the mob's attack had focused on him. Instead, as his eyes adjusted to the shadows, he saw everyone looking at him in a way he didn't understand—as if in awe or reverence. It was like everyone was waiting for him to say something ... something godly ... and give them direction. He'd had a fleeting thought that this was how Nyaho, the Spirit Man, must have felt when his predecessor, Ab Oh jsandata, died suddenly years before.

He had to say something, so after a hesitation that was way too long, he said in a weak voice only those nearest could hear, "The storm has passed." This didn't seem to do much of anything, and, as a result, the eager expressions remained reaching out to him. Then he composed himself, realizing that for some reason he was being exalted, and so repeated "The storm has passed," this time with a resonance that seemed to satisfy.

Only this wasn't enough either. He had had to say more; so after another pause, he said more of the obvious: "Darkness will soon be upon us and there's much to be done. Therefore repair to your camps and go about doing them. Tomorrow we must continue with tending the injured and honoring the dead. Hopefully, by the third day, we can assemble again to do those things for which we've come to this place." If he'd had a bent for the political, he would have taken those few thoughts and stretched them ad infinitum. But he didn't ... and what he said was all that was needed anyway, so after letting the directions sink in, he ended with ... "Now go!"

And so they went.

The Gathering had actually gone pretty well in those next days. It was if some poison had been drained from the different nations, with more open and receptive attitudes remaining. The exchanges were still awkward as there was an abundance of speaking-in-tongues supported by a shortage of interpreters. But patience, benevolence and the strange new regard for John combined to make things work.

Besides the building of trust and respect, there were also several meaningful agreements: one was that there must be mutual acceptance of cultures; another was that there must be peace; and finally there was that regarding Braga, the warrior Chieftain who'd been suspected of many intrigues in the past. It was agreed that Braga was in violation of all their principles and objectives, was guilty of promoting the horror that had been experienced, and was therefore banished, an outcast to all the societies gathered. Furthermore, if seen, that he should be captured and returned to the *Atjahahni* for judgment and punishment ... or justifiably killed. John cringed at the final thought, but the swell of testimony and the emotion resulting from it carried the matter to agreement.

On the last day, after days of idyllic conditions—clear skies and mild breezes that seemed an apology by the spirits for what had happened—the finale that had been intended actually happened. Special meals were prepared in each of the camps, the varied citizenry then circulating and intermingling and sampling ... and developing a semblance of rapport.

When the nations broke camp to start their long ways back, it was with sadness, as if a parting of old friends. The reality was that only a little over a week had passed, but the mutual experiences of maelstrom and frenzy and tragedy, followed by shared sorrows and healing, seemed to do the work of years. There was a particular bond among those who'd been a part of the channel-cutting to drain the flooded quadrangle where the Gathering's activities had been planned. There men from all nations had joined in an almost impossible task under abominable conditions, and yet had succeeded. Since then, with each of them, there was a certain glow as their eyes met, rekindling what had been shared. The same was true for those in that frail front line formed in the mud to quell the madness of the mob.

Most of the dead and injured were from the *Bjarla-shito*, who'd been inspired to act because of goading by Braga ... but none of the nations were spared. Among the *Atjahahni*, beside Matthew, there were many with cuts and bruises and broken bones. John's most visible hurt was a cut that crossed from above his brow to half-way down his cheek. Nyaho had been pinned against the rocks and pummeled, resulting in, among other things, broken ribs. The most serious injury was to old Da-hash-to, who'd been trampled in the frail first line he and other Chieftains had formed, suffering a broken hip. Like Nyaho, he stoically participated in the sessions of the final days; but since his movements and effectiveness were seriously compromised, he passed leadership and its symbols—a crude scepter; and a necklace of bear claws and canary feathers surrounding an amulet on which an impressive array of gemstones had been set—on to Dlahni. Dlahni accepted the responsibilities the actions represented, but only for the moment, refusing the symbols and wishing Da-hash-to a speedy recovery until he could resume his rightful place.

For the return home, the *Atjahahni* divided their delegation into two groups—those who would canoe the lake, and those who would walk the trail—generally the way they had made the trip northward. Dlahni led the fleet of canoes, taking Nyaho and Da-hash-to along in what was intended to be as quick a trip as possible. Among the reasons were reporting to an anxious nation the results of the Gathering, and getting the injured home to better care.

John chose to be a part of the baggage train on the trail. The trail, as it wound its way through the forest, was longer and more arduous, but John, much like Clifton Campbell, a fellow hiker eons before, wanted to get away. A long walk in the forest would do that, and might help to heal as well.

There was a great need for that healing. At sunrise the day after battle, the transformational ceremony for Matthew had been held. First thoughts had been to transport the body home, but given the speedy processes naturally following death, and the distances involved, doing so couldn't be considered.

Searching an area south of Pangaea—the direction from which the *Atjahahni* had arrived—a small hill suitable for the purpose was found. Preparations were made and near sundown on the second day the ceremony—first transcendence, the placing of the body on a raised platform over a small fire; then incantations by Nyaho; then conveyance of the body to nature; and finally the hanging of chimes—were conducted in accordance with the *Atjahahni* premise of life, death and regeneration.

Only this time there was a difference. Usually the ceremony was private and restricted to the family. But here, more then ever in the twenty years of experiences, an entire delegation of those that could be spared from other duties attended, feeling as a part of the family. They had watched Matthew grow, the product of the perceived giant among them, and had learned to love him in a way they never realized. Matthew had developed in a manner reflecting the stature of John, becoming agile and strong and a champion in all that he undertook. Only it went beyond athletics. Carefully tutored, he had become gracious and humble, whether with elders or peers, in whatever the situation. In individual contests, he would achieve levels of performance unbelievably outstanding; but in group matters such as races or team sports, he would hold back, and if managing to lead or win, would do so with only a small margin.

He had been a part of all the excursions to other nations, and in doing so had been a strong and positive factor in the impressions conveyed by the *Atjahahni,* which led to the acceptance of the Gathering concept.

When Matthew took the blow and died, all who saw were horrified, and upon recovering, became galvanized in both grief and resolve. They saw how his sacrifice brought John out of his curious stupor, turning him into a demon unlike any that had ever been seen—that would someday be compared to a certain Samson wielding a jawbone. This, followed by the amazing episode on the hill—the thunder and lightning and all—that elevated John to the extent that it had, also elevated Matthew, now to a place among the stars.

So a large group followed the family to the ceremonial site. They watched as Nyaho conducted transcendence, for which he moved with sounds and movements more touching than before ... which in turn inspired everyone else to join in the mournful cadences. After the body had been returned to an earthen platform and decorated, a procession formed for a final viewing, John and Matthew's sisters, Sara and Naomi, being the last. By this time daylight was coming to an end; but before the sun disappeared, by some miracle, its last rays penetrated the forest and illuminated Matthew's face, the pallid, spiritual glow causing a ripple of responses throughout the assembly, adding more detail to what would be the saga of Pangaea.

John cut a lock of hair, then gathered the sisters and left ... the three holding each other together.

*   *   *

Now, days later, John was on the trail, hoping in some way to heal, and at this particular stop, he was watching ants.

2

How?

Ants could only do so much. The entertainment they were providing ended with a thought that made John wince, causing him to spring back and slam into the trunk. The thump caused everyone within hearing to snap to, and in so doing, see his wrinkled brow and clenched jaw, which they understood but couldn't cure. Almost as quickly, they turned back.

The pain ... this time ... was Annie. *How could he not have remembered she was real? How could he not remember their last night together?*

*   *   *

Huston had made his final summary of their mission, and Reynolds had added his comments, and hugs and wishes had been extended all around ... and it was time to rest. A few of the Chosen retired to a bunkhouse, but most snuggled into sleeping bags, bundling in heaps around the campfire, where they watched its soothing effects until one by one they drifted off.

John and Annie went for a walk. The day had been pleasant with the march of seasons showing in a blaze of autumn colors; but now the night and its cool, dry air replaced that kaleidoscope. It was still beautiful, however, because the sky was clear and the stars were brighter at this location of remoteness and elevation than they were accustomed. They didn't have trouble finding their way.

They passed through the yard and past the turn of the hill accented by a rocky mass, then followed wheel tracks in an overgrown grass-scape—a service road extending from the complex—bundling together as pulses of breezes amplified the chill. Without a destination in mind, they zigged and zagged and bounced hips and kicked butts and occasionally twirled, always snapping back as if tied by elastic bands. About a half-mile away they came to a jagged rock wall that shot out of the ground like the head of a spear. Even in the dim detail in shades of gray, there was enough to see that it was out of place among surfaces otherwise gently rounded. The possibility it was a dumping ground of an ice-age glacier came to mind. There was also an expanse of boulders to one side of the spear that covered about half an acre, framing the crest of an incline sloping down and away.

They started up into this expanse, then stopped. With the footing here uncertain even during daylight hours, the risk of falling and being injured was something they didn't want to take. So they sat on a rock and looked at the sky and listened to the night. There were occasional flurries in the air, which they guessed were bats; an owl hooted its unmistakable refrain; running water somewhere below softly gurgled. It was peaceful and it was nice, but it was also sad; without needing to say so, they were mindful that the sights and sounds were possibly the last they would ever experience in this world.

The last conversations with home came to mind.

"Mom and dad were in great spirits," Annie said, wiping a tear as she held back from losing it. "They were so upbeat."

"No mention of the pandemic?"

"No … none at all. In fact when I called they were on the back porch sipping chokecherry wine, looking at the beauty of the newly painted barn. Dad even said farmers from all over the area had come by to admire the job. One even hung a large first-place blue ribbon on the barn door."

"Really?"

"Of course not. He was just funning."

John laughed and shook his head.

"What did you hear?"

"In a way, the same thing. Everyone's so cheerful you can't help wondering if all this is real. The Reverend was just bubbling. He asked question after question about what we were experiencing—the make-up of the group, the incubation complex, the special training we were receiving, and so on—and seeming to marvel at each of the answers.

"He also told how busy they were with church, and how the best of human nature seemed to be coming out in everyone."

"Yes, mom said that too."

"And of course, Mark was Mark. He was in the process of preparing another backyard barbeque, naming all the friends who were coming by and who was bringing what and what games were being planned. It sounded like so much fun.

"With regards to Bobby and Sissy, he mentioned that arrangements were in place and that other details were being added to give the plan a better chance of success. As could be expected, there were many who had come forward wanting to add their children, but at some point they had to say no. The result of this was that similar plans were being started wherever there was the opportunity.

"He also said he'd keep me updated by writing ever so often."

"Mom said she would as well."

"Seems odd doesn't it?"

"Maybe not ... while we're on ice, life on the outside will still be going on."

"I mean, whose going to deliver the mail?"

"Hmmm ... well, as long as there's life, there's responsibility. On the good side of human nature, there's also the wish to hoe to the end of the row."

"John ... what are you doing?"

"Oh nothing." While the conversation ambled along, he'd picked up a sharp stone and started etching on a flat surface beside him, the sound finally registering.

"You're doing something ... What?"

He ignored her, instead scraping away with more intensity until ... "There!"

"Let me see …." She leaned over, squinted, and then rubbed the stone lightly with her finger tips.

"John, it's too dark … What did you carve?"

He teased with a giggle, for which she elbowed him in the ribs …

Squealing as if in great pain, he relented, somewhat, saying, "I'll show you in the morning."

Back in a private room that had been reserved for them—one of the few married couples—they slipped into bed. As they shifted into their customary position of mutual comfort, John had in mind to simply hold Annie, another caution to avoid a last minute injury that could be deadly with what they were to experience in the morrow. Besides, holding her was just fine as he loved to hear breathing change and muscles twitch and relax as she slipped with ultimate trust into somnolence.

Only it didn't work that way. The soft kisses turned to something else and the gentle caresses turned to something else and the soft breathing turned to something else leading to extended violent movements and agonizing sounds … and finally brains all over the place. When a semblance of normalcy was once more restored, the fear that prompted the initial good intentions came flooding back.

"Are you okay, honey?"

She giggled and kissed him softly, "Of course … silly."

*   *   *

How could he not have remembered?

3

Sara

"Dad, are you okay?"

"Oh sure … just remembering things."

She looked at him in that way—not the normal open, trusting, loving way, but somewhat tense, one eye squinted. She parted lips as if to say more, then closed with a weak smile.

Damn, she's so much like Willow.

*   *   *

On the last day of the Gathering, the day of dismantling, packing and leaving, John had fulfilled his promise to Nyaho and Dlahni—a promise to tell. So he had taken them to the cut that drained the lake. He had shown them the semblances of an ancient roadway, and then told them what it meant … in all its detail … about a time so far in the past that it had yet to be measured. They had been stunned, of course, so much so that they hardly spoke. They couldn't envision the kind of world John was describing since there wasn't a common ground with which to make a link. John sensed this, recognizing a new dilemma, which was how to prove that the astounding things he told were true.

And this wasn't the case for just Nyaho and Dlahni; it was as much so for his family, who were probably on to something, or would be soon, and would need to be told, and convinced, as well.

The dilemma really started during the confusion just before the battle, when people were running about in all directions. Dlahni was screaming to get his men in line ... and at John and the group at the dig to get over in back, when all the while the wind blew and rain fell and clouds rumbled and lightning flashed and a demonic mass of humanity chanted and screamed and advanced.

Sara had her own problems at the time. She was in charge of the archers. That part started years before when Willow was killed. Sara was very young then, but she was the oldest; and although she'd been a good athlete, the first of all the *Atjahahni* to swim for instance, she was looked on not only to do well as an archer, but also to lead. All of this wasn't easy, particularly when challenged by the twins, who were right on her heels at every step, driving all of them to levels of excellence that none of them could have achieved otherwise. The accomplishments anchored her in that leadership position, so when the time came for the excursions, she became an essential part of two of them.

At the battle in the flats, she'd been in charge of the archers, and had been like Dlahni, screaming to get the squad in place above and behind the linemen. She hadn't noticed the peculiar state that John was in at the time, but heard about it later from Naomi. She did see Matthew step forward to blunt the attack, and had watched as Braga and Tsjanitca trapped him.

It can't be explained how anyone, who witnesses a horror for which the natural response is to scream and collapse in helpless grief, somehow holds together. Sara did; she steeled against those impulses and held ground, performing her duties like a seasoned veteran. She called her squad's attention to Braga as he threaded his way clear of the melee; then, when he reached Ah-ton-jacii, gave the commands that sent its deadly volleys. Only after the battle was over, and there was no longer a need in the line, did she allow a release of emotion. But then she quickly composed herself to do what had to be done.

Days later, during preparations for departure, she received another call. Dlahni had intended that John travel back by canoe; but John had decided otherwise, substantially changing arrangements. It wasn't that John couldn't manage the effort, because this was really nothing new. It was that now, more than ever before, John was a person of such station that there was a need to protect him. Dlahni, therefore, had to rearrange everything. From the three dozen or so in the baggage train, he formed two security groups, one of which was to be in front of John, who would then be near the center of the train, the other immediately behind. Both groups were directed to be vigilant at all times, and should it be required, to defend John to the death.

Sara was to be in charge of these groups. All of which couldn't have come at a more awkward time for both her and Naomi.

In Sara's case the awkwardness was a budding interest with Chjenohata, the young *Njegleshito* Chieftain.

Chjenohata had organized a group that not only assisted John at the dig, but also joined in the battle, helping to subdue parts of the mob and bring the matter to a close.

But the interest started before then. Four years before he'd been part of the six young hikers who'd secretly explored near the shore opposite the *Atjahahni*, only to be discovered by Sara and her girlfriends who came upon them while canoeing.

The six were caught napping, dropping everything and gawking.

Fortunately the canoes were filled with girls. Had they been boys or men, there could have been posturing or something stupid leading to a conflict. But as it was, the girls glided by, bug-eyed and stunned as well, then turned and left the way they'd come, not realizing what impact they'd made.

What caught Chjenohata's eye was the girl in back of the last canoe to turn around, who happened to be Sara. She seemed to be in charge of the group and less flustered than the rest. When she turned about to leave, she removed a ribbon from her hair, tied it to a branch in the water and waved good-by, flashing a smile that melted all of them. As soon as the girls were out of sight, the young men did what young men do—crossed-eyes, ooh-lah-lahs, swaggers and staggers and the like punctuating their actions. During the clowning Chjenohata had the presence to wade out and retrieve the ribbon, almost drowning in the process.

Then the reality of what happened sunk in, so they quickly packed and left. As for Chjenohata, the memory of Sara stayed with him every step of the way back. This sweet memory wasn't a help at the reception received in the land of the *Njegleshito*, however.

"They saw you?" said his father, Chief Mahacanta. "We told you to stay back and out of sight … we didn't want any trouble."

"Sir, we weren't even close to the lake itself, like that group years ago. We were way back on one of the inlets and were just surprised, that's all."

"Did anyone try to follow?"

"We don't know … we got out of there as fast as we could."

That's about as much as they could tell, so soon the matter quieted down.

Only the quiet didn't last. When a signal fire was first seen on a hill less that two miles away it was as if the world was coming to an end.

"The boys were followed! We're under attack!"

This had never happened before and understandingly there wasn't a plan of action. Everyone seemed to run in circles, grabbing whatever weapons were available, finally grouping in mass waiting for the order to charge.

The order never came. Instead Mahacanta calmed everyone down, sending scouts to first see what the fire was all about. When they returned describing the scene—with a giant, a small man and two girls waiting on a cleared slope, and a few dozen more relaxing on the crest with more girls among them—the panic subsided.

Subsided somewhat. Although the description hardly sounded like a war party preparing to attack, there were still those who wanted to go to battle, being very emotional and chest-thumping with their arguments. Again Mahacanta fought for reason, but in the end settled for a plan that was a compromise. The *Njegleshito* would organize into two wings and would surround the invaders. Then the Chieftains would confront them to see why they had entered their territory. If the response was not proper, then a signal would be given to kill or capture them. And so it went.

As simple as the plan was, however, it was unrehearsed, which meant there was a danger of it going out of control at any time.

The Chieftains weren't any better organized as those on the wings because when they got to the edge of the clearing, they could see what had been reported, but didn't really know what to do next. After a period where everyone was unnerved, Chjenotata came forward with a request. He'd seen that the older girl was the same one who'd left the ribbon, and requested that he be the first to approach them. His reasoning was that since he and his friends had been the cause of the problem, all of them should go forward for whatever was waiting.

Mahacanta nodded and indicated for them to go. Then all fell silent. Ears strained and eyes focused from every tree and vantage point as the boys trudged along ... to a result that had jaws dropping. The confrontation ended up looking more like a reunion with conversation and conviviality and finally even laughter.

So there was no war and the leaders met and all went well.

For Chjenotata the meeting was over way to quickly, because it wasn't long before everyone shook hands in friendship and parted, the *Njegleshito* returning to village while the *Atjahahni* started the long trip back. And she was gone.

But she wasn't forgotten. When he saw her again at the clearing, she was every bit as pretty as the first impression in the canoe, and what memory had pictured of her since then. This impression was immediately amplified as she also proved to be spirited and charming. And when translations revealed she was a champion archer who could put out eyes at 100 paces, he was lost forever.

In the years following he traveled to the *Atjahahni* in accordance with John's invitation; based on his findings of a peaceful nation, he lobbied for and won for the *Negleshito* to participate in the Gathering being planned; and, he worked to plan for the expedition required, including laying out and improving a pathway. For all of these he was elevated to the Council as one of the youngest Chieftains ever to be so honored.

At the conclusion of the Gathering, it was his intention to return by way of the *Atjahahni*, and to finish the trip with Sara as his bride.

With Naomi, a similar situation existed, which was every bit as eminent. She'd spent a year with the *Anlyshendl*, Willow's home, and had not only learned the language and culture, but had also made many friends, including one who was very special. She and La-sa-sena, a sturdy young man who'd also been involved in the dig and the battle, had already planned to make their announcement.

And there was more. In the bustle and confusion of packing and departing, many from the other nations lingered about to see the parties off. Among them were a few from the *Bjarla-shito*, also ones of the dig, who stood by, more than fascinated by not only the Giant, but also by the nation whose young women could go to battle. When they realized how arrangements were being scrambled and that John and the archers were walking, the scales tipped. A few of the more adventurous of them broke from their pack and asked if they could accompany the train. All of these became part of the group that made up the security forces. They were a veritable united nations … as dedicated to the assignment as any could be.

The complications didn't end there. Sara was reminded of the mystery of John's stupor, as reported by Naomi, when she was told of a meeting between John, Nyaho and Dlahni at the dig. Once more there had been observations of shock and actions in stupor.

There was a mystery … and there were questions.

*   *   *

Now Sara was before him and it was obvious she was on to something. He needed to tell all of his family, but wanted to do so when they were together, and when he had a way of convincing them. So for the moment he remained quiet, feeling like a shuttlecock caught in a game of intrigue.

"Well dad," Sara said, breaking the impasse, "I hate to disturb you, but we've got to get going. Everyone's getting antsy to move."

"Antsy … now that's appropriate."

"What?"

"Never mind." With that John got up, careful not to trample his friends.

When the last of the groups had passed the tree and disappeared down the trail, the vicinity settled to its normal … which was *not* one of inactivity. The ants continued doing what ants do, completely unimpressed or unaffected by the traffic; a chipmunk appeared from out of somewhere behind the tree, sniffed, twitched, and in a series of stop and goes, made its way across to disappear on the other side; and then soon after, only a foot from where the chipmunk passed, the leaves layering the ground parted and the head of a black snake appeared. After testing the air with its tongue and interpreting its messages, it slowly moved out, stopped, tested some more, then slithered across to disappear close to where the chipmunk disappeared. Finally, about fifty feet back from where the last group rested, a hand eased a branch back into place, then relaxed the tension on the arrow that had been primed.

4

How?

Left ... right ... left ... right ... eyes on trail ... carefully, carefully ... slip and slide ... climb and drop, climb and drop ... and so it went, mindlessly, monotonously, but in a way, therapeutically. The trail was anything but groomed. It had started a few miles north of the *Atjahahni* village where normal travel ended, then continued in generally a northeasterly direction paralleling the lake until the first major inlet was encountered, after which it ran in every direction at random, finally arriving at Pangaea. As crude as it was, it required a summer-long effort of two squads, who scratched and clawed and chopped with wood and bone and stone and muscle. The lead group tried to select the shortest and easiest route with the least of gradients, and probably did ... but it wasn't apparent ... because the trail went this way and that, doubling back frequently due to elevation changes or obstructions. Bridges were formed in a number of instances—at times a single trunk, at others groupings of them depending on the span. At one point where nothing else seemed to work, a rope bridge was put together, adding adventure to an otherwise tedious effort.

John trudged on, mentally multi-tasking with each footfall while bouncing between two worlds—the memories complicated by generous amounts of guilt and remorse. The next pain was Gary. *How could he not remember him ... or at least their last experiences?*

*   *   *

The two went back a long ways. Their acquaintance began with Scout Camporees, where they became aware of each other across troop boundaries, because Gary was energetic and loud, and John was athletic and tall. The natural distance between them, however, could have gone on forever had it not been for an incident.

On that occasion troops were gathered with the program much the same as the year before … except for one thing, the weather was near to freezing. After the last event of the evening, most scouts, at least those with sense, retreated to camps and tents into sleeping bags, which were heavily insulated for just that sort of thing. Some, however, undaunted in the face of adversity, chose to continue socializing, trying to stay warm by the side of a campfire … a difficult thing to do because there was only one side warm to three sides cold, and the warm side was smoky. To complicate matters, a good fire needed lots of wood.

John had started to stay up at the fire in his troop's site, but after a bunch of teeth-chattering shivers, decided this was foolish. He was on his way to retiring when he heard a commotion another camp over; so he joined the flood of the curious to see what the noise was all about. The "about" was near to a fight with four older and larger scouts fuming and stamping and occasionally prodding a smaller, embarrassed and unusually subdued Gary.

"You little bastard, we oughta knock your damned head off," was just one of the sentiments floating in the air.

Listening to the buzz, John learned that in an ill-advised quest for warmth, Gary had taken a totem that marked the other's campsite and burned it, the evidence contributing its last in the fire illuminating the scene. The totem had been old and not exactly a work of art, but it had been an heirloom, an object of identity the troop had cherished, and this was wrong.

Even though the infraction was fairly serious, the scene somehow struck John as being funny … possibly it was the look on smart-alec Gary's face, which reflected a rightfully embarrassed person definitely in a box. Without thinking, John laughed, then clammed-up as faces turned and glared, finding little humor in the situation. John restrained himself for a few moments more, then lost it … this was just too funny. The four tried to stay mad, but John's outburst became infectious, bringing others about the scene into laughter as well and the whole matter to a tipping point, which could go either way. Sensing this and while still in a giggle, John did the first intelligent thing he'd done so far … he walked over to Gary and put his arm around his shoulder. This almost evened sides as John was taller than any of the four. But John's intent wasn't to fight. Instead he said to Gary, "My dad has a pretty good workshop. I'll bet we can make a totem larger and better than the one that somehow caught fire here.

"What do you think?"

And they did. In a few weeks afterwards they researched the topic and sketched, then cut and fastened and chiseled and sanded and painted.

Mark took an interest in what they were doing and gave them ideas and assistance along the way. In so doing, however, he noticed that John and Gary seemed to be having way too much fun. After listening to more of the nonsense, a sixth sense told him that something was going on, the muffled giggles just didn't seem to fit in with what was happening—the project, after all, being a good bit of work. So at a time when the two weren't around, Mark stood the totem against the back wall and reviewed the unfinished assembly. He was actually impressed by what he saw, the artwork and craftsmanship being downright noteworthy. There was nothing wrong that he could see. Then he turned the totem over. He didn't see anything unusual on that side either, and was about to return the pole to where it had been left, when something struck him as odd. Looking again and turning it so shadows altered the impression, he finally saw it. Hidden amongst the otherwise legitimate designs, was the faint, ingeniously scribed form of a giant phallus.

The final operations of sculpturing were closely supervised, with certain essential alterations being made. Only after that, with no one being the wiser, the totem was presented to the victimized troop in a ceremony that achieved closure in a very commendable manner.

John and Gary had been like blood brothers ever since.

On the last night in the twenty-first century, as the Chosen were parting to rest, Gary was the last person, other than Annie, John was to speak to; and at the time he must have had that look.

"You're still concerned about being the first to be brought back, aren't you?"

"Yes ... of course I am."

"Look, John, you'll do fine. None of us would want it any other way. Besides, I'll be on deck ... I'll have you covered."

John nodded, only partially relieved.

"Something else," Gary added, "The first thing we're going to do as soon as we're set up in later-later-land ... is carve another totem to mark our new settlement, a totem bigger and better than ever."

* * *

How could he not have remembered him?

5

Braga

He stood in the shadows, carefully scanning Pangaea, its quiet expanse now ghostly with the only movements being trees and bushes as they ruffled to shifting breezes. It was hard for him to imagine all that had happened within its perimeter, especially in the flats, where the battle, which would surely be conveyed to legend, had taken place.

Braga growled under his breath.

He couldn't believe that it happened again—that he had moved forward with a plan that couldn't lose, only to see it upended. This time the result was far worse than with the others, because previously, although not successful, he hadn't been damaged. This time, however, he'd been thoroughly nailed and it hurt in more ways than one.

Years ago, soon after John arrived, he'd taken a new mindset regarding leadership and domination, deciding that a new game, a game of peaceful cooperation and existence, would in time gain him the upper hand. So he'd played the game; and in so doing had been patient … patient far beyond his natural inclination. And although there hadn't been any harm caused by this game, he'd really only treaded water—not really losing, but not gaining anything either. Then came the excursions to other nations, and the possibilities that might go with them. With the first, the *Njegleshito*, he saw there were elements of superstition and malice with which he could easily develop a rapport. But it was with the last trip to the *Bjarla-shito*—a large nation with several loosely organized federations—that held the most promise.

He'd then spent the better part of the past year with them—he and Ah-ton-jacii and Daj-na-soa, that is—helping locate a pathway to Pangaea, and pitching in with its clearing for a good part of the distance. In the process several things had been accomplished besides making friends: he had developed a good command of their language; and, he had firmly planted a seed that John, who was suspected of being a giant, was an ominous presence that needed watching. With regards to the latter, he also established that he'd dedicated his life to the benefit of all the nations by being on guard to counter any harmful action John might take. There wasn't a specific plan in mind with any of these efforts, except to lay the groundwork for an opportunity that might present itself. His mind was always working.

Then came the storm which provided that opportunity, and it was perfect. With the wind and rain and thunderously bolted light-show, it didn't take much to convince the *Bjarla-shito* that this was an action of the gods in protest to what John was doing, which in this case was bringing all nations together for evil purposes. From that primed point, superstition took over and away it went. The frenzied mob worked itself up to where blood was the only answer—exactly what Braga wanted. He remembered what Dresh-na-togl had done for him years ago, pinning arms back so a person was helpless. So intending the same tactic, he made his way to a place behind John as the mob converged. But then Matthew jumped forward, catching him by surprise and causing him to act instinctively against the son instead. With the main opportunity against John lost by Matthew's interference, he'd threaded through the melee to where Ah-ton-jacii stood, hoping for a second chance.

That didn't work either as Ah-ton-jacii never got a shot off. He was in the process of drawing back when a volley of arrows whistled into both of them. Stunned and in shock, they had hesitated enough to receive a second volley before fleeing the scene, now badly porcupined.

They didn't stop until well out of range, with Ah-ton-jacii

squealing in fear and pain. Braga, however, roared in anger and frustration, because the hurt was secondary to the fact that John was still alive. A few people from one of the delegations who lingered back from the madness, happened to be in position to see what happened next; and they were amazed. They looked on as Braga ripped at arrows that extended out of him like branches on a tree. One squarely into his chest had hardly penetrated his leathers, but others in his thigh and shoulder and rump were real. It didn't matter, they were all torn out. Then Braga went to Ah-ton-jacii, and grabbing him by the shoulders and glaring into his eyes, snarled "Arrows can't hurt us."

Ah-ton-jacii didn't agree. He screamed as Braga tore *his* arrows away, almost fainting.

Braga repeated, "The arrows can't hurt us ... do you understand?"

Ah-ton-jacii clearly didn't.

But Braga continued, as if he could force his will onto someone else. And in a way he finally did ... to the extent that they then, with Braga refusing to limp, walked and bled back to the *Bjarla-shito* camp where they picked up their totes and disappeared down the trail.

At a point well out of sight, the two cut into the forest and picked their way through a density that closed behind them, concealing the remaining part of their travel. During the trail-making process Braga had stumbled upon a cave about a hundred yards off the line selected for the trail. It hadn't seemed important at the time, so Braga hadn't mentioned it. But now as they retreated, he recalled the cave, remembering that its size, remoteness and cover made it ideal for what they needed; so that's where they went.

Now, many days later, he stood in the shadows at a loss as what to do next. He was about to turn and return to refuge when he saw, far in the distance, someone emerging from the beginnings of the *Atjahahni* trail heading south. He watched as the person got close enough to be recognized, then moved into the clearing and sat on a rock, folding his arms as if on a throne to give audience.

It was Daj-na-soa.

Daj-na-soa was one of those in his clique, though not outwardly so. He didn't lounge about wherever Braga happened to be like Ah-ton-jacii and others tended to do; instead he drifted around, almost as if being open to any association or issue.

But Braga knew better. Daj-na-soa had been one of the four in the hunting party years ago that really had been a trap to ambush John, Willow and Dlahni on their intended trip north. When the trap failed, it was Daj who had disposed of Dresh-na-togl when he became a problem.

Their long association, however, didn't put Braga completely at ease. Daj wasn't a large man; he was about the size of Nyaho, with short bandy legs and a slumped back that gave the impression he wasn't much to contend with. But Braga knew otherwise; Daj was daring and crafty, and probably, with this being the unsettling part, had less in the way of conscience that anyone he knew.

He shuddered.

When he told Daj to kill Dresh-na-togl and hide the body, he had no idea how cruel and ingenious the execution would be. Daj had gone to Dresh-na-togl and gained his confidence, telling him Braga was furious and that it would be better to hide for a while until he cooled down. And for hiding Daj had the perfect place, it was an abandoned bear's den under rocks in a thicket a mile across the river. He then assisted Dresh-na-togl with water and provisions, with orders to stay deep inside and not come out until he came to get him. What was perfect about the hiding place was that a large boulder at the mouth was loose; and when Dres-na-togl was deep inside, Daj and Ah-ton-jacii were able to dislodge it, sealing the tomb forever.

"Oh there you are," Daj-na-soa said. "I was hoping to find you."

Braga nodded.

"How are you doing? I heard that you and Ah-ton-jacii had been hit."

Braga smiled. "A few arrows can't hurt us."

"So I understand. There's a rumor going around that the two of you just pulled out the arrows and walked away. The people who saw it were really impressed, and have been spreading the word ever since.

"It's quite a story."

"We're doing fine," Braga said, passing the matter off as if it wasn't of consequence. "In fact Ah-ton-jacii's on a hunt right now."

Then he added, "Tell me what's happened since all of that. I know
that John's still alive, but I've been out of touch."

"You haven't talked to anyone?"

"No ... I heard John scream my name. With what happened to
Matthew and all the arrows, I thought it best to stay away."

"It's a good thing you did. You've been charged with inciting the
riot where so many died. In fact, you've been banished, which means,
among other things, you could be killed on sight."

Braga hardly reacted ... a subtle tightening of his features being
the only indication he'd absorbed the news. After a few moments
he nodded as if in acceptance, then, "Tell me everything else that's
happened. I've heard sounds from time to time ... they may have
been from ceremonies ... but I haven't ventured out to see what they
were about."

Daj-na-soa stepped to another rock nearby and set down his packs,
then settled in, stretching his legs and making himself comfortable.
He focused on Braga, who, to Daj, was obviously trying to appear as
if everything was normal. But things weren't normal and it showed
on his clothes: The effects of dampness and mud and the small tears
from thorns and occasional areas of wear were normal; but punctured
rips with traces of darker stains, and bulges that hid wrappings and
poultices were something else. Daj-na-soa saw all this, and saw that
Braga saw that he saw, and let it be. Instead, once set in place, he told
everything as he understood it, relating results of the fight in all of
its morbid detail ... its startling conclusion ... and then the things
that happened during the last days of the Gathering, none of which
made Braga feel any better. After several minutes while Braga was
mulling this over, Daj-na-soa changed gears ... "I tried to kill John
on the trail."

"You what?"

Daj-na-soa laughed, "It wasn't much of a try. When Dlahni
found that John wanted to walk the trail, he made sure he was well
protected. There's a group in front of him, and another in back, both
pledged to be on alert and guard him at all costs. I was only able
to get close at one of the switchbacks, but even then I'd have been
skewered if I'd tried. John's girls are part of the defensive groups, and
you know how they are."

Braga nodded, knowing all too well, saying as if concerned, "No need for that." Then after a pause, "What were you doing on the trail anyway? I guessed you to be in one of the canoes."

"I was supposed to be in the last one to leave; but when the time came, I said there was too much of a load on board, and volunteered to catch up with those on the trail."

"How noble of you," Braga said, but in a way more of a question than a compliment.

They both laughed.

"Well," Daj-na-soa said, "there were reasons. One was that I wanted to find you and see how you were doing. After looking around without success, I took off down the trail to see what could be done there."

"You mean like kill John?"

Daj smiled.

"You said that from what happened after the battle, everyone was in awe of John. Why weren't you?"

Daj-na-soa hesitated, mulling over the question. "Actually at first I was ... I mean the lightning strikes and smoke and rainbow and all were really something. But then I was close to the ledge where John stopped on his way down, and I could see the look on his face. It wasn't the look of a man who'd just been sanctified by the Great Spirit. He looked confused ..."

"Hmmm." Braga rubbed his chin.

"Is that it? Nothing more that might be of interest?"

"No, not really ... except maybe ..."

"Yes ... "

"Remember that cut that drained the lake?"

Braga nodded.

"Well, there's something strange about it. You may not have noticed because you were pretty busy at the time, but there's something in there that shocked John ... it put him in a stupor just as things were coming to a head. Then on the last day while everyone was making preparations to leave, John went back to the cut. He worked on it for a while, digging to expose more of the dark material that obstructed the initial dig. I was curious so went over and asked if he needed any help. But he said "no", saying it in a way that meant he didn't want me around. A little later he called Nyaho and Dlahni over, talking to them at length. I have no idea what he told them, but the looks on their faces as they passed by were like being in shock."

"Hmmm ... everyone's being shocked. Let's have a look."

They got up and walked across to the corner of the quadrangle, Braga moving slowly without gasping or limping or revealing the pain that went along with the effort. But near the cut the level surfaces ended; things were a mess with dirt and bushes and even trees piled every which way on both sides. It was a while before they could thread their way over and through all of this, with several moves that had Braga sucking air before getting to where the cut could be seen. Finally there, Braga scanned the length of it, really appreciating what had been done for the first time. After scanning, he turned his attention to the special part Daj-na-soa had mentioned— the additional excavations John made for the benefit of Nyaho and Dlahni. He looked at the dark jumbled mess, trying to attach some meaning to it; he looked at Daj-na-soa, who only shrugged, finding as little in it as he did. They discussed what was there, but in the end what they could see didn't have any meaning to either of them.

Braga didn't stop with those first impressions, however. He repeated scanning and scrutinizing what had to be a key part of it all. The blackness was pitted and broken with many sections missing or out of alignment, so much so that the condition tended to mask the fact that it described a generally flat plane. A small section, retrieved by Daj-na-soa, crumbled away as he tested it. Looking back at the rough surfaces, he noticed that the sides were in alignment; he reasoned by that that the sections interrupted by the cut were once tied together. Other than the alignment he couldn't see anything else of significance.

Braga shuffled back and forth along the edge for several minutes, absent-mindedly kicking pebbles into the chasm as he did. Finally he said, "If there's a mystery here, we're not even close to solving it....

"So let's do this. Stay with us tonight and get some rest. We can discuss what we've seen here some more and maybe come up with something."

Daj-na-soa nodded, still trying to see through to the mystery. "I wonder who else has been told ... besides Nyaho and Dhlani?"

Braga shrugged.

"My guess is that John isn't telling anyone else."

"Why do you say that?"

"Just a hunch … From what I've seen, which isn't much, he's mainly keeping to himself."

"Do you think he might be priming for a grand announcement when he gets home?" asked Braga.

"Maybe so … which means it may be very important."

"Which means we've got to be there."

Braga laughed at his own comment. "Obviously *we* can't go. Anton-jacii and I wouldn't be welcome right now, would we?

"So here's what we do: You return and join the baggage train. It sounded like they're moving slowly, so catching up shouldn't be a problem. When you find out what this is all about, come back and let me know. I'll stay here for a good while more … at least 'til I've heard from you. Right know I don't have anywhere to go anyway."

With that they crossed back to the shadows where Braga had been before, then went farther, the woods closing in behind them.

6

How?

John fell. Not like this was the first time, but this time it was special—feet up, landing square on his ass, spinning and sliding backwards into trees which stopped him before it got worse. Since nothing was broken, it was really kind of funny, especially the bug-eyed reaction of those who came to his rescue.

But everything was okay and in moments they were back on the trail. The incident reminded John of a hike years ago ... actually several thousand years ago. At that time equipment was much more sophisticated, with hiking boots in particular coming to mind. They were light-weight, waterproof, and with deep-lugged soles for traction. On that trip one of the hikers scorned the technological developments that made life easier, and opted for casual instead—blue jeans, cut-off sweats, deck soles, and so on. The result was that he was all over the place. In fact in a game devised by unsympathetic witnesses, he was credited with a Guinness record for the frequency of falls on a downward slope.

John's footwear, nor anyone else's, wasn't much better in the here and now as those deck soles he remembered, since materials weren't yet on hand to make anything better. Footwear was basically a moccasin-like leather wrap, which was fine on dry, level ground. But the trail on this occasion was rarely level, and was still damp and slippery because of the storm. If this wasn't enough, the trail was also a mess with leaves and twigs and branches and even trees downed along the way.

All of this was contended with without much in the way of expression because other thoughts were now on his mind, continuing to cause pain. This pain was about the rest of the Chosen. *How could he not have remembered them?*

*   *   *

When John and Annie first arrived at the French Broad, they met with a number of friends or at least acquaintances, but most of the group—almost fifty in number—were first meets. A few weeks later when the sixteen Chosen assembled in those final days of training, however, it was like a meeting of old friends. The partying, the intense exercises, particularly the whitewater rafting, combined with the unbelievable calamity overshadowing the world, had done this.

John smiled as he thought of one aspect of the group—their height. If the *Atjahahni* thought upon first seeing him that he was a giant, they would have been convinced of this had all of them been on hand, as most of the men were over six feet tall.

Roland Thompson was the tallest at six foot five. Very strong with wide shoulders that seemed out of proportion to his narrow waist, he had scouts from many schools salivating at his prospects ... which happened to be in several sports. The scholarship he selected was crew, in which he was a natural talent. He went on to be at stroke seat, and captained a team that was tops at both the IRA Collegiate and the Henley Royal Regatta in England. A third generation member of a noted construction family, Roland graduated in building sciences, intending thereby to extend the line.

Both Anton Stordahl, an agronomist, that is a farmer, and Rodney Snedecor, a chemist, were also taller than John. Rodney was notable because his chosen field couldn't have been more appropriate. He often took the look of a mad scientist, as in the movie *Back to the Future*, with an Einstein hairdo, popped-eyes, elastic impressions, and large hands that wildly gestured to emphasize his expressions. A real character, his antics, usually hilarious, never succeeded in masking the fact that he was not only a serious scientist, but also a gifted athlete in several sports, including volleyball and hoops.

Anton was one of those who had flipped out during the white water episode. Rather being angered or scared and intimidated by it, he had hooted and laughed the rest of the run, and was still beaming several drinks into the end of the day. It was one of those events that gives a person an impression in one's eyes. So that now and probably forevermore, whenever those who were there meet, thoughts return to that defining experience, with smiles and good feelings about the modern farmer, whose ruddy complexion, gangly, two-furrow stride, meaty hands and sparkling smile are so prominent.

Then there were Devon Noveyak, a biologist with interests in forestry, and Abram Cone, a historian specializing in ancient cultures, both over six one. Abram was thin and hawkish in appearance with a mop of intensely curled hair. An energetic person, he had been involved in many extra-curricular activities on campus including being captain of the cross-country team. It was also rumored he was a closeted black belt, but as there never was a show of macho, nobody knew for sure. With John the memory of Abram always coming to mind was the look of frustration and panic on his face just before lunch at the *Easter Armageddon* conference. Arrangements weren't ready and deliveries were just arriving when the doors opened at the break. John and Gary had been like the Seventh Cavalry to the rescue—helping get everything in place before the mob of hungry students got to them—and the fact of that would never be forgotten.

Devon didn't look like a scientist at all, at least not like Rodney. He was much more at home outdoors then in the lab, and had a dark tan, bleached and tussled hair, and an otherwise weathered look as evidence to where he'd been. These features, along with thick eyebrows, a handle-bar mustache, natural leanness, an ubiquitous guitar, a surprisingly good voice with a repertoire of backwoods songs, and an easy, open, informal manner gave him a strong identity.

The shortest of the men was still taller than any of the *Atjahahni*. Bruno Kinnaman, an architect, was about five six. The "Bruno" part, that puzzled everyone, was really a nickname which since early years had obscured his real name of Elroy. It seems that as a laddie he'd been well into the rough and tumble, and had been labeled Bruno after an instance where he'd huffed and swelled in an imitation of the Incredible Hulk. In the years that followed his peers grew past him, but somehow, more as a joke, the name stuck ... and so it went. A further contrast resulted with his vocation, in which he was creative and artfully talented, while his main sport continued to be rough and tumble—both *Tae Quan Do* and wrestling in the lightweight division.

Even the women were taller than the *Atjahahni*. Mona Picconi, a registered nurse, was the shortest at five two. Rebecca Sweberg, a musician, Judy Vester, a teacher with a specialty in philosophy, and Terry Noveyak, a botanist married to Devon, were increasingly taller, with Annie at five ten being the tallest.

It was a good group; a group with a wide range of specialties, bonded by common traits of adaptability, camaraderie, conditioning and environmental concern. They had linked arms on that last night and made a solemn pledge, while a fire burned in their midst and the stars overhead with their attendant spirits witnessed, to commit themselves with all their energy, ability and honor to the challenge Huston had put before them.

*   *   *

How could he not have remembered them?

7

Where?

There were many revelations in the history unlocked at the drainage cut. Among them was where. John still couldn't pinpoint anything exactly, but now he could get much closer.

In the confusion of the first months twenty years before, he'd tried to reason, among other things, his locatiion in the world. About all he could conclude then was that he was in the eastern mountains. Now he knew more. He knew, for instance, the location of the French Broad; the Conference Center where the Symposium was held was just off US64 ten miles out of Brevard and thirty from Asheville. As for the Cryogenic Complex, he could only get close. After a week of goodbyes, the Chosen had reassembled at the French Broad, where they boarded a bus on which all windows had been covered. While this secrecy added a mystery to what was unfolding, their natural curiosities had them collectively recording turns and stops and goes and time intervals and sounds and the like. When they shared observations later, the conclusion was that they were fifty to sixty miles northwest of where they'd started. That could put them somewhere north of Highlands.

*   *   *

Highlands.

The very thought made him smile ... because it wasn't the first time the area had come to mind. The excursion to the *Negleshito* four years earlier had been the first time a sizeable group—around four dozen—had traveled cross-country through these forested mountains. Although minor by comparison, the problems of the trip *and* something in Highlands reminded him of Hernando de Soto. De Soto had been a part of studies in high school, but like so many other bits of learning, had been relegated to memory and forgotten. Then later, while traveling through Highlands on a scouting trip, a historical marker along the main route through town caught his attention.

It read ...

> In 1540 an expedition of Spaniards
> Led by De Soto, the first Europeans to
> Explore this area, passed through here

This fascinated him and grabbed his interest, so much so he couldn't be satisfied until he'd researched the topic. He learned that de Soto had led the first large-scale exploration on North American soil. In doing so, he'd first landed at what was later called Tampa Bay on the west side of a land called *La Florida*. *La Florida* had been named at its discovery by Ponce de Leon, who first saw it on Good Friday during *Pascua de Florida*, the Easter season.

De Soto was no ordinary person and his exploration was no ordinary adventure. Ignoring aspirations his parents had for him, de Soto instead, at the age of 15, sailed to the new world as a page. Developing quickly, becoming an excellent horsemen and one of the finest lancers in Spain, he rose through the ranks and was a Captain by the age of twenty. When John later read of George Washington, he was reminded of de Soto and of the fact that many great personalities of history, without the distractions of movies and television and computer games and instant gratification, had become so accomplished at such early ages.

De Soto had been involved in the wars of the notable conquistadors, and, with the policy of that time of sharing in spoils, had become wealthy. Being relatively young and still hungry for more adventure, he petitioned for and received exclusive rights to explore, subjugate and control *La Florida*, which was thought to be an island at the time.

The expedition that resulted—10 ships, 600 soldiers and cavalrymen, 200 or so pages, servants and clerics, 225 horses, a herd of pigs and large amounts of armor and supplies—was financed by De Soto, with the same carrot of sharing in the wealth inspiring the group he'd assembled. Moving in what had to be a difficult journey, de Soto and his entourage left Tampa Bay and traveled north, averaging around two miles a day. During the first 16 months they snaked through *La Florida*, and what is now South Carolina, western North Carolina and eastern Tennessee.

As with most of the conquistadors, the object of the exploration was more for gold and spoils than anything else. Those who had conquered the Aztecs and Incas in Central and South America had found fabulous wealth ... literally roomfuls of gold. But in this part of the world nothing remotely similar had been found in the months that passed. Turning south into what is now Alabama, de Soto entered the territory of the Choctaw nation led by Chief Tascaluza. The meeting and immediate relations between the two cultures began peacefully as the Chief's son, accompanied by over 100 nobles decorated with skins and large feathered headdresses, first met them with open arms. The retinue then guided the Spaniards deeper into Choctaw territory to the fortified village of Mauvila and Chief Tascaluza. The Chief was a most imposing leader, almost seven feet tall with a muscular well-proportioned body; unlike most of the natives, he was neither impressed nor intimidated by the horses or the armor or the devices of the Spaniards, none of which he had ever seen before, even though obvious attempts were made to do so. Despite some tactics, like charging forward in fearfully feigned attacks, which could have been viewed as effrontery, Tascaluza took it in stride. He welcomed de Soto and his advance party with attractive young women in songs and dances, and gave thoughtful considerations of food and lodging.

The friendly start, however, soon degenerated into something else. The battle that ensued, a struggle that may have been the most significant battle ever held on the American continent, even though only a handful have ever heard of it, seems to have been initiated by the Indians; but was probably in response to actions by de Soto and his men. Although supposedly trying to avoid conflict, the Spanish most likely treated the Choctaw like the conquistadors treated the Mayans and Incas and other natives earlier.

Mauvila, one of the largest native settlements north of the Rio Grande, with 15 feet high timber walls and guard towers and extensive defensive features, was so completely destroyed that traces of it had disappeared by the time settlement began again in the area 200 years later. Approximately 8,000 Indians died, as did Tascaluza and all of his nobles. In a horrible, hard fought battle of charge and counter-charge and hand-to-hand combat lasting nine hours, more were killed on the American side than in any other day in American history, including those of the bloody Civil War ... or of Pearl Harbor and D-Day and 9-11 combined. The result was that one of the most advanced civilizations of Native America, a civilization that stretched from Central Alabama to the Gulf of Mexico, was reduced to a few scattered survivors.

The Spanish also suffered. Over one hundred were killed and many more wounded, and badly needed horses and equipment and supplies were lost. And the horrors of the day were not limited to the physical. One of de Soto's cavalrymen, a Portuguese Knight who hadn't been injured but who'd been a party of and a witness to the slaughter—of his own men, of the Indians who fought to the end, of the maidens who'd greeted them so delightfully at the onset, and finally the last brave, who seeing the hopelessness of the situation, hung himself in full view with the string of his bow—was so disturbed that he lay down the next day and remained in the same position for three days. Neither eating or drinking, he quietly died.

The Spaniards had to stay at Mauvila a month afterwards to reorganize and recover before they were able to continue.

If this battle and its horrors had been the extent of the damage to the Native Americans, it would have been bad enough. But there was much more. Mauvila and other battles and acts of cruelty, such as cutting off the hands of Indians that had been captured if they wouldn't tell where gold was hidden, were completely overshadowed by the diseases the Spaniards carried for which there were no endemic immunity. Millions died as a result and entire areas were depopulated, destroying most of the indigenous peoples' ability to form a unified resistance against the European expansion that followed.

So whenever John traveled like the little caravan was doing now, he would invariably think of de Soto. On the first trip in particular, he worried about the complexity of coordinating the actions of several dozen people of differing ages, sexes and responsibilities. But then he'd think of what it must have been like for the Spanish. The challenges for de Soto had to be far greater. He had to manage 800 to 900 people, hundreds of horses and even 200 pigs. *And how do you keep pigs under control? It must be like herding cats!* Regardless of the difficulty, de Soto managed his challenge through terrain with hills and rivers and swamps and forests that couldn't have been much different from what was in the here and now.

There were other lessons in the recollections. One was about weaponry. The lesson was that if both sides in a conflict are organized and fierce and brave, as they were at Mauvila, the outcome will be determined by weaponry. This had been true at Tenochitlan with Cortez and Cajamarca with Pizarro and countless other places. The Indians with Tascaluza, who had bows and arrows and stone-headed tomahawks, were no match for the Spaniards, who had body armor and helmets and swords and arquebuses and crossbows and halberds and daggers and lances and armored war horses. Even though the Indians were superior to the extent of 10 or 20 to one, the result was defeat and slaughter.

This, as well as everything else John knew about war, bothered him very much. He had held back from developing weapons more advanced than he could already see in the village, as he was wary of advancements going to someone who would use them in the wrong way. He had organized the village for defensive purposes, but that's as far as he could see to go. This little bit, however, had been a godsend at Pangaea. He hadn't planned for combat, being optimistic that all would go well; but it had happened. And although the mob had been crushed, he hadn't done it alone. There's no telling what would have happened if others hadn't followed their training and performed the way they had.

Then there was body armor, which John had neglected because it was part of the proliferation he was so concerned about. De Soto and his men had armor of interlocking metal plates and coats of mail. The latter, however, had proven to be ineffective against the arrow, so early in their campaign, they had replaced the mail with thick quilted coats. The change worked ... At one point in the battle at Mauvila, 20 arrows had been pulled from the coat de Soto was wearing.

Now John began to think a protecting vest was reasonable to consider. During the battle in the flats, the forces assembled under Dlahni's direction had been put in harm's way. As much as he hated to think about it, it could happen again.

*   *   *

John returned to the matter of location, finally realizing the information gained was of little help. The mountains themselves had probably changed very little in the time that had passed ... since a few thousand years is only a blip in the millions of years these particular mountains have existed. But the lakes ... they *were* different. Previously there'd been many lakes, but most were man-made reservoirs. There had been nothing, however, to compare to those that now extended for hundreds of miles in meandering northeast-southwest directions. In remembering what had been said about the snows that never melted, he guessed there'd been a period—possibly a few thousand years—when glaciers formed. Over time, with huge pressures in relation to their thickness and with movements into the valleys as glaciers tend to have, a great many features in topography and construction would have been pulverized, and the landscape gouged to form the lakebeds now a part of the world. So it didn't matter if he could pinpoint a location from what he'd learned. What had been most likely wasn't there anymore.

There was a commotion back on the trail that brought all but the most forward elements of the caravan to a halt. That included John, who found a convenient ledge, dropped his pack and sat to hear what it was all about.

Then Naomi appeared, hurrying by on an obvious mission. John gave her a quizzical look as she passed, but she shook her head so as not to be bothered. Then she returned, this time with Sara in tow, both moving past him as if he wasn't there.

John shook his head in amusement. Here he was the man of the house, and somehow somewhat exalted within the community, yet he was being excluded from whatever the matter was back on the trail. The mystery hung in the air for several minutes, while sounds of conversation managed their way forward. The sounds weren't loud or emotional or seeming of a critical nature. *Whatever it was wasn't life-threatening.* So he relaxed, opened a small pouch attached at his waist, and ate the last of the blackberries picked earlier that day. He was spreading some bush branches in search of more food of any kind when traffic doubled back again. This time there was a third person ... as if the person was being escorted.

The third was Daj-na-soa.

"Daj," John said, "what a pleasant surprise to see you," his daughters registering a subtle look of disbelief with what he said.

"What are you doing here?"

Daj-na-soa laughed, then stopped at ease, leaning against his walking stick. "As I've just explained to your girls ... I was going to return with the last canoe, but the damned thing was so heavily loaded, that someone had to walk. I volunteered."

John nodded, "Well good ... welcome to the party," then snorted at what was obviously absurd.

"How are you doing ... everything okay?" Daj-na-noa said.

"I'm fine ... but as I'm sure you've noticed, the trail's a mess."

"That's a fact ...."

"Did you see anything of interest behind us?" John wanted to ask how Braga was doing, but that would be an insinuation revealing more of his mind than he wanted, and would most likely be met with a lie anyway, so he held back, knowing full well Daj knew what he meant.

Daj-na-noa did and lied, "No ... I must have been the last person to cross Pangaea, as there wasn't anyone in sight." Then he joked, "It hasn't been easy being the last one on the trail playing catch-up. I usually don't have trouble finding food in the woods, but all of you have picked the place pretty clean."

John smiled at that, "Probably true … We're working pretty hard at scrounging. But as you can see, we're not getting fat either."

"Dad," Sara butted-in. "We've got to keep moving. I've asked Daj-na-soa to help up front as there seems no end to the mess."

With that they disappeared down the trail, everyone else picking-up and resuming the hike.

John thought as he walked, almost smiling, that the girls had gotten so serious-minded, becoming almost as suspicious of certain persons as Dhlahni had been. Then a crushing thought hit him … a thought that was to descend on him from time to time the rest of his life … If he had been more suspicious and less trusting, then maybe someone who's beautiful essence now floated in the ether of the unknown, would be walking at his side.

8

What?

It had been twenty years. And the reason he'd been in this world was not only a rare privilege, but also a responsibility of gigantic proportions. Only he hadn't really understood the extent of it until the numbing recollection at the cut. Now as he plodded along, another question surfaced to bother him. The question was ... if he could somehow find the Cryogenic Complex ... and if all of the others could be brought back .... what could he show them to justify all those years?

John wasn't happy with the answer.

He thought of *Tschtaha-tata* and Sundays and canoes and Craft Fairs and swimming and Home Guard, all of which were noteworthy ... *I guess*. Then there was the Gathering: This had taken four years and tremendous amounts of work, and although it ended on a high note, the cost had been so horrific he couldn't think of it in a favorable way.

The mission the Chosen had pledged was to *start mankind all over again*. This was such a simple statement that it tended to mask the far-reaching and all encompassing nature of the challenge. It meant all of mankind's experiences, at least the four or five thousand years before the pandemic of the twenty-first century, be studied to understand the good and the bad and the net result leading to a failure of the human experience. As Patrick Henry said long, long before … *You can hardly prepare for the future if you don't understand the past.* This meant the challenges would be much like that that had faced the Founding Fathers, who were very familiar with different forms of government, and were trying to shape a new one without the drawbacks those before had proven to have. From the lessons of all of this, including the successes and failures of the 1776 experience, a new, more encompassing, self-perpetrating system was to be formulated—a system with three legs in support of one another to achieve the ultimate in effectiveness and stability.

One leg was ecology—an appropriate consideration of all creation—because the stability of the ecosystem is dependent on a healthy diversity … a consideration never before included.

And what had he done about that? Basically nothing. He'd been well aware of the problems in the twenty-first century, and of the movements on many fronts to counter the momentum of global practices. But had he carried his learning forward into the here and now? Actually not; actually the world of now was basically bio-degradable. Furthermore, he'd received lessons from the *Atjahahni* on several aspects of ecology: Like the Cherokee before them, they were respectful of everything in the natural world … and gave thanks for any part they used in surviving; they were already aware that over-killing or over-grazing were not in everyone's best interest; and finally, as if to underscore their commitment to their beliefs, they returned their own physical beings into the cycle of life, death and regeneration—which was the premise of it all.

He'd hardly impacted this leg of the challenge.

Another leg was the peaceful coexistence of cultures. For some reason he'd worked hard on this, even though he didn't have an awareness that it might fit into an overall concept. With the *Atjahahni* nation, the blending of cultural concepts had gone very well. And even with other nations, as they were brought to familiarity, the soft approach to acceptance of differences was working … until with the wind and rain of the tempest, they degenerated into the most violent, tragic episode in the memory of any of the nations.

John shuddered as the recollections in the flats played on his mind.

The third leg was governance—the process by which populations are organized and directed so that creativity and productivity are enhanced ... and that an optimum good comes to the largest number.

John had clearly been no more than a spectator in this arena. The *Atjahahni* were only a few hundred in number ... and on the surface as unsophisticated as could be. But then subtleties in their culture and its leadership began to play out. With finally a command of their language and an understanding of community workings, first impressions of them remained that they were primitive and simple ... but not ineffective. In a way it was like in *Shangri-la* ... where there was a rule of moderate strictness, and in return were given moderate obedience. The result was that the people were moderately chaste and moderately honest. But there were differences. In the fantasy world of *Shangri-la* there were abundant gardens and fine wines and pleasing temperatures and eternal youth. The reality in the world of now was the opposite in every way. Despite the apparent benevolence of the basic culture, there were pressures related to survival that strained the bonds of the community. Because of this at times there was thievery ... at times there was malicious mischief ... and at times there was battery and murder.

All violations of acceptable behavior, which were usually minor grievances, were brought before the Council of Chiefs, where they were managed with impressive wisdom and fairness. One thing John noticed, or really gravitated to awareness after discussions with Nyaho and Dlahni, was the strength of public opinion. The conscience of the community was powerful, and was a big factor in controlling obverse tendencies that are a part of everyone.

Serious matters were different. In one instance in particular, a man had invaded a hut and raped a woman. When the husband returned and learned of it, he sought the man and attempted vengeance, only to be killed in the attempt.

Not surprising, the news spread like wildfire ... in response to which the Council quickly met and took action. The man was chased and apprehended and trussed.

John had watched this without getting involved; but as the man was brought in he wondered what was to happen. Would they consider that the man was deranged? Would they debate *ad infinitum* the intricacies and circumstances of what had happened ... with duels between defending and prosecuting advocates? Would there be learned testimonies and expert witnesses and process and delays and appeals and horrific energy and provision? Would they send the man to exile? Would they confine him in some manner?

The answers to all of these were no, no, no and no. Sane or insane, considerations that didn't exist in the awareness of these times, the inescapable facts were that atrocious acts had been committed, it was known who'd done them, and, after reasonable testimony, it was apparent there wasn't justification for what had happened. With these truths the Council decided on the sentence. Banishment or exile wouldn't work ... the person would be a threat to anyone who ventured beyond the periphery of the community. Confinement wouldn't work either—the community didn't have the facilities for doing so ... and the thought of caring for someone when the rest of the community was in a constant struggle for survival didn't make sense. All of these options had been discussed for similar situations generations before, and the answers were always the same. Life is precious ... it is the ultimate treasure; but it carries obligations of equal measure—it must be justified by good works. For the person who commits a crime for which restitution can't be made, justice is a terrible swift sword ... the person must die.

With this unavoidable conclusion it was hoped that the guilty party would recognize his sin, express his regrets, and redeem himself by performing a final and honorable act. To set the stage the man was brought a poison; then as all in witness moved to the periphery of the room, he was released.

The hoped for conclusion, however, didn't work. The murderer immediately kicked away the poison and dived into the men guarding the doorway in an attempt at escaping. He was then tied again, this time to a pole in the room in addition to being simply restrained. While in this helpless position, his wrists were slit and then left to let gravity do the work.

John was horrified ... a feeling most likely reflected on his face, because during the process, Dlahni looked at him and their eyes met, neither going beyond the link. But the stare was like a question ... *What would you do in a situation like this?* John broke the connection and shook his head ... he didn't know. He then thought of what would have happened in his make-believe other world ... finally accepting that under the circumstances, the justice in the here and now was as good as could be contrived. He even considered that it might be better than in that other. But he did nothing to influence the process one way or the other.

With such a mixed bag of feelings he gravitated to something that was probably the most significant achievement in all of those years. It was the fact he'd successfully brought all four of his children to adulthood.

In this world, although idyllic in some regards with a backdrop of an Eden-like forest and a beautiful lake, death was a constant companion. John's family experience was rare as almost every family had suffered death, for some more than once. Childbirth and childhood diseases led the way, but even when those early years were cleared, there were other threats like pneumonia and dysentery and a bunch of maladies relating to constant exposure. There were malnutrition and starvation. Despite the fact there were fish and game and more and more success with gardens, the difficulties rarely rested. Long hard winters that exhausted reserves and limited hunting raised their form of havoc; and diseases and injuries for which treatments were primitive or non-existent did their thing. Therefore, for all these reasons, an extent of medical problems, although varying, was evident in a good part of the population at any one time.

For John the real eye-opener to all of this came during the first horrific winter. With this and other experiences, he soon understood how difficult conditions were to overcome on a continuing basis.

Then came the ridiculously bad situation in family planning that resulted in four children in three years. The problems because of this were so monstrous it was even suggested that the last pregnancy be aborted ... a practice that wasn't unusual in the usual struggle for survival. That struggle included other grim practices, such as that relating to the infirm who'd become a burden—like people in a lifeboat who recognize someone must leave so others can be saved. In the village it was not unusual that persons in this situation give those in their sphere a final gesture of love ... and then take a walk into the cold. This sort of selfless act added an admirable quality to the culture that wasn't discussed, but was nonetheless there. Despite that being the case, John rejected the thought suggested to him, and instead steeled himself to the almost impossible challenge ... and Matthew was the result.

The years that followed were consumed by an endless list of needs for a young family. The situation wasn't much different from a nest with young hatchlings, where there's a wild clamoring for fulfillment whenever a parent approaches.

Early in the experience John thought of a movie seen in his childhood. It was a catchy story of a family marooned on a tropical island called *Swiss Family Robinson*. In it, shortly after a shipwreck, appeared a cheerful scene of an attractive tree-house and ingenious automated moving devices with ropes and pulleys and waterways, and a yard glamorized with tamed animals and children riding ostriches. But that was a scene concocted by specialized set designers and built by teams of craftsmen. In contrast, John was alone with the roughest of tools. While hunting and fishing and planting and doing all he could for food, he also did everything he could to provide enhancements to their lives. He added features—a latrine, showers, cisterns, covered decking and the like; he altered his tent-like home, improving light and ventilation in the process; he covered the dirt floor with carefully selected and fitted flat stones, which were in turn overlaid with woven mats and furs. Along with this he implemented the habit of frequent cleaning and airing—the floor and coverings, all blankets, cushions and wearing apparel ... and especially each other with bathing and showering and examining for ticks—as part of the routine. The result didn't look at all like the images in *Swiss Family Robinson*. There were ropes and pulleys and a few impressive looking features, but mainly it was a weird assortment of sticks and stones and frames and trellises and works in progress, much like what you'd expect from a loony scientist just passed beyond the Neanderthals, that was a daily source of amusement to the passing *Atjahahni*.

There were two main results of all of this: One was that many of the features found their way into other homes ... with perceptive benefits to them; the other was that the efforts worked. They kept the family protected and clean and warm ... and alive.

And that was something.

9

Dlahni

The day was calm and the lake smooth as the canoe skimmed the surface, sending a gentle wake spreading out on both sides. Dlahni pulled with deep powerful strokes. It didn't matter that his muscles ached and his partner up front groaned on occasion, there was so much on his mind that the only relief from the anxieties they caused was hard work ... which this was. In the center rode Nyaho with his ribs wrapped and his body cushioned for as much comfort as possible. A ways behind followed another canoe, this one carrying Da-hash-to with provisions much like those for Nyaho, trying frantically to keep up. The two canoes were now at least a day ahead of all the others and were on the last leg of the return home.

*　　*　　*

At the stop after the first day on the water, Dlahni had gotten a jolt that put all of his muddled thoughts and concerns into one more focused bundle. He'd already wanted to get Nyaho and Da-hash-to back as soon as possible because there'd be family and food, and the comforts of home where better care could be provided. But then he'd stood on the bank at that first landing, and watched as one by one each canoe arrived and was pulled ashore. Then there was the last one and the shock. Daj-na-soa wasn't aboard. For several reasons Daj was someone Dlahni didn't trust, and although he'd often been chided for being overly suspicious, his feelings toward Braga had more than proven out, and that strengthened some of his other feelings ... most recently towards Daj. Now Daj was still back somewhere around Pangaea, and the story given that he'd volunteered to walk since the canoe to which he was assigned had been overloaded, didn't fly. Dlahni's senses told him the man could be teaming with Braga and At-ton-jacii, who were last seen walking away on the *Bjarla-shito* trail, or stalking those on the caravan ... or both. So now he couldn't rest until he'd gotten back ... and then some.

The last week and a half had been something else, with any one of a number of happenings—the storm, the killings, the burial ceremonies and then the final meetings—being events that would live forever engraved in the minds of everyone who'd been there. They were boggling. But even any and all of them paled in comparison to what happened just before leaving.

John had called him and Nyaho over to the drainage cut, which he'd almost disappeared into an hour before.

"Sit here," John said, pointing to edge of the excavation over the ledge of black surfacing he'd just exposed.

They did as asked, Nyaho needing help before gingerly settled into position. John looked away as they did as if carefully selecting words, which he was. Then he turned back ...

"Years ago I was asked in Council where I was from ... Remember?"

They nodded.

"And do you remember my answer at the time?"

"Yes, of course."

"Well ... I lied."

They fidgeted and looked at each other and smiled to acknowledge they already knew that, but there was also a nervousness as they realized something, possibly momentous, was happening. John had admitted before that he didn't really know where he was from ... but he'd said when he found out, they'd be the first to know.

Was this that time?

John was nervous as well. He took a deep breath, hesitated, and turned away, then spun back to face them with a look that answered the question. "The fact is that back then I really didn't know; I didn't know for sure where I'd come from, or how I'd gotten here, or why ... if there was a why.

"That was then ... until a few days ago. Now I know.

"It all came to me when water gushed through and exposed this black layer you see here," tapping the surface with a stick.

"As you can see, the edges of the surfaces exposed on each side of this ditch line up. The portion that the water tore away connected these two parts ... Do you see that?"

They studied the sections, following his pointer as it traced an imaginary line from one side to the other. After a repeat of the description they nodded again.

"Okay ... now if you can visualize the torn away portion being back in place, you'll see a black surface about twenty feet wide. If we were to follow the direction of the sides in either direction, we would continue to find this same black material. *This* is an ancient roadway. By the shape of surrounding hills, my guess is that the road continues fairly straight in this direction," pointing away to the west, "and then goes along this line bordering the quadrangle, turning left and passing through near where the *Anlyshendl* were camped.

"Do you understand?"

They didn't really ... until Nyaho interpreted what he thought John meant and then John nodded as if in "close enough".

"Alright, now comes the hard part ... and I don't have a way to prove what I'm going to tell. This roadway ... where I now stand ... was used by a nation of peoples thousands of years ago. Maybe ten thousand years."

He waited until he thought that might have sunk in, then added, "I come from that people and *that* time."

They blinked.

"Look ... Nyaho ... each year at harvest you give a lengthy history of peoples and snows and struggles that goes way back in time. The farthest point in that time is the same time I'm talking about."

"You mean the time of the giants?" Nyaho asked.

John grumbled "Maybe what you *call* the time of the giants."

"Then you *are* a giant!"

"No dammit, I'm not a giant ... I don't know what the hell they even are. All I can guess is that they're some figment of imagination. I'm just tall that's all."

There was a lull then as both sides seemed to jockey for points to understand and express. Dlahni finally broke the impasse. "How John? ... How could you come from such a time? Since Nyaho found you and brought you home, you've aged like everyone else. I'd like to believe, but how can this be?"

"Good... that's a good question," John said beginning to shuffle back and forth on the narrow ledge. "It's very complicated but I'll try to explain ...

"You know that each winter things freeze ...."

They nodded.

"Well, some of those things are living creatures ... like frogs in particular. Frogs freeze solid, then in the spring they thaw and come back to life. We were all put through a process very much like that."

"We?"

"Yes ... there are more of us. In fact there are fifteen more."

"Where?"

"That's what I have to find out. I believe they're still in their winter home, so to speak, in a special building inside a mountain. Now that I know what's happened, I've got to try and find them and bring them back to life ... even if it takes all the rest of mine.

"I'll need help with this ... and I was hoping you'd both give me whatever support you can."

This was too much. The two looked at each other but neither could think of anything to say ... only subtle, confused whispers. This time Nyaho responded. "John ... we're trying to understand. Let me repeat what I think you've said. First, this black stuff you're standing on is a road."

John nodded.

"It was used by a people thousands of years ago. A time that may coincide with our time of the giants."

John flinched but nodded again.

"And you come from that time."

"Right."

"What happened to all the people?"

"Another good question. There was an epidemic that ravaged the world and killed almost everyone. Remember a few years ago when a flu of some kind had almost everyone sick, with many dying? This epidemic was like that but much, much worse."

"How many ... How much worse?"

"Oh my ... I think the numbers would only add to your confusion. Words like thousands and millions and billions have no meaning to you. When you look at the sky on a clear night, how many stars do you see?"

"They can't be counted."

"The number of people that were here thousands of years ago are almost like that. Around the world there were nations with many people and cities with beautiful buildings beyond my ability to describe. The people died ... It was awful. I lost my family and many friends. And, I suppose, in all that time the buildings crumbled and disappeared."

"But sixteen of you were put in a winter home?"

"Yes ... that's all there was room for."

"If there were people that numbered like the stars ... out of all of them, why you and the other fifteen?"

"We were very fortunate."

That wasn't a good answer, and John looked up and sighed after he said it.

"Are any of the others as tall as you?" Nyaho continued.

John snorted, trying to make light of it, "Why yes ... In fact some of them are even taller."

"But you're not giants?"

"*No dammit* ... as I've said before, we're just tall."

"And why again were the few of you picked?"

"We were chosen to be of help to any who survived the epidemic."

This wasn't going well. John was trying to confide in two of his best friends, ones he'd shared experiences and challenges and joys and heartbreaks with over the past twenty years, and was not finding the right words.

This story is too incredible ... I'd feel stupid but Nyaho is having the same problem ...

"Look," John said, "I told you at the start that the truth was going to be shocking ... and that I couldn't prove it at this time. In that regard I don't think I've done anything to either of you or to the *Atjahahni* that represents a violation of trust ... except for that lie years ago that you knew about. So somewhere here you'll just have to go on faith.

"As for the people still in winter, they're good people. They're good, they're strong and they're dedicated to helping in a variety of special ways that can be of great benefit. All of them are my friends, and in fact one, a beautiful young woman with a heart of gold, is my wife."

If Nyaho and Dlahni weren't in shock before, they were now, and it showed ...

"Wife?"

"Yes, I know ... me too.

"Well ... that's the story. I've told you all I can as best as I can. So think about it. I'd like your help, but if you decide otherwise, I'll understand. As for me, with or without you, I'll have to press on with finding my friends ... I've just got to. I do have a favor to ask of you now, however, and that is not to tell anyone else about this. I haven't told my family yet, so you see I definitely have another bridge to cross.

"And that's it ... Let's get back to the things we have to do."

At that point Dlahni had been in a stupor. He did have things to do ... the final arrangements for both those who were leaving in canoes and those who were taking the trail being among them. There had been more than the usual confusion because of his state of mind, but things finally got in reasonable order. The caravan left first. Dlahni watched as it rambled toward the trail, then as the last of them waved and disappeared, he grabbed a shovel and said to Nyaho, "Come with me."

They walked back up from the shoreline where all the canoes were gathered, the riders on ready wondering what this was about, 'til they came to one of the staging areas ... now deserted like everywhere else.

"John indicated that the roadway uncovered at the cut ran through here somewhere ... How would you interpret what he said?"

"You intend to find it?"

"Exactly."

"Hmmm." Nyaho turned back to get a fix on that ditch, then shook his head and walked all the way over to it. There he repeated in mind what had been said and tried to follow what he could interpret. With that he walked the way back, ending pretty close to where Dlahni was standing.

"I'd say it would pass through right around here," waving his arm to indicate a location. Then as Dlahni was about to dig in, he noticed something farther on.

"Wait ... water draining from the hill during the storm has sliced through on the same line," Nyaho said, pointing to the depression almost fifty feet away.

They didn't have to dig. When they got to the little gully, they could see at the deep end of it the same black rubble John had been standing on as he told his story.

Finally in the canoe and launched to lead the way, it wasn't long before the quiet rhythm of the effort opened the door in Dlahni's mind to what had happened just a short time before. Every word of the meeting at the cut came back to him ... over and over again.

Could what he heard be true? He found much of it was beyond his ability to understand. But what bothered him as much as any of that was his own skepticism. Here John had opened his astounding secret to he and Nyaho, his best friends, and they had doubted him. They had doubted the word of someone who'd been steadfast beyond belief; they had doubted someone who'd always been on hand to help; they had doubted the word of a person who directly and indirectly had changed so much of their lives ... all for the good. And finally they had questioned someone who'd spoken to the Great Spirit, a fact they had witnessed in the electrifying aftermath of the battle.

Earlier that year, before sunrise on the day when the hours of sunlight equal the hours without—a day John had come to call

Easter—many had assembled in *Tschtaha-tata* before daybreak. The night before had been clear and calm, a pleasant condition continuing as the show unfolded in a cloudless sky. First there was a glimmer of dawn, beginning ever so faintly; then the sky segued to red which reached its own crescendo, as if laying a carpeted runway; then the red faded as the sun burst from the horizon. The show didn't last long, but as the sun broke free, its rays flooded through the eastern open side of the structure and exploded against the rocks that formed the west. For a few magical moments, the light illuminated the faceted surfaces, as well as the flowers assembled along the tier, into a show so scintillating it was as if the spirits were among them.

Experiences had accumulated to indicate something special was happening in their lives ... and they were ignoring the signs. For all of these reasons he felt ashamed.

At the first opportunity away from other ears he discussed all of this with Nyaho, and found he felt the same.

Then came the issue with Daj-na-soa, and his course was set. He revised canoe teams so his and the one carrying Da-hash-to had rowers with the most stamina. Then early the next morning, before the rest were ready to go, the two canoes were launched and on their way. From that moment his obsession was to get home and then to backtrack to John and pledge him his support.

*   *   *

The days after that seemed like an eternity, but now more familiar landmarks came into view, one after another, and then there was the final turn and the dash home.

It was a wonderful feeling. After the grueling effort, which in his case included anxiety and shame, the thought of home and family and friends was like a balm. Looking back at the other canoe, he could see the same look reflected in their faces. But then there came a cloud over their expressions. Pivoting around he was able to see why. Something wasn't making sense. There wasn't a lookout on hand to spot them. There weren't people descending on the landing to give them a hero's welcome. What he could see was a shock ... he saw mobilization. Back from the shore nearer the Commons there were squads in formation fully armed with shields and spears and auxiliary units beside them.

Only this wasn't the time for Home Guard exercises.

Was the nation under attack?

They were almost into the cove before they were spotted ... and as they approached the bank he heard a cry that sent a chill and scrambled everything in mind ...

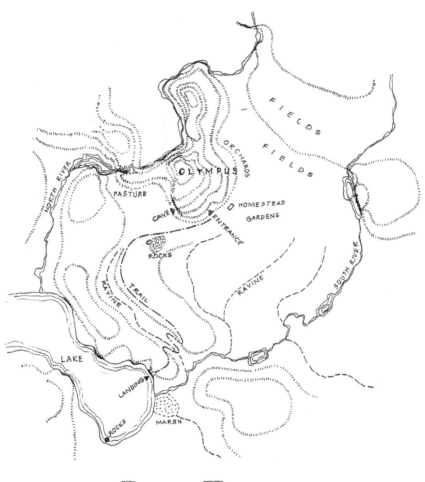

FIELDS

FIELDS

OLYMPUS

ORCHARDS

NORTH RIVER

PASTURE

CAVE

ENTRANCE

HOMESTEAD

GARDENS

ROCKS

SOUTH RIVER

RAVINE

TRAIL

RAVINE

LAKE

LANDING

ROCKS

MARSH

PART TWO

10

Easter – Six months earlier

"Wake up Gary; it's time to get up." This was the first sound he heard and it barely registered. He reacted with a twitch but slipped away again.

"Wake up Gary," the voice repeated … then again and again.

He mumbled something unintelligible in protest.

"Gary, wake up, it's time to get up," this time the order was barked.

At that moment, a few more winks was the most important thing in the world. He slowly edged into consciousness, but really not wanting to go there … the bed feeling like a magnet of cuddle comfort. He slurred "Lay off, dammit, give me a few more minutes."

"Gary … wake up, it's time!" The words like from a drill sergeant.

"The lights … turn down the goddamn lights! I can't see a thing."

"Get up Gary, it's time to get up," the bed now being rocked.

The harangue continued until finally he responded. With sloth-like movements, he kicked and flopped and lifted until he managed to sit on the edge, head in hands and almost falling over.

My god, what happened last night? I feel like a zombie….

"Gary, grab the railing and stand up!" There were encouraging remarks from several voices. As the sounds began to penetrate his muddled senses, he became aware of people moving about.

He groped and found the railing; then grasping it with fumbling hands, he wobbled to his feet.

"You're doing fine, Gary, now come this way..."

Starting slowly, he lurched along holding the rail until told to stop. "Good going ... good going," the closest person said, while others moving about behind him added their "way to goes" and applause.

"Do you know who I am?"

Gary squinted ... tried to focus. He shook his head, "I can't see very well ... the lights are too bright."

I'm Doc Walker ... Darby Walker." Then he laughed, "You might remember me better as "Bones"."

"Hi Gary ... welcome back, It's me, Huston ... Huston Burner," said the dim outline standing in the shadows beside Bones.

Then one of those moving around, a sturdy man with a wild tangle of hair and a handlebar mustache, stepped forward smiling from ear to ear, "Recognize me Gary? I'm Reynolds ... Reynolds Bascomb."

"Reynolds?" Gary croaked, a slight connect being made.

"Yes Gary ... remember that meeting a while back. You and John and Annie and Mona and a dozen others, and all of us, were together at a final meeting before the start of the journey ... a journey where no man had ever gone before ... Remember?" He related other details of that night, throwing in more names like Georgi and Anton and Devon and Abram and Bruno.

"Well, you're through with the first step in that journey, and you've arrived in fine fashion. "You're back.

"Now Doc here ... I mean Bones," laughing, "is going to walk you through the next step, which is a kind of orientation."

And Bones did. While Gary sputtered and mumbled at some of the instructions, the doctor ignored his protests and pressed on. One of the first tasks was to step onto a stationary walker and spend several minutes on it; then he was directed to a vending machine where was told to drink; then back to the walker; then to another drink; then to a console with handles for each hand like an early gaming device. While there, Bones proceeded with "yes" and "no" questions, which he responded to accordingly, using one handle for "yes", the other for "no". Gary did as he was told, but after a while, the simplicity of the process made him feel like a horse stomping in a circus show.

It also seemed that with each step, whether exercise or drink or question, the scene about him became clearer. He noticed that the area in which all of this was being conducted was like a large play pen with the equipment and devices being used built into and around its perimeter. He saw that the bed he'd been roused from was more of a low casket-like affair with lines and pipes and valves … and a domed, elaborately rimmed canopy, now wide open. A few feet from the one he'd been in was another just like it … also open and empty.

Then it hit him … he *was* back. Everybody had already told him that, but it hadn't sunk in. *He was back!* He was back and with him were Reynolds and Huston and Bones, which meant the world hadn't gone to pot after all. On that last night, they had prayed that the pandemic would stop … like the 1918 thing … and that they'd be brought back to a world where their friends and loved ones were still alive.

He was about to drop the handles and jump around and shout, but instead held back, sensing something strange. The strange was Bones, who kept asking questions and waiting for answers … without variety or personality in the process. It also dawned on him that the only real communication was being conducted by means of the "yes-and-no" machine; because if he said something or asked a question, there wasn't a reasonably expected reaction; instead Bones would proceed as if the script were etched in stone. Gary also noticed that Huston and Reynolds and the technicians who rambled about behind Bones occasionally looked over to see how things were going, which seemed natural enough; but if he smiled at them … or waved … there wasn't a reaction as should have been expected from any of them either.

The parade of questions, along with the observations, began to paint a picture that was somehow out of sync. He recalled a time when he'd placed a call and gotten an irritating automated response. He'd followed the instructions and selected the options as best he could until a question came to mind … and without thinking he'd asked it. The response was that he had to answer as directed for she couldn't "talk" to him … she was only a machine.

Ohmygod!

He let go of the handles and stepped back. Then he walked through a gate to where Huston and Reynolds and the others moved about ... *and walked through them!* They were a mirage, a smoke and mirror holographic display programmed to greet him in the new world.

Now he understood ... and the elation he'd felt deflated like a leaking balloon.

"Shit!"

Bones, who was now a vague mist as Gary was behind him, kept asking him to return as the orientation wasn't complete. So he kicked at dust that wasn't there and shuffled back. He shook his head, now with sad wonderment, as the simulations reformed and went into their routines. Bones drove on with his appeal, which Gary almost responded to, but then he backed-off. His eyes became misty and his lips quivered, so in an effort at control, he went to the treadmill instead. Thirty minutes later, gasping and dripping, he stopped it and stepped off. Only it didn't work. When he cooled, the scene, with Bones pleading and spectators revolving in sequence, brought reality back like a rogue wave and he lost it.

*   *   *

The *Easter Armageddon* Conference had made a definite impression on him, as it had John, but in a different way. John had been turned to a new calling, the environment, which the conference was all about. For Gary, however, it was the mystery surrounding Huston that stuck and wouldn't let go.

A few weeks later, not able to resist the curiosity that kept building, he did the brass-balled unthinkable, he gave Huston a call. He didn't get through, as were expected, but he managed to reach an assistant to whom he flat lied.

"What's that again?"

"My name's Gary Edson. I'm a good friend of Clifton Campbell and Reynolds Bascomb. I didn't get a chance to speak to Mr. Burner at the recent Conference, but I really wanted to. You see, I'm in my first year at medical school, and while this direction isn't relevant, another interest is. I'm speaking of Cryogenics. I think what's been done to date is only on the surface of what's possible. I happened to mention this to Reynolds and he said "talk to Mr. Burner ... he's been working in this field for years and could tell me a head full"."

"Tell you a head full?"

"Yes … he even gave me this number to call."

The conversation didn't go much farther than that, so when he hung up he'd thought no more would come of it. But then a few days later, the phone rang.

"Is this Gary Edson?"

"Yes."

"This is Hal Barnhard, assistant to Huston Burner. If you're still interested, Mr. Burner would like to meet you. He said "any friend of Reynolds is a friend of mine"."

And so it went.

When he was escorted into Huston's office, his first impression was a surprise. It wasn't elegant or ostentatious as could have been expected for a person of his accomplishments. It was a hodge-podge. There were no hunting trophies; there were no framed certificates and awards; and there were no grand smiling pictures with presidents and dignitaries. Instead there was an assortment of items representing the interests and accomplishments of a well-traveled person. The pictures were compositions of natural settings—a tropical jungle; a mountain meadow; a herd of bison on an endless plain; and many more like them. The accent pieces were complementary—a large bronze of an Indian on horseback appealing to the spirits; an ornate globe of the earth with an exaggerated relief of mountains, and forests and savannahs and deserts and oceans in vivid colors; a well-worn cowboy's working saddle on a stand; and an assortment of spiritual Indian artifacts. The décor was interesting and comforting rather than intimidating.

And then there was Huston, who got up from behind an ornately carved desk, which had to have an interesting story tied to it, and met Gary half way into the room. They then sat and sipped tea and exchanged pleasantries, with Huston prodding him about his interests and the details of his medical studies. It was all going so well Gary almost forgot how he'd gotten in the door.

He didn't have to remember. At a pause, Huston sat back into the cushions and for a few moments just looked at him, before saying, "Gary, why again did you call? *And let's cut out the bullshit.* Your good friend Reynolds didn't even remember you at first … and Clifton swore, but then said you were okay. So what's up?"

Gary flushed and didn't know which way to turn. He hadn't been in a spot like this since he'd been caught burning the totem pole. And just like that time he didn't have a place to run. So he fought to compose himself, swallowing, stuttering and finally speaking, the thoughts and words slowly coming together.

"Mr. Burner..."

"Call me Huston."

"Yes sir ... I mean Huston sir..."

They both laughed, which restored Gary's ability to breathe again. Then in a further moment of brashness, he decided he'd already dug a hole, so he might as well go for it.

"Sir ... you've been working with applications of cryonology to put people in time suspension. You've even built a secret facility in the mountains to house your program."

He was going to continue but Huston's reaction stopped him. First it was a poker player's blank stare, which segued to a twitch, then pursed lips, and finally a head turn with eyes squinted, "Who told...?"

Gary didn't smirk ... He didn't dare. Instead he wilted as a stare drove into him. "No one told me," the first words catching in his throat. "As I've said I have an interest in the same arena; my research came up with bits and pieces that eventually formed a possibility. Yes, I was guessing ... but it all seemed to make sense."

Huston got up and took a step away as if looking for something but forgetting what. Turning back he said, "So no one told you?"

"No sir."

Huston snorted, and laughed in a way, muttering only "Damn."

There was a short, awkward impasse, which Gary couldn't stand. "Sir, I'm sorry if I've upset you. There's no need to worry ... I can keep a secret. I was only hoping that if I was right, there might be some way to get into more of the detail of it all.

"The more I learn, and not just in school, the more uneasy I feel about planet earth ... Yes, the whole thing like that beautiful globe over there. It isn't just what the Conference told me, which was a lot. It's that and what I've learned in separate studies about what's happening on that globe, the billions who are wrapped up in their own needs or interests or ambitions, completely unaware or unconcerned about the grim possibilities unfolding. It may take time, but with what's being done, and not done, the world as we were given and would like to keep … is, in my opinion, doomed. Then there's that whatever in Indonesia killing everyone. If that gets loose, it could …"

Huston had turned away again, pacing as Gary spoke, but with the last comment spun around gaping, stopping Gary in mid-sentence. This was too much … too many scores on a mission he'd treated with utmost secrecy. *If a college kid can figure this out, who else is out there?* He plopped back in the chair, shifted, more to get his thoughts in order than to get comfortable … then looked up, face pinched.

"Come again, Gary?"

"Sir?"

"What do you want?" Leaning forward, he added, "What are you after?"

"Nothing. Nothing … except that if it's appropriate, I'd like to learn from what you've done, and possibly get involved. If it's not, I'll understand. And please, please don't worry about confidentiality, I haven't shared my thoughts with anyone."

Huston sat eyeing him as he spoke, remaining silent for a few moments. He nodded, smiled, and then broke into a laugh that started as a snicker, built in spurts, and finally rocked the room. He slapped his knees as he settled down, "Damn, if this isn't the most interesting meeting I've had in a long time.

"Gary … are you *serious* about wanting to get involved?"

"Yes sir."

"Okay. Okay, but first we must have an understanding. What you've guessed about is not just confidential … it's top secret. And it's also just the tip of the iceberg. So if I invite you to join us, it must be with your pledge to secrecy. You must not tell your family or friends or sweethearts … *no one.* Do you understand and pledge this on your honor, with the only assurances from me being that our actions will not be harmful to anyone, nor will they be disloyal to the country we pledge our allegiance. Do you pledge?"

Gary gulped and got a little dizzy, feeling like the man in the fable with two doors to open, one hiding a hungry tiger. But there had to be a great adventure tied to all of this, and the thought of being a part of it was just too much. He swallowed, then stammered "Yes sir, I mean Huston, sir … I pledge."

"Great," Huston said laughing some more. "Then hold on to your hat … it's going to be a wild ride."

And it was.

Before a week had passed, Huston invited Gary to an informal meeting at his offices, indicating that Eugene and Clifton and Reynolds and a number of his associates would be there. True to the description, the meeting started as a social with pleasantries and wine and no other disclosed reason than to allow people of similar interests to get acquainted. Gary had seen some of the associates at the *Easter Armageddon* Conference the month before, which was of some help, but regardless he was nervous amid the amassed credentials that were all about the room.

The occasion was a reunion of sorts as Gary hadn't seen anyone since the Conference; it was also an opportunity to meet men whose backgrounds led to interesting conversations. One of those was Doctor Darby Walker, who Huston made a point to bring by and introduce. It just so happened the doctor's specialty was Cryonology, sparking an immediate barrage of questions. Darby smiled at the enthusiasm, and answered a number of them, but then excused himself when another signaled for his attention. For Gary it was exhilarating just to be there, but there was also puzzlement, and in that he wasn't alone. Eugene was at the table of hors d'oeuvres picking over the choices when Gary stepped over to hear him whisper, "Why does it seem everyone here knows what the hell's going on but me?"

"You're not the only one in the dark," Gary said as he pretended to sip on his drink, "but I may have an idea." He was about to tell of this meeting with Huston when there was a clinking of glasses …

"Gentlemen, may I have your attention."

It was Huston. "Please fill your glasses if need be and follow me. We have some things set up for you that should be of interest."

With that the molecules of people bumped and bounced and reformed to funnel through to another room down the hall. Gary stayed by Eugene who sought out Clifton who'd been by Reynolds, so by the time the awkward process was over, he'd managed to be seated among the comfort of the few people he knew.

His mind and its curiosities couldn't rest, however. The chairs, arranged in gentle arcs focusing on the front of the room, were ergonomic concoctions of webbed plastic over molded framing, with various controls for motion and comfort. After settling-in and testing the possibilities of the chair, Gary looked at the room, which was richly wainscoted and paneled and quite attractive, but after scanning a few times, didn't seem right. The surfaces before him were like one of those pictures that if you press your nose to them and focus properly, will change to reveal a surprise view in three dimension.

"What do you see?' whispered Clifton, who hadn't been surprised at Gary's reaction.

"I'm not seeing much of anything … and somehow that doesn't fly."

Clifton nodded and smiled. "Just hold on … I think that curiosity of yours will soon be satisfied. I'd heard this room had state-of-the-art conferencing with moving panels and screens and monitors and projection equipment and recorders and assorted what-nots, all controlled in unique ways. State-of-the-art's a moving target with advances coming so quickly these days, so some of it may now be passé … but I think we'll enjoy the show, whatever it is."

When everyone was settled Huston began. "A lot has been going on at Burner Enterprises … some of you are familiar with parts of it, but none of you are with all of it. There have been projects we felt needed every confidentiality that could be maintained; and in that regard we were doing pretty well … at least I thought we were. But then Gary here came by recently and asked why we were doing what we were doing … and seemed to know exactly what that was."

Gary cringed and sank into his seat as heads turned and Eugene gave one of those looks.

"*Helloooh!* … If Gary could see what was up from the bits and pieces coming his way, then it wouldn't be long before other speculations would be on the streets. So some change is needed, and that change starts with us today.

"Now, before I get to the meat, let me back up a bit …

"Clifton, didn't you and Eugene and Gary and ... the tall, good-looking guy ..."

"John Anderson."

"Yes, the preacher's son."

"Don't let that fool you," Gary said.

Everyone laughed.

"I'm just kidding. He's a straight arrow ... my best friend."

"Okay ... well anyway, my understanding is the four of you camped out a while back, and while sitting by the fire, discussed various natural disasters like volcanos and meteors and things like that, which really did raise hell on earth a few times in the past. The odds are pretty slim for a happening of any of them anytime soon, so there's no need to go there now.

"Isn't that what you concluded at the time?"

Clifton nodded ... "Yes, but there were others, however, that could be a threat in our lifetime."

"Right ... and that's next.

"At *Easter Armageddon* we hit hard on the environment, which is a problem whether ninety-nine percent of the world recognizes it or not. But you all know about that."

Huston pushed a button and a wall surface moved into an indiscernible overhead recess, exposing an eighty-inch monitor. The monitor displayed a two-dimensional image of the world. "This is a study of population growth over the last century, prepared by an organization called Zero Population Growth." Another command began a program in which dots began to appear on the map representing parts of that growth, with background sound emphasizing the cadence. As the years rolled by the dots came at an increasing rate, hitting all land areas but accumulating more in China and India and within emerging nations.

The program was short, but in the few minutes it ran it built to a crescendo that suddenly stopped, the stopping and the silence afterwards emphasizing the fact that this was a problem.

"This you all recognize as population explosion. Since World War Two the earth's numbers have tripled. I won't say anymore about it except that it's the root of many of our problems ... and I really don't know what to do about it, because there's no doubt in my mind each additional person is endowed with the potential of any other. But let's combine this growth with other things that have happened."

Another click cleared the map of dots, then "Over the same period here are the nations who have developed atomic weapons capability with the number of warheads superimposed ..."

Here again the progression started slowly with first the United states, then Russia, then other nations following in quickening order, and within those nations the stockpiling of weapons shown with white dots. As a finale certain rogue nations were shown in pulsating form to show they were developing the capability.

"The next exhibit relates very definitely to what you've already seen." The screen cleared a second time. Then, after an interval, there was a simulated explosion on the map that faded to a red dot. Then there was another, then another and another in similarly increasing tempo to the present day, ending with dots scattered over most of the world with heavy concentrations in the Middle East.

"Now let's put them all together."

Starting with the blank map, the programs for population growth, nuclear proliferation and terrorism were run simultaneously, to a crescendo of sound that was more than three times any one of them, further emphasized by the introduced smell of cordite. There was a lengthy pause as the affects settled in.

"Yes," Huston said, "we do have a problem with the environment, and we do have a problem with population, but I think you can see there's another concern that's just as scary ... and more immediate. Terrorism is a madness that's hard for us to understand. George here can give you a better idea. He was on special assignment in Indonesia and was only a block from a bombing ... and this is what he experienced ... George."

George was Doctor Georgi Dvylas, a pathologist. George, a small man with graying hair that thinned to a scraggly veil on top, which contrasted with a well-trimmed, pointed beard, giving an impression somewhere between Einstein and Lenin, was someone who looked like he'd be more at home in a lab coat.

"A block isn't really far away," he began, "but far enough to allow me to be here. The concussion knocked me down ... Glass and debris were bouncing all around. You've all read about it, and know 107 people were killed and over 150 injured. As awful as the statistics sound, there's no way to describe the reality of the horror.

"There was lots of smoke which initially masked the scene; but as I moved into it to give a hand, the reality—blood and body parts and hanging innards and staring eyes ... in such abundance—stunned me like nothing before ever had. Then there were the injured, in many cases only slightly better off than the dead ... with looks that ran the gamut from stupor to fear to pain. The scene was quiet at first but soon the sounds of the injured began, growing into a mournful chorus.

"Words fail me. For anyone to do this to innocent people—men, women and children—is beyond comprehension. And yet that's what we are contending in these supposedly enlightened times.

Georgi struggled to say more, but he couldn't. He turned and sat.

Huston picked it back up. "Terrorism ... It's hard for us to understand how anyone can justify it as a rational action. And yet it's here. If we delude ourselves to think it's so unusual it's going to disappear on its own, we have a rude awakening. History gives us many examples of men, with their movements, who've been cruel or senseless beyond our ability to understand. The twentieth century had its share, with Stalin and Hitler and others leaving bloody trails. A while farther back were the Mongol hordes, who set their own standards. One of them delighted in capturing cities, then in the course of slaughtering tens of thousands of the populations, lopped heads to form grizzly pyramidal monuments to their victories. How can we fathom the horror among the hapless prisoners waiting their turn to make a contribution?

"What we have shown underscores a simple point. If terrorists gain access to atomic weapons, they'll use it at the first opportunity ... without regard for who is killed or what might follow. Some say it's not a matter of *if*, but of *when*.

"None of this is new ... we've just packaged the details in a way that gives the truth more impact. But it does bring us to the next level, the point of this meeting.

"With what we've just seen, there's an ominous threat to the world because of terrorism. I wish this was the worse thing before us."

Someone in back whispered "You've got to be kidding," but in the quiet following the last comment, it carried.

"No, I'm not!"

The world scene on the monitor came back to life, but not with the progression of threats as previously shown. Instead there was only a subtle pulsating glow from somewhere east of Java in the Indonesian archipelago.

"The spot you see may be worse ... far worse ... than anything else that's happened or can be anticipated, like an atomic bomb. We don't have a firm grasp on it yet; but we do know that it, I mean some virus, killed everyone on a small, remote island in that location. The island's been quarantined by the government and the incident treated as if it never happened; so nothing more has come of it. But it has scared the shit out of me. Although we only have bits to go on ... and Gary, you should appreciate this kind of reasoning ... it has all the characteristics that point to catastrophe. If this "whatever" was to get loose, it could wipe us out, I mean *everybody!*" His hands waving to emphasize, "It's potentially that bad.

"I've had a team with Georgi heading it in the vicinity ever since we heard of it, to find anything that would give us a leg up to counter it if it cropped-up again. The fact it happened at all has shaken us to the core and forced us to accelerate one of our programs. Most of you are already involved. The rest of you will be have the opportunity for additional positions that have opened because of the urgency this incident has made us consider.

"Here is the plan."

Huston then described the work of Cryonology and the recent successes after thirty years; he showed pictures of an astounding secret hi-tech complex nearing completion in the mountains; he told of all of this coming together for the purpose of sending a dozen or more carefully selected young men and women ... where no one had gone before ... into the future; and he explained why.

The plan and his involvement in it changed Gary's life. He'd been busy before, but after the meeting it was as if the demands on his time had been doubled, with hardly room for rest. He was assigned to Darby and his team, and cast into the world of Cryogenics with all its complexities. He was present when a certain Ahmad Barakzai was brought back after five years in suspension, seeing first hand the awakening characteristics and the methods used to bring a person back to normal function.

Time became lost to him with the intensity and challenge of all the involvements, which meant some things had to go ... like the weekend trips to see Mona, with whom a definite attachment had been developing. And events just blew by: There was John and Annie's engagement, which caught him by surprise; then the wedding; then the horrific nuclear mess that created the apocalyptic summer; and finally near the end of that summer, the awful news that the greatest fear of all, the dreaded pathogen, was alive and had struck again, this time in a manner indicating the tiger was loose.

It was as if all of Huston's fears proved to be prophetic.

Their efforts had come to a head at the French Broad, and all of it in less than a year's time. But what a time. So much happened, with so many bonds of admiration, respect and friendship forming as a result, that he didn't realized the extent until much, much later.

*   *   *

Now, alone in the antiseptic confines of the orientation chamber, it hit him. The world he'd known and loved was gone; gone were his parents and all his friends; gone were all those he'd labored with during those hectic months, including Huston and Reynolds and Darby and Clifton and Eugene ... all of them.

And he lost it. He'd never thought of whether or not he could cry ... real men don't cry, at least that was conventional wisdom. But here, alone, as reality imbedded itself, there grew a sorrow somewhere between heart and mind that grew and grew and burst the bonds of control, venting itself in deep sobs. Helpless, Gary staggered to the rail and grabbed it before falling, staying there until the volcano of hurt within him had reasonably quieted.

He walked back to the console, stepped on the platform and grabbed the handles. Immediately the apparition that was Bones changed and returned to the place in the program where the interruption had occurred.

Soon it was over.

The final questions were asked twice. It was like with a computer where a selection is made, and then a dialogue box pops up so the action can be verified. The questions were: "Did he understand he was the first to be brought back from the twenty-first century, and now had to assist bringing back the others?" And, "Was he now ready to get on with the mission?"

With the final verified "yes", several things happened: A series of lights flashed and horns blared around the room; and whistles and claps and waves came from the spectators. Huston spoke first, "Gary, by now you've figured out we're not real." Huston's eyes were focused on where Gary was standing. Gary realized this, knowing that if he moved he'd break the bond and the spell, so he stayed where he was. "We've been dust a long time ... that's just the way it is and that's okay. Our thoughts and good wishes, however, are real and are sincere forever. You're back and are about to embark on the greatest challenge ever put before anyone in the history of mankind. May the grace of God be with you."

Then Reynolds stepped forward. "Gary, since you're the first, it can only mean something went wrong with John. I hope he's alive and only missing ... but whatever the case, please help Annie in whatever way is needed. She's my girl.

"Now, as you know, there's a tremendous amount of information and research material at your disposal. What you don't know about is the daily log we're keeping that should add to those resources, and the letters from loved ones that kept arriving for weeks after your departure. I hope they'll be of help.

"God bless."

Gary shook his head, choked and teared-up again as the orientation came to a close, the much respected and loved apparitions before him fading into nothingness. And, in the adjoining area with its rows of casket-like cocoons, each with its disciplined array of wires and tubes and devices, sounds could be heard.

Gary knew what had to be done ... the instructions before and the reminders now were loud and clear. The first steps following the orientation were to strip from the space-age jump-suit he'd worn during the freeze, to sponge bathe, and then to change into the fatigue-like clothes packed in his locker. With these completed, he was to take a nap, as the next of the scheduled "resurrections" were going to begin early the next day. From then on it would be hectic, with groups of two following in quick order, and a great deal to do.

All that being understood, there was still the one reality pushing all others aside and bothering him. John had preceded him. At least it appeared that way because John's cocoon was empty.

But where the hell was he?

When Gary went to the locker room, he checked John's locker; it hadn't been touched. Then he searched every room he could, the power chambers being the only places that weren't accessible as they required a special key and access code. He went through an arrangement of doors through the decontamination chamber to the entrance vestibule and its adjoining spoils storage room. He looked over the massive entrance door, which appeared more like a blast-resistant vault door, but left it alone as opening it was complicated … and he could see it hadn't been attempted. He retraced his steps past the orientation arena to the library and media center and assorted support spaces, ending at the far end of the complex where a series of doors finally opened to another vestibule that had at its far wall an exit door boldly labeled "CAVE". He stopped there. A sign beside the door warned that the strike needed to be unlocked otherwise it could close and lock-out anyone who'd passed through. There were, however, keys, thoughtfully hanging conspicuously on the wall beside the sign. There was also a cabinet with ropes and tools and manually generating flashlights, all neatly arranged as originally placed.

The exit-way was a double-door, one swinging to the inside, the other out; both with closers. The doors were of steel, obviously sturdy, but not nearly as bulky as the single entrance door up front. The inner door had a peep-hole, through which Gary couldn't see much of anything, so he opened it enough to see the outer door, which had a small view panel that must have been bulletproof to match the structural integrity of the rest. He peered through the panel but saw little here as well. Then he flipped a switch, which turned on outside lights whose illumination partly clarified a mess of webs and stalactites and fluttering movements and glop, the light mostly disappearing into the expanse of the cave's volume.

With that he stepped back to close the inner door, but stopped.

On the last day all of them had been given a tour of the facility. They'd started with decontaminations where overalls and hair caps and antiseptic light had been a part; then with Huston and Reynolds and Bones alternating descriptions, the group had woven from one room to another to where he now stood. Along with John and a few others, he'd gone through both doors, stepping down to a landing from where a view of the cave opened before them. A stair dropped from the right side of the landing, following the foundation wall down to the cavern floor. There a trail began with standards and ropes that snaked their way through the contours and stalagmites that made up the convolutions of the cavern floor, disappearing from view at one of the bends. They were told that the trail eventually led to a surface opening, and that it could be an escape route should one be needed. The area they could see from the landing was relatively clean about areas of recent construction, but was a musty, reeking mess everywhere else ... the obvious result of bats and critters and lots of time.

So what was the cave like now? A second look revealed the railings were gone, which meant they'd probably rusted or rotted away, and may have meant other things as well. He really wanted to see what that might be; but he just couldn't take the chance of opening the outer door and stepping out ... he was alone with everyone depending on him.

But there was something about the door combination ... and about the warning sign beside it.

Could John have blundered through?

Returning to a bunking room where cots were lined in close array, Gary reviewed the high points. For one thing he was alive; the system had worked, and the orientation that had been so ingeniously choreographed had brought him up to speed, eliminating the short-term memory aspect that would have been a problem. For another, John had also been brought back to life, but wasn't there; he'd looked from one end to the other and hadn't found anything, which was half good because at least there wasn't a dried skeletal remnant along the way. Now at least there was hope ... even if it was wrapped in mystery. And finally, there was the time; when he passed the library he saw a clock with its seconds in relentless motion. The hour and minute and second were of little concern, but the other information was; the clock displayed the day as March twenty-second in the year of ten thousand twenty.

Ten thousand twenty?

And a message panel above the clock read in pulsating multi-colored letters that couldn't be ignored …

"HAPPY EASTER."

11

Two Days Later

"Hey, you guys, come look at this," Roland said as he ducked through the door.

"Can't now … You come here, things are starting to happen … *shhh.*"

Gary had seen it before, first with Ahmad in what amounted to thousands of years before, then with Abram and Roland two days ago; but it was an experience that would always be amazing. Although similar events were occurring in nature all about the planet from single cells to the largest of creatures, duplicating it remained one of the science's greatest challenges. The challenge was creating the spark that was life.

Roland walked over. He looked around, careful not to interrupt again, and saw there weren't bubbling vials or electric flashes or cacophonic pulses as might have been expected—like in the Frankenstein dungeon. Instead, the scene was quiet, with only faint muffled sounds and subtle movements on overhead monitors.

A lot was happening, however. Within the bulky enclosure, in a variety of sequences that had started hours before, the body within the cocoon was thawed from extremely frozen to normal; at which point cryoprotectants were extracted and fluids infused to replace them; lungs were drained and refilled with oxygen-rich air; and organs—including brains, heart and lungs—were stimulated by individualized and synchronized electro-chemical impulses. When all works were completed and balanced, connections to the body were extracted and openings sealed.

For the observers, the only awareness to all of this was on the monitors, which one by one moved to one-hundred percent and began to pulsate. Agonizing minutes after the last one indicated its operations finished, the lid to the cocoon emitted a long, low, hissing sound and disengaged, opening slowly to expose its content. The content was Anton. He looked natural enough, but could have been just a corpse as there wasn't anything to indicate otherwise, the only movements being slight reactions to externally applied electrical impulses.

The cocoon was also being mechanically shaken, which together with the impulses didn't seem to be doing anything other than increasing tensions to a breaking point ... everyone holding breaths waiting for the magical spark.

There was a twitch ... then another.

"Did you see that?" in a whisper.

They wanted to jump around, holding back only because they couldn't be sure. Then a loudspeaker overhead boomed "Wake up Anton, it's time to get up."

That was the cue. The three took it from there, jostling and ordering and encouraging until, like a babe slapped on the butt, Anton blinked, moved, groaned and blubbered in protest. Without a letup in the harangue, he eventually staggered to a sitting position and flopped his legs around.

"Come on Anton, it's time to get going ..."

Anton sat on the edge, weaving and nodding and squinting, slowly bringing those around him into focus. He tried to speak again but only slurred.

"You're doing fine ... doing fine," Gary said, his voice breaking. He stepped back as his eyes misted and blew his nose. *Would I ever get used to this?* There were exhaling sounds of relief, followed by all of them looking at each other and laughing.

Gary moved forward and grabbed Anton by the shoulders, "You lazy bastard, do you know how long you've been sleeping?"

Anton squawked again, managing a weak smile.

Abram and Roland added their jibes, and when enough of the

nonsense had done all it could, Gary added, "Stand up now ... we've got work to do. In fact Doc Walker ... you know, "Bones"?"

"Bones?"

"Yes, Bones; he's going to walk you through a program that'll put that head of yours back on straight. Grab the rail here and do exactly as he says."

The three stepped away then and let the program—a modified version much like the one Gary had experienced—run its course. It was to take a drink, walk the treadmill, drink, walk, 'yes' and 'no', drink, walk, answer some more, and on an on. Tommy and Abram went to the area where holographic images of the orientation cast were doing their thing, blending in and making it look like quite a group was on hand.

In time the program was over and lights flashed and horns blew and everyone clapped and cheered, setting the stage for Huston and Reynolds, who gave their final statements and faded away. When things settled, Gary asked Roland to take Anton around and get him reacquainted with the surroundings, while he and Abram moved back to where the sounds and signs in the next cocoon holding Bruno were reaching a critical point.

And so it went.

Later there was a time to relax, with all that had been resurrected gathering in the lounge. It would be the final stop before the rest period ... which was a planned sequence to prepare for the next round of retrievals.

"What is this crap?" Anton said as Gary pushed his first meal towards him.

"Whatever it is, don't complain," Gary said. "It's the best we've got." The best was a tasteless mush of freeze-dried, vacuum packed granules added to water and heated. It was a meal specifically designed to provide basic nourishment, as well as to encourage getting out and finding something better. In the latter regard it did very well.

"So what's going to happen next, Cap'n?' Anton drawled after he'd swallowed a few spoonfuls, his movements, thoughts and words still being difficult to manage.

Gary sighed. "Actually, quite a lot. But first we need for you to rest."

"Good … I'm bushed."

"Me too," Bruno said. "And I haven't done a damn thing."

"That's natural. Hey, it's going to take a while before we're back to speed with strength and stamina … okay? So we need to go slowly and take rests."

Gary looked at his watch. "In six hours, another cycle will begin for Devon and Rodney, which means we'll then have all the muscle we're going to have to get out of here. Even so, the program will continue without a break with the girls. Everyone will therefore be back in a few days."

"What's the hurry?"

"It's simple. This place has a lot to offer, especially with the library, media center and laboratory; but it was never intended as a home. It'll be pretty crowded when everyone's on hand … You'll see. For many reasons, we need to get out and set up outside."

"How soon is "need to"?"

"Don't know exactly," Gary said, answering Bruno but speaking to everyone, "I don't think there's a problem with air or power; as I recall those systems had the capability for ten thousand years, so there's room to spare. But the amount of water stored is what it is, and the food—that mush we're eating—definitely is as well. All we have to do is divvy up what's on hand to see how long it'll last. Not long I'd guess."

"Reynolds said a week."

"That sounds right … and the time will go fast."

Bruno leaned forward, still struggling to accept what had happened and curious as well. "Another question … maybe some of you discussed this before, but isn't there an elephant in the room?"

"You mean John?"

"Yes, John. He was supposed to be the first one brought back, then you. The two of you were going to team-up, with you assisting in getting us back and John concentrating on getting us out. What happened? His cocoon's empty but his locker isn't; it hasn't been touched."

Everyone looked up.

"I wish I knew. From what I can see, I'm sure he was resurrected; but I can only guess at what happened after that.

"In my case, I went through essentially the same orientation each of you did. The only difference is that when I answered the last question, the answer triggered the mechanisms starting the process for the rest of you.

"However, John was supposed to be that trigger. Since the trigger wasn't pulled after him, I can only assume he never completed the orientation. It's possible he didn't even start it."

"Why do you say that?"

"Well ... it's the program. It's very cleverly composed. Once you get into it, you're pretty well hooked, and therefore continue until you're done.

"Wouldn't all of you agree with that?"

Everyone nodded, but Bruno wasn't through. "If John didn't trigger our returns, how soon afterwards were *you* independently started?"

"I don't know ... Don't have the faintest idea. Why?"

"Well, think about it. What year is it now?"

"Now? The monitor in the library says ten thousand twenty. So?"

"Just a hunch. Huston had some strange ways and he liked to be in control. If the year now is really ten thousand twenty, it doesn't sound like a number he'd have picked ... and also not some random happening. But the year for John, who was first, might have been a special selection. If that's so, what year do you think he picked?"

Gary shook his head, "I'm still not following you."

"Okay ... Let's say Huston can pick any date he wants, and that he likes noteworthy, even numbers. Ten thousand twenty is hardly it, so what year is?"

"I guess you want me to say ten thousand ... even."

"That sure sounds better."

Gary thought for a moment. "If your hunch is correct, then John would've been resurrected twenty years ago. Is that what you're thinking?"

"Yes. It just seems to make more sense that way."

"Wait a minute, why a twenty-year difference?" It was Abram. "Why not a day, or a year, or two years, or ten? Twenty years is quite a gap."

Gary shook his head while the others shrugged. Finally Bruno suggested, "Maybe no reason ... Maybe when you're dealing with thousands of years, the next notch in the timing system just happens to be twenty."

Anton, following the discussion and trying to grasp the significance of it all, said, "This is all very interesting, but whatever the time, where is he? There's not a trace of him around here."

"That's true, but some things are clear," Bruno said. "If John came back, regardless the time, it's obvious he didn't stay around. That leads to ... Did he make it out? And ... did he survive? If the answers to these are "yes", then what happened? John isn't the kind to abandon anyone ... especially Annie."

"Ahem." All eyes turned to Roland, who'd finished all the mush he could stand and had settled back, hands clasped behind his head. "I don't know whether he survived or where he went, but I damn sure know where he didn't go. I wanted to show you something a while back when Anton was coming on line ... Remember?"

"Oh yes," Gary said. "What was that all about?"

"Well, while you and Abram were obsessing over what was going on with hayseed, here ..."

"What? Watch it," Anton said with a grin, tossing an imaginary missile.

Roland flinched, then sat up. "Anyway, I took a peek at what getting out of here was going to involve."

"And?"

"It's not pretty." He stood and walked to the door, turning to say, "All of you need to see this."

They followed him through doors and hallways, including the decon chamber, then up a flight of steps through more doors to the entrance vestibule, stopping in front of the huge portal at its end. Roland worked the latches, just as he had a few hours before, slowly swinging the creaking, over-sized, vault-like door to rest against the wall on the hinge side. The opening exposed a problem. It was a cruddy surface solidly packed against where the door had been, a surface with clay and dirt and sand and pebbles and rocks and boulders; and tunnels of critters; and interlocking webs of roots ... the whole collage seeming to be cemented together.

"This is the way out?"

12

A Plan

Designers had no way of knowing what conditions would be like thousands of years in the future, so they considered a worse case, and proceeded accordingly. Access to the underground compound began within a large wood-roofed building that looked like a machine-shed—a rambling, rustic part of the farmstead. The interior, rather than being open storage, was state-of-the-art workspace vital to the operation. This access led into a gabled section which extended from the shed, penetrated the hill rising from the base of it, and ran to where the roof plate and the slope of the hill intersected, where it seemed to stop. The extension, sturdy in itself with concrete retaining walls below grade, didn't end as it seemed; it connected to a tunnel, ten feet by ten feet in cross-section, that continued into the hill another thirty feet to an end-wall with a vault-like entry door. This part of the long hallway was of heavily reinforced concrete like the rest of the compound, with an overhead slab two feet thick.

Provisions within the entry were just as well considered. Although Huston had a bias against metals in the new world, or at least a desire to minimize their use, he caved-in to the argument that his whole noble experiment might fail if the Chosen were resurrected, only to die entombed. Therefore there were tools. There were shovels and axes and picks and sledges and hammers of many sizes; there were saws and chisels and cutters; there were crowbars and jacks and come-alongs and chains and cables; there were electric power tools like chain saws and jack-hammers and drills; and on and on with supporting hardware and accessories. There were provisions for exhaust and filtered fresh air, which was necessary for messy operations in an enclosed space, with linkages to cave volumes. There were, resting on extenders at the top of the equipment array, several steel rods of varying lengths to twenty feet—similar to the kind used as probes to locate bodies buried in winter avalanches.

Things had been provided in response to situations that imaginations could envision, which had been good. All of them would come into play.

The first few feet of excavations went easily—Roland and Anton and Gary alternating to dig and fill a wheelbarrow-sized, four-wheel cart, then dumping in the adjacent spoils reserve.

"Okay, my turn," Gary said as Anton returned from one of the first rounds. Then he attacked where the other had left off, dislodging bits and pieces with reckless abandon.

"Hold it there," Anton said.

"What?"

"You're making a hole in the middle."

"So? Aren't we trying to get all of this crap out?"

"Yes, but if you go too far and create a tunnel, the stuff above could come crashing down."

Gary stepped back and caught his breath, "Oh, I see and you're right. We've got to be careful."

They continued to take turns, working until lungs and muscles, which still hadn't returned to normal, gave out; at which point they'd step back and let the next take over. They tried to keep the cut in safe proportions by clearing to the ceiling, then excavating along it to maintain an angle downward that wouldn't tend to collapse.

The initial easiness soon got difficult. Root systems, for one, went from tangles of feeders to increasingly larger sizes. "Looks like the business end of a giant octopus," Roland said after sawing off the latest portion. "What do you suppose is above it all?"

"It's got to be a pretty damn big tree."

"Or trees ..."

"Or trees."

Rocks and boulders were also jammed in to contribute to the blockage, each one being its own unique problem. For the largest managed on this first day, shovels and pry-bars were used for loosening; a cable was wrapped around; and then, using a come-along, ratcheted and pulled forward onto timber planks, from where it was coaxed through the doorway. In similar fashion the boulder was forced onto runners over a bed of sand and slid to the spoils pile.

"This may have been how they moved those rocks at Stonehenge," Gary said.

"Which means we're back to the past as well as the future ... Right?"

Roland groaned at the play on words, "Something like that."

When four hours passed and it was time to quit, they were spent. They had cleared a volume through to each sidewall and to the ceiling slab ten feet back, but they weren't in a mood to celebrate. The root system had taken on larger and more menacing proportions; final actions had exposed a boulder larger than any before; and the ceiling slab, which was supposedly indestructible, had instead been like the Titanic, collapsing with two-thirds of it adding to the rubble somewhere in the remaining mess.

For all of these reasons, the crew that returned to the lounge to greet Devon and Rodney, the newest arrivals, were not only dirty and tired, they were also discouraged.

Later Gary couldn't sleep.

It wasn't as if everything had gone wrong, because that wasn't the case. He'd assigned Bruno and Abram to assist with the arrivals ... and the change had worked fine. The two added a nice touch by announcing to the diggers through the intercom when all monitors were pulsating, which allowed them to be on hand and celebrate another companion's coming back to life.

It was really a bunch of things.

One was that theory Bruno voiced soon after being brought back—the one about the time difference between John and him. Gary knew more about the process than anyone else, having spent the better part of a year with Bones and his team; so without a reason to think otherwise, he'd assumed the gap in timing to be only half a day, just as it was for everyone else.

Could Bruno have a point with the year being at ten thousand twenty? True, Huston could be squirrely, so an even number might have been important to him. Another factor was the day itself. Huston wasn't outwardly religious, but he did have deep beliefs, and the concept of Easter—of renewing or being born again—had a special meaning to him. Gary knew Huston felt the traditional process for determining Easter didn't make sense, so in his mind the Vernal Equinox was it. Besides, by bringing everyone back early in the year, as much as five weeks earlier than by traditional Easter reasoning, the Chosen would have at least six months to adjust to conditions and prepare for the winter.

Huston had emphasized the importance of timing. "The Pilgrims, for instance, were put ashore in early November in the cold of winter. It was a dreadful time because they not only had to find a place to settle, they had to find food, build shelters, and prepare for the next growing season. By the time that season arrived, half of the party that landed—just over one-hundred men, women and children—were dead."

He had added, "Don't take the challenge of surviving too lightly. The lessons from the earliest settlements—Plymouth and Jamestown—were that it wasn't easy and may take years to become established. Since there are so few of you, and since your mission is so important, we can't afford to lose half of you or take a long time. Therefore to give all of you a better chance in this, we've assembled young, strong people—people with survival skills—and put them in a place where game is plentiful."

Even with all of Huston's cautions being considered, one day more or less on the calendar shouldn't make much of a difference. But the fact was *his* date *was* Easter, and most likely John's was too, which meant at least one year had passed for this coincidence to happen. This also made the twenty year gap more and more probable.

The next thought had to do with the girls, who were next in line. He really wasn't ready for them, but maybe he could assign the first of them—Mona and Rebecca—to replace Abram and Bruno so there'd be more men in the dig. And how he looked forward to seeing Mona again. The last year B.P.—Before the Plague—had been so frantic a definite wedge had been driven in their relationship. Although he'd texted her a few times, he felt he hadn't handled the situation very well, making it awkward when they finally saw each other again at the French Broad. The situation didn't improve much there either as the schedule and his role in the proceedings continued to keep them apart.

It had come down to the final night when all of them gathered around the fire. They'd sat together then, and during the hours of songs and stories, had sidled closer to become wrapped in a blanket, and not just because of the night air's chill. When in the wee hours a number parted to sleep, they'd joined those who chose to stay by the fire in sleeping bags. Only they didn't sleep. They talked and snuggled and hugged and talked some more. He tried to apologize but she'd hushed him saying she understood ... saying she felt blessed to be among those who had a chance to represent so many ... saying she was there for him and that they could work things out later.

Now later was at hand and it was hard to wait any longer.

It was with relief he remembered that the two married girls were among the last to be revived. Someone decided it was best this way in case something went wrong with a spouse; it would give more time to prepare.

The consideration was nice, but prepare to what? What was he going to tell Annie that would mollify the truth? All the time in the world wasn't going to help, because right now he could only tell her John had been successfully revived, as much as twenty years beforehand, but was missing.

Then there was that damned plug that blocked the entry.

He remembered what had been intended ... because Reynolds had explained it. "One of the last things we'll do to help all of you along is to build a timber wall across the beginning of the concrete tunnel. With the time being considered, the shed and hallway extension will be so obliterated little trace will be found of them. The timber wall, however, should act as a buffer from all else that's happening, and before it comes apart, limit the amount of stuff working its way in. Digging out shouldn't be difficult."

So Reynolds had worked it all out … everyone thought. Unfortunately he was wrong. Over all the years, things had happened to fill the tunnel in ways much different from his assumptions, and now they were stuck with the result.

In keeping with Reynolds' assumptions, the plan had been to break out quickly, then get on with the mission. That plan already had a few hiccups—first John, and now the plug. He didn't know what to do about John; as for the plug, they could keep hammering away, and could eventually work through; but there was just as big a chance that the more they cleared, the more they'd expose themselves to dangers they couldn't foresee. They weren't miners, so he didn't have that to fall back on; but he could still visualize problems with the boulder and the tree, and he shuddered at the thoughts.

Another part of it all was that they not only had to break out, which a small opening would do, they also had to clear out. That meant clearing the entryway to its original dimensions, because there needed to be long term and convenient access to the resources within the compound—the library and media center in particular—in order to do what was needed.

What should he do?

Since conditions were so different, it might be that the problem needed to be attacked from both directions. Both directions meant getting outside in order to get outside; and getting outside meant either tunneling vertically from where the roof had collapsed, which was risky, or finding a way through the cave. These were the only options.

He would discuss tunneling with the diggers at the start of the next work period. As for the cave, however, he shuddered again. He remembered the impression millenniums ago when several of them stepped onto the landing; he remembered the view a few days ago when he looked through the port in the back door. It wasn't pretty in either case. And he was mindful that since John wasn't inside the complex, and hadn't gone out the front door, he must have gone into that mess. If so, John went in befuddled, and … he was probably still there.

That thought made him twist and almost roll off the cot.

He looked at his watch for the umpteenth time and could see it was approaching eight o'clock—*eight a.m. that is*—which was perfect because the light of day might reveal an entrance to the cave... if there still was one. Anyway he had to go there; but he needed help. There was no way he was going into that place alone.

Who?

After reviewing the who, Devon came to mind. Devon was a good choice, not because he was suited physically, as any of the others were equally so, or because he was such a character, which he was ... a special bonus. When the diggers cleaned-up and joined the rest in the lounge, Devon had just finished his first meal of mush. Despite this tasteless introduction to the new world, he and the other three were having a good time ... the resounding success of Huston's systems being more than enough reason to celebrate. But then the diggers made their report and gave a tour of the entryway, where the yawning hole looked like a monster's snare.

That would have killed the mood had it not been for Devon. On returning, he stopped by the locker room and picked up a package. Back in the lounge he unwrapped it in a process that captured everyone's attention. It was a guitar—a three-quarter sized one with enough dings and scratches to indicate something well traveled. He tinkered and strummed, adjusting turns until satisfied with the sounds. Then he launched into several ditties, the first slow and elemental as a further test; the second picking-up the pace and changing the drift; and the final one from a collection by "Walking Jim Stoltz" that had been played by the fire on the last night together.

> *There's a place that I know,*
> > *where I'd like to go,*
> > > *the rivers all run so crystal clear;*
> > *and the trees are growing tall*
> > > *and the critters have it all,*
> > *and the wild birds are all that you can hear.*

> *[Come walk with me*
> > *through the big pine trees,*

from the mountain tops,
to the shining sea;
where the critters roam,
breed on their own,
in the wilderness,
we'll be right at home.]

There were several more verses, and after each one, just as they had at the campfire, the others joined in with the chorus. And as they did the slouching body languages perked to be replaced with smiles and sparkling eyes.

The last song was a particular favorite of Terry's, which he loved to play as it may have been the song that tipped the scales in their acquaintance and began a mutual interest.

They'd met in as strange a way as any. He'd been hiking the Appalachian Trail with a group of college friends, with their hike of several days ending at the Nantahala Outdoor Center where they'd planned to do some refreshing, white-water rafting.

It was an easy ride in an eight person raft, simple enough for families with younger children, with only a few low level rapids—just enough to cause screams and get riders wet. But it was a beautiful day and the cool water and the passing scenery made it perfect. Adding to the fun was the guide, who had named himself "Fatal", as if to emphasize the great, but fictitious, danger of the adventure. He, like Devon, was also a character, with a cheerful patter that made the trip much more interesting for most. But patter can get out of hand, because when it's repeated day after day, there's a danger of infiltrating exaggerations building to ridiculous extremes, as the story-teller tries to be more and more impressive.

Devon was relaxed and hardly listening as the raft approached a high bluff around which the river bent. The guide, Fatal, was pointing out, as an item of interest, that dropping from the vegetation crowning the bluff was a special vine, a vine so rare in the botanical world that scientists from all corners came to study its particulars. As they passed nearby, and the description was reaching its zenith, Devon was startled by an incredulous *"What?"* from a girl up front, who turned to express herself at the same time the raft hit a minor dip. The combination flipped her out, a happening quickly accompanied by a chorus of screams.

Devon was on the same side and tried to reach her as she glided by, but the current pushed her away, so he simply rolled out to give assistance ... knowing there was little danger and welcoming the chance for excitement.

As it happened the girl didn't need his help. She was laughing hysterically, but had turned on her back with her feet pointing downstream, and was floating in parallel to the raft just as she had been instructed. Anyway, they were both pulled back into the raft and it all added to the fun.

Later that night at a bon-fire near the Center, there was an opportunity, along with many beers, to strum the guitar and sing a few songs. After one of them, he was adjusting the stops when he recognized the girl who'd just joined the fire as the one in the raft ... much prettier now than when bedraggled in a wetsuit.

He then had hit with *Come Walk With Me* and was further moved by her exuberant participation, which lifted him in return. Besides her name, Terry, he found she was studying to be a botanist, and that the exotic vine Fatal had described was a common mountain variety.

A year later they were married.

Devon was the choice because as a biologist he might make a better assessment of conditions above ground, and therefore help in guiding the next move.

Gary was ready.

13

The Cave

They assembled in the vestibule before the cavern doors, with Abram and Bruno assisting in what was similar to pre-flight operations. First was equipment. Gary and Devon would each carry a length of rope coiled about the shoulders; each had a small backpack with rain gear and snacks and water and assorted stuff; each had a hand-crank generator clipped to one side of the waist, a machete to the other. The generator was wired to both a head-lamp and a walkie-talkie, which seemed crude by way of twenty-first century standards, but for a time eight thousand years later was a marvel. Each carried a pistol holstered next to the machete.

The next step took them outside. The inner door opened easily and stacked against the wall; and surprisingly, the outer door, which had been assumed to be a problem with frozen hinges and weather-sealed edges corroded shut, swung away almost as readily. And with the opening came the smell. They had stepped from antiseptic clean to cool, damp cow barn and it hit like a wave.

"*Peeeuh!*"

"Welcome to the nether land, the world of guano … Come on, we'll get used to it."

Then came the cleaning—the view panel on the outer door, building flood lights, electrical outlet and switch covers, and communication devices—all of which were a mess.

With this completed and tested, the two assisting them said their goodbyes, wished them luck, and left for the cocoons which were making noises, shutting the doors behind them.

Alone now, the two stood, viewing the ghostly expanse whose details drifted to nothing as the light dissipated. "Now let's hold on a sec," Gary said, uncertain of the next move. They'd seen it all before; but then they were in a small crowd under the safest of conditions, so now the impact was greater, numbing senses for a while.

"Weren't there railings here before?" Devon asked.

"Yes, but nobody thought they'd last. Now we know. But it really doesn't matter." Taking a deep breath, he added, "Let's get on with it."

They did, descending the stairs while staying close to the wall, and then slowly stepping their way into the soft, collapsing surface. Only a few steps past the bottom, Gary happened to turn back and look up, only to realize they may already have screwed up ... *"Damn!"*

"What is it?"

"Just look at that." He was looking at the steps, which now had footprints all the way to where they stood. "I wasn't thinking."

"You mean about John?"

"Yes ... I didn't think to see if there were footprints anywhere around before we messed the place up. Did you notice any?"

"No, I wasn't thinking either."

Devon looked past where they were standing, "Don't see anything ahead of us." Then he walked back to the steps, "Gary, there are only two sets of tracks here ... it's pretty clear; in fact, it's almost as clear as those moonwalk shots. But hold on."

He ran back up to the landing. "We stayed close to the wall here too, didn't we?"

"Yes, why?"

"Come take a look."

Gary retraced his way to the landing to see what Devon was looking at. The landing surface by now was well trampled over the half of it nearest the wall, but the rest still had its coat of dust and grime intact except for an elongated skid-like gash at right angles to the wall centered on the door.

Gary sucked air, then exhaled "Oh no" in a whisper. He stepped to the side of the skid and looked to the cave floor in line with it almost fifteen feet below. At first he couldn't see anything because the area was boxed-in by a large obstruction at the base of the steps and a foundation wall extending from the far side of the landing.

He stared until his eyes adjusted to the light, then he saw ....

The normal smoothness of the glop coating everything on the cavern floor was definitely disturbed, like it would be if someone had fallen down into it. There was more. He told Devon to stay put, then raced down to the floor and around the obstruction to the area he'd seen from above. He cranked on the generator for his headlamp and then drank in the details.

"Oh Jesus!"

The glop was disturbed as if by a trapped animal trying to escape. On the wall were signs that something or someone had tried to climb it, the highest ones being clear finger marks streaking down.

Gary sank to his knees as if punched in the gut.

"You okay?" Devon said, not able to see what Gary was looking at. "Have you found him?"

"No ... no, John's not here ... but he's sure as hell's been here."

Then after absorbing all there was to see, he said, "Devon ... turn off the lights."

"Can do ...."

In an instant darkness descended the equal to anything they'd ever experienced. Gary stood and turned, waiting for his eyes to adjust and allow details of the cavern to come into view, regardless how faint ...

But details never appeared.

He tensed and squeezed fists as if to shut out the horror of what an absolutely hopeless situation this must have been. Everything else became magnified—ears, the nose, even the skin unconsciously strained to find some awareness. Gary held out his hands and fanned them in hopes unused but latent sensors would come to life. After all, bats used sound, like radar, to tell them all they needed to wind their way through darkness; snakes used tongues to test the air and gain a picture from temperatures and movements and what-nots.

It eventually unnerved Devon, who hit the switch, momentarily blinding them. "That's scary as hell. What now?"

"Come back down, we've got work to do." Gary said, sighing, "If there's a way out of this God-forsaken place, we need to find it."

He'd intended for the two of them to work together, and, beginning at the foot of the stairs, retrace and replace the roped line that had been in place thousands of years before. Not surprising, the rope and the stanchions were gone, the work of caustic droppings and alternating periods of wet and dry doing their thing. But after locating where the first stanchion had been, Gary left Devon to proceed on his own and went back to where John had landed. It was easy to pick up a trail leading from that point. The trail, however, was unusual. He had expected something like tracks in snow from someone who was confused and staggering. Instead there was a shallow trench that meandered in and around the numerous convolutions. At times there were markings of a slip or fall or bump on walls and stalagmites, in which instances there were hand prints. Gary could imagine John, completely blind, shuffling along with arms outstretched seeing with his feet and fingers.

But why the shuffling?

At the same time Devon was slowly making his way, finding where a stanchion had been, uncurling a length of rope to tie it to the one before, and continuing on in search of the next. His course was more regular than Gary's, and at times they were not just close, they crossed.

Everything about the cavern was irregular, with the floor generally dropping, which was unnerving because as near as could be reckoned, they were already thirty feet below entrance grade at the base of the stairs. The ceiling was the more dramatic. It had been high at the complex, providing a space that needed little alteration to accommodate its dimensions, but then it contorted and plummeted to an area where the two had to stoop to clear. There was a space past that to the right that appeared to go nowhere, and another turning left. They turned to the latter, which seemed another long and irregular volume. But once past the turn, they were completely in the dark. The light from the landing, which was already dim because of distance and obstructions, had disappeared.

"Weren't there fixtures along the ropeway?" Gary asked. "I seem to remember illumination way in the distance when we saw it the first time."

Devon had given his generator several good cranks and was probing for the next stanchion. He didn't answer until he'd found it, then, "There were and still are, but the lines tying them together are almost gone. See" ... pointing to a remnant that followed above the ropeway.

"By the way, hand me your rope; mine just played out."

Gary did, saying, "Well that's an encouraging sign."

"What?"

"The bats. I noticed them for the first time when I looked up for the lines."

"Oh there have been several pockets of them. And yes ... it's a good sign. If there are bats around, there's a way out."

"Right."

Devon tied the ropes together, then uncoiled a ten foot length, which was about the distance to the next stanchion. "Aha!" he said as he found it, tying a loop to mark the site.

"It looks like we're going left."

"Good." Gary had been standing still while Devon worked on, trying to determine if this direction held the best promise. The right seemed to drop away, and he could hear dripping sounds. Right could be an abyss or a pool, so that tended to rule that out.

He looked back down at the shuffle marks. It was as if John had stopped there too, then turned and moved in a direction following Devon. For a while that is. As he caught up to Devon he heard him swear.

Gary cringed, thinking of a body in a teal-green garment, like the ones all of them had worn in the cocoons, "What is it?"

"Look at this ... John must have fallen on his ass and slid all the way down." Down was almost twenty feet away, ending in a messy pocket that was otherwise harmless. But there was no body. "Don't you know that scared the crap out of him?"

Right beside the slide were other prints that looked like a frantic climb to get back where the slide had started. Once there the shuffle marks continued on.

"Now it seems he knows where he's going," Devon said a little later.

Gary thought on that a moment and said "Turn off the lights."

They did and were immediately returned to the paralyzing darkness experienced earlier, the complex lights now totally obscured. It seemed like a long time, but may have only been a minute, then "I see light … *dammit Gary, I see light!*"

Now inspired, Gary forged ahead, still following where John had gone, whose tracks had changed from shuffle-marks to footprints. Then he understood. While John was blinded, he'd shuffled so he could retrace his steps if he had to double back. Gary hadn't caught on to that even though it had happened several times. Now the tracks moved with confidence. The way still wasn't easy because of obstructions and level changes, but it became clearer.

It was also different in another way—the cavern floor was rising. Gary had trouble controlling himself as the way out was in sight, and possibly an end to the mystery; and it was getting the best of him. Forgetting Devon, who continued to systematically search for stanchions and lay out rope, Gary clawed and climbed his way up the incline. The way changed from the smoothness of damp and slime, to more and more rubble with dirt and branches and leaves and vines. There was something else … it was the air, which changed from the rancid dank they'd become accustomed to, to a special, welcome freshness … a woodsy fresh. Finally, after an effort that wasn't noticed in the excitement, Gary reached the top, spread branches that partially blocked the way, and fought his way into the clear.

Except that the clear wasn't an open expanse. It was an obscure, poorly defined area with bushes and vines in amongst rocks. A large outcrop framed the top of the well concealed opening, which was wide, ascending dozens of feet higher before disappearing in more of the hill's vegetation. Below, an uneven slope similar to that on the inside, fell a dozen feet to a semblance of level ground.

Gary saw hardly any of this. What caught his attention was the incredible forest that filled the space before him and almost blotted out the sky. He was sitting on a rock, scraping crap and catching his breath, when he heard a struggle behind him.

"Thanks a lot, you bastard ... You left me," Devon said as he fought his way to where Gary sat. He threw the last of the rope down to the forest floor, then, after drinking in the view, said "Wow!"

"Yes, isn't this something?"

Devon didn't answer just then, his eyes drinking in the view.

Gary gave a few good cranks and picked up the walkie, "Abram, Bruno ... can you hear me?"

He repeated a few times before a crackled reply was received, "We hear you, Gary, but not too clear ... how's it going?"

"Just wanted to let you know we're outside, and we're doing fine."

"Great ... And John, what did you find about him?"

"Good news. We didn't find him ... and that's good. But we found his tracks; in fact, his tracks led us into the light."

"What did you say?"

"I said John's not here. He made it out."

"*That's wonderful!* We'll want to hear all about it when you get back. By the way, it's good here too ... Mona's up without a hitch. She's going through orientation right now."

Mona! Oh god. In all that had happened, he'd forgotten about her turn.

"Gary ... Did you hear me? Mona's fine."

"Yes, I heard," he replied, avoiding eye contact with Devon. "Thanks for that. Give her my love ... over and out."

They rested for a while, scanning as much as they could, with Devon making a host of observations. Then he said "What now?"

Gary looked at his watch. "It only took us about an hour to get through the cave. It sure seemed longer."

"It did. So where do you think we are. Recognize anything?"

Gary looked around, then up. "Doesn't look like the same world, does it? But that rock above us seems familiar. What do you think?"

"My guess is we're on the west side of the hill. There was something like that there."

"Could be. That means the farmstead was somewhere left of here ... and with it the entry door."

Gary nodded. "Okay, let's head that way and see what we can find. We should get back before noon, which will be when everyone takes the next break."

As they started into the tangle, Devon drew his machete. "I'm glad we brought these along."

"No kidding."

Devon shook his head, laughing as he did. "I feel like a kid in a candy store. Just look around … We're in a pre-historic, deciduous rain forest."

"Hopefully that's good news."

14

A Theory

"Long time no see ..."

It wasn't exactly the first words she hoped to hear, but then it was an awkward moment for her as well, and when she saw the smirk and twinkle that accompanied the words, she shrieked and fell into his arms. "You idiot ... I'm expecting roses and get a comedian instead."

They both laughed, and kissed and hugged some more, until the quiet from everyone else in the lounge was interrupted by "ahem!"

It was Devon, who'd been the last to enter the lounge, making the fact he was holding something behind his back easier to conceal. Then as everyone turned he brought them out—two beautiful bouquets of dogwood, rhododendron, mountain laurel, trillium and other spring flowers. "Your comedian friend insisted we bust our asses to bring these back for the girls."

As the rest of the group, now eight in number, assembled, he continued, "All of you are in for a treat when you get outside. It's absolutely beautiful, unlike anything you've ever seen, with colors like these sparkling up the place."

"Beautiful?' Roland said, "I get something of a picture by the flowers, but what about everything else. I was just leaving the locker room when you two dropped in ... remember? Both of you were a god-awful mess, and you stunk."

"Oh that, that was the cave. I was talking about the forest. It's dense with huge trees and shrubs and vines and ferns and wild orchids and all kinds of stuff."

"And I suppose lions and tigers and bears ..."

Devon laughed, "Don't know about them, but we did see lots of birds and squirrels and chipmunks."

"Don't forget the deer. When we were cutting our way around the hill, we flushed a couple deer ... scared the hell out of us," Gary said, releasing Mona just enough to get into the conversation.

Everyone had heard about the message "We're outside", and wanted to hear more details; in fact, were trying to find a way to celebrate it. So there was foolishness like "I guess you never found a pub."

Regardless, the topic went on longer than it should, until finally there was a lull at which time Bruno said, "What about John? We couldn't understand everything you said through the talkie, but we got the impression he'd been in the cave."

"Yes he had, and that was easy to see. The cavern floor, and some of the wall surfaces as well, are covered with dust and crap, in some places over a foot thick; so while Devon was relocating the ropeway established when this place was built, and laying a new line, I followed where John had gone. In the end his trail led to a light which was the opening to the caverns."

"That's amazing!" Bruno said, his comment accompanied by nodding heads, with everyone eager to learn more. Bruno continued, "But if John could do all that, why didn't he walk up the stairs, open the door and return. In other words, do what he was supposed to do?"

Gary looked away as if to compose an answer, but when he turned back, he asked a question. "Answer this for me, Bruno, what was on your mind when you were first resurrected?"

"What do you mean?"

"I mean, what's the first thing you remember?"

"The first thing?"

"Yes, the first thing. What do you remember? How did you feel?"

Bruno sat back, his eyes losing focus, "Not much. I really didn't want to get up ... I remember getting mad. There were lights and noise and I wanted to sleep."

"How long before you realized where you were and what had happened?"

Bruno twisted in his chair. "This is kind of embarrassing."

"Why?"

"Well, I have to face the fact I'm not as quick as I'd like to be. It was well into Bones' orientation before the reality of it all sank in. I was a real dunce."

That hung in the air for only a moment. "No you weren't." Abram said. "It was the same for me."

This was followed by a chorus of "Me too, me too, me too ..."

"Exactly," Gary said, "It's been the same for all of us, and it was most likely the same for John."

"Which leads to?" Bruno's curiosity rekindling.

"Where this leads to ... is something I've thought about it a lot. John's my best friend, and I know he wouldn't intentionally desert us. He's also a man of action, and in this case that side may have been the cause of what happened."

"And so what happened?" A chorus mumbled nearly in unison.

Gary got up and paced, speaking to everyone but no-one in particular. "This is as near as I can figure ... John is awakened, but he doesn't want to get up; there are bright lights and noises and voices and the situation makes him mad ... just like it made all of us. Only he doesn't simmer down and stay put and follow directions and find out what's happened; he gets up and stumbles off in a huff.

"Now with that action, his mind still isn't working, not the conscious part of it, anyway ... He's more like sleepwalking. He doesn't remember any of us; in fact, whenever he does come around, he most likely doesn't remember the last years of his life before Armageddon. All of us received a bunch of reminders to bring that part back. He didn't get any of it ....

"Anyway, he blunders around this place, probably opening doors and bumping into all kinds of things while working off his anger. Somehow he ends up at the exit doors to the caverns, and opens them. The inner door opens easily, but it has a closer, which forces him against the outer door.

"Now the outer door has been almost sealed shut by mold and corrosion, which resists opening; and with the inner door crowding him, he gets madder. He pushes the inner back and crashes against the outer with all his might, and it gives way. His momentum carries him onto the landing where he only gets two steps before passing where handrails had been.

"He falls fifteen feet into a pile of soft, stinking shit, and a world that returns to total darkness as the doors above him close. Now he's in a panic and tries to get out by climbing the wall … which he can't do. Remember now, parts of his mind aren't working. He doesn't realize there are steps leading back to the doors. If he had known that and tried, there would have been footprints.

"Instead his sleepwalking mind collects itself and he starts off in the only direction that seems open to him; then by hook and crook, following touch and smell and sound, he makes it out.

"At that point the trail ends … and so do any theories I have to share with you."

15

Connecting

"That's pretty far-fetched," Abram said.

"I know, but it's the best I've been able to come up with. If any of you have something better, speak up."

"It's hard for any of us to do that. We didn't see what you saw … except for you Devon. Does this make sense to you?"

"Actually yes. Gary and I discussed it on the way back, and reviewed the trail John carved. Except for the sliding step on the landing, the trail really begins at the bottom of the wall, where it's a mess. Imagine falling fifteen feet into a shit-cushion, then being in a panic trying to claw your way out in total darkness. Since he's hemmed-in on three sides, there's only one way to go. This first part tears your heart out … but the next is miraculous. John somehow calms down enough to develop a strategy that gets him out. It *is* hard to fathom."

"But it *is* possible," Rodney said, finally getting into the discussion. "The brain's amazing … and sometimes does things that are hard to explain." With this opening remark his hands and long fingers and piercing expressions went to work, putting a spark to every thought. "A friend of mine played quarterback in football. In one game, near the end of the third quarter, he took a hard rap that dazed him; so the coach wanted to take him out. But he convinced the coach he was fine and wanted to keep playing. He stayed in and had a great last period, winning the game … only later he didn't recall any part of it."

Anton laughed. "I once had been hours behind the wheel, and should have stopped and taken a break as my eyes were getting heavy … you know how that goes. But I didn't, and at some point slipped into functioning like a zombie. I came out of it when startled by the loud swoosh of a semi passing by, which really shook me up since the last recollection on the road was five miles back."

Abram nodded in a way of conceding. "Okay … so it's possible. A long shot, but possible. If that's the way it was, then what's next Capt'n?"

"What's next? Well … we probably need to forget about John for the moment. I mean, if he's only a few days ahead, then that would be different. But I don't think that's true. There were a few instances where his tracks and ours were side by side so we could make a comparison. Ours were sharp whereas his were dulled by dust and droppings, which meant an interval of some sort. Anyway the difference was more than a few hours or a few days worth, so Bruno, your take on time looks more and more the case.

"That brings us back to getting out of here. Yes, technically we're out, the cavern being such a godsend; but it is what it is and we can't operate from its hazardous, contorted half-mile of shit.

"But first, Mona and Rebecca, you two have to rest. It's part of the recovery program and it's not debatable. So off with you. The next round will involve Judy and Lisa, and you can get involved in helping with them."

The girls protested at first. "We just got here!" But after a few exchanges, they admitted some sleep sounded pretty good, gave hugs to everyone, clutched their bouquets and left.

Gary then settled back to collect his thoughts. The others— Bruno, Abram, Roland, Anton, Rodney and Devon—relaxed as well, and outside of a few quiet conversations, sat in wait for what was next.

His thoughts settled on the six before him. Although having only a short real-time acquaintance, the stress and uniqueness of their situation was bringing them together as a team. In some regards there was sameness, like in clothing. In preparing for the mission, each had to pack, but to do so with limitations. There could only be a few changes of clothes, and these would have to be flexible and able to bridge the changing conditions of seasons. Many selections were therefore taken from outfitter shops where light-weight, wash-dry fabrics, like nylon, spandex and polyester, and cargo pants with detachable leggings, predominated. There were also variations that suited preferences and backgrounds. Anton, for instance, had changed to a denim overall with a checkered cotton shirt, which wasn't unusual as shirts and jackets with materials and colors and patterns every which way were picked after basics had been selected. Shoes were mostly light-weight hiking boots, with moccasins the favorite for casual wear.

"Devon and Rodney ... how are you two holding up?" Gary asked.

Devon, who'd been yawning and was due for another rest period, said "We're pooped, but we're fine. Lead on."

"Good. At eight tonight, the next round starts. Mona and Rebecca should be able to help, but since it will be their first, if Bruno and Abram can stay on, it would be great."

"Glad to," Abram said, "but we don't need to sit around twiddling until then. Put us to work now ... the afternoon hours shouldn't be wasted."

"You're right and thanks; we can use the help. I know this twelve hour schedule we're on is weird and isn't in sync with a real day, but that will end once everyone's up and we're out of here.

"Okay ... Roland, how did it go with the dig?" With the spirited goings-on that had followed the break-out, this part had been almost forgotten.

"Not too good. You didn't stop by when you got back, so you need to come and see ... We're at a point where we don't know what to do next."

Anton added, "We worked pretty damn hard at it, really; but we didn't get as much out as before. We dug around that boulder, and cleared back to some of the concrete that had collapsed. But it got scary."

"Scary?"

"Yes. The stuff we're exposing has nowhere to go but down on top of us. 'The root system seems to be bridging everything for now, but it could come plopping down if we take out too much below it."

"Gary, we need to be tackling this from the outside," Rodney said, his big hand spinning to point away. "Were you able to find anything out there that would lead to here?"

"We tried. We hacked our way around the base of the hill for over half a mile, which we thought covered where the entry corridor would be. Along the way we banged on rocks with that "Shave and a haircut, six bits" routine in hopes of getting a reaction. Didn't any of you hear it?"

"No."

"Wait … there was a sound one time," Roland said, "but it was faint, and I thought it was just a critter. And I never heard it again when I stopped to listen."

"Were you able to see anything of the farmstead?"

"Oh no … Maybe if we dug things up and sifted every bit, we'd find something; but there was nothing obvious to see. It was all trees and bushes and more trees."

Later everyone climbed the steps to the entry and looked through the door opening to understand what the dig team had come to. There was only silence until Bruno came up with what was on his mind. "Is there a way we can punch through to the surface with these rods?" He was looking at the array still hanging on the wall.

"I don't know," Roland said after everyone else shrugged, "but I see what you're getting at. It's worth a try."

Several attempts later a penetration was made. Then the longest one was substituted to continue the penetration, finally hitting something solid.

"If we keep butting against whatever we're hitting, do you think you'll hear it on the outside?"

"That's it!" Gary said, slapping his leg. "This just might work. Roland, Anton, you two stay here and work the probes. Everyone else grab a tool and follow me. If we can find the other end we'll have something to work on. We'll get out of this place yet."

In only minutes an excited group passed through the double doors and down the steps to the cavern floor. Devon took the lead and started out without hesitation, but then had to stop ... the others breaking away to see first hand where John had fallen and his trail leading away.

While this was happening, Gary had an afterthought, "Oops, someone needs to stay behind on the landing. I don't know what can go wrong, but we may need to be in communication if something does. Bruno or Abram, it should fall to one of you."

There was hesitation as both were eager for what might be ahead, until finally there was a sigh from Abram, "Oh hell, I'll stay ... this time."

Abram leaned on his shovel as the rest caught up with Devon and started down the ropeway. What he saw for the next few envied minutes was a diminishing show. Head-lamps and hand-held flashlights bobbed and weaved and searched every which way among the exotic variations of cavern workings, until direct line-of-sight disappeared, and finally light as well.

He was about to start back up the steps when the condition of the surfaces made him cringe. *What a cruddy mess!* To make use of the time that was otherwise lost, he started to clean, scraping with the square-edged shovel he'd chosen to carry, and dumping the crud out of the way. As he worked he was careful not to alter any of the markings John had made, the markings having become, in only a matter of hours, relics of importance. When he got to the landing he was especially mindful of this, clearing all of its surfaces other than a neat square preserving the sliding footfall from which John had catapulted.

The soundbox crackled, "Abram ... you there?"

"I'm here, Gary. How's it going?"

"Everything's going fine ... and we're out. Tell Roland and Anton to start banging away in fifteen minutes. We're heading around the mountain and should be in the vicinity of the entryway by then. Okay?"

It wasn't a simple walk in the woods. The marginal clearing made hours before was just that, with the path zigzagging in accordance with least resistance. They got to what could be considered the vicinity, which was more of what they had just passed—trees, some of them huge, bushes, vines, ferns and rocks, with earlier generations of them down every which way in varying stages of decomposition.

"Not much we can do until we hear something," Gary said as they came to a stop. "Let's start here ... it's as good a place as any."

They split up, taking positions about ten yards apart along the base of the hill, and sat still to listen. When Devon put his ear to the ground, everyone else did the same.

An hour went by without results, even though moves were made to test different locations. Gary looked at his watch ... It was three-thirty. "Damn!" He looked over at Devon, "Any ideas?"

Devon shrugged. "I've been trying to remember what rocks we'd beat on earlier. Roland said he'd heard something once."

Gary nodded. "But he wasn't sure. Besides, I think we've covered that area. Let's move on, it looks like there's ...."

"*Shhh!*" It was Bruno, holding up his hand for silence. Then he motioned everyone over.

They all put ears to the ground; they moved about and repeated the process, drawing together until Bruno stood up with a broad grin and pointed down.

The celebration was short lived. The next step was to turn and look about for what work was involved, and if they were hoping for the worse possible circumstance, they came close to getting their wish. Looking towards the slope, a huge oak towered from almost within reach, its roots fanning out, embracing several boulders, one squarely where the tunnel would be; small trees grouped at odd intervals nearby; a toppled relic lay covered with moss and lichens and mushrooms that suggested its own world of workings; and bushes were everywhere.

Gary looked around and forced a sick laugh. "Why are you all just standing around ... I never promised you a rose garden?"

"Thanks a lot 'cause we sure didn't get one."

"Okay," still shaking his head. "Let's do what we can in the next few hours. We at least want to get to where we can shake hands with that rod."

By the time they started back, the area had been cleared of shrubs and small trees; a dig had been started roughly ten feet in diameter, the going slow with a thatch of roots complicating every shovelful; a section of the log laying over part of the dig had been chopped out and rolled away; and a depth had been reached to expose crumbling remnants of concrete—a foundation wall from the maintenance shed extension that had collapsed. Digging down beside this remnant brought them, finally, to the rod that had been thumping away. This gave Devon another chance to play his tune ... which was repeated from the other end.

The heavy work had hardly begun.

16

Reality

At first light the next day, all seven men wound their way through the cave and around the base of the hill to the hole above the entry. There was so much to do that deciding who does what took only minutes before everyone was at work.

Roland led a group attacking the hole, where with pick and shovel and saw and lever, the external part of the dig slowly expanded. As it had been from inside, the going was complicated by roots and stones and boulders and disintegrating sections of concrete. Now, however, the fear of something crashing down wasn't a factor.

Devon and Abram took on the oak, determining how it would be cut and where it would fall. With that in mind, they first went about clearing the area involved of other trees and bushes. Bushes were stacked for a controlled burn as soon as a cleared space was available; and trees were trimmed and stacked to the side, with the material organized by caliper for future use. One of the uses, for which smaller one to three inch sizes were suited, was to replace the ropeway in the cave with wooden stanchions and rails.

Gary and Bruno generally coordinated what was happening. They also pitched-in to find the perimeter of the storage building, which they hoped would have enough in the way of useable slabs and foundations to provide a base for the first structure they would need.

By the end of the day the site had been transformed from a primeval tangle to a mess of another kind. The outlines of both the shed and the entry corridor were established, with digs along many of its points and considerable volumes in between removed. Corridor foundation walls were crumbled and generally in removable segments. The shed slab was also fractured; in one case a corner was above ground, looking in its eroded state like a battered outcrop of rock. Within the corridor, the stage had been set to attack the two main obstacles blocking the way—the tree and the boulder. A penetration of the mass following the line of the thumper rod, with enough dimension so words could be exchanged with the girls on the inside, had also been made.

And with all that they were exhausted.

"Devon, we've got a problem," Gary said as the group came together preparing to wrap up and head for the cavern.

"We've got lots of problems," Devon laughed. "Which one's on your mind?"

"Food."

There were unanimous mumblings and nodding. They were hungry and didn't need to be told that the kind of work they were doing required more than what the mush could sustain much longer.

"Yep ... my stomach's growling too," Devon said.

"Any ideas? You're the expert."

Well, my "expert" needs a little brushing up. But I hear you. Actually, Abram and I discussed this a while back when we were chopping away. So we scoured the area for what we could find, which wasn't without incident, by the way."

"Without incident?"

"Yes ... we were a ways into the woods in that direction ...."

"That's the way back to the cave."

"I know. Anyway, we were walking along, spreading bushes and scrounging for anything edible, when I came face-to-face with a large wolf standing in a crouch less than twenty feet away."

"Why didn't you shoot it? Wolves are food."

"Believe me, I forgot about the food thing, except not wanting to be a provider; but I did think of shooting, because the damned thing wasn't exactly wagging its tail. As soon as I could collect my wits, I grabbed for the pistol … almost dropping it while fumbling with the lock. When I looked up to aim, the wolf had disappeared; there was only the rustling of bushes where it had been.

Abram added, "I was a bit behind and saw it all. I got a fleeting glimpse of more than one … and there may have been several of them. Wolves tend to work in teams, which is pretty scary when you realize they may have been creeping around watching us for some time."

"You're right … that *is* scary; it's also a good reminder. It's easy to take in all this as if it's a safe and sound paradise, when in reality it may be a dangerous place."

Everyone nodded again.

"So what happened after that? What about the plants? Find anything?"

"Oh sure. There were quite a few things picked; that stack of greens over there are all edibles. We'll take them back and concoct something to go along with the mush.

"It's a start."

"It's *just* a start," said Anton who'd sat back on the dead trunk still in the area, fidgeting with his shovel until everyone turned. "There's a lot of work right here to complete the connection we need … Lord knows what it's going to take to get that tree down. But it *is* just a start.

"The shed's been located, so it shouldn't take much to find the rest of the farmstead. Remember now, besides the house and barn and a few smaller out-buildings, there were orchards and gardens and corrals and pens and fields all around here. The farm was pretty complete … like they were in the good-ole days. Some of those areas aren't important right now, but the fields and gardens are. We need to get them cleared and planted soon if we expect to harvest anything in the fall."

"What do we do if the seeds stored away don't work?"

Anton shrugged, "I don't care to think about that."

"You're right, Anton," Gary said. "We'll have to come up with a contingency plan if the seeds don't take; but let's assume they will.

"All of you might not be familiar with this part of what's been done in preparation, so this is what we're talking about.

"Huston was just as concerned about plantings—for both gardens and fields—as he was about human beings. He felt that if a group could jump in time, they may have to take along a way of producing food as well. So he started experimenting with varieties of seeds, just as he was with the human body and its separate parts."

"We heard a little about that," Bruno said, "but why didn't he just do what the Norwegians were doing with their seed bank on that off-shore island?"

Anton snorted, "You mean the Svalbard Seed Vault?"

"Yes, I guess that's it."

"Well, the Svalbard thing isn't the first seed bank by far. However, it is unique. There are hundreds of them worldwide, but some are in politically unstable areas, and most don't have the natural temperature advantage the Norwegians have.

"Back to Huston. He had started years before the Norwegians and had already solved most of the problems before they developed an interest. They actually borrowed some ideas from him."

"Could you define that success for me so I can sleep better tonight?"

"Well, let's see now … Basically it's temperature again, with the degree not nearly as severe as with us. The seeds are also heat-sealed to exclude moisture and then specially packed. This combination worked fine for many of the seeds, especially grains; but for others it got more complex in order to achieve similarly extended times. In those cases something like cryoprotectants were developed, in a way like they had been for body parts; then they were put into the freeze. The revival process was just as complex and individualized as with flesh and blood stuff, including their share of frustrations and failures. But the proof of the pudding came when finally, after a five year test period, they were brought back to room temperature, planted … and *voila!*"

"And you think five years will hold for eight thousand?"

"Bruno … It worked for us didn't it?"

"Okay, enough of this," Gary said. "Let's pick up and get back. We shouldn't leave anything around here, so let's carry what we brought out and leave them somewhere in the cave."

They were about to get going when Rodney, who'd been quiet

during the exchange, which was unusual in itself, said "It didn't work for everyone."

The remark didn't register at first. Gary had picked-up his shovel and several of Devon's make-shift stanchions, and was turning to leave, when he stopped … "It didn't what?"

"It didn't work for everyone … at least not today," with that exploding his hands upwards as if to say *"poof"*.

Gary turned pale, finally stammering … "Who?"

"Jim … James Wilson."

"How'd you find out?

"Who told you?

"Why didn't you tell me?"

"Now hold on … okay? A while back I was down in that hole," his hands whirling to double point out the main excavation, "digging away until I was able to talk to the girls. Actually I was scared as hell thinking the tunnel would collapse, so as soon as contact was made, I started scooching back, when something was said that stopped me. I said "What was that?" and then heard crying … I think it was Mona. Anyway she told me the story. The bottom line is … Benjamin's okay but Jim's not; he didn't make it. Apparently he didn't look right to the girls from the moment the canopy opened, and nothing the system did or what the girls were able to do changed anything."

"I wish you'd told me. I should have been there."

"Hell no, Gary, there's nothing you could have done. When I finally crawled back, Roland asked me if I was okay. I didn't even tell him."

Gary sank to his knees and covered his face …*"Damn!"*

"Look … it's not your fault; it's nobodies fault. The system's been amazing and has worked for all of us; but it's worked on its own. The help we've given by jumping around and clapping to greet the person coming-to has been nice, but those actions didn't make or break what was happening. Furthermore the cocoons Benjamin and James were in were the last ones made as Huston strained to include as many as possible. He wanted Benjamin on board because he was a personable and well-rounded guy, whose interest and training in psychology might be a good fit for the purposes we're all gathered. The same had been for Jimmy, who was well on his way into law, another subject that'll be getting our attention.

"Now remember this ... both knew they were taking more of a chance than the rest of us because their units hadn't had the same amount of testing; there hadn't been time. Still they jumped at the chance, and probably would have even if the alternative hadn't been so grim.

"We need to be grateful that at least Benjamin made it.

"As for telling ... everyone was busy at the time and there was nothing you or anyone else could do.

"But now you know and it *is* time ... so let's head back."

They wound their way along the convoluted pathway, drawing closer together this time than they had earlier. If the awareness that they weren't alone in the entanglements that still amazed them wasn't enough, the winds picked up, and from the sky which they could hardly see came flashes and deep rumbles. Before they got to the incline leading to the cave, it began to rain.

17

Last Ones Out

"Come on baby … come on," Devon whispered as he paced back and forth within sight of Terry's cocoon, where the girls—Mona, Rebecca, Judy and Lisa—were grouped. Most of the men, who'd showered, changed, washed clothes and eaten, had drifted off to their cots. It was after eight, and although not late, had been a long, hard, exhausting day. Gary intended to stay up with Devon, and especially to be on hand for Annie, but he'd gotten comfortable on a bench cushioned with a pillow and had fallen asleep.

On the monitor, gauges inched their way to completion, the workings subtle sounds becoming amplified in everyone's minds. Although traumatic in normal instances, emotions were further exaggerated by Jim Wilson's result that morning, which was still on everyone's mind.

Then came that magical moment with its hissing sounds, when the cover, in agonizing slowness, opened to expose the sleeper. The sight was so serene and beautiful Devon came near to buckling. Then there was more to the wait as the workings measured internal aspects outside the understanding of the group. Finally, after time and action seemed forever in suspension, came the automated direction everyone was waiting for, *"Wake up Terry, it's time to get up."*

An hour later, after the orientation, they were in each other's arms.

The same sequence repeated soon after that; this time with Annie. The girls, doing double duty, were again on hand, as was Gary, who was roused when monitors reached critical levels.

Annie was the last, and except for the Wilson experience, was also successfully resurrected. But this time, after the orientation, there was a difference. Gary watched every part of it, and knew that moment when all of the back-story came together in her mind.

She had answered the final question and the horns had sounded and the lights had flashed and the good-byes had been expressed. Those still up, for it was now almost eleven, moved in to congratulate and celebrate, and during this there was a radiant look with a pearly smile and flashing eyes. Then while sharing the moment with hugs and squeezes, those eyes scanned the group, leading to the inevitable.

The smile faded. "Where's John?"

Even though everyone knew this would happen, there wasn't a plan or a rehearsal to cope with the situation. So the celebration turned to gritting teeth and evading eyes.

"Mona ... Gary ... where's John?"

Gary stepped forward then and reached out to grab her shoulders, looking up for she was slightly taller, and seeing the eyes wide in anticipation beginning to water.

"No, no, now don't jump to conclusions."

"But he's not here ... Where is he? *Is he okay?*"

"Just hold on Annie ... hold on. It's not easy to explain."

Annie put her hands to her head, shuddered and looked away.

"His cocoon's open ... Wasn't he brought back?"

"Yes ... he was first."

"So where *is* he? Is something wrong?"

While the girls circled awkwardly, Gary led Annie to a couple chairs, where they sat while he told her everything, including the speculations.

"He just left us?"

"Hell no ... He wouldn't do that. Like I said, we don't think he knew what he was doing."

"And you said it may have been twenty years ago."

"Annie, that's part of the speculations. We're just guessing."

"I want to see the footprints ... *now!*"

"No, not now. Look ... you've got to eat and then get some rest. That's doctor's orders. Besides, it's near to midnight, everyone's had a hard day, and except for the few of us here, everybody's sleeping.

"We can show what you want to see in the morning."

"You expect me to sleep?"

And so it went.

18

A Woods so Wild

Anton sat on his haunches at the mouth of the cave, watching the dawn slowly evolve to give detail to the rain hitting the treetops. He could see that it splattered every which way as it filtered down. There was only a slight semblance of a wind where he was sitting, but every now and then the branches high above twisted and turned to show that something serious was happening. In addition to the canopy of trees, he was further protected by the contorted outcrop forming the mouth, so he remained as dry as the falling mists would allow.

"You shouldn't be here by yourself," Bruno said, puffing as he finished the rubble climb from the cavern floor. The other men, with the exception of Gary, were strung out behind. "I thought we'd all agreed that no-one would strike out alone."

Anton nodded. "I was only going this far … but you're right. Sorry."

"Everything okay?"

"Yes … sure. Slept pretty good last night."

"Pretty good?"

"Just restless, that's all. There's so damn much work to do. There's a lot of forest covering the acreage we've got to clear, and we can't get started because the entry's plugged. Now this rain. In the middle of the night, I opened the front door and saw flashes through that tunnel we opened yesterday; water was leaking in many places."

"Saw it too," said Roland as he made it to the top. "There's a lot more dripping in parts of the cavern. Did you notice how water had risen back there?"

"Yes … That could be another problem."

"Must be a mess out here."

Anton's talkie crackled, "We're on our way." It was Mona.

"All of you?"

"All but Annie. She's with Gary …They're going to lag behind so she can see the footsteps; but they'll be coming."

"Okay."

A few more minutes passed as one by one the others arrived and strung out to see first hand what was all about.

"Don't you imagine the lions and tigers and bears are too smart to be out in this? It might be a good time to get that work done that's bothering you."

"You're thinking this is like what only mad dogs and Englishmen might do?'

Bruno laughed. "The analogy had to do with the heat in India, but I guess it fits."

Everyone began to fidget; the game plan was action, which the storm had stalled, and for direction, which wasn't at hand. Gary, who'd inherited the leadership role by returning first, was still somewhere behind. This indecision didn't last long. Anton said "Look, there's stuff we've got to do. If we don't get with it we may end up drawing straws to see who's next for dinner."

"My God, now that's a pleasant thought," Roland said, laughing, as he grabbed a shovel and started down. "Damned if I'm going to be the short straw."

That's all it took; a rag-tag formation, almost skipping that something was happening, caught up to Roland and disappeared into the trail.

In the area cleared the day before, the rain and flashes and thunder were more pronounced than under the canopies, but it didn't matter. Shovels dug and mud flew, exposing more and more of what the years had covered; and axes slashed doing their thing. It was serious business with little interruption, so when arms turned numb, another stepped in to take a place. And so it went. The tree—the main problem—massive and tall with at least six feet in its diameter, stood firm while the ants of men worked at cuts that seemed unlikely to matter.

It was during this time, when conditions could hardly be worse, that one of the events happened that would make the day remembered in the forever of a lifetime. Rebecca, who like all of the girls was just as busy and just as bedraggled and dirty as the men, saw something ridiculously funny in the situation, and, possessing a beautiful voice and ready wit, started a soft shoe shuffle with her shovel in the mud. She whispered to the girl next to her, the message spreading, and soon all the girls were following suit. Then she belted out *High Hopes*, leading the group in a chorus line of uncoordinated, interpretive dancers around the tree singing the song with all its inspiring lyrics like … *everyone knows an ant, can't, move a rubber tree plant.*

From that point on there were cat-calls and insults and laughs to fill the day.

By late afternoon it was time to quit. Despite the foolery, a great effort had been made—the tree had an impressive gouge on the fall side and the start of another opposite it; the boulder had been coaxed out of the way; and a section of the shed floor had been exposed. Unfortunately, most of the work was masked by surface flows and rivulets that layered mud as soon as something was done. It was what it was, however, and they headed back in good spirits, not suspecting the day had more to offer.

The return was as usual—rambling but with certain conditions; a few men led the way, the women next, with the rest of the men in the rear. At the cave it happened that Bruno was the last to start up the incline. When he saw something he hadn't noticed before, he did an about face and walked to the right instead of where the trail went.

"Hey you guys … have you ever taken a good look at all that makes up the opening to the cave?"

Most had already started down the other side but the last of them stopped in track to hear what this was all about.

"What's the problem?" Devon asked.

"No problem. I just noticed that the mouth isn't just a simple opening. 'The whole thing is masked by bushes, but if you look beyond them, you'll see that it's actually a contorted leer, like on a Halloween lantern. We've been coming and going through the big side of that leer."

"And your point is?"

"Don't know … it's just odd, that's all."

"Anything of interest on the other end?"

"That's what I'm trying to see … it's pretty well covered."

Bruno made his way farther to the left, then started upwards parting the bushes and almost disappearing as those at the mouth strained their necks to see what he was doing … really a courtesy as everyone was tired and hungry and anxious to move on.

Then it happened.

Bruno froze as the face of a cat emerged from the tangle, a cat several times larger than a tabby with eyes focused and ears flattened, accompanied by a shriek as it burst out like an apparition in a 3-D movie.

He put up his hands, the shovel flying in the air, as two-hundred pounds of evoluted killer crashed into him with claws and fangs and muscles coordinated to do its deadly work, which could have taken only seconds. And would have, but as Bruno fell his head buried in the leaves and mud, and together with his hands, kept the lion from both his throat and back of neck, which were the instinctive kill zones.

The sounds—impacts, thrashings, snarls and screams—hit like a shock wave.

"Whaaa!"

Devon fumbled for his gun, nothing learned from the time before, lurched forward attempting some semblance of control, lost it on the slippery down-slope and pirouetted in mid-aim, jerking the gun skyward as he squeezed to make sure he didn't hit someone. The last move toppled him backwards, and in this way he slid to the bottom to complete a somersault in the mud.

Missing everyone and making noise were the only things he did right. The gun-sound was a thunder clap, igniting, if not action, at least an awakening as the bullet ricocheted off the outcrop with a loud *twaaannng.*

For most of the others, the next moments were frozen, but fortunately there was Abram. At the first dreadful sound, he reached into the rubble, grabbed rocks, and, screaming like a banshee, raced down past Devon towards where Bruno struggled. His first throw hit the lion on the rump and got its attention; the second missed completely, but worked anyway, the lion disappearing in a blink, bushes hardly moving as it vanished.

Bruno was a mess. He staggered to his feet with eyes wide, not yet comprehending the seriousness of what had happened. His sleeves were shredded, and hands, ears and side of head were oozing; but as everyone crowded to help out, he relaxed and smiled as if embarrassed by it all. Gary and Mona, who'd been half-way down inside and had raced back, moved to the front, and while the rain thinned the effusions, saw up close the damage.

"*Damn!*"

Gary turned Bruno's head and parted hair to get a better look.

"How bad is it?"

"Well, it's not good, but you're lucky it's not worse. Another inch down and one of the fangs could have cut the cord."

"One of...?"

"There are several gashes, Bruno. Your ears are a mess and ... *oh sweet Jesus* ... look at those hands ..."

With word of the attack spreading like wild-fire, the whole party was on the scene in moments.

"What can we do? Do you need any help?"

"No, I'm fine ... Scared the shit out of me though."

"How do you feel?"

"Like a fool."

Gary broke in, "We're all fools to be standing in the rain longer than we have to. Let's get back and get this man sewed up."

"Where the hell did he come from?" Rodney asked as they made their way back up to the mouth, his hands drawing pictures in the air.

"It was a she."

"How'd you know?"

Anton edged through the bushes away from the entrance, drawing out his machete. "I've a hunch we've been just a few feet from a lion's den since day one. When Bruno moved in that direction, he may have threatened a mama."

He threaded his way to the far corner of what Bruno had called a sneer. A well concealed opening there led to a deep, dark, pocket that didn't seem to be a part of the cavern itself because of the rocks and branches that formed a barrier on the side that might have connected to it. He stuck the blade inside and shook it around, generating a squall of hisses and squeaky snarls. Without hesitating, he reached in with a gloved hand, grabbed what was there, chopped a few times, and finally turned to hold up two carcasses still twitching.

"They're only kittens!"

Anton walked back and stopped in front of Rebecca, who'd made the comment. "Look … this lovely forest with all its pretty flowers is a *verrrrry* dangerous place. Even Daniel Boone was afraid of it in the good ole days. He's reported to have said *the woods are so wild and horrid it's impossible to behold them without terror.* If Bruno's close call isn't a reminder of that, I don't know what is.

"Besides, these cute little creatures are food. After we've skinned them, we're going to eat every part that's edible—the meat, the organs, everything. That's just the way it's going to be from now on … and if that doesn't work, we'll be eating bugs, or each other."

"Yes, that *is* the way it is," Devon added, somehow acting normal, his Keystone Kops performance going unnoticed with all else that had happened. "It's much better to eat them, then the other way around. There's also something about the forest and its creatures you don't realize, and it might make you feel better. It's that nature has a way of recreating itself. An animal, a female, who loses its young, like this mama lion just did, will go right back into heat, and probably will be pregnant again before long.

"As for the den, that's another matter. We don't want one at our back door if we can help it." With that he motioned to the men still gathered, who in keeping with his suggestion took turns parading by the den and peeing.

"Men!"

"If any of you don't understand about this, let me explain. Many animals mark their territories this way. While it's mostly to keep away their own kind, it may discourage other animals as well.

"I don't know if doing what we did will do any good, but it was worth a try. We want that lion to be just as afraid of us as we are of it."

"Oh hell," Gary said. "No way that lion's going to come around here again … not as long as we have Dead-Shot Devon and Ab-Rambo to protect us."

"Right on … no way!" Was the beginning of chants and jibes as Devon turned red, and Abram, who saw this coming, was already half-way into the cavern.

19

First Hurdle

What was that? Bruno sat up with a start ... sucking air as a thousand reminders told him not to do that. He hadn't slept well, a combination of dull hurts from sore spots made it difficult to find a comfortable position, so he'd left the flatness of the cot and settled into an armchair in the lounge, softening it with a pillow and blanket.

He was still a mess, but now more neatly packaged. The seventeen stitches on the back of his head, and the ten behind his ear were covered in bandages that left tufts of hair sprouting along and between the wraps. His ear, also sliced and sewed, was covered in a separate swathe that crossed his head and circled under his chin. His hands, particularly his right, had combinations of stitches wrapped in corresponding combinations of ways. In addition, there were a number of welts and bruises, including one on his lower left side that may have cracked ribs at its core, that made comfort elusive.

The *what* was a *whomp* like a sonic boom that resonated throughout the complex and left anything loose momentarily quivering.

Bruno struggled to his feet, groaning, his movements causing low-level cove lights to automatically turn on.

Anton, who was a light sleeper, appeared before Bruno had fully regained his balance, "What was *that?*"

"So you heard it too ... I wasn't imagining things."

"Sure did. Whatever it was shook everything. Do you think there's a problem in the power room?"

"What's up?" Roland and Devon came out, yawning and rubbing their eyes.

"Don't know. I don't smell anything, so hopefully it's nothing inside here … but let's look around."

They made a quick inspection, room by room, seeing nothing that could relate to what had jarred them awake. They stepped into the cavern, fearing a section of the hill forming the ceiling had collapsed, but it was normal except for the dripping which had been noticed earlier. They looked into the view panels to the power room and saw nothing like sparks or smoke that might indicate a problem; and an ear to the door picked up only soft humming, which was no different than before. Then they climbed the steps to the entryway.

"Normal here."

There was nothing to see through the porthole, however, which wasn't good. Even with the outside lights turned on, a film of mud covered what there might have been to see.

"Let's open the door and take a look."

Roland grabbed the latch, then hesitated …

"What's wrong?"

"I'm a little leery. It should be okay because we've cleared the first ten feet away, but if the "whomp" came from here … who knows? A couple of you come here and brace against the door and I'll ease it open."

He turned the latch, then with a slight pull broke the seal, at which point water sprayed from the lower perimeter.

"Would you look at that," Roland said slamming the door back in place. "What could have happened?"

Bruno forgot himself and slapped his side, then winced and shook his hand … *"Ow!"*

"Nice move … does that mean you've figured it out?"

"Can't be sure, but a best guess is the tree came down."

"The tree? Hell, we didn't cut half way through."

"That's true, but a combination of those cuts and twisting gusts may have done the trick. If it did come down, that would explain the shock that woke us up; it could also have torqued the root-ball to do all kinds of damage ... like rearranging the plug and putting water at the door."

Whomp.

Gary thought to himself ... *so that's what the whomp meant.* For some reason it triggered a thought from way back. It was something his grandfather had said about the good 'ole' days. Pappa was talking about radio, and how much more enjoyable it was than the "boob-tube" the latest generation is locked into. He spoke of the mysteries that put imagination to work and enthralled them; and how when something happened that was a clue to something significant, there'd be an audible "whomp" to make sure you got the point.

They poured out at first light and soon verified what Bruno had predicted—the mammoth tree was down. It was easy to see that in falling, its tremendous weight, in addition to creating the quake, toppled the stump and root-ball, crushing more of the corridor structure, reshaping what had been excavated and forcing mud and water back against the door.

In a way it was a sad sight, particularly about the corridor, where the work that had been left in such good order the day before was now a demolition pile. But none of this was a disappointment or considered a setback, because now the means to an end was in sight.

Once more the ants went to work; axes chopped and saws cut and shovels dug and slowly the pile diminished. At noon during a break the rain stopped, the sky cleared and the sun broke through. "Hey, lookie here," Roland said, lifting his hands to the sky. "*Ooohie*, this feels so good!"

And it did ... inspiring more that any sports drink could ever do.

By the end of the day the corridor was open. Only it wasn't just open, it was clean. The root-ball, reduced to a ponderous stump, was rolled out of the way to a point beside the trunk; the surviving concrete foundation walls and roof slabs were cleared back to their structurally sound remnants; and the corridor slab was brushed clean all the way to the shed floor, with much of the latter cleared as well.

The work also followed several planned objectives. Bruno, who couldn't do what everyone else was into, busied himself with seeing to what logic the efforts could be directed. As the work progressed he reasoned that the shed slab would relate to a permanent new structure—one of brick and stone and concrete and well-crafted décor—and therefore one that couldn't be considered at this time. With this premise, he began a programming exercise, sketching in the sand the considerations for what should evolve, considering from memory where buildings of the farmstead had been, where the fields and orchards and gardens had been, and evaluating those locations. He didn't make conclusions just then, the problem needing more data and much more study, but he did bring to the surface processes that needed to be considered, and did locate where the first structure—a log structure—would be. For this he directed that excavated materials be placed in a particular location, then shaped and compacted for the construction that would follow.

Towards the end of the day, there was a brief period of awkwardness. Work was coming to a close with the most obvious objective nearing completion, when it seemed there was a sense that the moment being approached was something special ... even momentous. Gary, who was shuffling as he struggled with the thought that a ceremony was appropriate, approached Rebecca, who seemed to have a bent for that sort of thing. Whispered moments later, they motioned Annie and Bruno to join them. After more of the same there were nods, the four moving to the front of the door while the rest gathered nearby.

Gary led the way.

"We've had several difficult and exhausting days during the past week. Muscles are aching, hands are bleeding and all of us have lost weight. The effort has brought us past the first hurdle, and if Huston and Reynolds and all our loved ones are watching right now, my guess is that they're very proud.

"The chronograph inside in the library says that tomorrow is Sunday, and that's good ... all of us could use a day of rest. But it's more than that. Bruno has thoughts to share in that regard."

Looking more like a mummy than a fellow traveler, Bruno stepped forward. "The problem I had with the lion yesterday was nothing compared to the abuse I had to take from all of you today. I can only conclude that when you're mentally challenged, it's hard to understand that thinking and composing is actually hard work."

Gary, Rebecca and Annie jumped to the side as mud dobs flew. Catcalls and insults later, Bruno continued.

"Taking the day off tomorrow is a great idea. There are too many other challenges before us to attempt to elaborate right now, but there are a bunch of them. While sketching, one thought invariably led to another, then another and another into a series of objectives that are all tied together.

"It would be good tomorrow to have an open forum to discus some of these and to determine the next of priorities. Devon wants to make peace with the forest … Anton wants to get into the fields … Roland wants to start construction … and, knowing why we're here, all of us want to know how best to proceed.

"It would be good to get a better idea of our surroundings. In all that's been done we've hardly moved beyond the pathway from here to the cave, and we need to do that.

"And finally, it would be good to have a decent meal. With a few of us able to shoot, other than Devon, and with a hardly tapped abundance hiding all around in the woods, a little effort might correct the empty hurt we're feeling.

"These are things we can discuss in the morning … As for now, Annie …"

Annie stepped forward and started to speak, and then choked, tears surfacing. Then she gritted and composed. "Religion is a topic that's usually avoided, so I don't know how each of you feel, and can only assume there are differences. But let's agree for the moment that there is at least an essence that can be recognized, an essence who we should now address.

> *The Lord is my shepherd;*
>   *I shall not want.*
> *He maketh me to lie down in green pastures:*
>   *he leadeth me beside the still waters.*
> *He restoreth my soul:*
>   *he leadeth me in the paths of righteousness*
>   *for his name's sake.*

Yea, though I walk through the valley
    of the shadow of death,
    I will fear no evil:
for thou art with me;
    thy rod and thy staff
    they comfort me.

"Dear Heavenly Father, we give thanks for the incredible blessings granted to us. You *have* made us lie down in green pastures; You *have* led us beside still waters … on a journey like never traveled before. We are humbled to even be here, and recognize that we couldn't be without the work and genius of others, and without the providence that had to be a part. May we never forget all those, including our loved ones, who frame our past and guide our future.

"And along with remembering, may we be ever mindful, and dedicated, to do the works they call on us to do.

"Amen."

Rebecca was last.

"We all know we're on a mission, the nature and complexity of which we will in time address. If we were to put to song a vision of what that mission represents, it would be difficult to do so in a more appropriate manner than one that has already been composed. Please join me in singing the first verse of America."

The sound, expertly led, resounded from the hill and was beautiful, far more fitting than for just the few assembled, including the assortment of species hidden within hearing.

Gary then opened the door, everyone stomping shoes and brushing clothes and filing in.

20

Next?

They couldn't sleep.

They'd cleaned and laundered and eaten and chit-chatted, and, normally after such a hard day, would have yawned and drifted away. Only it didn't happen that way. The ceremony outside the door had been moving and could have been the reason, but something went beyond that. The beyond may have been the completion of the first hurdle, which was a combination of rising from the dead and escaping from the tomb. The second part had been scarier than most cared to admit, because time had gummed-up a carefully contrived plan and trapped them. The cavern had been a godsend, a ridiculous stroke of good luck, but even here there had been uncertainty and risk. Then the tree fell … which meant that ants could.

So without realizing the reason, a great weight had been lifted. And although each knew a lifetime of challenge lined up behind the one just completed, they wanted to bask in what they felt … and linger … and talk.

Gary scanned the room, at the moment not engaged with anyone. The lounge was nice, but nothing like the Ritz; in fact, it was Spartan. All furniture was of wood; there were no lounge chairs or couches, instead there were a few benches with backs and arms, and a scattering of matching chairs, only two of which had arms, adding up to seating for only a dozen. He knew why. The Caretakers never used the room, or any of the other facilities for that matter; for the only ones who came down after the icing had been completed were those who checked-in to see if everything was working. Secondly, Huston wanted it that way; he didn't want the Chosen to get comfortable, feeling a need for them to get out and get on with their mission. Decoration was also sparse, the only bit being a series of pictures on one wall: a seaside view with palm trees and a lighthouse; a wheat field stretching to the horizon with a farmstead to the side; an orchard and garden rich with a ready harvest; majestic mountains with bison and antelope in the forground; and a palisaded, rocky shore.

Arrangements weren't a problem, however, as there was plenty of floor space and the group was a malleable one. Roland seemed to prefer the floor as he looked perfectly comfortable sitting against the wall with his long legs pulled-up to support his elbows; Terry sat on the floor cradled between Devon's knees; and Rodney parked on a back-supported, swivel-stool taken from the lab, which suited him fine as the freedom of motion it provided fitted his expressive mannerisms.

He shook his head slightly without realizing it as he thought how well the group scattered about the room had performed. They'd began to form bonds of friendship at the French Broad, and had strengthened them during the tense and emotional orientation before icing; but all of that paled before the experiences of the last week. They'd moved quickly from the stupor of resurrection to full participation; they'd pitched in without hesitation and had worked hard under frightening and abominable conditions; and they'd done so with an attitude and humor that made it all bearable. There's nothing like winning a tough football game in the mud.

When the chit-chat drifted to an awkward silence, much like what had happened at the end of work outside, eyes eventually drew to Gary, their acknowledged leader, who seemed to be deep in thought and not paying attention. Most noticed this, and in a few moments of nods and winks and smiles, made him the butt of a silent joke, which Bruno brought to a head by saying "Ahem …"

Gary came to with that, saw he was suddenly in the spotlight, and did the only thing he could think of, which was to smile and nod in return.

"What's happening?"

"That's what we're wondering," Bruno said. "When we wrapped-up things earlier, you'd asked me to make mention of an open forum tomorrow. Since we're all here, could you share what you intended now? We seem to still be wide awake."

Gary hesitated … This isn't where his mind had been going. But then it wasn't difficult to regroup, because he couldn't escape thoughts about all that had to be done.

"Oh sure … The biggest issue is to gain consensus on what to do next. There are choices. Before we get into that, however, there are a couple items to go over first.

"The week has been so hectic, I've hardly had time to touch on ones I know will be of interest. One is the fact a log—a Captain's log, if you will—was kept, first by Huston, and then by Reynolds after Huston died. The log documented day-to-day actions by the group who watched over us and this complex. They called themselves the Caretakers.

"When we were put on ice, there was a question as to whether a vaccine could be developed in time to extend the life of the Caretakers, who were only a dozen in number. Obviously they succeeded, because the final entry by Reynolds is twenty-five years later.

"I've only read the last few entries, so have little yet to share. But surviving as they did for so long was great for us, because they were able to make many more instructional videos, most in holographic form, to help us with what we've got to do.

"I'll get back to the log and read the entries—every single one— whenever time permits … and will report on the ones that might be of interest.

"There's also the matter of letters. There's a stack of them waiting for each one of you, so anytime you want them, just let me know. I've only read one of my own so far," then he stopped with eyes misting and voice beginning to garble. Regaining control, he said "Someday I'll get to the rest. One thing of interest is that letters are written, not email copies. That was surprising because letter writing for most had become a lost art. When was the last time you received a written one? But think about it, writing had to be in everyone's minds as being more personal and engaging.

"Let's see now. Jim Wilson. Some of you asked what we intend to do with him. Nothing has been planned as yet; I'd advise we wait until we're more settled. We've sealed the cocoon and have reset temperature controls to a preservation level, so for the moment, there isn't an urgency to do anything.

"Now for the main event. Because of a hell of an effort, we're now free to move out and move on. So the question is how should we proceed? There are basically two ways: we could, after minimal preparation, strike out and find people, determine what condition they're in, and then make our plans; or, we could solve our problems first by becoming self-sufficient, and then strike out.

"I want everyone's thought on either this or any other topic you feel important. Who wants to start?"

A few moments passed as minds went to work. Terry broke in first. "It may seem like it's a coin flip, or that we can try both approaches and see what works best. I have a gut feel about that though."

"And that is?"

"Well, we all remember how remote this place was in the twenty-first century. What's there to think it's any less so now? People most likely are a good ways away. If that's the case, then minimal preparation might be pretty damned extensive.

"As you know, my field is botany. We have a fair idea of edible plants and have already picked some to spruce up our meals. But we need to know much more about this. Towards that end, I intend to compile an extensive list of plants we can expect to find in these mountains, complete with pictures, and present a program for study by all of you. It may be a key part in our survival."

"I'm on with that," Devon said. "I was only in the third cycle brought back, but I guarantee I'm as sick of the mush as anyone. And it's not just that we want something different, we *need* something different. The supply on hand may only have another week to run.

"There's a caveat with plucking from the forest, however. We can't forget that one of the premises of our assignment is to live in harmony with Mother Earth. We can't repeat what has been done since we climbed down from trees and ambled out of Africa. Rather than picking the place clean and moving on, we'll have to take what we find in the forest and make them parts of our garden ... in other words sustain them"

Anton signaled to speak.

"We hear you ... and there's more. You know what's on my mind as I've already expressed it a few times. Right now I feel the fields are our top priority. Getting that first crop in will take a staggering amount of work, which needs to come from all of us.

"As for finding people who are already self-sufficient and able to take us in ... that's a long shot. A long shot with two down-sides. One is that if we waste time in the search and don't succeed, we'll miss the chance to get our own crops in, and will be forced to face a winter without stores. Remember what happened to the Pilgrim's that first winter.

"The second also has to do with Mother Earth. Our fields will be in a sense like laboratories; and if we're successful, we'll have something really significant to pass on to others."

"Like what?"

"Well, the obvious is that we won't be using many of the practices used before. Some of it was okay, but a lot had definite drawbacks. We'll basically be applying organic means to what we do, some traditional, others unique and exciting. I could go into detail, but it's all a moot point until we get the forest cleared."

"Bruno ... you look like you're going to burst. What's on your mind?"

Bruno laughed, "I hate being so obvious. Now, about the options you mentioned. I think it's also a moot point whether or not we find people. I mean, we've got to ultimately find them, that's true; but it's also true that we're stuck to this place. The library is a treasure trove of thousands of years of human accomplishment—a trove of chemistry, biology, botany, geology, medicine, psychology, history, humanity, government, agronomy and every field of study you can think of—and a trove we can't pick up and carry to another place.

"When I was sketching in the sand this afternoon, playing silly games as some of you called it, I stopped at one point and climbed the hill. Not far, you understand ... that damned lion was very much on my mind. I wanted to find a vantage point and get a better feel of the area; but the attempt didn't work ... there were too many trees.

While sitting on a rock, however, thoughts came to mind that are worth considering.

"Someday we'll find the descendents of those kids who survived; only then will we know what condition they're in. Remember now, the oldest of them at the start were only three years old. That means they knew practically nothing. For a hundred years or so they had clothes and books with pictures and buildings with stuff, but they didn't have anyone to explain any of it to them … and in time all of it rusted or rotted or collapsed. John told me before we went on ice that his brother was trying to teach his kids how to use a can opener. *A can opener!* With so little to go on, it could well be that they're like the pitiful hunter-gatherers in *Planet of the Apes.* Even if they're more advanced than that, we'll still be worlds apart; this place will be like the home of the gods … like Mount Olympus."

"Well, just listen to EtchASketch boy. I suppose you want this place to look like Emerald City in *The Wizard of Oz.*"

"Oh good grief," Bruno said as everyone laughed.

"Actually, I think you're right," said Roland, who couldn't resist pulling Bruno's chain. "And I also agree with Anton. My natural inclination is to start building something, but building can wait. Besides, the clearing that needs to be done is an opportunity to stockpile timbers for when that time does come.

"Right now my main interest is that big meal mentioned for tomorrow. Toward that end, at first light tomorrow morning, I'd like to take one of the rifles and see what I can bag."

"Count me in with that," Benjamin said. "You may not have noticed this morning because the rain and mud had erased most of what there was to see, but there were still quite a few tracks in the area we'd cleared. If that amount of traffic is normal, it shouldn't take long to bring in something."

"May I come along?" Asked Lisa. "For your information, I've been into archery all my life… and was a state champ while in high school. I'm probably a little rusty because I didn't have time to devote to it while in college, but I'd love to get back into it. There are a couple compound bows in storage that would fit in perfectly for the hunt you mentioned. "

"Well I'll be darned," Roland said. "Of course, come along. I'd forgotten you'd mentioned that before … but that was eight thousand years ago."

With that bits of nonsense bounced around the room. When it settled, Gary said "Anyone else with something to say? Rod, you've been quiet so far …"

Rodney straightened up, his stool spinning and hands going into action, "I've been waiting for a point to contend, and so far haven't found one. My hands and arms and back and legs are aching and telling me to shut up, but since you've asked, I'm forced to agree with Anton that we've got to get on with clearing and planting … Ouch! Ouch! Ouch! Ouch!

"I also agree with Bruno in that this is the center of the universe. It certainly will be for me. I don't know yet how the wonders of chemistry will fit into the new world … but they will, and seeing that they will will keep me anchored to the facilities and resources right here. Actually, I'm just as interested in getting out and seeing what the world has come to as anyone. Doing so will just have to be fitted in later."

"I'm interested in that too, Rod," Abram said. "I think all of us are curious about what's around here, even though for different reasons. To me it's the next thing to do. Bruno, you piqued my interest with your small climb. Tomorrow I'd like to go all the way to the top. Who knows … there might be something really interesting to see. Who'd like to make the climb with me?"

Most everyone raised a hand.

"Hey, that's a great idea," Gary said, "but can I make a suggestion? Let's split into groups, with each group heading in a different direction. Each group can have a walkie, which on the outside should carry a few miles, and each should carry a gun. When we get back in the afternoon, we can share what we've been able to find. The findings might be interesting."

The suggestion hit a common nerve. In the scramble that followed, groups were formed and directions chosen. The action also put a cap on the day that satisfied what had been missing before. So when the first person yawned, the yawn became epidemic. Soon everyone drifted away

It was after midnight.

21

A Day of Rest

"See anything?"

"Not much. It's beginning to lighten-up, but there's ground fog complicating everything."

"Oh hell, let's go anyway ... and let's be quiet about it. With all the tracks yesterday, there just might be something hanging around today."

With that, the three—Roland, Benjamin and Lisa—eased the door open and stepped into the early morning's chill. Roland, who was leading, only got as far as where his head cleared the sloping grade into which the corridor had been carved; then he froze, holding up his hand in a signal to stay ... There was movement beside the branches of the tree that fell and woke everyone two nights before.

Squinting to focus, he saw the movement become movements gradually coalescing into form. The wolves were back. Two of them were clear of the tree, also frozen and staring back in a ready-to-flee pose, while ghostly shadows behind them indicated more.

Roland eased his rifle into place, aimed and squeezed. The explosion immobilized everything in the area except the closest wolf, which was slammed back and upward before it fell into a disjointed heap. The second wolf tensed for a fraction before instinctively taking flight, but that was too long. A second bullet tore into its rear, knocking it down and paralyzing its hind quarters; and while it thrashed to gain control, a third killed it.

In less than a minute the first hunting expedition was over.

"What's going on?" Said Gary, who'd been among the early risers, but was still in the lounge when he heard enough to know something had happened.

Soon most everyone else had made it up the stairs and through the doors to the outside. There they were treated to the story, which was impressive enough to need no embellishment, and to the spectacle of two animals being skinned and dressed.

"It looks like the banquet tonight is going to feature *Canis Lupus* on the spit."

With the hunt over before the day had really begun, arrangements made the night before were scrambled a bit, generally following the same purposes. There were the hill climbers—Bruno, Abram and Judy; there was the group exploring east where the main fields and gardens had been—Anton, Devon, Terry and Roland; there was the group heading south—Gary, Rodney, Mona and Rebecca; and the group retracing the trail to the mouth of the cave and continuing west—Annie, Benjamin and Lisa.

There was a little foolery as the groups assembled outside the door, but mostly it was serious business with a few signs of nervousness.

"Walkie-talkies?

"Check ... check ... check ..."

"Weapons?"

"Check ... check ... check ..."

And so it went until everything Gary could think of had been covered. "Looks like we're about ready. Remember now, stay together; it will be easy to get separated and lost. Hopefully the lions, tigers and bears have gotten the message with what's happened the last few days, especially this morning, but be on guard anyway ... you never can tell.

"Be sure to make sketches of what you find as you move along, properly oriented of course, and with estimates of distance. When all of the sketches are combined, they'll be the start of the map we need to be making.

"Anything I've forgotten?"

"Yes," Terry said. "Be sure to include with your notes the kinds of edible plants you see …"

"The same for animals," added Devon. "They're all food."

Gary looked from group to group, but there were no more comments. "Okay, let's head out. See you this afternoon."

With that they parted to the four directions, the forest swallowing them by sight and sound in only moments.

*   *   *

Bruno arched back, trying to see Abram who was somewhere eighty feet above. As he did, both his back and head silently screamed.

"How's the weather up there?"

Abram laughed as he clung to a clump of branches, nearer to the top then he cared to be. He yelled back, "The weather's fine. But can you turn down the breezes … I'm getting sea sick."

"Can't help you there. See anything of interest?"

"I see a hell of a lot of topography—hills and valleys and more hills, all covered by trees. If that's interesting to you, then yes."

"Tell me more. I need more information."

"Okay … hold on. Let's see now. There are a number of outcrops. There's a large cliff with a small waterfall to the left … that would be west … no northwest. It's really pretty."

"How far?"

"Can't tell … miles."

"Anything else? Any sign of people? What about water?"

"I did see water … yes, to the southwest, two or three miles, that's got to be water, it looks like a lake. I don't see anything to indicate people, however. But that gives me an idea."

"Which is?"

"Why don't you build a fire, and then throw wet green stuff on it to make smoke … as if in smoke signal. I'll stay here and see if anyone answers."

Bruno looked at Judy and groaned. She'd been a real trooper from the beginning as they'd hacked their way to the top. It wasn't a big hill, but it still had rocks and topographic convolutions and every kind of snag to make the trip difficult. He had hoped the top would be pronounced, with an impressive pinnacle of rocks so they could stand tall, plant a flag and make some grand announcement. But there were no rocks, instead the top was more of a camouflaged knob—trees and bushes everywhere—that fell off in cliffs to the north.

It was obvious that if there was to be anything seen, the seeing would have to be from atop one of the trees. Judy quickly volunteered, but Abram said no, he'd do it because he used to work for a tree trimming company, and that climbing was right up his alley. He was lying, of course, which plainly showed before he'd gone very far, but he won the argument and was somehow still alive.

Clearing an area for a fire was easier said than done, especially with hands that were already bleeding. Another complication was that there wasn't an area of any consequence free of trees. There weren't more large ones like the one Abram was riding, instead there were many smaller ones of varying sizes, all struggling for a share of light. Had it not been for Judy, the suggestion Abram made would never have happened. But it did, with the two of them working together until enough small trees were downed to fashion an opening. Then bushes were cleared, and finally rocks, which were plentiful, were piled into a circle.

Next came the fire; and when green bushes stacked from clearings were piled, a white curling calling-card rose from the trees into the mountain air. Only then did the two retire to a comfortable spot near the tree Abram had climbed.

Judy wasn't the type you'd expect to see pole dancing. Rather than trim she was on the stocky side, but not in a soft or pudgy way. Willing to tackle anything physical, she'd excelled in several sports that required more than an interest. As a scuba diver she'd deep-dived to reefs and wrecks on several continents. In one instance, an unnerving for most cave dive in one of the endlessly tunneled springs in Florida, she found and rescued one in the party who'd made a wrong turn and was headed to hopeless oblivion. As a skier she joined the ranks of those who dropped from helicopters unto the upper reaches, and then challenged the powder down seemingly impossible slopes. She was also a seasoned backpacker with adventures equal to any of the others. When the group had been tested with white-water rafting, the loudest screams had come from her, but they weren't screams of panic … they were screams of joy during the roughest parts the run presented. Her hair was long and dark and usually in a pony tail. Boasting a fraction of Indian blood, she would at every opportunity for costuming, wear a beaded headband complete with feather. With all of that, other parts of her make-up were something else altogether. She was a deep thinker well engrossed in philosophy—of logic and aesthetics and ethics and metaphysics and epistemology and all they contained. She had graduated in the past spring, and had been eagerly looking forward to her first hire, which was as an instructor at a Community College. But then the bombs dropped and the plague surfaced.

"I thought you had a point with what you said last night," she said after they'd gotten settled.

"Which one?"

"The comment that we might be perceived as Gods, and that this place might be like Mount Olympus. You got kidded about that, but what *did* you have in mind?"

Bruno picked a stick and started to scratch in the dirt as he collected his thoughts.

"In your studies you're basically delving into the way people think … right?"

"Yes … that's part of it."

"That had to take you back to the earliest recorded thoughts … that's thousands of years ago. Did you ever visit the physical remnants of those civilizations?"

"A few. So?"

"I'm getting at how monumentally the ancients were able to think. I mean they didn't have radio or television or any form of mass media or communication, and yet separate societies made expressions that are absolutely mind-boggling. Upon graduating from high school I made my first excursion and got hooked. That one was to the pyramids and temples of Ancient Egypt. Each summer thereafter, I went to see more. There were the ruins of Greece and Rome; Angkor Wat in Cambodia which covered miles; Persepolis in Persia; the Mayan complexes; the Incas. Most of the wonders no longer exist … like the Hanging Gardens or the Colossus of Rhodes or the Lighthouse in Alexandria. One of the Greek temples had columns one hundred feet tall. Even on Easter Island, the statues call *moai* got bigger and bigger until the last being carved weighed over 140 tons.

"How were they able to think on such a scale?"

"And you think we should be moving towards the monumental on a scale similar to what they did?"

"Not necessarily. I just don't want to underestimate the significance of what we've got here … and not address it skillfully and impressively in what we do."

"Well … okay, you have a point … but think about this. Every civilization that amounted to anything didn't just happen. They evolved over hundreds of years, in some cases thousands, and eventually numbered millions of people. But I see what you're saying and agree what was done by the ancients was boggling. Some have said that the works have been so amazing that extra-terrestrials had to be involved to assist the societies to such levels of achievement. I don't happen to think that's the case. In my mind it's mankind's tendency, or maybe obsession, to wanting more. When a person gets something, he's satisfied for a short time … but only a short time; then he wants something else, or something bigger, especially if someone else has it. This tendency invariably peaks, and then seeds its own destruction as the more and more and bigger and better implodes for lack of cultural and political complements. As for artwork, monuments and buildings, these evolved along with everything else. Something would be well crafted, better than anything that had gone before. Then others would see it and make a copy, adding a twist or making an improvement … and so it would go. My understanding is that in many cases buildings were initially constructed of wood and reached high levels of artistic expression in that form. But because wood didn't last, the next step went to brick and stone, with many of the features of decoration and construction copied as if they were still of wood."

"That's true. Greek temples, for example, mimicked their wooden predecessors in many ways."

"Yes. Bruno, the things we build are going to be important, and I don't want to diminish that. But we're only fifteen people with many things to do, so we're not going to build an Acropolis. A part of human history that can't be ignored is that buildings survive much better than the societies that build them. The human animal has done so many great things, and not just in what he's built. There's art and music and theater and literature and, of course, all the technologies. The record of all of it is preserved in the complex inside this hill; culturally, however, we've sucked. There's never been a political system or cultural structure that's stood the test of time. The grand experiment Washington and Jefferson, and that bunch we call Founding Fathers, undertook, was well studied and debated, with thousands of years of history to reference, before it was implemented. It wasn't perfect, but it was pretty damned good. So what happened? By the time the bombs fell, the systems and guidelines and safeguards had been substantially eroded, with the result that the once great nation was near to bankruptcy, with policies and programs completely at odds to what those fathers intended. It's as if there's something in the human animal that leads to his self-destruction ... and *that's* the most difficult problem we've got to solve."

"Hey, did you hear that?" Abram called from above.

"No ... What?"

"A sound from the southeast ... That would be Anton's group. Could have been a gunshot."

"We didn't hear ...

"Anything come into view yet?"

"Nothing, except for a few birds always being in the air. A line of hills to the north blocks the view in that direction. One is pretty high. I'll bet the view from it is a lot better.

"Put more green stuff on the fire. I'll keep looking."

*   *   *

When they passed the cave, Annie stopped and looked about.

"What are you doing?" Benjamin asked.

"Thinking ... and while I'm at it, what do *you* think. When John came out of the cave, what direction do you think he'd take going away?"

"I'd say the one we're taking right now ... It's almost a straight shot."

"That's what I thought."

With that the three moved on, Benjamin wielding the machete in front, Lisa in back, awkwardly following with the bow—cables and pulleys and attachments—tending to snag at every opportunity. They hadn't gone far before they came to a clearing, which was like discovering America to Annie. She'd hoped to find a place like this that would provide a connection to the previous world; and here it was, an irregular tumble of boulders framed on one side by a jagged rock that shot from the maze like the head of a spear.

She left the others and entered the rocks.

"Annie ...?"

"I've been here before ... I'm trying to find something." She tried to visualize where they had been on that last night. *Let's see now, the spear-head had been to the right ... and we went over about here.* She stepped into the rocks, remembering how careful they'd been so they wouldn't get hurt. Reconstructing what had happened wasn't easy because it had been dark with only stars lighting the way. As she passed each rock she stopped and bent over to examine the surface.

"What are you looking for?"

"John and I were among these rocks on the last night. He carved something on one of them."

"What was it?"

"I don't know ... It was dark and he was teasing and wouldn't tell me."

"Annie," Benjamin said, "that was eight thousand years ago. It's doubtful there's anything left to see." But then he saw the look on her face and knew he was pissing in the wind.

The other two joined in the hunt, with the only direction Annie giving was that "We were sitting somewhere around here, and John was carving on a flat surface between his legs."

It seemed a hopeless hunt—wind and rain and freezing and mold and crud and god knows what doing their thing over thousands of years—but then Lisa sucked air.

"You found something?"

"I think so, come here and take a look."

There it was. The markings were faint, with the workings of time and all, but there was still enough to discern a carving. It was two overlapping hearts, each about six inches high, with the letters "A" and "J" inside the overlap. Annie drew in close, lightly touching the lines until the design became clear … and then she lost it. Ever since that moment after resurrection when she realized John wasn't beside her, she'd held it together for what needed to be done. But this was too much and she sobbed uncontrollably, collapsing in the arms of the other two who came to the rescue. Finally the dam emptied and she broke away, smiling weakly, saying "Whew … sorry."

"Don't be … there's nothing to be sorry about."

"We've got to get going."

"No we don't," Benjamin said. "We're in no hurry."

"Look, this has got to be pure hell. As much as we're able, we understand that. If it'll make you feel any better, there's some scuttlebutt among the men …"

"Which is?"

"It's that coming into this world the way John did, so confused and all, had to be one humongous challenge. The feeling is that if anyone could make it under those conditions, it would be John."

"Thanks."

*   *   *

The group heading south moved along even slower than usual. They hadn't gone far before coming to a small gully whose flow had diminished, but whose sides were still soggy from the rain. There was another like it a quarter mile away, and then a stream a similar distance beyond that.

"What do you think?" Gary said. "What we've covered so far seems to drain that way," pointing to the southwest. "Maybe there's more of interest for us there."

"Sounds good to me." Rodney said as he stepped on a few rocks and gazed into the water, which was hardly moving at that point.

"See anything?"

"No, nothing here. But I like the idea of following the river … Wouldn't it be great to add fish to our diet?"

With that they followed the bank through its contortions and entanglements that seemed worse than the forest beyond the banks. There were toppled trees, boulders galore, sharp drops, rapids and waterfalls, such that following closely wasn't always possible. So they veered away at times, always returning to stay in contact. There were also pools where the waters seemed to take a breather, and at one, a large, quiet pond that ended a string of swirling drops, Rodney found fish. While the others undid packs and rested, he took out a pad and updated the sketch he'd been keeping, adding to the pond's depiction the words "eighteen-inch trout".

"How far do you think we've gone?"

"At least fifty miles," Mona said, rolling her eyes as she sagged against the bank.

"Seems like," Gary laughed. "It's hard to tell since there's been so much zigging and zagging. We've been gone two hours, but my guess is that we've only gone a mile and a half or two."

"Just look at this place," Rebecca said. "It's beautiful. The sizes of the trees aren't larger than those we've already seen; but here by the pool with its opening to the sky, everything's so much more striking."

While resting and being quiet, they began to notice they weren't alone. Besides fish there were birds, which were everywhere, and more. Other movements became noticeable, like a family of otters that surfaced on the far shore and began to do their thing. Then Mona put her finger to her lips and pointed. On a rocky formation upstream half hidden by the bushes, a doe and two fawns stood watching them, their only movements being their ears, which slowly moved like radar screens. When their eyes linked, the deer turned and disappeared.

Rodney scribbled more on his pad.

"You're right ... this place," shaking his head in wonder, "this world, is something else. And we may be the first to ever look on it."

In another hour they saw reflections through the trees that lifted their spirits ... It was a lake. They were on the edge of a rise out of sight of the river at the time, and to finally get to it, they had to negotiate a drop and then cut their way through a thicket. The shore where they emerged was a raised shelf, void of vegetation, which ended in a weathered edge ten feet above the water. From the edge a clear view of a gorgeous body of water could be seen, the view indicating they were near the end of a lake about a half mile wide, that extended to the right and then turned west, its shape and length lost in the configurations of the shoreline.

Gary reached for the binoculars, this being the first good opportunity for putting them to use. While Rodney sat updating his sketches, and the girls dropped packs and began preparations for lunch, he stepped to the edge and swept the area, starting on the left. The nearest feature was the river, which emptied into the lake about one hundred yards away; then a marshy area of aquatics like lilies and reeds and rushes; beyond that a typical density of shrubs and trees extended to the end of the lake. At the end a notable rise stood out with more trees, one in particular very tall; a small off-shore grouping of rocks were at the turn; and more bushes and trees extended from there, along with more outcrops and off-shore rocks and so on to the right.

There were many signs of life—fishes jumping and birds flying and a bear and its cubs in the distant shallows trying to catch a meal. There weren't any people in sight, however, or anything to indicate there ever had been any around.

The lunch, such as it was, was the usual mush, somewhat enhanced by assorted greens. But it was hardly enough. They were at a point where the need for more food was definitely opening attitudes for the acceptance of alternatives. With this in mind, Rodney made his way off the shelf down to the rocks making up the shore below it. He was looking for snakes, lizards, frogs, clams or anything that could be considered edible, and picking stones that might be used to stun fish moving in close enough. He found a few clams and threw them on the shore, but everything else he got close to easily got away.

"Dammit," he shouted. There were fish in this lake and he could see them—big, nourishing, salivating fish—and there he was without a rod or gig or anything useful. *"Damn, damn, damn!"*

Gary walked over … "What's the problem? Want me to take a shot at one?"

"No, dammit, the bullets are too precious for this. Once they're gone, they're gone." With that he threw a rock, the release accompanied by a few more choice words.

They watched as the rings from the splash spread and dissipated; then the surface settled back with enough clarity to see the rock in the last of its fall settle amongst the boulders deep below. Only that's not what caught their eye. There was a color; a color that didn't belong ten feet down miles from where it had last been seen. Gary climbed to where Rodney stood and peered into the shimmering surface.

Whomp!

"Are you thinking what I'm thinking?"

Without answering, Gary stripped and eased into the water. A deep dive later he was back, handing the object to Rodney, who carried it to a flat surface and untangled it.

There were gasps above from the girls who'd come to the edge and seen everything. There was no doubt what this was—it was John's jump-suit for travel through time, a fact verified when it was spread out to reveal a label with ANDERSON patched above the left breast.

Gary made his way over, unconsciously shivering as he tucked in his shirt. He put his hands to his head as if he could squeeze out the reality of what was this was, then said "Is any of him in there?"

"No," Rodney said, shaking his head as his hands probed inside. "There are nasty tears on it though."

"Oh Lord, oh Lord," Gary said speaking more to himself. Then he moved away and sat on a rock looking back at the remnant, "Where do we go from here?"

"You think he's dead?"

"It's not looking good. If he wasn't killed by whatever made those tears, he'd at least be naked, which could add up to the same thing."

"Gary," Mona said, "let's not underestimate him."

Gary closed his eyes and rocked. It was hard to imagine anything positive from the discovery, but then he nodded, saying "Okay, let's do this ... Let's keep our finding a secret until we can find out for sure, one way or the other, what happened.

*   *   *

"Do you smell something?"

They were just passing the mouth of the cave when they realized something special was in the air. This was verified when they broke into the clearing and exchanged cheers with the other three groups who'd returned long before.

After exchanging hugs and slapping hands the final four turned to what had quickened their pace over the final leg. It was a glistening carcass on a spit, over a fire whose aroma laden fumes just happened to waft in the direction they'd come.

"What in the world is that?' Gary said, hardly believing his eyes. After detecting the smell, he'd expected to see one of the wolves being barbequed; but this wasn't the lean body of what had been killed outside the door that morning, it was a plump full body of a creature in the swine family.

Roland and Devon were tending the spit and so he could guess what had happened, which Devon verified.

"You're not going to believe this, but I didn't shoot it."

Everyone laughed, and from the look on Roland's face, one of feigned humility, it was obvious who'd done the shooting. It seems the east group had been a mile out when they heard a sound that indicated game. Creeping forward they spotted within range a wild hog at work on some roots. Without hesitation, Roland once again proved marksman, dropping it with a single shot. There was more. The hog turned out to be a sow, and not far from the scene were five piglets, still small enough to be captured.

"They're here?" Gary said.

"Come take a look," Mona said from the other side of the entry corridor where the girls had gathered while the men chatted around the spit.

And there they were, lightly squealing and poking around in a small enclosure that was something quickly thrown together.

"I'll be damned."

"Yes, aren't they something? Anton said, just as proud about this as Roland had been, and rightfully so as he'd orchestrated their capture and penning. "Didn't expect to be in the livestock business this soon, did you?"

"But you can't leave them here."

"Oh no … They wouldn't last the night. I've started another pen inside in the spoils area; that should do for the time being. We've got a bunch of things to work out, though.

"Incidentally, what's that you're carrying?"

Gary had almost forgotten what his group had managed, which now didn't seem like much.

"A few dozen clams."

The banquet was actually much better than anyone expected. Besides the roast pork, which was plentiful and clearly the star component, there were a variety of greens which all groups had contributed, steamed clams, and of course mush. There had also been an opossum, which Lisa speared, but after seeing all else going on the table, it was dressed and put in the cooler along with the wolves.

After the meal and the cleanup that went along with it, everyone got together in the lounge so each group could comment on their experiences. Most of it was common knowledge by this time because of conversations over the past few hours, but Gary felt that reports should nonetheless be formalized.

"Abram, tell us again about you and the tree."

"Well, the two of us spent a lot of time together and got very close. Other than that, there's not much to tell. I saw the lake the south team ended up on, and lots of forest … that's about it. Bruno and Judy built a fire that created a lot of smoke, but I understand none of you saw it, and apparently no one else did either as there wasn't a response.

"There's more to be done up there though. I'd like to climb the tree again late some afternoon and then stay the night. If there's any light to be seen, it would tell us where to find people."

Gary nodded, "Good idea. Rod, you're next."

"Okay … Group South didn't do much in that direction because of the many gullies we had to cross. The last was a stream going more to the southwest, which would take us off course, but it looked interesting so we took it. The stream led to the lake Abram mentioned, and that was quite a find. We didn't see people or any signs of them, but we did see lots of fish and game; the clams were the least of it.

"We took a different route coming back because we didn't want to retrace the way by the stream, which was a mess. In doing so we rambled a bit, but if we can manage to find the best way, I don't think it would be much over two miles. We need to find this route right away, so we can have an alternative food source that's readily accessible."

"That's another good idea," Gary said. "You've got to see the fish. Rod almost went nuts 'cause he didn't have a way to get at them. There were also deer and beaver and otter and bear along the way."

"Annie, I understand your group had quite a day."

"We sure did. You've all heard by now about the carvings John made in the rocks. They're faint and not completely intact, but the fact they're there at all is pretty amazing when you consider how old they are.

"You also need to know that Roland isn't the only sharpshooter around here. We didn't see much in the way of game ... lots of small stuff like squirrels and chipmunks and rabbits and raccoons, though. The opossum was the only chance for Lisa to show her stuff, and she nailed it on the first shot ... really impressive. We'd discussed it on the way back ... I mean the idea that many of us should learn to shoot with the bow, the bullets are only so many in number, and once they're gone, they're gone forever."

"The only thing I'd add," Benjamin said, "is what we found about two miles out where we turned around. Pretty typical for these mountains are the occasional rock planes where nothing grows, and also boulders and crop-out ledges. On one of the latter in plain view, was a monument. It was made of a half dozen flat stones stacked with the largest on the bottom and the smallest on top. It's a generally recognized trail marker among trekkers, and it didn't just happen ... To me it means someone in the past, and I don't mean eight thousand years ago, came by and put it together."

Gary heard this but it was hardly recorded. Annie's mention of the etchings took him back to the lake and his own finding. They had buried the garment and piled rocks over it so no one would be likely to uncover it. As they started back his mind had been on the dilemma of what to do next. He had to find John or find what had happened to him. If he'd been killed, the event had most likely occurred close to where the jump-suit was found. If that were so, there may be something laying around to verify the fact. Under the right conditions bones can last hundreds of years. But conditions by the lake were something else. Every kind of animal and critter that would be interested in the remains of a kill, so there would either be little left, or whatever remained would be scattered, possibly over a wide area. *How do archaeologists work?* They section-off an area of study, and then patiently and systematically inspect every bit of a surface to a certain depth to insure that anything that can be found, will be found. He'd have to do something like that, but he couldn't use anything obvious to section areas off because Annie might see and guess what he was doing. The only thing certain was that he had to get back to the lake and he had to search ….

His mind had wandered, and didn't snap back until there was an awkward silence after Benjamin made his points.

"Yes … good, thank you," he managed to say.

"Okay Anton, we know all about the pigs, and we know generally what you want beginning tomorrow … so clarify all that for us."

"I've got a sketch here," Anton said, holding up a well scribbled paper. "It outlines the area that we believe needs to be worked. We only went out about a mile and a half and then looped around; but even though the area was heavily wooded … no surprise there … we got a pretty good idea where things should go.

"The important thing now is to get started. When we get the smaller stuff out of the way, we can refine the plan and go from there. But whatever the arrangement, we need to get seeds in as soon as possible. Towards that end, I'd like everyone who's available at it in the morning."

"I agree, Gary said, "that what you're proposing is our top priority, Anton, but it's not our only one. The lake is also important.

"Remember what Rod said. My suggestion is that we do as he suggests—that he and I cut that trail back to the lake and see what we can harvest from what we've seen. I'd like to have Lisa along because her arrows, with strings attached, might be one of the ways to bring in the fish. I've also asked Bruno, who's useless right now anyway … "

"Useless? Thanks a lot."

Gary laughed, "I mean for hard labor. But you could outline the trail we pick and coordinate all sketches into a map. You can have everyone else.

"How does that sound?"

"Sounds good."

22

Underway

Blazing a way to the lake was fairly easy, and by the end of the second day the trail was set. Aiding in this was the fact the first part out from the front door had already been traveled twice by the west group and once by the south. Beyond where a turn off that path was necessary, it only took the testing of a few options before a route with the least of problems, including switchbacks, came to favor.

With that the way was improved—small trees were cut, bushes were removed and grades were eased. In a few places where steep grades fell away from the sides, rails were set; and, as an aid until the trail was clearly shaped, trees were marked.

Those parts went well. Others, however, were mixed.

At the ledge along the shore—the end of the line—fishing had been the objective everyone seemingly understood, which led to an awkward moment. Camp had been set-up, Lisa had made ready with arrows and lines, and Bruno had settled on a rock, laying out a sketchpad and preparing to update it with the latest images. As he did he couldn't help noticing Gary and Rodney, who stood to the side and spoke in whispers.

"What's happening here? I thought we were going fishing."

Gary turned then and was about to speak, when he noticed Lisa moving away. "Lisa ... before all of us get wrapped-up in fishing, give us your attention."

She stopped and looked at Bruno, both raising eyebrows.

"Rod and I discovered something yesterday that we've kept to ourselves. Oh ... Mona and Rebecca were with us at the time, so they know too ... but that's all. We'd like to share it with you two now."

Rodney went to stones stacked on the far end of the ledge, lifted away a few, and extracted something which he unfolded and laid on the rocks before them.

"Ohmygod!"

"Yes, we were just as shocked when we found it."

"Where was it?"

Rodney walked to the edge. "It was ten feet under water among the rocks down there."

Bruno picked up the garment and turned it over. "These aren't ordinary tears. They had to come from an animal ... a large animal."

Gary nodded.

"Any blood ... or, you know ... parts?"

"Nothing we could see. If we had a chem-lab at our disposal, we might be able to do forensics, but we don't."

Bruno settled back, setting the sketchpad to the side, "So what's the plan ... other than keeping this a secret?"

"Well, we now know John made it this far, which is amazing. What happened next? The possibilities are that he either was killed, killed right here ... or that he somehow survived and moved on."

"Moved on ... naked?"

"Yes, naked."

Bruno shook his head ... Lisa put her hand to her mouth.

"I take it that's as much as you know."

"Yes ... We made a quick search around here Sunday and didn't find anything; but I don't feel we can settle with that. I'd like all of us to take a better look today. If in an hour or so we're still not successful, the rest of you can get on with fishing, which everyone else thinks we came here to do. We've got to bring something back.

"While you're doing that I'll keep searching, but in a more detailed way, until I'm convinced one way or the other. The area involved includes from there to the shore, from this ledge to the river, and a smaller area on the right side. I know that's a lot, but if his remains are anywhere, they're most likely in one of those spaces. What makes it hard is that remains means only what's left after twenty years. If I can't find anything with a detailed search, we can assume he survived past here. That being the case," speaking as he walked to the edge to sweep his hands at the expanse, "we'll try to pick up his trail somewhere out there."

The second search didn't find anything either. Gary then began the systematic process he envisioned archeologists using. Setting stakes at intervals, he joined them with strings to isolate an area. Then within the selected area, he sifted the top few inches, meticulously eye-balling every composition of dirt and leaves and roots and such being turned. It was tedious, but the work would become an obsession, an obsession which would also become awkward as there were other concerns for which, as the acknowledged leader, he had to give attention.

There were two needs cropping up, however, that allowed him to be involved for much more time by the lake than would have been expected. The first surfaced Monday as they reassembled on the ledge and made preparations to start back. Gary had stopped what he was doing and placed a marker to indicate where his searching ended. Only a dent had been made in the search area, but it was the most proximate, and at least it was successful ... nothing was found.

Rodney returned about the same time, having worked his way along the shore all the way to where the stream emptied. There in the slow-moving waters of the rocky shallows that characterized the intersection, he'd had good luck with the gig he'd improvised; and he was beaming.

"What you got there? Looks like four pretty good trout."

"You got that right. The biggest is a least twenty-four inches ... and there's more like 'em that got away."

"So that's what all the shouting was about."

"You *did* hear me then."

"Yes, but I was deep in bushes with my face in the dirt, so didn't want to get up to see what it was about."

"Thanks a lot. I coulda been killed for all you guys cared," addressing all of them as Lisa and Bruno approached from the other side.

"Could've been killed?" Bruno asked.

"Yes. Here I am minding my own business on those rocks over there, when I look up to see a couple bears come out of bushes nearby."

"Nearby?"

"Damn close …"

"How close?"

"Okay, so they were upstream a ways … maybe a hundred feet. But it *felt* real close … and one of them was big," all said with bug-eyed expressions exaggerated by flaying arms and hands.

"And that's what you were yelling about?"

"You heard me too?"

"Yes, but we were out of sight around the bend. Keep going, what did you do?"

"You mean, outside of crapping?"

The three looked at each other with skewered faces, knowing the direction this was going.

"I did everything I could think of. I jumped around flapping my hands. I yelled and threw rocks. All of this did bring them to a stop, at which point they stood and looked at me like I'm a damn fool. I swear to God the one was ten feet tall! I didn't know what else to do and was unbuckling the holster when they dropped, turned and lumbered away."

"One bear must have said to the other, "That looks like one of those humans we've been hearing about … real bad-ass"."

"Something like that …"

And so it went until Bruno changed the subject.

"Gary, between the three of us, the fishing's gone pretty well. All told there are over a dozen keepers to take back. We worked hard at it though, and scrambled along the shore almost a hundred yards in each direction.

"The lake's proving to be quite a resource, one that'll remain great as long as it's worked right. If other foods become hard to come by, I could see us returning almost every day. We were lucky this time though, because the fish seemed to have gathered on this side. That won't always be the case. We need a few boats."

The next day was to be about the same as Monday, but it got much more complicated, mainly because of Bruno, who saw additional work to do along the way.

Monday's totes had been simple with only two machetes, an ax and a folding pruning saw being carried in addition to basic packs. This time a shovel, another ax—a fireman's type—coils of rope rescued from the cavern, and a tarp were added. The work could have been easier if the route selected before, which followed the path of least resistance principle, were followed. But this time Bruno saw things differently. He saw that improvements could be made that had long-term benefit. The problem was this meant simplifying grade changes and straightening lanes, and a lot of work. So they chopped and dug and pried and moved, bringing all the tools into play. Even though with what they were attempting, they could see how the end result would be worth the effort, only a dent in most of it was accomplished, except for the fact the trail was now down to one major switchback. In this instance the trail worked its way down a ravine that was so deep and lengthy there wasn't a convenient way around it. The flow at the bottom was normally a trickle, so a few logs were all that was needed to cross to the other side.

This was frustrating.

It wasn't the work. Everyone was pitching in, including Bruno, who occasionally gasped at a movement that aggravated his ribs or pinched his hands … often causing blood to seep through the wraps. It was the time. A trip that could have taken an hour was so extended they didn't reach the shore until noon.

Anxious to get on with what they'd come for, they parted company, only to have the time they had left shortened further by rain. It wasn't just rain, however, it was a deluge, far too heavy to be contended with, so they gathered at a cramped shelter along a raised ledge fashioned with the tarp and a few leafy branches. After waiting for several hours in hopes the rain would stop, which it didn't, they started back in order to return before dark.

"Oh, lordy, look at that," Lisa said as they turned through an archway cleared in a thicket and started down the incline. The short footbridge had disappeared, and the trickle was now an ominously slurping, fast-moving, brown body over twenty feet wide.

Gary continued down to the edge.

"I know what you're thinking," Bruno said. "Let's not forget the power of moving water."

"Damn ... we don't have good choices here. The rope we have left may not be strong enough for a life-line; without that, trying to cross isn't worth the risk. At best we'd lose stuff we can't afford to lose."

"We can stash the equipment back at camp," Rodney said.

"That's true, but I still don't like trying to cross here. And if we tried to hack our way upstream to find a better place, there's a good chance we'd end up in the forest after dark."

"If you're worried about me, don't," Lisa said, "I'm a good swimmer ... probably better than any of you."

"That's good to know."

"Ahem ... Do we have some water wings?" It was Rodney.

"What?"

"Water wings. Can't swim ... not good anyway."

Jesus!

"It looks like we should go back and spend the night."

"We wouldn't be in this pickle if we had a bridge," Bruno said.

By first light the flow had abated, and Roland, Devon and Abram were waiting on the other side. "Don't you people know when to come in out of the rain?" Devon said as the miserable campers came into view. You're about as sorry a sight as I've ever seen."

"Still a sight for sore eyes," added Abram, whose wide grin erased the lines of concern that had been the night.

"Rave on ... Rave on. The fact is we were having a private party."

"Right!"

Getting serious, Gary said, "We tried to call you on the talkie to let you know what was happening, but couldn't tell if we were getting through."

"About all we heard was static," Roland answered. "When you

still hadn't shown up hours after dark, we guessed what must have happened."

In quick order a rope conveyer was fashioned and gear shuttled across; then one by one the marooned team was pulled through.

All of this was reason for a real day of rest. Both groups—Anton's in the fields and Gary's on the trail—had worked hard and could use one. In addition to the sore muscles and bleeding hands, there were also an assortment of coughs and wheezes and sneezes from being wet and chilled.

So everyone got clean and dry and warm and relaxed. A fine dinner was prepared, which not only capped-off the day, but also signaled a milestone of sorts. There were several kinds of meats, fish, mixed greens laced with animal fat and wild mushrooms, and of course mush. But it was also the last of the mush, and although not regretted, was sobering in that it made everyone realize that now, for the first time, they were completely on their own.

After the meal and clean-up, the fourteen straggled to the lounge, as had become the custom, to discus further the scattered topics broached at dinner. Hot tea extracted from one of the plants was on hand to add a nice touch.

When all were settled and small-talk at an end, Gary got things moving ..."Anton, you mentioned some things to me at dinner that everyone should hear ... please repeat them for us now."

"Actually, Gary, mine may be long-winded, and since we were all on edge when you didn't show last night, how about you and your group going first with what really happened."

"Okay ... this won't take long as you all know the story by now. The ravine was so flooded with fast moving water we decided to stay the night. It wasn't pleasant because we hadn't prepared for it, but it was the right thing to do. We're all here, which might not have been the case if we'd tried to cross that damned torrent at its peak.

"The others may have a different slant on this ... Lisa ..."

Lisa sank into Roland, whose frame spread in several directions from the inadequate confines of the corner of the bench, and hid her face in her hands, finally saying "Squeak."

Cat-calls and proddings later, she sat up with a grin to continue.

"Last night I retired to a warm, cozy log cabin, with a wood-burning fireplace and candlelight and red wine and white sheepskins covering the floor ... and proceeded to shack-up with three handsome, virile men. It was wonderful."

The lounge came to life.

"Were we at the same place?" Bruno asked.

"All right, so it was wet and cold and miserable ... but I can dream, can't I?

"As for fishing, that went pretty well, particularly on Monday. Didn't all of you enjoy what we caught?"

There was clapping and whistling and creative versions of praise.

"Well, some of them were mine. The arrows with strings attached did the job all right, but a few fell off the first day because the points were the wrong kind. I needed to use something like a barbed or gig point, a smaller version like what Rod was using. That night he helped me fashion something better, and in the few hours we were able to fish yesterday, the arrows did much better.

"And that's about it from me. But Rod had an interesting story from the day before, so Rod, take it from here."

That was a mistake. It was as if the report he made at the lake was a dry run for a comedy routine. Not only was the report not even needed since everyone had heard about the bears, it was long in the telling, and minutes before the room quieted enough for Gary to get back on track.

"I'll be damned ... a miserable night without sleep seems to addle some people's brains. Bruno, is it possible you have a way of telling your story that isn't off the wall?"

Bruno, still laughing from Rodney's rendition which creativity had turned into a combination of exaggeration and fantasy, had to compose himself before beginning. "If I could think of a way to put a spin on what comes to mind, I'd sure do it. Okay, here goes. I seem to be seeing the need for construction at every turn. When I got to the top of Mount Olympus, I had visions of a Tower of Babel."

"Mount Olympus? Tower of Babel?"

"Be careful what you say," Judy said with a tease. "He's serious."

"Okay, but that's another story.

"Anyway, with regards to the pathway to the lake, there are several needs. First of all, we need a steady supply of food … you all know that. Now that the mush has run out, and Anton's fields are still a dream, the sources are the plants and animals we can harvest from the woods, and the fish we can catch at the lake. The fish may well be the most reliable and most renewable over a long stretch.

"And, it just so happens, we're here for a long stretch.

"So back to needs …"

"The distance from here to there is going to be traveled a lot, making a need for more than just a winding path. We need a small road, or at least we *will* need one sometime in the future. If we find horses, which have probably survived somewhere, we'll be able to develop all kinds of efficiencies to help us along. So although we don't need one, I mean a road, right now, my suggestion is we think in those terms as we move ahead.

"One thing that *can* be used right now is a bridge across the ravine. The ravine's a pain on even a good day; and on a bad day, like yesterday, it's pretty damned dangerous. I don't know yet how high or how long or just plain how, but I'll be working on it. Roland, you might have some ideas there.

"The last project in mind is actually the most pressing. We had good results with fishing on our first attempts, like Lisa said; but we all recognized that it will be much easier with a couple boats. The lake is almost a half mile wide, which is something; it's also several miles long, which is great. All of you might get tired of fish, but at least you won't starve. In addition, there's no telling what we can find that might be of use by being able to explore the miles of shoreline. So at the first opportunity, I'd like to start on a boat, even though I don't have a clue how to build one. If any of you have ideas, please let me know."

"What are you thinking … a canoe or a sailor or just what?"

"No, not either of those. A canoe would be hard to make and tricky to manage. Since we have a few tools, I'm thinking of something simple in wood … probably flat-bottomed with oarlocks and oars."

"That's it … Gary, back to you."

"Okay… Thanks, I think. Anton, are you ready now?"

It was really a silly question, although no one could guess it or why. Anton was, if anything, overly prepared with so many thoughts clogging his mind he didn't know where to start or what to leave out.

He knew *so* much.

He had been weaned in the life of farming and had taken pride not just that he was five generations into it, but that the operation was so successful. The family and its wide-spreading operation were on the cutting edge of what had become Industrial Farming. They could quote systems and processes and yields with the best of them. Animal Husbandry, which once had been a vital component, had disappeared a generation before, and had been reduced to a hobby, almost as a token to what it had been. This wasn't the case in the fields, where the specialists rode high and did their work.

Damn the torpedoes.

All had seemed well and good and perfect and could have been accepted without challenge forever, had it not been for a few college instructors, and others in smoke-filled rooms with pilsener-inspired minds, who raised questions. Good questions.

So he studied beyond the curriculum.

He had read *Giants of the Earth*, required reading at one Minnesota University, which had given him an appreciation for the incredible struggles of the first generation. The author said near the conclusion …

> *Many took their own lives; asylum after asylum was filled with disordered beings who had once been human.*

In all the story was very impactful, but it didn't raise the specter of fallacy as was to be hoisted later.

He read more; he became familiar with concepts like ecology and the environment and biodiversity, which he could not help but make comparisons with to family operations. The family was all for it, of course, and put up bird houses, and recycled trash to county bins, and planted a stately row of Italian Cypress along the long driveway to the stead. Other than that the probing conversations were either stared down or changed.

He came to realize that so much he was in the middle of was wrong. He would see the loads of fertilizer; he would see the machines for distributing herbicides and pesticides and know. He would walk the lanes about the family holdings, picturing in mind how it had changed from what it had been. From a rise he looked down into a depression that except for its contortions was in a sameness blending into the fields on either side. He knew that at one time this was a coulee that swept for several miles to a small river snaking through the countryside. Generations before, the coulee had been considered too poor to plant, and had been fenced-off with its grasses and shrubs and occasional trees left undisturbed. The coulee tied to a barn at the stead, and each day the livestock—horses and cows and sheep—would meander back and forth in keeping with the workings of the farm. Now the barn was gone, as were the fences and grasses and shrubs and trees. Rough edges within the last remnant of the original biota were smoothened, and with the application of fertilizers and methods of continuous cropping, soil fertility became redundant.

He came to know that mono-cultural, continuous cropping, which admittedly was impressive with tall, uniform, abundance, came at a price. Although pesticide use increased over three thousand percent in the last sixty years, crop loss actually increased; and although fertilizer usage, which at one time was hardly a factor, became such that the costs of production doubled. The effects of these chemicals draining to streams and leaching into the aquifer, ultimately reaching our tables, has been more difficult to measure, but was significant.

It was sad. According to a few, one of the deepest wounds on the planet was the gash made by till agriculture; but to most, the new developments were so, so progressive.

He knew that all the animals that were once part of the farm scene instinctively had lives. They roamed and enjoyed open spaces and had names and personalities and mated and tendered. The chickens clucked and pecked and crowed and fought over imagined domains and left eggs in the damndest places. Now, in the industrial way of doing things, those animals were removed from roaming and culture. Chickens were confined to less than a square foot for entire lives, and each of the others were treated in a similar fashion, ending semblances of what they naturally had been. Instead, with the use of antibiotics and hormones and special feeds and conditions, they were heartlessly funneled to the objective of impressive yields.

He knew that till farming and Industrial Animal Husbandry weren't the only parts at odds with new awareness. Open range practices have also been ignorant of basic understandings in biodiversity, and have suffered similar detriments. Up until the mid-nineteenth century there was a balance in the prairies. The balance was of several grasses and rain and fire and wind and predators and prey. Most noteworthy of them was the bison, which once numbered about fifty million. Into a situation that was much like manna, came concepts extended from Jefferson, the founder of the West who never crossed the Appalachians, and other visionaries and theorists, including those espousing manifest destiny.

And what happened? An animal in sync with the characteristics of the prairie, and which provided healthy, lean meat and quality furs at no expense, was traded for beef cattle. These cattle were not natural to the biota, degrading natural grasses and leading to the importing of exotics which compounded the problem. Cattle were then fed on those grasses, and fattened on grains and chemical additives, all of which led to fatter meat with heart-stopping cholesterol. A summation of the disparity in the exchange was the fact that seventy percent of the grain crop went to livestock that replaced the bison, which didn't require feed or supplements of any kind.

That puts American Agriculture on the cutting edge?

He suspected that America's diet, thoroughly laced with agricultural products boosted by herbicides and pesticides and antibiotics and hormones, and a smorgasbord of preservatives and enhancements, was central to what was happening to its population. Basketball teams sixty years ago, for instance, were normal people with few over six-feet tall. The Minneapolis Lakers, a première team in early professional ranks, featured George Mikan at six foot ten, and jumping Jim Pollard at six foot six, who dazzled crowds with their size and ability. They probably wouldn't make roster on a good college team today.

But height increases, which had averages raised several inches during this period, wasn't all that bad ... nothing like some of the other effects. Obesity and diabetes instances sky-rocketed, along with a host of related debilitations; cancer and heart disease increased; and developmental obstacles, like autism and ADD, which had previously been of little incidence, became problems like never before..

He knew that one author, who had studied the industries that put beef and pork and lamb and poultry and fish and shrimp on our tables, came to the conclusion that the practices were so inhumane and unhealthy that "you couldn't call yourself an environmentalist if you weren't a vegetarian."

Which led to his interest in the environment. When he heard of the conference called *Easter Armageddon*, he had to go. The interest wasn't just the topic, it was also that Huston Burner, a hero rising in his mind, was going to be there. Huston had acquired large land holdings in the west. In that area he had removed fences; he had replanted historically native grasses while eradicating the exotics; and then he had reintroduced bison and elk and other animals that once prevailed. By recreating what had once been, he had proven the positions that recent studies had made regarding natural biodiversity.

When that conference was followed months later by an invitation to the Symposium on the French Broad, he was further elated ... then stunned, because the ending hit like a sledge. It was too much ... that out of millions, only sixteen were selected *"to start mankind over again"*, with the crosshairs of responsibility seeming to be aimed at him. The possibility that the others felt the same about themselves never occurred to him.

But then at the secret complex, he was called out, along with Devon and Terry, to meet with Dr. Ansgar Kjemsrud, a botanist part of Huston's team, who had not only headed the seed program, but also had served as coordinator with the Norwegian Svalbard Vaults. In the days before icing, they spent a good amount of time together. On one occasion, foregoing an available jeep, they mounted horses and made a tour of the farm, which had passed its heyday and was really an illusion of legitimate activity, but was still impressive. The nature of the setting was not unusual for the range in general, with hills and ridges and gulleys all part of the immediate vicinity, as well as extending in every direction *ad finitum*. Buildings of the farmstead were juxtaposed along the southern and southeastern parts of the hill, which although not particularly high, was of a bulk and shape that determined all other arrangements. The hill was more than a round glob. From its crown it dropped north to a ridge that extended to a smaller knob. This complex sloped down at an easy decline on the south and east sides, but on the north it dropped sharply to a river, small most of the time, that snaked its way from the north, turning at the hill to continue more west southwest. To the northeast about a mile and a half away, another stream cut out of the hills and made its way southward, eventually bending to the southwest like the other. These—the hills and rivers and flatter planes in between—were the main features shaping the farm. To the northeast of the buildings was the largest of the flats, an impressive area in two levels, irregularly shaped in a configuration a half mile wide at its widest, amounting to the better part of a section. To the north, on a rise, were orchards; and to the east, clearly visible from the farmhouse's terraced lawn, but at lower levels, were gardens. South of the farmhouse was the barn, and continuing the sweep around the hill to the river on that side was land that had seen its best use as pasture. All of it, wrapping the hill as it did with lower elevations extending to the south and east, was ideally oriented to enjoy the full benefit of the day's sunshine.

Dr. Kjemsrud explained how the farm had been planted, which was generally impressive with few of the detriments included with Industrial Agriculture. He went on to describe the seed bank, and what selections they tentatively recommended for the future, given the present state of temperature, soil type, rainfall and so forth. He discussed concepts of biodiversity and polyculture and provided a quick-study on what had been developed with them to that point. With regards to the recommendations, he said "These are only guides. What conditions will be like around here thousands of years down the road are anybodies guess. You'll just have to take it from here."

Anyway, it was good to have a jump on what needed to be done, and particularly good to be part of a team rather than standing alone.

"Anton, are you ready," Gary repeated.

"Oh sure … just trying to collect my thoughts.

"Like Bruno, I'd like to put a spin on what I've got to say because it's mainly hard work. With the rain coming as it did, we've only had two good days, which is surprising as we've done quite a bit in that time. In little over an acre, ground covers and vines and shrubs were grubbed ... and small caliper trees were taken out and trimmed, complete with root-balls. Only one of the larger trees was taken down with several more to go. The one downed was trimmed, but the root-ball is still in the ground.

"What we've done gives us a good indication of what's left to do, and unfortunately, it's a lot. We need to clear many times what's been done so far. We not only need enough area to develop our orchards and gardens and fields, we also need to trim back the trees so the sun can get in and do its thing. For that we need all the manpower we can muster. This isn't a reflection on the girls, by the way, who've pitched in and worked as hard as any of us. It's just that we need more hands. We're also losing one. As you probably know, one of the piglets died. They represent a rare and unexpected opportunity, so if we can save the rest, it would be great. Terry is now full time trying to do just that, which besides TLC consists of trying to replace mother's milk with a thinned and warmed puree of water and mush and greens and animal fat."

"I thought we were out of mush."

"We essentially are. The last that we had was put aside to give the pigs a chance.

"Anyway, Terry's not only up to her ears with that, she's scrounging the woods for anything edible; and whenever they're found in the area being cleared, she digs them up and transplants them. She's also working with me reviewing the seed bank, and has started seedbeds for trees and bushes slated for the orchard.

"Let's see now, where was I. Bruno, Gary ... I know the lake and its fish are important, but we can get by the way things are for the time being. We can't do that in the fields. The work there has to be done as soon as possible, and like I said before, needs all the hands we've got.

"Can't the bridge and boats and trailway improvements wait for a while?"

"I hear you," Gary answered stoically. *Obsessions don't make way easily, especially when the most important thing in the world is finding a best friend.* "We can pitch in for a few days, and then depending on how much food's on hand, break away when needed. Bruno's projects will really make a difference; but I agree, they're not the critical path at this time."

"Thanks.

"Now ... some of you have asked what will be planted when the clearing is finished, and I haven't been able to answer. I still can't ... *we* still can't," pointing at the others involved. "Way, way, way back before we were put on ice, one of Huston's specialists spent time with Devon, Terry and me going over the seeds in inventory ... as well as giving a bunch of advice. We're reviewing all of that and hope to have an outline of selections, as well as a plan of action, on hand in another week or so."

"How much needs to be cleared, Anton?" Rodney asked, his hands sweeping as if to include the world. "There was a lot of open ground as I recall, certainly more than we will ever need."

"Don't know for sure. Hopefully there's an area much smaller that'll do for us. But complications are already coming to light. We're finding a lot of rock, boulders even, in the area we've worked. And during our sweep of the area on Sunday, we came across a long, low ridge that was nothing but a piling of rocks. These weren't there before. We don't know why and we don't know what other surprises are waiting for us.

"Anyway, that's as specific as I can get right now. There are some generalities that might help you understand what we intend to accomplish ... besides putting food on the table, that is. So step back in mind a minute; and remember that part of our challenge is to live in harmony with the natural world. That means in every way, including agriculture. To put that in perspective, I need to start with some of the history of agriculture and how well it has fitted with the harmony bit.

"Let's use the twenty-first century as a reference point, okay. I mean, the last eight thousand don't really fit in.

"From that point, say year two thousand twelve, go back another twelve thousand years or so, to ten thousand B.C.; that's about when the hunter-gatherers settled down by starting the Agricultural Revolution. Now it's natural to think of those first farmers as primitive and crude, and in other words ... not too smart. But somehow, by the time of Abraham, around two-thousand B.C., most of the crops being eaten today had been developed. That means that in a six to eight thousand year period before them, those crude, ignorant people had taken nondescript perennial grasses and somehow cross-bred or cross-pollinated them until there were the wonderful wheats and ryes and oats and barleys we have today. They did a lot more, and although there isn't a written record to tell how it was done; we know it was done. They took animals that hardly resemble what we're familiar with, and gave us horses and cattle and sheep and goats and chickens, and varieties of each of them. They took wolves and gave us dogs of every size and feature. They domesticated cats.

"But back to the crops. In the years of development, the breeding moved the plants from being hardy perennials to specialized, domesticated annuals.

"The four thousand years since then basically continued with whatever had been accomplished; and although farming moved from hand-and-hoe to ox-and-till to tractor-and-plow, the concept remained the same.

"We have become aware in recent years that the concept may have been wrong all along. It certainly hasn't been in harmony with the natural world. Even though there were signs to read along the way, which have been ignored, the gap has become wider and wider.

"When the states were first settled, woods were cleared, much like what we're doing, then planted year after year until the soil was exhausted ... and in many cases eroded.

"When the prairies were reached, sod-busters did their thing and followed suit. A Sioux Indian watching this was reported to have said "Wrong side up." He was right, for the rich, wonderful sub-surface entanglements of biodiversity were destroyed. It was a continuation of what some have called one of the deepest wounds on the planet—the gash made by till agriculture. By plow and disc and drag, the way was opened for the erosion of top-soil, followed by the dust bowl.

"Some changes were made—such as soil banks, crop rotation, contour plowing and shelter belting—and these things helped. But then family farming with its diversity of product such as cattle, sheep, poultry and gardens, began to disappear sometime after World War I, segueing to what became Industrial Agriculture.

"Parts of this latest form, particularly after World War II, were truly impressive, with monster air-conditioned machines, satellite guided control systems and legions of round, corrugated metal granaries. With all of this, farm yields became greater and greater.

"Farming also moved farther than ever from the natural world.

"Because of the demand for more and more, traditional ways of managing land, including banking or rotating, were abandoned for continuous cropping. This soon diminished soil fertility and opened the way for weed and pestile invasions. Countering these problems required herbicides, a petroleum-based product, oil-based chemical pesticides, artificial nitrogen fertilizers and often irrigation. It was as if farmers were growing crops in oil rather than soil.

"I just happen to be the fifth generation in a family that's been in farming since the mid-nineteenth century, and have been a part of what I've just described.

"Our family goes back all the way to the sod-busters, who did exactly what the Indian said. But they were hard workers and suffered unbelievable hardships to start the greatest farming empire on earth. They and the next generations progressed from oxen to horses, and then to large cumbersome steam-powered iron monsters with steel wheels and lugs, to equipment with combustion engines and rubber wheels, and finally to those with air-conditioning and computers.

"When I was in my teens, I was convinced my family was on the cutting edge of farming sophistication with every humanitarian and ecological benefit. But then in the schooling that followed I became exposed to other thoughts about the industry. When brought up at home those thoughts were met with a respectful but stony reserve. It was as if the smart college kid hadn't caught on to the way things work in the real world.

"But as much as I love them, and as proud as I am of the good hard-working generations that have gone before me, I know in heart and mind they were following a premise, that, although thousands of years in its development, was wrong.

"We're not going there.

"There are certain natural laws that we're going to work to observe, such as:

Nature uses only what it needs;
Nature recycles everything; and
Nature banks on diversity.

"As I said in the beginning, we don't have the perfect plan yet, but with a target in mind, there will *not* be petroleum based pesticides or herbicides, there will *not* be chemical fertilizers, and there will *not* be plant or animal hormones. We're going to work with nature, and, we're going to get it right."

23

August

Almost four months had passed since Anton outlined his agricultural program, and they were all still alive ... and that was something. Maybe it was more of a miracle. Anyway, it was a special day for Gary, with a special possibility, and he couldn't sleep.

He dressed quietly and tip-toed out of the cubicle he shared with Mona. Like Terry, Mona was pregnant, which simply goes to prove that when things are as stressful and difficult as thought possible ... watch out.

Up and outside, he was greeted by the cool mountain air, and the vague forms of things he recognized, faintly painted with light from a clear, starry sky. It was quiet and beautiful.

The tents were almost two hundred feet apart, one just outside the entry beside the shop, the other nearer to where the farmhouse had been. The locations weren't random, but were placed for what would hopefully counter encroachments by critters, which had become a problem.

Encroachments, Gary thought ... anyway that's what it had been expressed at one meeting, which drew an immediate response. "Oh you mean like the Indians encroached on the settlers?" The remark coming from Judy.

No one picked it up from there and Gary had let it die. But the point was a good one. They had invaded an ecosystem that was biodiverse and doing very well. He couldn't help but smile as he thought of the analogy, all the while stirring the ashes in the pit beside the near tent, adding tinders and coaxing the fire back to life. With that underway, he set-up the cooking frame, filled the pot, and made preparations for a spot of tea, such as it would be.

He crossed to the other tent and got that fire going ... the encroachment problem continuing to nag him.

It had taken almost three weeks to get enough land cleared to satisfy Anton, an area that only amounted to about fifteen acres. But Anton had to get seeds in the ground, so he said the fifteen would do for now ... everyone knowing that when the planting was done, he would continue to work the edges.

Gary returned to the first fire, where the water was near to boiling. Putting crushed leaves into a cup, he poured water, then settled back, his mind still reeling.

To say the work had been hard was an understatement. It was damned hard ... and dangerous too. Thank God for Roland, who unlike most of them who were still neophytes in their field, was well seasoned to the ways of the working man's world. He was a bug on safety, taking every opportunity to describe how things should be done, with warnings about carelessness and over-exuberance and fatigue that can lead to accidents. Like what occurred the first week. Judy was hard at work with an axe, trimming one of the felled trees. She had removed a branch with several well placed strokes and continued swinging to remove the nub that remained. Only the next stroke was too flat; the side of the axe hit first, bouncing with such centrifugal force it tore from her hands and catapulted counter-clockwise towards Annie and Lisa, who were faced away with what they were doing. Judy screamed but the axe and sound arrive around the same time. The handle hit Lisa hard in the butt, reversed its spin, the blunt edge of the head then hitting Ann a glancing blow before bouncing into the ground past them.

The screams and cries of pain brought everyone nearby in to help. But in this case the girls were lucky; nothing was broken, and outside of rubs to soothe bruises and bandages to cover minor cuts, the girls shoved the helpers away and picked up where they had been.

There were many other minor accidents that led to stinging and bleeding and bruising and limping. The result so far had always been the same. The person simply sucked it up and continued. It reminded Gary of a story John had told. It seems one of his great-grandfathers was a blacksmith, a man renowned for the prodigious amount of work he did. For fifty years the sounds from his anvil and trip-hammer awakened the town for a good mile around, because he'd be at the forge by five in the morning. He'd start the day in clean over-alls, then return, often after dark, blackened with his shirt zebra-striped with salt. One day, while grinding on a cultivator shovel, which was curved and difficult to manage, he was pulled into the wheel. Besides a gouge, the muscles on two fingers were twisted on the bone and split. He stopped and turned off the grinder, then walked a block to the nearest doctor who reset the muscles and sewed the breaks. Returning in less than an hour, he put back on his gloves and continued to work.

Gary shook his head. Everyone around him was acting like a bunch of god-damned blacksmiths.

He took another sip, exhaling with an "aah" as he finished, not thinking how something so simple was so pleasurable in the absence of much else.

What caught his attention was movement over at the other fire. That would be Anton. He waved but couldn't tell if there was a response. That was okay … it was early and he wasn't ready for company anyway.

Returning to mind, he thought the worst part of the last months. Worse than the discomforts of weather or work or injuries, were the maladies. The great outdoors has a good wholesome sound to it, but with it comes healthy portions of cold and damp and chill, and then colds and flues and assorted combinations. And to aggravate all of this, there wasn't much he and Mona could do. The pharmacy, such as it was, was limited, like all supplies, as part of the challenge to live by what was available outside the incubator. So they did the best they could, getting a jump start in part from information in the library, particularly a book of plants with medicinal capabilities, the result of a study of Indian civilizations. Maladies ranged from inconveniences to the more serious requiring bed-rest and treatments. As in Abram's case. He had wanted to stay the night near the top of a tree, the same one climbed earlier, from where he hoped to find lights that would lead to other people. So at the first opportunity he did, only to have temperatures drop and light, cold rains fall. The exposure gained nothing as lights weren't seen, and he developed pneumonia. Abram was out over two weeks.

He thought of Mona, shaking his head on how he had almost screwed up something terribly important. He and Mona worked together on many things, the injuries and maladies and all, but were usually apart during the day. On one Mona had been with Terry and Devon, carefully sowing precious seeds under Anton's direction. The day had been unseasonably hot, with the result that by the end of it, Mona was a mess with dirt caking her clothes, her hair wet and stringy, her hands and nails abominable, and her face sweat-streaked with a wide smudge across her forehead where she'd wiped with a dirty hand.

When Gary moved to greet her, he found the situation funny. Without thinking he cropped her face in his hands and said "You're absolutely beautiful … will you marry me?"

He had intended to be funny, but then he saw the look of hurt flash to tell him he'd broached a tender subject in an insensitive way. As the tears began to form, he managed to recover. "Look, I'm sorry … I've been thinking of proposing a lot recently and it just came out. I hadn't planned it this way, but since I've asked once, I'll ask again. I love you and want you for my wife … Will you marry me?"

"Seriously?" She asked, the words in a whisper as conflicting emotions rippled under the mud decorating her face.

"Seriously," his words having less meaning than his eyes which were beginning to mist over.

There was silence … then the unfortunate awareness that everyone else had filtered in to surround them, realizing what was about and anxiously waiting a response.

Mona collapsed laughing. She tried to hide in her hands, bumping her head against his chest, while Gary wondered whether he'd done it again. He thought of the Totem Pole. After a time that seemed forever, Mona finally slid her muddy hands to his face, tilted her head back with eyes glistening but hardly seeing, and squeaked the sweetest "yes" he'd ever heard.

The explosion of cheers with feet stomping and hands clapping was so loud a covey of quail hiding nearby burst into the air, and the piglets slopping in their little Eden stopped and perked.

That had been three months ago … and so much had happened since.

The highly anticipated planting had been completed; and then came the wait, which didn't last long before buds began popping everywhere. There was the orchard, a long-term interest that wouldn't bear fruit for several years but needed care from day one; there were the fields, where a few experiments were being conducted in addition to large areas of wheat and corn and smaller plots of oats and barley; and there was the garden with its wide variety. The whole farming bit was exciting as each green spike was like a promise for the future.

It was also exciting for most birds, and for critters like rabbits and deer and others—those damned encroachers again—who were drawn to the well organized smorgasbord of delectables.

This complicated Anton's life to no end as he felt it necessary to constantly police the area, which meant late to bed and early to rise and trip-wires and noise-makers and not a great deal of sleep.

Fortunately there was help which was totally unexpected. While reading a part of the Daily Log, as Gary did at every opportunity, he came across comments by Reynolds about taking down Homer and Jethro. These turned out to be animatronic guardians that had been assembled for the very same problems Anton was facing. They had been carefully deactivated and cleaned and then vacuum wrapped and stored along with instructions for their resurrection. The comments led to a hunt into the often confusing bundles packed in storage, and excitement when items were found labeled with descriptions like "photo-voltaic cells", "motion detectors", "pneumatic activators", "voice simulators", and so on. Rodney, who took on the role of mad scientist at the slightest inspiration, was beside himself in leading the effort to put the scarecrows back together and into operation. When installed and turned on, the two proved to be the most hilarious displays any of them had ever seen. The instructions mentioned that voice simulations had been programmed by a spirited group of designers, but that subtle explanation didn't prepare them for the antics and comments that emanated. They were a hoot.

He thought of Bruno, who along with Rodney and Abram, was inside the tent. Bruno had been as busy as anybody in a group of very busy people. In the normal course of the day everyone would be into their priority responsibilities. Then there'd be a filtering back, showering, eating and occasionally a gathering in the lounge. But most of the time there'd be continuing pursuits of individual interests. In Bruno's case it was master planning, as well as specific project design. For the former he created a base model of the farm, with the hill and orchards and gardens in as near to accurate three-dimensional scale as he could determine. Using clay to shape most of surfaces, he added small rocks and chiseled stone to emulate outcrops and cliffs; and used sphagnum moss, lichens and miniature junipers combined with cuttings to represent vegetation. When completed it proved to be invaluable, not only for him to visualize specific arrangements, but also for the others to understand the scope and relationship of all the considerations. After putting finished touches to the model, Bruno spent hours before it, sketching options for housing and manufacturing and storage and every other need coming to mind. These he carved into scale models that could be composed in various ways into the base. What he hadn't gotten into yet, but which everyone suspected was on his mind, were concepts on a grand scale, with soaring buildings and promenades and eventual aspects of a sophisticated society, including provisions for transportation and security as well as beauty. Although he avoided the topic, the thought of the ultimate Olympia never left his mind.

For the moment there were specific projects. The first was a roof over where the machine shed had been. It had been assumed this location would have a prime use, such as an operations center or a meeting room; but needs and conveniences won over. With electricity available on the entry wall, and with limited extension cords on hand, the space became a fabrication shop.

Another was a tower for the top of the hill, which never got beyond a model of a sculptured masonry spear the equivalent of six stories high. Bruno saw several reasons to think of this feature, but for the time being never pressed the point.

There was the bridge. Like with the master plan, Bruno carefully measured contours, depicting them as accurately as he could into a study model. He further explored the geology of the area with pickaxe and shovel, leading to assumptions that were as good as he could get for foundations. Given these, he then, with sticks simulating timbers, assembled a model of a trestle spanning the ravine. The bridge was more exciting to everyone than some of the others, probably because bridges are just that way, or because climbing up and down and fording streams gets old real fast. It was especially true for Roland, who was faced with many works to build, but none as dynamic or challenging.

Most of the items hoped for, however, would have to come sometime in the future. Priorities being what they were, the first project after the shop canopy were boats.

And that was the root of Gary's excitement.

A few days before, the second of the boats, after labor-intensive sawing and planing and drilling and pegging and trimming and caulking, were finally ready. The next day they were carried to the lake. This required all eight of the men as the boats, despite efforts to thin the boards, still weighed several hundred pounds each. Any arguments against the bridge were dispelled at the ravine, where the normal difficulty was substantially multiplied. The launching was also more difficult than anticipated, leading finally to trial runs and re-caulking, before tying up and covering for the night.

"I guess you're going to want a dock and boat-house next," Roland said as he saw the difficulties along the shore.

"That would be nice," Gary agreed. "This place is going to see a lot of use. And you can see that if we take care of the boats, they'll last for years."

Roland grunted, thinking of all the projects on his list.

"When can you start?"

"Let me think on it?"

Gary stood and paced. Looking east he could see only the faintest suggestion that dawn was on its way. What's taking so damn long? Today was the day he'd been waiting for a long time.

He'd made many trips to the lake, but each one was made only after some other priority had been satisfied. Despite the interruptions, he'd finished with the archeological sifting, and had been elated that in the last portion there still hadn't been a remnant of John in its makeup.

Then he'd stood on the ledge above where the jump-suit had been found and gazed across the lake, saying to himself "Okay, John, you made it this far ... where did you go from here?"

The day after the launch, Gary, Rodney, Bruno and Abram returned to the lake. Everyone knew what Gary wanted to do, but Bruno suggested an overview first, with arguments that could hardly be denied. So they pushed off, choosing to the right, and began exploring.

It would take all day. The lake snaked its way west for a few miles, then turned south for another good ways before ending at an outflowing depression. The mists and sounds from beyond that point suggested rapidly running water and possibly some serious drops, which they really didn't want to tackle ... not then anyway ... so they paddled away. The way to the outflow, and the return to base, were both characterized by alternating sections of sand and rocks and ledges and forest. Several ravines carved their way out of the surrounding topography, and half-way down the north shore, another river similar to the one near home base emptied. In all the travel was less than eight miles; but at times they slowed to fish, and at times they came ashore to explore points of interest, especially at the outflow where curiosities were peaked. By the time they made the turn at the last mile, the sun was low with shadows blotting out detail in the nearest corner. In all they had seen, which included many plants and animals of interest, there was nothing they could tie to John.

That was yesterday.

"How long you been up?" Bruno asked as he made for the pot.

"Awhile," Gary said, knowing he wasn't fooling anyone. They were all aware of his obsession, an "all" that hopefully didn't include Ann. He'd avoided discussing John in general conversations, probably too much so, but he didn't want to face her with speculations, which put more urgency to finding something that had a definite meaning.

An hour later the four were back at the lake and in the boats. This time they moved to the left, passing the creek and marsh, and coming ashore just beyond the latter. "At least we're not going to be sifting sand the way you did back there," Bruno said, really as a suggestion.

"That's true, but we'll still have to be thorough. Rod and I will jump out here ... You take our boat and tie up about a hundred yards ahead. We'll search the area between and meet, and if nothing is found, will move on to the next hundred ... and so on."

It wasn't easy. They worked with machetes, criss-crossing land that put up every defense to criss-crossing. As half expected, and in some cases hoped, they didn't find anything—bones, fire pits, monuments—or anything to indicate a person had passed this way. When they returned to where the boats were tied, it wasn't necessary to say anything because eyes already said it all, like "You mean this is what we're going to do all around this damned lake?"

But nobody protested. And as the sun marched its way, they chopped-off another hundred, then another and another and another. Nearing the far corner of the lake, Gary looked up, shielding his eyes as the angle of the sun was in line with where he was looking. "Just look at that ... That's some tree."

"Sure is," Rod agreed. "I've been looking at it since that first day fishing. What is it?"

"I think it's an oak."

They continued chopping, weaving back and forth, until they realized the tree was no longer in view ... they were under its canopy. And Bruno and Abram were waiting for them, sitting with their backs against the huge trunk which disappeared into an amazing structural system that seemed to reach forever.

"We're bushed," Bruno said.

"Me too," added Rodney.

Gary went to a rotting, fern-covered remnant of a log nearby, and finding a solid part on it, plunked, saying, "Same here ... Damn, this is harder than I thought. Where are you two tied?"

"The boats are back a ways," Rodney said pointing with his head. "It looked nice and cool under here, so we cheated."

"Want to call it a day?"

"No, not yet," Bruno said. "I've got an eerie feeling about this corner. When I stand at the ledge where the jumpsuit was found and tried to visualize where John would go if he had to swim, this corner is one of the places that seemed to make sense."

"So?"

"So, let's look at another section or two. When we swept by yesterday, the shadows blotted out most of the detail."

"Okay, sounds good. How much ground around here did you cover?"

"We went over this side of the tree pretty well ... starting back at the boats. But we hadn't gotten into that thicket yet, so that would be a good place to begin."

With that the teams groaned, got to their feet and parted, Bruno and Abram disappearing towards the lake.

The thicket, which had been suggested as a point of interest, was hard to figure. It seemed like there were several smaller trees that had somehow collected all sorts of debris—dead limbs, vines and the like—and packed them into more than the usual obstruction. "Okay, let's give it a try," Gary said, going to the left while Rodney veered right.

But they didn't get far ... something exploded!

"Holy shit!"

A blur burst out at ground level as Rodney approached and rocketed upward, not settling until ending ten yards higher somewhere in another mass of leaves and vines.

Gary ran over, "Rod ... you okay?"

Rodney was white, wide-eyed and fumbling around for something the nature of which he hadn't determined.

He mumbled something.

Moving closer, Gary looked back and up. There was a hissing. Then there was a movement and a face and their eyes met.

"I'll be damned, it's another panther!"

Rodney began to giggle, "Jesus ... it happened so fast ..."

"You okay?"

"Yes. Yes, but that *was* something. I must have almost stepped on it. Had no idea."

After a few minutes looking about, they ignored the animal that seemed content in its new hiding place and moved on, hacking their way to the to the left and leaving the thicket around the trees alone. Wading through the bushes, footfalls were often on uneven ground. At one depression, Gary kicked up black cinders and rock, but they were blended with leaves and other debris and he failed to see them. Another sig-zag took them inland a ways and then back to shore.

"Let's take a look at those rocks offshore. From what I can see, we can get over without getting wet."

They crossed a series of stones and made their way to a high point among the jumble, when Rodney said, "Well lookee here."

But Gary wasn't listening. He had returned to the stepping stones and was eyeing them. The stones were far too regular, with layers having been carefully placed by someone. *That someone could have been ....*

Whomp!

"Over here," Rodney repeated.

"What is it?"

"A firepit. There's a ring of stones and lots of ashes. Someone's been here."

Gary jumped up and down and waved and yelled, getting the attention of the others, and soon both boats were over and tied.

When Bruno and Abram were shown the findings, the balloon of excitement deflated somewhat with the question "What does this mean, other than that someone was here?"

"It must have been John."

But it could have been someone else."

"Jeez."

"Let's look around. Seems John had a bent for etching. Maybe there's more."

At almost the same time, Abram, who had spotted something on a flat surface a short ways away, said, "You want etchings, I've got etchings."

"What is it?" as they gathered.

"Damned if I know. There's kind of an arc with some other

scribbles. It doesn't appear to be artwork ... like a petroglyph, I mean."

"Here's more ... but just a bunch of marks."

"Looks like someone counted days, like on a prison wall ..."

There were seventy-two marks.

"There's more," Gary said, pulling away an old rotted branch and dusting away accumulated leaves and twigs. He went to his hands and knees, cleaning with his nose almost to the stone until the marks blended into something telling, at which time he shouted and jumped to his feet, hopping and dancing and twirling, the last movement taking him too near the edge, where he stretched out, let go and did a back flop. As he surfaced spitting out a stream, the others, who were more embarrassed for him than laughing, said "What the hells wrong with you?"

Gary yelled again as he struggled to his feet in the shallows, shouting "Those scratchings ... those scratchings tell it all!

"Read'em! Read'em! ***Read'em!"***

They read:

LEFT FOR NNE PEAK 6/22 JEA

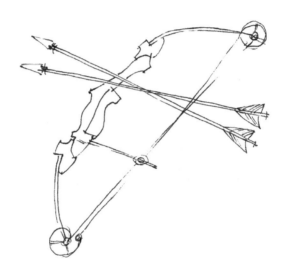

PART THREE

24

Drums

"Here's what we now know," Gary began to everyone excitedly crammed into the lounge, "and Annie, I apologize for keeping you in the dark, but we didn't have a picture that could be shared until a few hours ago."

He turned to a map Bruno had hurriedly sketched and tacked on the wall. "Okay, since early on we've known John was brought back successfully, and that he made it out through the caverns. Later we found that he'd made it all the way to the lake; and Annie, that's the part we never told. You see, we knew he was there because we found his jumpsuit ... but it was in ten feet of water and had several tears.

"Here it is." He reached behind and brought the garment out, now cleaned and neatly folded. He gave it to Annie, who sat without making an expression.

"Now we know more ... and know that the tears may not mean anything. What we know is that John spent the next few months almost a half-mile away in the vicinity of off-shore rocks right about here," pointing to the map. "Then, on June twenty-second, he left for the large peak we've all seen north of here."

"You mean June twenty-second, twenty years ago."

"Probably ... but we don't know that for sure."

"Here's what we're going to do. As soon as preparations can be made, in two days if possible, we're sending a party of four to that mountain. From that peak, and depending on what we see, we're going to continue further until we find people ... and John."

"I'd like to go," Annie said. "I know it won't be easy, but nothing can be worse for me than staying here waiting."

"Annie, everyone wants to go."

"Let her go," Lisa said. "You talked to me about it because of the need for a good archer. Well, most of the girls have been practicing with me and have really gotten good at it. Annie is one of the best.

"Let her go."

Three days after starting, the four—Gary, Roland for his strength and marksmanship, Annie, and Judy as her logical companion—reached the top. It took longer than anticipated, even though they alternated in the lead to share the load, and kept at it from dawn to dusk each day. At the crest they almost jumped for joy, finding something to go by—ashes. The ashes were on the north side in a ring of stones among a confluence of boulders, now weeded over.

The view atop the boulders was spectacular, every bit as grand as they'd hoped—more hills and ridges descending to the north; a series of lakes to the east and northeast; and woods everywhere disappearing into the haze that was the horizon. There was also disappointment; there was nothing to indicate people.

Roland sat back, swept the panorama with binoculars once more, and then dropped them to his side and shrugged, "I don't see a damn thing, Gary."

Gary nodded and sighed. They hadn't known what to expect, but they were hoping to see something ... anything. He looked at the girls, particularly Annie, who was sifting through the ashes as if making some connection, then back to Roland, "We can't see home from here, can we?"

"You mean Mount Olympus?"

"Yes, Mount Olympus," Gary said smiling. "Bruno and Abram were going to set up a platform in that tree at the top, so we could see each other and communicate."

"I know. They asked me about it. I suggested they cut off the top third, then build a platform sturdy enough to hold dirt and rocks, and on which they could make a signal fire. But no, we can't see each other from this side. We passed a spot back a ways that will work, though, so let's go there and set something up."

"Sounds good. We could start the fire now; the plume would let them know we're here."

"No, let's wait 'til after dark. By then we'll have seen if there are lights to the north. That would be pretty exciting to report."

Just then a gust blew in, rattling the branches and kicking up dust.

"Whoops … looks like some weather moving in. We'd better set camp and batten down first.

"But not here. We don't want to be on top if high winds are a part of it. Let's find a place down the slope. Hey girls!"

They worked their way off the top and down the north face, finding an outcrop over a hollow that with a little clearing provided a good cave-like shelter. After setting up camp, they retraced steps to the rocks where they could watch as the day faded. Before this, however, they continued to the south face, cleared an area and made preparations for a fire. Occasional gusts fanned them as they did, causing them to look up to see what might be happening. They noticed stars beginning to disappear from the south. This meant clouds moving in and possibly weather, but for the moment it was still pleasant.

"Let's get it going," Gary said, "I don't like the wind we're catching, but we should be able to put up a fire long enough to let them know we're here."

After getting it going, he stepped aside and stared into the nothingness the shadows were forming on the landscape below. It wasn't long before he laughed. There was a faint glow breaking through from a point far away and below them.

"That's got to be Bruno."

The letters "OK" were spelled, soon followed by the same from below. Then another gust hit and sparks fanned out beyond their ability to control. "That's enough. We don't need to light up the whole damned mountain. Besides, there's nothing else to report."

They doused the fire and covered the embers; then groped their way, aided by hand-generated lights, over the crest towards camp. The winds, which may have been lesser at lower elevations, compressed and accelerated as they crossed the top, making further stay not only difficult, but also next to impossible.

At camp, the girls had tucked into their tiny, two-person backpacker tents, with Gary and Roland preparing to do the same, when Gary doubled back to the vantage point for one last look. His shouts brought everyone back out.

There on a peak, seemingly forever away ... too far for an estimate of distance, but definite enough to have a meaning ... was a light.

Whomp!

Gary and Roland awakened early, and while laying all wrapped-up in the pre-dawn darkness, discussed the light and what it could mean ... always leading to the same thing—people. But people were what they were after, so the sighting was an important and exhilarating something.

The obvious and only conclusion they could make was that they would press on towards it, working the ridges and ravines before them the best way they could. While they were talking, coffee came to mind, and as often happens, the power or suggestion took over. So Gary slipped out to restart the fire and set things up. Before the pot got to a boil, however, he heard sounds and felt gusts of some kind of weather. It wasn't just any ordinary kind, as it grew quickly, alarmingly so, becoming like the rumble of a giant herd. The rumble, growing to a banshee pitch, then hit with a wet wave that blew the fire away and everything else not tied down. In an instant, wind and water became one, and Gary, who stood briefly in the tempest as if it wasn't real, had to scramble back to shelter.

The storm raged through the day and next night, coming in pulses of wind and rain that varied from momentary calm to blasts of hurricane velocity, ripping the landscape every which way. It also rotated so a place in the lee at one point, came to be in the brunt in another. During the morning that followed a day later, the storm left to the northeast, exiting the area almost as fast as it had entered. They woke to a beautiful sky and only whispers of breezes, which was good, but the world around them was a mess. Many trees were toppled, and those that stood were twisted and broken with leaves and branches and debris in every array in all directions. The mountain was also saturated, and although surface water wasn't a problem where they were, sounds from below made it plain that serious flooding was working its way to lower elevations.

They stayed at camp that day, drying out on a day so pretty and clear it was as if the God's were making an apology. At dusk they returned to the south side and rekindled. Their fire was answered atop Olympus a short time later; which led them to send the following message:

ALL OK ... LIGHT FAR N ... GO MNY WKS

The going was slow. Climbing before had been difficult, but by comparison, fairly good time had been made. Now toppled trees and debris, combined with previously dry gullies turned to torrents, added complications at every turn. In time, they reached a place where they could see that the lakes were tied into one gangly body in a generally northeast direction, with frequent fingers extending from its sides. Their only option was to skirt the fingers as they were encountered and press on, hoping the choices available to them would be somewhat efficient.

A week passed.

On the eighth day they were strung out along a comparably open stretch. As was their custom, they followed contours to the extent possible to ease the way, marked trees, and looked for vantage points. At these they would stop, with Roland, a head taller and with binoculars in hand, would sweep whatever the view. The views were always the same—nothing new—continuing to make it hard to believe the world could be so devoid of people.

But they kept moving. During one stretch, Judy dropped back to Gary who was bringing up the rear. "How far do you think we've gone?"

Gary shook his head, "Hard to say. I jot notes every so often ... you know, direction, time and distance. It seems like we're covering a lot of ground; but as the crow flies, it may not add up to much. Certainly twenty miles, possibly thirty or thirty-five."

"That isn't anywhere close to the light, is it?"

"Oh no. We haven't been in a position to see it since we left the peak, so it's just a guess at this time. We're probably only a quarter the way."

Judy nodded. "That means it may be the end of September before we turn around."

"Getting tired of this?"

"No, just talking. You said before leaving that this could be a long trip. I'm here for whatever the duration."

"Thanks. How's Annie doing?"

"She's fine. She'll walk 'til hell freezes if that's what it takes. Her world is somewhere out ahead."

They'd been lagging back as they talked, so when they made a turn and climbed a small incline, they found Roland and Annie on a log waiting for them.

"Want me to take the lead for a spell?"

"No. Heard you talking back there, so guessed you hadn't noticed," Roland said.

"Noticed what?"

Roland pointed to where they'd come, then continued pointing to where he stood and past.

"A trail?"

"It's not much, but yes … it's a trail. Since it's so faint, it could be the end of the line."

"Or something from animals?"

Roland shrugged, "Could be that, I suppose. Whatever it is, it's the first I've seen."

At noon they stopped for a break, dropping totes and finding comfortable spots to stretch out.

"It's a definite trail now," Roland said, "and from people, not animals. It's not only more pronounced, it's also having off-shoots, which are probably to different spots on the lake."

"Saw that. Could mean people a lot sooner than expected."

People? … What people? … How many? … Peaceful?

"So what's the plan?" Judy asked. "Any strategy?"

"No," Gary answered, "none other than to keep going."

The others looked at each other, generally expressionless. With that he added, his hands trying to form a picture, "We can hardly make one until we find what we're up against. Look ... this is what we came all this way for, isn't it? We're not turning back, so let's just press on ... I'll take the lead."

"I don't like that," Roland said. "If there're people up ahead, there might be trouble. And if there's trouble, I should be up front."

"Let's not be planning for a fight," Annie said. "Sure it's a possibility; but can't we at least *look* like we're coming in peace. Judy and I should be leading, to give that impression."

The argument bounced back and forth, but in the end, the last idea won out and on they went. Not to be completely unassuming, Judy checked her machete to be sure it was set for quick release, automatically gripping her walking stick with a new resolve. And Annie did about the same, even though her bow appeared to be casually draped over her shoulder.

The last discussion caused several other changes to what had been a light-hearted journey: casual patter ended; eyes became more focused; and ears reached for every sound. When a harmless chipmunk burst across in front of them, heartbeats skipped, followed by nervous giggles.

"Did you see what I saw?" Annie whispered a bit later.

"No, what?"

"Can't be sure ... I thought I saw two people up ahead. When we made the last turn, I thought there'd be a better view of them, but they were gone."

"No matter," Gary said as he and Roland caught up, his voice low and pinched. "We didn't think we'd be catching anyone by surprise.

"Keep going."

The trail became wider with more frequent offshoots.

"This has the look of a main pathway paralleling the lake."

Gary nodded, "Keep going."

"I saw people up ahead again. For sure this time."

"I know ... keep going."

A mile later they came to a clearing off to the right. It was an open expanse formed mostly of flattened rocks, with an escarpment springing from the ground almost separating it from the trail. Within the clearing, a panorama opened up with woods to the sides, the lake stretching out before them, and the mountains and ridges beyond completing the view. They stepped off the trail for a moment to see if there was something they could learn. As before, they didn't see anything of use ... but then the sounds reached them.

"Jesus ... those are drums!"

Annie recoiled, putting hands to her face. "If John were there ... there wouldn't be drums."

It was frightening and logical, but before it took hold, Judy said "Now let's not jump to conclusions. Maybe John's not there right now. Maybe it's just their way of calling everyone to assembly. Maybe it's them who are scared ... and maybe they should be. After all, we've got a marksman with a blunderbuss, and an archery queen, who together can raise royal hell if they want to play rough. We can't turn back because they know we're here. Let's go!"

They did, but then stopped when Gary burst out laughing.

"What's so funny?"

"I don't know ... I do that sometimes when I'm real nervous. But hell, what you said sounds good to me ... As you said, let's go!"

They started again, their footfalls, not hurried but steady, seemed to pick up more authority as they moved along. Gary remembered a concept from World War I—that if a force moved forward slowly and steadily, showing no fear, the enemy would panic and flee. He also remembered that it didn't work; the slowly moving ranks were simply mowed down.

Some concept.

Regardless, the four moved along; but like in most armies, each continuing because the person beside them kept moving.

The drumbeats got louder. Mouths went dry. Roland, tall, resolute, a tower of strength with a granite-solid jaw-set, ignored the warm trickle down his leg.

They came to a bridge over a small ravine. Past there through thinning segments of forest, they could detect movements and hear growing bits of chatter.

"Stop here a minute, girls," Gary said. As they did he looked at Roland. "Any thoughts?"

"No. We're on the edge of a village, that's certain ... and the village is preparing a reception."

"Lordy. Okay, let's keep moving. If arrows start to fly, take cover."

This is crazy!

They pressed on, crossing a small bridge. The first thing Gary saw, with eyes darting from side to side, was what appeared like a homestead a ways to his left. It was a complicated affair with poles and lines and gardens and shelters, all of which fronted on an oddly shaped, thatched house. The house reminded him of an overgrown backpacking tent.

They passed another tangle and turned past the remaining vegetation blocking their view. As they did, the subtle impressions took solid form. They gasped. The form was an army ... an array— squad after squad in stiff military formation, extending from as far as they could see in each direction, each squad different in dress and shield and spear and color and decoration.

The squads stood rigidly, faces barely showing above shields, with only eyes betraying any feeling. The array appeared at first to be immoveable; but then there was a chink. Behind the screen there was excited conversation ... a lot of it. And although there was nothing understandable, it was obvious there was disagreement.

At first lull, Annie handed Judy her bow and stepped forward, moving several paces before a stunned Gary could think of what to do ... which was nothing. She stopped and lifted her hands to the eyes, now close and bugged and easy to read. Then speaking slowly, loudly and firmly, she said, "My name is Ann. I am the wife of John Anderson. We come in peace. We mean you no harm. Let us talk and be friends. We seek your leaders. Please come forward so we can talk."

The ranks, except for shuffling, stayed in place, while in the back the chatter, which had momentarily stopped, picked up again.

Gary, who'd been looking about for any direction, finally went to where Annie stood and said, "That was wonderful, but I can't tell what good it's doing or where this is going. We shouldn't stay here ... it's like we're standing in the bulls-eye. Roland spotted a structure of some kind behind those weird looking rocks. Let's head that way. It's got to be better than here."

Annie wanted to stay, but after some pleading, she consented, joining the others as they turned and walked away as if there was nothing to fear.

"For gosh sakes, look at this," Judy said as they passed a low eave and entered the expanse of *Tschaha-tata*. The building had changed since its original construction: it was now festooned with a variety of beautifully crafted wall drops and decorations; the gable ends were closed-in with multi-colored mosaics of organic materials, which sparkled on the south side as the sun's rays penetrated it; and candle assemblies dropped at uniform spacing along the east-west line. "We can forget about these people being like the remnants in *Planet of the Apes*. This is cool … Bruno would flip if he were here."

After being impressed by the building and its internal workings, the girls were drawn to the rocks into which the western gable was framed. It was such an unlikely part of it all, yet the more they gazed, the more they were moved, particularly Annie. She climbed steps to the stage-like tier and came to a plant—a small tree that clung to the side of the wall—and its two crafted white doves. Seeing a series of candles attached nearer the center of the wall, she dug into her pack for a starter kit and lit them.

Then she dropped to her knees and prayed.

Judy watched a few moments from below, then turned and left to give her privacy. Extending her tour, she stepped out on the south side to view the arena-like yard that dropped in a series of steps and extended to the forested perimeter.

Just then she saw movement in the bushes on the far side. The movement was from two young boys who'd frozen too late, and, realizing they were spotted, stood with eyes as big as saucers. Judy correctly guessed they'd been far from the village when the drums sounded, and hadn't made it back in time.

She sat on the top step and smiled …

They didn't move.

She said, "Don't be afraid … come here, I'd like to talk to you."

They shook their heads.

My god, they understood me!

Judy, stunned, was trying to think of what to do next when Annie stepped out, all five feet ten of her, carrying her compound bow. The boys vanished in a blink, sounds of crashing bushes telegraphing their escape back into the forest.

Meanwhile Gary and Roland had only glanced at the interior and turned back to keep a vigil. When they couldn't see anything of significance, they moved to a bench under the north gable, which seemed to be the main entry. But then things began to change. The squads, while still in place, began to shift about. It was weird. *Where was the leadership?* The only semblance continued to be sounds of bickering from behind the shields. After a time of bouncing knees and strumming fingers, Gary got up and paced, his stomach in a knot. He didn't hear the commotion on the other side of the building.

Roland stayed put, forcing himself to stretch his legs, lean back against a column and even yawn. While in this act, he occasionally lifted his binoculars. At the last of the liftings, he sat up with a start ...

Gary froze.

"Two canoes just came into the cove on the right ..."

25

Finally

Dlahni rammed the canoe into the bank and jumped out. "What are you talking about?"

"We've been attacked … attacked by *Giants*!"

"Attacked? Where's the fighting? Has anybody been hurt?"

"Well … there really hasn't been any fighting yet."

"How many of them are there?"

"We can see only four … two men and two women; but there could be many more."

Dlahni almost exploded. "Whose in charge? Where are Brundahni and Ruth."

"They're over by the Lodge with the Chieftains. No one seems to know what to do."

Nyaho limped forward, pushing away those who'd helped him out of the canoe. "Did I hear something about Giants?"

Dlahni stopped and fought to settle down. "Sorry, are you okay?"

"Yes, I'm fine. But let's look to Da-hash-to. His canoe came in right behind us and he needs help."

With that, many hands gently lifted the Grand Chieftain out and onto a stretcher.

"How do you feel?"

Da-hash-to smiled. "It's good to be home. But we seem to have a problem, don't we. Let's get on to the Lodge and find out what it's about before someone does something foolish."

The procession, growing as they moved up the slopes, wound its way to the Lodge, where the Chieftains who remained behind were in a heated exchange with Brun-dahni and Ruth. The groups, including a crowd of bystanders, were so into the arguments they hadn't seen what had just happened at the landing. Then one by one heads turned and jaws dropped, the contenders sputtering to a halt.

The silence didn't last. Everyone began speaking again; some asking "When did you get back? Why are you limping? What happened at the Gathering? Where are the others? What did you learn?" Others saying "Giants have arrived ... We don't know why they're here; therefore we've mobilized for defense. Our squads are in place with our archers and slingers behind them ...We want to attack ...We don't want to attack, but no one moves to greet them." All of the comments blending into a dissonant combination of sounds defying understanding, until Da-hash-to shook his head and held up his hand.

He let things simmer for a while, then said "The Gathering was a success; but it was also a tragedy because there was a battle and many were killed. When everyone's back, which will take several more days, we'll make a full reporting. There's much to tell, but now isn't the time.

"As you see I'm injured and weak and can no longer lead. I've therefore appointed Dlahni-de-njsata-uta-Slahama Grand Chieftain.

"Hear now *his* words."

Dlahni stepped forward. "I've accepted what Chief Da-hash-to has requested, but only until he recovers. As he said, we'll share all the news when everyone has returned. There is one thing, however, that must be shared now. The tragedy at the Gathering, resulting in the scars and injuries you ask about, was the work of Braga. The blood of many from all the nations is on his hands. Therefore the Council of Nations has been deemed him a traitor to all mankind and banished him. That means he can be killed on sight, or captured and brought before the Council for justice."

This brought another explosion of comments and questions until

Dlahni held up his hand as Da-hash-to had done, and soon everyone quieted down again.

"We'll answer all of these questions ... but later."

"Now, what's happened here? Why are we mobilized? We don't want more fighting."

One of the Chieftains spoke, "We've been invaded by Giants."

"Giants you say?"

"Yes. One of them is taller than John."

"I see ... and how many of them are in their army?"

The Chieftain mumbled something.

"How many? And were there women like we've been told?"

The Chieftain looked down and couldn't answer.

"You thought the *Atjahahni* were in danger so you mobilized, right?"

He and the other Chieftains nodded.

"Okay, that's good ... to show strength. But you didn't attack, right?"

They nodded again.

Then Ruth, who was agitated and couldn't hold back any longer, said "Chief Dlahni, the four who approached from the north have done nothing to cause us either harm or alarm. They said they come in peace and only want to talk. Your fellow Chieftains here wanted to attack. We were in an argument about this when you returned."

"How do you know they just wanted to talk?"

"They said so. They speak my father's language, which half the people understand."

Dlahni exhaled, half whistling, not yet making sense of it. "Anything else?"

"Yes." As Ruth struggled to say more, Dlahni noticed her anger turning to something else. She stammered ...

"What *is* it?"

"One of the women, the tall one who spoke, said she was the wife of John ... John Anderson ..."

Whomp!

Dlahni looked at Nyaho, whose features had frozen. He looked at Da-hash-to, whose wrinkled brow said *what is this you know that I don't?*

Dlahni had to take control, and after a moment he relaxed and did.

"Where are they? I didn't see anyone as we walked up."

"When we didn't reply to them," Ruth said, "they went into *Tschtaha-tata*. I guess they're waiting for us there."

Dlahni nodded, then speaking to the Chieftains, said, "Nyaho and I happen to know who these people are," a comment that drew another explosion which had to be quelled before he could continue.

"They come from the south, as did John. They're our friends ... There *is* no danger. So dismiss all squads and auxiliaries and thank them for their performance; they've done well. As we've said, there'll be a report on all of this, as well as of the Gathering, when the time is proper.

"What's happening now," Roland said, inching towards his rifle.

"Relax; it looks like they're dispersing."

As they watched, the disciplined array of squads shuffled and turned and began to mingle, some disappearing, but most regrouping as spectators. The movements were so extensive that at first something else wasn't seen ... the emerging from the mass of a strange delegation—one man limping, two others carrying a third on a stretcher, and a woman with a toddler holding her hand.

Roland stood to join Gary, who'd stopped pacing. They were joined by the girls.

Dlahni stopped when they were about ten feet away and hesitated ... It was awkward. He set the stretcher down, then, along with Brun-dahni, helped Da-hash-to to his feet where he stood on one leg holding onto the younger man.

Turning back, Dlahni tried not to show what he was feeling, for what he was facing was awesome. In the years since first seeing John, he'd gotten used to his size, eventually coming to feel he was one of a kind. But now before him was another ... another even taller. And although two others were more nearly "normal", there was a fourth, a woman, who was the tallest he'd ever seen. If that weren't enough, there were the clothes they were wearing ...

Dlahni swallowed. *What was it John said?* "*There were fifteen more*" ... "*They are good people*"... "*They are my friends*".

He looked at Nyaho, who was almost expressionless, but then Nyaho flashed a slight smile and nodded.

Dlahni looked back at the four, focusing on the taller woman, and in so doing seeing eyes that were large and questioning and on the verge of tears.

He swallowed again and composed himself, almost choking on the first words, however, before saying in almost perfect English, "Welcome to the land of the *Denas Atjahahni*. My name is Chief Dlahni; this is Nyaho, our Spirit Man. We have been carrying Grand Chieftain Da-hash-to, who has suffered a broken hip. With us is my son Brun-dahni, and his wife Ruth, daughter of John Anderson, and his grandson Andrew.

"I know who you are. We are all friends. We've a great deal to talk about, so let's go inside and get comfortable. "

*   *   *

Two days later the sun was beginning its dive to end the day. The groups in the baggage train then did what they always did, they dropped totes, set up shelters, started fires and prepared meals, working efficiently and quickly, knowing the speed in which darkness descends in the forest.

John was all set for the night. He was cordial to those around him, and loving to his daughters, each of whom stopped by as usual to make sure he was okay. But mostly he was quiet, settling back and returning to the thoughts he couldn't suppress. He'd told of the other world to Nyaho and Dlahni, and it was clear they were skeptical. *Well, why not* ... he found it hard to believe himself as there were parts to it he still didn't understand. And there were his daughters. He hoped Dlahni or Nyaho would tell Ruth about Matthew, so at least he wouldn't have to break that bit of news. Regardless, he'd have to assemble all of them to tell the revelation—the Armageddon for the world that was, and the Easter for the Chosen that remained.

Oh my. He shook his head trying to see how he could do this in any way that would be believed.

He heard a disturbance in a camp further up the trail, but ignored it. There were always free spirits who seemed to have energy left at the end of the day. *More power to them.*

The disturbance, however, didn't drift away, it grew louder. Looking up, he saw in silhouette against the fading light the forms of a group coming his way. The voice of one he recognized immediately, giving him a lift. It was Dlahni, his best friend in this world. The other sounded familiar, but he couldn't place it or the face … or realize, even after the man stood before him in the light, that this was a person with clothing and equipment he hadn't seen in thousands of years.

Not even when the face said with a tell-tale smirk …

"Mr. Anderson, I presume."

26

John

"*Whaaaa ...*" John looked at the man, shocked beyond his ability to comprehend. He looked at Dlahni, who was somewhat bland except for the sparkle in his eyes and the curl to his lips. He looked at Sara and Naomi, who were back a ways but still in the light, both reflecting a near explosion of curiosity.

Struggling to his feet, he grabbed the tree against which he'd been sitting, then turned and looked down at the person who appeared little more than half his age. His face contorted with the question, "Who *are* you?"

Gary laughed, although in truth his eyes were just as probing, the man before him not only tanned and slightly craggy, but also white-haired and bearded and scarred and crudely wrapped. Beneath all of that, however, were the voice and eyes and stature that echoed a person he couldn't forget.

"John ... it's me, Gary."

"Gary?"

"Yes John ... it's me, Gary. I'm back ... We're all back. And I need help."

"Need help?"

"You don't expect me to build that totem all by myself, do you?"

John's jaw dropped, eyes almost popping. He reached out and grabbed Gary by the shoulders ...

"*Gary!*"

"Yes John, it's me."

"You're back? Everybody's back?"

"Yes."

John held him for a few moments longer, fighting to believe against the disbelief that continued to linger. He shook Gary, his eyes penetrating and expecting the image to disappear. He shook again, then said, "You're back. Everybody's back."

"Yes John, we're back."

"And Annie ... she's back too?

"Yes, Annie's back."

"She's okay?"

"She's fine and full of vinegar. She's back at the village right now, waiting for us to return."

Dlahni interrupted, "She wanted to come along, but we were in a hurry and didn't want a girl holding us up." When both John and Gary broke out laughing, he said, "I'm missing something; what's so funny?"

Gary turned to explain, "She's a champion runner. She would have left us in the dust if we'd given her the chance. The real reason to leave her behind was to give John time to prepare. I figured one shock at a time would be enough."

John looked down and surveyed himself, "Thanks for that. I'm a mess ... I don't want her to see me this way." He stepped back, turned and took a few steps to nowhere and back, shaking his head as if to test whether this was real.

"You *are* a mess," Gary jabbed. "No doubt about that. But you know, with a good shave and a haircut, you might come close to being presentable."

John tried not to smile, searching for a come-back. Not coming up with one, he said "Well damn, I don't care what *you* look like, which isn't that great either, but" ... running out of words, he grabbed Gary again and gave a great big bear hug ..."*Damn it's good to see you!*"

Then they parted and held each other at arms length, grinning from ear-to-ear.

"Who's Annie," Sara asked, edging forward as the reunion played out.

John motioned for the girls to come to the fire and then made introductions. After that, he said "There's so much to tell, I hardly know where to begin. I'd planned to sit down with all of you when we got home, and share what I told Dlahni and Nyaho the day we left Pangaea. Now Gary showing up like this has changed everything. *Everything!* I'm still reeling ... this is unbelievable. Right now he and I need to talk. You can listen in if you wish. I just know what you hear will confuse you even more, but whatever ... we'll get it all straightened out later."

They moved back to the tree where John had been, making the place as comfortable as possible with packs and totes for cushions. As they settled-in Dlahni left, taking the girls with him, at the same time dispersing the group that had been edging in all around.

Knowing Dlahni and his concern for security, John guessed what that was all about, promptly forgetting about it with the unbelievable turn of events.

"Tell me everything."

"Everything?" Gary laughed, "There's a lot to tell."

"Everything. When, how, everything. What happened?"

"Okay ... for starters, the systems brought me back several months ago, on Easter, March twenty-second, to be exact. I was the first and the rest followed by twos in a matter of days after that."

"I'll be damned ... on Easter. That's when I first became aware of things ... twenty years ago."

"How'd you figure the day out?"

John shook his head, "I'll tell you later. Keep going?"

Gary did, telling him about the holographic orientation and the trials and tribulations of getting out into the open and of all the work that had been done. Dlahni and the girls returned and quietly joined them while he was into the telling, but they let the conversation go without interruption. It wasn't really a conversation as John said little, only asking an occasional question and prodding for Gary to continue.

This went on for hours until John laughed and said, "So you found the marks on the rock?"

"Yes, we'd been searching high and low for anything that would give us a clue to your whereabouts. That was only a few weeks ago.

We hit the forest heading north as soon as we could after finding it."

"Where were you when the storm hit?"

"Atop the mountain you directed us to. The storm was something else. We'd seen a light far, far to the north, which was the first indication of life we'd gotten ..."

"That was probably the signal fire on the hill above Pangaea."

"Whatever ... We were elated to have something to go on and had gone to bed. Hours later ... *wham!* We were pinned down and couldn't move for the next twenty-four hours or so."

John nodded, trying to ward off the bitter memories. "But you found our village. That had to be a surprise for them."

"Actually, for all of us. Dlahni, you might be able to tell what happened better than me."

Dlahni had gotten up and gathered wood from a pile nearby, and was stoking the fire when Gary turned to him. He groaned, remembering his own impression of that time.

"John, our canoes had just pulled up on shore and were almost too late. There was a lot of confusion. Evidently the appearance of the four strangers, oddly dressed and tall, especially the one called Roland, terrified everyone. The Chieftains on hand should have handled the situation better, but they panicked too, mobilizing everyone as if the village were under attack. They would even have taken the offensive had it not been for Ruth and Brun-dahni and some of the women, who seemed to be the only ones with cool heads."

"It was impressive," Gary said, "seeing the line-up of squads spread out so far; it was also pretty damned scary. Fortunately,we had a champ. At a time when tensions were about to break, Annie calmly stepped in front and addressed everyone. It was beautiful."

"So what happened?"

When Gary shrugged, John looked at Dlahni.

"I didn't see that part," Dlahni said. "After coming ashore we managed to get everyone settled down. Then Ruth told me what the woman who called herself Ann had said. John, up until that point, Nyaho and I were having a tough time accepting what you'd told us at Pangaea. When she repeated Ann's words, "wife of John Anderson", it settled the matter in our minds. So we dismissed the squads and went to meet the visitors, finding them at *Tschtaha-tata*.

"Somewhere along in the discussion that followed introductions, we realized the problem you mentioned—to find the others and bring them back—was no longer a problem. The visitors *were* the others."

"In fact, with what I've told you about our troubles," Gary said, "you must realize you couldn't have ever found us, because the mountain and forest had buried the front door. I mean *really* buried it."

John thought of that and nodded.

"It was a good meeting. Da-hash-to mainly listened because I understand he doesn't *speak* English, but he was very interested and asked a lot of questions. We learned all about the Gathering, the storm, the riot and all."

"I made a mistake during the telling of that," Dlahni said. "Without thinking, while talking about the battle and injuries and deaths, I told about Matthew.

"Ruth shrieked at the news and ran out, followed first by Brundahni, then Ann and Judy."

"Ann was somewhat in shock, too," Gary added. "First she's introduced to Ruth as your daughter; then she finds you also have a son, a young man idolized by the whole community, who's just been killed. Finally she learns of your returning with the baggage train with two more daughters. She spent a lot of time with Ruth to help her out ... but I suspect doing so was helping her as well."

John looked at Sara and Naomi. Their eyes locked briefly, but nothing was said.

"There's not much more to tell about us, John. You know most everything now. What about your story? You've got twenty years to explain."

"I can do that, but there's a part of it that I'm really having trouble with. From the start, being lost in the forest, that is, and at times along the way, certain triggers brought back corresponding bits from memory. Most of it was helpful, except there never was a complete picture; there never was anything tying those recollections to why I was here. I finally came to an assumption, and a wrong one, that the memories were programming and not reality. I'm still missing parts to fully understand."

Gary nodded and said, "We guessed something like that had happened."

"Like what?"

"Like not recalling. John, all of us went through an initial stage during resurrection when there was confusion and anger and belligerence; the orientation, however, guided us through this until we were well grounded with short term and long term tied together. You evidently blew by the orientation and were left with only the emotions and not the connects.

"When we get back to Olympus we'll show you your footprints in the cavern. They gave us a pretty good picture of what happened."

"Olympus?"

"Yes, that's what Bruno has named our little mountain."

John grabbed his knees and rocked, staring into the fire. "You may have it right with the orientation ... damn ... look at all the trouble that's been caused because I didn't settle down and go through with it ... *Damn!*"

"It may have been better that way."

"What? Dlahni, why'd you say that?"

"It's not what I said, it's what Da-hash-to said. At the meeting in *Tschtaha-tata*, I mentioned how badly you felt that you hadn't remembered, feeling that not doing so had caused all of the problems. When Da-hash-to shook his head, I asked him what was on his mind. He said this was another action guided by the Great Spirit."

"I don't follow that at all."

"I didn't either, but then he explained it this way. When you first came to the *Atjahahni*, you came in escorted by Nyaho and me. We apparently paved the way by explaining how you were gentle and knew of things that could help us. Even so, as you recall, there were attempts made on your life.

"Then there were the years we've lived in harmony.

"Da-hash-to said had it not been for all that, if and when any of the Chosen had appeared, they would have been declared the hated and feared "Giants" and killed. Then he repeated that the hand of the Great Spirit had clearly been guiding how this had come to be, the same way he'd looked over you in your trips to the nations while preparing for the Gathering. Da-hash-to finished by saying he didn't know why the Great Spirit had been so involved."

After a lull Gary added, "That's true … that *is* what he said. We didn't understand at first because they were speaking *Atjahahni*, but both Nyaho and Dlahni conveyed the meaning.

There was a longer period as John seemed to drift away, his eyes misting; then he shuddered and shook his head, wrestling with something internal and shaking it off. "By the way, how is Da-hash-to? We've all been concerned about him."

"He's not fine; he's in pain … but he's hanging in."

"Were you able to help?"

"I tried. When our meeting was essentially over, I asked if I could take a look at his hip. And this is where it's frustrating. Without an X-ray to go by, it's hard to tell what's happened. I put my hands on his leg to see if I could feel anything, but the leg was swollen so I only succeeded in hurting him … during which time he didn't make a sound. The best thing for him, assuming the bones are in place, is to immobilize the break so it'll heal. But we don't have plaster for casts or flat boards for splints or gauze for wrappings or any of the things we need. *Frustrating!* I did call for a paddle from one of the canoes, which I shortened to act as a splint. This I tied down with padding in places to hold the leg in line from knee to armpit. We'll just have to see if that does any good.

"Also frustrating is how everyone is thinking of me as a doctor. Hell, I'm no doctor. I've only finished Pre-med and one year of Med School, which had good stuff in anatomy and physiology and psychology and pharmacology, but the real meat had yet to come and residency was three years away. I still have a long way to go."

"But Gary, you're the best we've got, and you know more than you're letting on. I'll never forget that canoe trip to Lake-of-the-Woods in Explorers, when you got a deep cut on your thigh. We were days away from help, so you pulled out a special needle and put in four stitches without the benefit of an anesthetic. Freaked us all out."

Gary laughed. "What you don't know is that I almost fainted. But you're right. I come from a family of doctors, and Dad had me practicing stitches the same time you guys were doing carrick bends. He even let me in to the observation chambers a few times to look down on operations in progress.

"But that's enough of that … I want to hear what you've been doing."

With prodding from Gary, John started with his first recollections, then proceeded chronologically. He attempted to skim over parts, but Gary, who was forever curious, kept asking for more details.

It was long into the night before fatigue trumped curiosity and the group curled up for a few hours sleep.

Conversations continued along the trail all the next day. At the stop for the night, which happened to be along a small stream, John stripped down and bathed; he washed and patched clothes; and finally he had the girls cut his hair to something more manageable, and trim his beard to a short crop.

There wasn't as much conversation later as had been the case the night before … the few hours sleep finally taking its toll. For all but John, that is. He tried to sleep but tossed for a long time. The night before had resulted in an incredible weight being removed from his conscience … only for that weight being replaced by another. The weight was Annie—his wife, the light of his life, who had disappeared in the relentless march of the seasons—who now was back. Annie was such a straight arrow. She probably knew everything by now, and if so … how did she feel about him? How did she feel about his family? Could she believe how it had happened? How could she forgive him when he was having such a hard time forgiving himself?

And she was brave and courageous. He could picture her stepping out front to confront an army. She was also young and energetic and proper. How could a person like that accept a dirty, smelly, weathered man almost twice her age?

The baggage train would reach the village early the next evening.

27

Home

In a community where the news of the day is a repetition of the extremely unemotional, unexciting and ordinary, anything of significance reverberates seemingly *ad nauseum*. So it was with the combination of events that occurred quickly one after the other—the storm, the strangers, and the return of the Gathering delegations.

Previously, there had been the excitement of the preparation, and then the leaving, of the delegation to the Gathering. Almost a fifth of the village left, the leaving being at different times depending on mode and responsibility. Soon thereafter, the ordinary set back in. But then came the storm, the worst in anyone's memory, with its variety of damages—torn trees, collapsed shelters and flooding. The river bordering the village on the north, which was normally shallow and a murmur, became a roaring torrent overflowing its banks and tearing out the bridge near the mouth that started the trail in that direction. Every minor cut and ravine, including the one by John's home, followed suit and went on a rampage.

For the next week anxieties regarding the delegation were forgotten as the community, like those in a highly disturbed ant farm, banded together to shovel and clean and repair until most of the damage had been corrected.

Activities had hardly returned to its trudging normal when two boys, who'd ventured far south on the trail, came racing back wild-eyed and shouting to the first people they met. They could have calmly announced that four strangers—two men and two women—were coming this way. Instead they screamed with imagination fueled enthusiasm that "Giants were invading." Not stopping there, they kept running, making the same announcement to everyone along the trail all the way to the village.

Two men went forward to see for themselves, more than a little influenced by the boys. When they saw the tallest woman they'd ever seen, carrying something looking like a weapon that could destroy them all, they gasped; when they saw behind the women a broad-shouldered hulk even larger than John, they almost left something on the trail. They also ran, corroborating the panicky message the boys had conveyed. And so it went, emotion running amok until the drums beat and the people gathered and the squads formed and anyone not conditioned to an orderly response ran in circles.

Fortunately all this happened at a time when some of the people, who they'd justifiably been concerned about and had been waiting for, happened to return.

War was therefore averted.

But the buzz continued. Never had so much happened over such a small interval of time. Insatiable curiosities magnetically drew to the first canoers returning, then to the strangers, and then to each other canoe as it returned. It didn't matter that each person relating an experience of the Gathering was repeating something heard several times before, it was still different in place or time or viewpoint and therefore relished.

With the strangers, it was the same. Those that remembered how John looked when Dlahni and Nyaho brought him years before, spoke of impressions then: John had looked like a savage monster carrying primitive weapons—a perfect rendition of what was in mind regarding giants. The new strangers were also tall, but there was a marked difference—they were neatly dressed with weapons so unique they were a puzzlement. Their clothes were a revelation: fabrics unlike anything they'd seen; pockets sewed to the leggings with threads so fine they were hardly visible; flaps that anchored shut by magically textured catches; straps and belts and ties with equally amazing characteristics; and certain parts, sometimes in tiny sizes, of materials that were hard, sometimes shiny, and seemingly indestructible.

The strangers were much like John, however, in ways other than size. They were friendly and quick to smile, with a sincerity that reflected in their eyes. They were easy to engage in conversation, and readily answered most questions posed to them. Some noticed, however, they were guarded about other things. When asked, for instance, about what was contained in the sheathes—machetes and Roland's rifle—heads were shaken or conversations were redirected, usually in questions to the persons asking.

One young man, tired of not getting satisfaction, grabbed at what Roland was carrying, almost creating an incident. Roland held firm, continuing to smile, saying in a calm voice "Not yet young man, everything in good time."

This happened on a day after Gary had left with Dlahni to meet the baggage train and John. Dlahni was the strongest and most calming among the leaders, and was also the appointed "Grand Chieftain", so his presence on this occasion was missed. Fortunately there still was Nyaho, who made it a point to be nearby at all times. There were also Ruth and her friends, who had quickly bonded with Ann and Judy the way women are prone to do, and Brun-dahni, under orders from his father, who never wandered too far away.

When Nyaho came forward and raised an eyebrow, Roland said "We're okay. I can't blame him for being curious … I would be too in his place. But there are things we're not getting into yet. Rest assured that like John, we're here in peace, and only mean to help in any way we can. At this point we'd like to wait until we meet with John, to make sure what we do is okay with him."

Nyaho nodded. He turned to the young man and said something in *Atjahahni* that wasn't exactly a snarl, but the affect was such there was no doubt about the message.

There were no problems after that.

The last of the canoes and the excitement they created had hardly abated when news came from runners that the train was only a day away. The buzz started all over again.

Several messages came through the next day, so by the time the first in the train appeared across the river, the Commons was full. With the bridge gone each one had to negotiate an improvised array of stepping stones, during which with each step the person was given encouragement, and at the final one a hero's welcome.

Amazingly each story and rendition was new again, and the time it took in the telling was perfect because every part was relished all the more. The problem became the lateness of the day and its advancing darkness, which put a shroud over later crossings, even though occasional bobbing torches were improvised to help. A large fire was therefore lit at the nearest place that made sense, which turned out to be the Council House, and wasn't close. Nonetheless, that's what happened, and the random torches were fixed at intervals between it and the river to guide the way to where receptions would be formalized.

The crowd likewise moved to congregate around the fire, with the result that only a few remained to greet those still to make their way across.

Da-hash-to and Nyaho and the Chieftains conducted the greetings, the darkness and fires giving the whole process an impressively mystic nature that had never been planned.

While all this was happening, Ann, Judy and Roland stayed to the far side of the Commons, which was nearest *Tschtaha-tata,*. They were accompanied by Ruth and Brun-dahni most of the time, but when they could see in the dim light that Sara and Naomi and their betrothed were making their way across, Ruth broke away. Soon the excitement of greetings and meetings could be heard, along with, as expected, crying as the tragedy of Matthew was addressed.

Winds picked up and occasionally clouds puffed with flashes and rumbles. The threat of weather and the fact most everyone was back had their influence, and soon what was once a crowd dispersed, even at the Council House, as other fires began to appear at scattered homesites.

By now, the evening had progressed to forest darkness, with a result that the group alongside *Tschtaha-tata* missed the fact that the last in the train had made a crossing. But then Gary, sensing there had to be confusion with all its anxieties, sought them out. He said

"Dlahni and John have gone to the Council House to complete the needed formalities. They'll come this way as soon as they can."

He added, "Ann ... he's okay but very nervous."

"So am I."

"Look, John and I've spent two days on the trail and he's told me twenty years worth. Until the day of the storm, he didn't know any of us existed. Finding out hit him pretty hard ... and, as a result of the stupor it put him in at the time, his son, defending him, was killed."

"He's carrying quite a load."

"I know. Dlahni explained that when we first met."

"Yes, of course ... but there's so much more, some of which I'm sure Ruth told you."

Annie nodded, "You mean Willow?"

"That's part of it," Gary said, his voice dropping, then rising again to say, "It's all going to work out."

"Sure."

"Let's get out of here before the Gods decide to throw some rain our way. We can go to John's house; the rest can catch up with us there."

"Get a load of this," Roland said as they settled around the small re-kindled fire. He was wrestling with panels hanging to the side of the house. Sensing there had to be some logic to them, he pulled at the ropes hanging loose beside the panels, which lifted them until they combined to form a cover over the fire-pit. Then he tied the ropes to cleat-like improvisations seeming to be located for the purpose. "Isn't this the damndest jerry-rig you ever saw?"

Hanging like they did, the panels danced with every gust, and together with the light flickering as light from fires do, created a scene somewhere between exotic and peculiar.

Time passed and conversations, which in a way were a reaction to nervousness, dwindled. With an obvious elephant about, no one knew what to do or say, putting everyone on edge. Making things worse, sounds from across the way at the Council House, where activities had been providing a backdrop of at least something, also dwindled, segueing to a silence that was now deafening.

It also drove Ann deeper into her thoughts. She didn't notice, for instance, when the men left; and hardly reacted when Judy, who'd been faithfully beside her, gave her a hug, kissed her cheek and disappeared.

Now she was alone, a fact that took a while for her to realize. She heard an animated flare-up somewhere in the darkness beyond the foot-bridge, but the comments were hushed, and then that ended too.

She sat and stared, drifting away again. She thought of the conversations she'd had with Ruth since coming to the village, and all she'd learned. She learned of a young girl named Nshswanji, a captive from a nation far to the north, who was to be given to an ugly ogre of a man in what would have been a horrible fate. But John had risked his life and fought for her and won … and in so doing became a husband—a husband to Nshswanji, a name he changed to Willow. She was told of how difficult life had been for the two with almost freezing, then starving, experienced the first winter. Then there had been four young children in three years, making survival ever so much harder. She heard about how hard John worked, not only for the family, but also for the community; how he'd done so many things which others observed and copied to their benefit, like showering and cleaning and habits of hygiene; how he'd taught the people to swim; how he'd made canoes, which allowed the villagers to travel far and wide so much easier; how he'd started Craft Fairs and Sunday fellowship and the Home Guard and defensive training; how he'd designed and supervised the construction of *Tschtaha-tata*; and how he'd organized efforts culminating in the Gathering. She was told how the four had been raised with a combination of love and discipline and responsibility; how Sara, at 18 months, had been the first in the village to swim; how the girls had grown and excelled in so many things, all the while competing with one another; how they'd doted on Matthew, the baby boy, and then given him such a hard time as he grew older; how Matthew had grown like a beanpole, passing the girls and becoming almost as tall as John; how he'd become a champion in every event, setting standards that would possibly never be matched; how John had worked with him so he'd be considerate and humble and respectful … and how all of that had resulted in adoration. And she knew from all of this that in every part there was a special person involved … a wife … a thin sprite with courage and determination who was by John's side for fourteen years … until she gave her life so one of her children could live.

Ann rocked as all of these thoughts rode roughshod through her: twenty years of effort and hardship and accomplishment; fourteen years of solid marriage; and danger and tragedy and war and killing and heartbreak.

She groaned, her own memories seeming to pale in comparison. *How did John remember her?* Their courtship had only been a few months; the day they met to the last night together had only covered a year; and in that time there had been school and love and family, and although on the other side of the world there had been a horrible nuclear mess, and then a looming plague, they were almost surreal; all together the events of that year were nowhere near to what had been experienced during twenty years in the wild. She thought of how cold it had been on that winter's walk on New Year's Eve, a memory that was so dear. She thought of the all the little things that made John the world to her. She thought of the last night when they'd walked under the stars and hugged and squeezed and giggled. It was like yesterday; but what would it be to John? After twenty years would he even remember?

Then there was a something: not a sound because the gusts whistled and the panels bounced; not a sight as eyes misted and flickers from the fire created a kaleidoscopic of indefinables. But she was no longer alone. The something sat beside her. She wanted to turn and look but couldn't; all she could do was lean … and in doing so came in contact with a shoulder.

"John," her voice a crackled whisper, "I know what and how everything happened … and it's okay, I understand."

He tried to speak, only to stutter and stop. Then he picked up a stick and leaned forward. He started to scratch in the dirt, and as he did his voice came back. "I promised to show you an etching in the morning … Please forgive me for being so late."

Below them crudely drawn were two hearts entwined over the letters "J" and "A".

28

Reunion

A swirl of wind rattled the panels and blew dust and ashes and embers all around, driving them inside. There the light, whose only source was from vent openings, was so faint in the gloomy expanse that after John tied the flaps and turned, there was little Annie could see of him.

They stood in the dim vestiges waiting for eyes to sort out more detail, neither able to think of how to begin. Ann broke the impasse and moved forward, gently taking his face in her hands. She traced the curls of his beard, then skimmed his cheeks and brow, wincing as she felt the remnants of scab that connected them on one side; she touched his lips, then his hair, her finger tips slowly reassembling the mosaic of features she'd longed to see. Then she slid her fingers into the tangle of his neck and drew him down to a kiss, noticing by way of faint reflections that his eyes stayed open.

She led him to some cushions, where they reclined and got comfortable as best they could, with swallows and coughs leading to only a few words. The words, mumbles really, were interrupted by touches as they attempted to jockey, without being conscious of doing it, to some common ground. The problem was mainly John, who although wanting closure as much as Ann, had a twenty-year glitch that made this more of a reunion than a morning after. The mumbles eventually coalesced into dialogue, mostly in response to

•

soft encouraging questions from Ann. It became, in a way, like
the exchange on the trail with Gary, but with a major difference.
While Gary had been interested in broader, impersonal topics—
characteristics and differences of the nations, the Home Guard,
canoes, *Tschtaha-tata* and so on—Ann was more into the personal.

"You okay? How did you get that cut on your head? Does it hurt?
Were you burned by the lightning?" ...

When that had run its course, she moved to others that had been
a part of his life.

"Nyaho was the first person you found, wasn't he. What's he
like?" ...

"Dlahni seems like the epitome of staunch. Do I have that right?
You're not going to believe this, but when I first saw him, his walk
made me think of you." ...

"Ruth is a dear. She was as shocked as anybody upon our coming
here ... especially, I mean, when she found out I claimed to be your
wife. But we hit it right off, and after a few rough spots, were together
talking like a couple of sorority sisters." ...

"Your other daughters are Naomi and Sarah, right? I haven't met
them yet. Do they resemble each other?" ...

John became more and more at ease. It was as if talking was a
balm, as if by answering questions the bigger issue of twenty years
was being circumvented. Besides, the truth was he wanted to talk; he
had a great deal to say and he wanted her to understand.

"Oh they're alike all right, in fact Naomi is an identical twin
to Ruth, and Sarah's only a year-and-a-half older. But they're also
different in ways."
And on and on.

"They must get their looks from Willow."

John nodded.

"Tell me about her."

John knew this one was coming. He knew Willow, alive forever in his mind and with him by way of the lock he carried, would be a prime topic, yet the conversation that had been moving along nicely came to a halt; he stumbled, once more in a bind. He sighed and settled back.

"It's okay," Annie said, kissing him accidently on the scab, "It's okay."

John shook his head; no it wasn't okay. He wanted to talk but couldn't find the words. Finally they came.

"One day, early on here, I was particularly on edge, which wasn't unusual in the beginning. Anyway, I went for a run. At the end of it a group of youngsters passed me doing their thing. One of them was a girl who ran with a nice, easy stride. The sight stunned me; she reminded me of you and brought back a whole bunch of memories. Only there was never a connection between the world of those memories, which was a part of the twenty-first century, and the world I was in. Things just didn't make sense. And so Willow became you, and, as it turned out, she was also a wonderful person."

Inevitably there was the name that had been avoided, but couldn't be ignored. There was, in fact, a build-up created by the ignoring, so when, after a lull, Annie said, "And Matthew?"

A dam burst.

John had held it together with regards to Willow, but a build-up had started six years before on that awful day, a day, when for the benefit of the family, emotions had to be buried. Then there'd been Pangaea, and not only family but also the Gathering of Nations was in need, so there was another reason to suppress. The long walk back was supposed to help with healing, and in a way it did, but revelations at the drainage dig had added the Chosen and Annie and the guilts regarding them to the anguish being repressed. It all churned in the deep recesses.

The breakdown wasn't immediate. John fought it; he tried to

speak, but the words were few and forced and jumbled, generating into blurts and halts that finally gave way to deep shuddering sobs.

Annie held him tightly as the emptying ran its course, patting and rocking.

There really wasn't much more John needed to tell about Matthew. Dlahni had explained about the mob and the battle in the flats that killed him, and Ruth had gone on at length during her grieving. Then there had been the days spent in the homestead while Gary was off on the trail to find John. Inside the dome was a wide and wild assortment of mementos that spanned twenty years of family living. There were feathers, beads, bones, teeth, furs, gemstones and leathers in all sorts of exotic combinations. They were awards; they represented achievements of everyone in the family, but a preponderance was credited to Matthew. One large section of wall was virtually his trophy case. So when Annie mentioned his name in question, it wasn't to learn about him, it was to acknowledge someone who couldn't be ignored.

The conversation drifted eventually to mumbles; for the time being it had gone as far as it could go, and that was okay—it was late, they had gravitated to mutual comfort with each other, and they were tired. John finally sagged, the emptying plus the sleepless nights taking their toll. His going to sleep had the opposite effect on Ann, however. Alone with all she'd been experiencing, her mind raced. So much had happened: She'd returned to life by way of Huston's incredible system; she'd spent months in an equally incredible new world; she'd met the *Atjahahni*; and she'd reunited with John. Even the structure covering them was a unique experience. In the daylight hours she'd tried to reason how it had been put together. There were large laminated diagonal trusses as primary support; then smaller trusses at third points; then horizontal bridging members; then grass roofing. It was completely organic. She imagined when it had been built twenty years ago, individual pieces making up both the laminations and bridging had been green and supple and easily bent to the shapes. All of it had long since dried and stiffened, with a result that when gusts buffeted the exterior, the structure creaked in a soft symphony. These sounds would be accompanied by flecks of dust drifting about, the dust clearly visible in light rays streaming through openings.

Ruth had told of the regimen about the household over the years, which Ann guessed was John's idea because of his awareness to germs and critters and their effects. Anyway, each day when weather permitted, blankets, cushions and skins were taken out, shaken and hung; and, floors and surfaces were dusted and swept.

She gazed at John, or at least what she could see of him, still unsettled despite how well the most trying situation in her life had gone. For one thing, she hadn't yet seen him in the light … although that was minor. The bigger part was that the big bearded shadow breathing softly beside was still struggling, and she wasn't sure of the next step.

During these reflections, Ann noticed that the structure had stopped creaking, which meant the weather, whatever it had been, had moved on. Then she heard birds coming to life, which meant a new day was on its way. Easing out of their entanglement, she tip-toed through the flaps. Once past the panels, she was able to see, as suspected, that all was quiet and the sky, the portions visible between the ever present canopy, was ablaze in the clear mountain air.

"Are you okay?" John said, yawning as he opened the flaps right after she'd taken her first few steps away. Obviously no amount of fatigue or depth of sleep could suppress a mind conditioned by twenty years on guard.

"I'm sorry. I tried not to wake you."

He stepped out, shook as the morning chill checked in, "You shouldn't be about in the dark. These woods are nothing to fool with."

"I'm not going anywhere … just wanted to check the weather. It's cleared up."

"I see that."

"John … I want to see the sunrise."

"Where are we going?" They'd left the compound, passed *Tschtaha-tata*, crossed a bridge and wound their way south. Even in the bits of starlight that filtered through the breaks, she recognized they were on the trail traveled when they first came to the village.

It was a while before John answered, and when he did he moved over and put his arm around her. She almost melted as this was the first unsolicited show of affection he'd made. Soon they were moving in a way like they had on that last night.

"This trail … It holds memories." He almost lost his voice with those words, but then composed. "Four years ago, in a night just like now, Matthew and I jogged to a special place, a favorite of mine for many reasons. There we watched the sun come up."

"Oh."

"There's more. Twenty years ago, the day before that fight for Willow's hand, she and I had a run together along here. The run's what convinced me that she was you in some inexplicable way. I know it sounds crazy …"

Ann didn't say anything … she just gave him a squeeze.

He tried to say more, but only blew out as if to relieve some pressure. The release earlier had helped a lot, but there was more and he had to fight it. "I thought that repeating this experience with you might help putting things back together."

"You mean run?'

He laughed. "No, I didn't mean *that*. Why? Don't you run anymore?"

"John," she said jabbing him in the ribs, "I haven't run in over eight thousand years. It would be silly. These clod hoppers weren't made for running."

"Then let's be silly."

She almost stopped at something so ridiculous, but then said, chuckling "Silly is good," breaking away into a trot.

They soon sounded like a couple of kids as the run degenerated to shoves and bounces and giggles and laughs, which extended all the way to the place called Lookout Point.

"Where have you guys been?"

When they crossed the small bridge and entered the home compound, there was a small group waiting. All of John's daughters, Judy, Roland and Gary were milling about.

"Here your girls have fixed a nice breakfast and you two are nowhere to be found."

"Annie wanted to see the sunrise, so we jogged out to Lookout Point."

"Jogged? Lookout Point?"

Ann laughed. "Lookout Point's that place on the trail about two miles south of here."

"You mean that open area we almost stopped at on the way in?" Roland asked.

"Yes ... and Gary, we did jog, that's what runners do."

"Annie, you look better than you've looked in months ... you're absolutely radiant. Is jogging all you did?"

Ann blushed and kicked dirt at him.

"Good grief," John said, "I was about to say something nice, like how good it is to see all of you, but ..."

Before he could finish, Roland stepped forward and approached him, saying nothing at first, just looking him over real good.

"Last night I couldn't see much except to think you looked like crap. Here in the light of day, all I can say is ... you look actually worse. Tell me, how does Annie like being stuck with an old man."

"You bastard," John said, bopping him first, the two big men then falling into a misty-eyed, gigantic, twisting, bear hug. "God, it *is* good to see all of you ... you have no idea." Then he went to Judy, who was laughing and crying at the same time,and gave her a hug.

John's daughters didn't quite know what to make of all this. It wasn't as if humor wasn't a part of *Atjahahni* culture, as that was far from the case, but this seemed to bring it to a new level. So they giggled and grinned, staying to the side until the nonsense subsided.

Then Ann was introduced to Naomi and Sarah, who obviously had been primed by Ruth, because from all appearances, there was an immediate bond.

Breakfast, which had taken a good deal of preparation, almost became an afterthought. This was a shame as it was quite good. With all else going on, it happened to be September, which meant crops had ripened and most gardens were being harvested. Besides an assortment of dried meats, there were mixed greens, berries, fruit, tubers and flavored drinks.

Afterwards, the men split and went to *Tschtaha-tata* while the girls stayed together to do their thing.

"You went all the way out to, what did you call it, Lookout Point, to see the sunrise?"

John nodded, "Yes ... and it was a beauty."

"We know; we were here in the chapel, and it was quite a sight here also."

"It's that time of year, Gary. *Tschtaha-tata* is oriented to the four directions. So twice a year during the equinoxes—Easter and about now—the sun rises due east. When it does, its rays hit the east gable just right, and explode against the rocks at the far end. I'd like to take credit for the effects because the building's my concoction, but that part was purely accidental.

"If the weather holds, we'll have a few more times to see it. In fact tomorrow would be perfect because it's Sunday,"

"Sunday? How'd you figure?"

John grinned. "You telling me it's not Sunday?"

Gary and Roland looked at each other, Roland shrugging, "Of course not, we're just asking how you figured out the day."

When John told them he'd shot an arrow straight up over a seven-segmented circular target in the ground, letting the day be determined by which one it fell into, the two literally rolled on the floor.

"We're not going to argue with a process as brilliant as that," Gary said. "We don't care what Huston's space-age computer says, tomorrow is certainly Sunday.

"So what's happening tomorrow? In fact where are Dlahni and Nyaho and Da-hash-to? None of them have been by today, which seems kinda unusual."

"There's a lot going on in the community next week. The three you asked about are all at the Council House working on arrangements. As for tomorrow, my guess is that it's going to be special. Our Sundays aren't church services in the sense you might expect. Villagers simply come together in the morning and socialize. Sometimes there are messages or topics for discussion or even programs; sometimes not.

With everyone back from the Gathering, I think the focus will be on that, even though it's been beat to death already.

"But that's just Sunday. Fields and gardens are being harvested, so in the next few days there'll be a festival making distributions of that harvest, followed later after dark by special services, most notable of which is the all-night memorial to the dead. These are core events in the *Atjahahni* culture."

"Did you say all night?"

"Yes ... It's fortunate you're here at a time when you can see the ceremonies, as words wouldn't begin to do them justice. It's important that you see them and I'll tell you why. We've been chosen, and given life, to give mankind a second chance ... to start it all over again ... Right? Gary's told me about the struggle you've had to get above ground and make preparations for survival. So I don't imagine there's been much thought regarding the actual mission.

"The fifteen of us have a wide range of familiarities with religions and cultures of the old world. *Old* ... that doesn't seem the right word. What should it be called?"

"Somebody called it "World B.P.", B.P. meaning "before plague", which sounds as good as any."

"Okay. Anyway some of them certainly have merit and have done a lot of good; some have been absolutely awful. Here we have a society that was near to being as primitive as one could get, where survival was a constant problem and death a common event. Yet with those circumstances, and with the same human capabilities and aberrations all generations have had, they developed a culture with aspects well worth understanding."

"That's quite a pitch," Gary said. "Count me in ... I'll sit in on it."

"Not just sit in on. The all-night thing is a dance in which you've got to participate. The purpose of dancing to a point of exhaustion is not only to honor the people who died last year, it's also to connect with the spirit world and its ancestries, possibly getting guidance from them. You'll be glad you took part."

"Mission control," Roland said, "ahem ..."

"What's the problem?"

"These," pointing to the sheathes. "We can't dance all night carrying these things; and we can't leave them lying around. If someone were to steal them, it would be really, really bad ... in more ways than one."

"Oops ... you're right about that. We'll just have to work out something, that's all. By the way, which of the rifles did you bring along?"

Gary laughed and Roland made like hiding his head.

"You didn't"

Roland nodded, grinning sheepishly.

"You brought the blunderbuss? That thing is hundreds of years old and weighs a ton."

"First of all it's not a blunderbuss, it's a Girandoni air rifle, and yes, it's old ... Lewis and Clark carried one like it on their little hike. And it's heavy, but it was my decision and I had to carry it. The other rifles are great, but they make a hellova lot of noise. One shot and every animal in the vicinity is a mile away as fast as it can go. The air rifle is quiet, shoots a 46 caliber slug at 800 feet per second, is accurate to one-hundred yards, and can fire damn near a shot a second. It's pretty impressive. We ate a lot of squirrel and rabbit and pigeon along the way here, and in most cases were able to recover the slug."

John shook his head, half nodding to indicate the possibility it made sense.

"Is that it then?" Gary asked when the matter of the gun was over. "A Sunday meeting and then the memorial ceremony."

"No, there's more ... there's a lot more. I happen to have two unmarried daughters, both of whom are going to get married next week after the other events. If they do it the *Atjahahni* way, it'll be pretty simple; but if we do otherwise, I've got problems ... which means Annie and Judy couldn't have come at a better time.

"The grooms, by the way, aren't from here. One is a young chieftain from the *Njegleshito* to the east; the other is a fine young man from the *Anlyshendl* to the north. I think you can see that it's important that all this be done right. Both of these men were shoulder to shoulder with us during the worst part of what happened at the Gathering. So we're honored to welcome them to the family."

From that point Roland guided the conversation. Gary had told him as much as he could recall of what he'd learned on the trail, but it had been late and everyone had been tired. So many questions remained, and he wanted to hear the details first hand.

And so it went.

The conversation could have gone on the rest of the day, but it ended when Nyaho entered, followed by Dlahni and Brun-dahni carrying Da-hash-to on the stretcher.

"You're not going to believe what the girls are doing right now," Dlahni said as the stretcher was eased down.

The three just looked, waiting for more.

"They're having an archery contest."

"Oh lordy ... Whose winning?"

"Can't tell, but they're drawing quite a crowd."

"I'm not sure it's a contest," Brun-dahni said. "They're trading bows as they go; I know all your girls want to try that so-called compound bow Annie carries. Anyway they're having a great time."

"Did you get everything worked-out? Gary asked. "John just told us about the events coming up."

"There are still problems to solve, but we're pretty far along, Dlahni said. "Some of them, however, have to do with all of you, and that's why we're here."

John looked at the other two to register he didn't know what this was about. "Well, come in and get comfortable. We'll help in any way we can."

Once settled, Dlahni continued. "John, before Gary and I set out on the trail to find you, Nyaho and I sat with Da-hash-to and told him everything you'd told us before we left Pangaea ... all in secret of course. He was just as astounded as we were, but I think he's more fascinated than disbelieving." As he spoke he looked at Da-hash-to who nodded. "But there are valid concerns. For instance, tomorrow is Sunday, and because of what's happened, we expect most of the village to be at the meeting. The Gathering will certainly take up most of the time, but your friends coming here will also be of interest. Who'll be the spokesman for your group?"

John pointed at Gary and Gary pointed back.

"No," John said. "You take it Gary. They've listened to me for years. Besides, if you can say things that match with what I've told in the past, everything should be fine."

Dlahni, Nyaho and Da-hash-to all shook their heads.

"What?"

"John, we can't get by with what was told before. Your story crumbled the moment Ann said she was your wife. Think about it. Ann's a young woman, my guess only a few years older than your daughters. That means when you came here twenty years ago you had an infant as a wife. You'd also said you were alone on a quest to find people and help them out. None of that makes sense now and everyone is seeing it. So we have a problem. We also think the truth is too astounding to be told.

"And there's more than what we've been told"

"More what?" John asked.

"What is what Gary and Roland have been carrying in their sheaths. Not revealing them to anyone has raised a lot of questions. Since we don't know what they are either, all we've been able to do is shrug and change topics."

John hesitated for a few moments, then got up from the squat he'd been in, "I'm glad all of you came to us with these things. We've been pretty absorbed with our own reunions and haven't given any of this a thought."

He paced for a bit, once more in a bind trying to find the right words. "Brun-dahni, would you please step out and bring me a small log, something about this long and this thick," making gestures that indicated four feet long by six to eight inches in diameter.

When he left John continued.

"I know what I told you that last day at Pangaea was startling, but it was only a part of the whole story. I told you about the many people, the great cities they'd build and a few things like that. There was so much more to tell that trying to do so would have been overload. I don't even want to do that now, because I feel, and I think Gary and Roland will agree, that we have to be very careful with not only what we say, but how we say it. I've been told that even the clothes my friends wear have caused a stir. And Annie's bow … that's amazed everyone.

"Those things only scratch the surface of wonders. The world thousands of years ago was truly amazing. It wasn't that the people then were any smarter than now ... not at all. It was that the people, through trial and error, learned from one another, constantly improving products and systems, until with billions of people over thousands of years, reached levels of achievement that were mind-boggling. Yes, men could fly," at this point hesitating as the impact registered, "but they didn't fly by magical powers or by flapping arms; they flew by making machines with materials and systems and technologies that enabled them to do so.

"You should understand how this can happen. In my lodge is a collection of pottery. Each year at the Crafts Fair I've selected a piece to add to that collection. Each year the new one is a little better than the one before. By making a comparison between the first and the last you can readily see how much progress has been made. That's what happened before; and that's what's been happening here in a smaller way. Before that evolution, which is what it's called, had some major flaws. Despite the wonders of all those achievements, those flaws would have eventually destroyed most life on the planet, even if the plague hadn't come along. But I'm getting ahead of myself and making everything more complicated than can be explained right now."

By this time Brun-dahni had returned and placed a log to the side.

John motioned to Gary, who extracted his machete and handed it over. John took it to the log, and with a few vicious chops, sent chips flying and cut it in half. Then he handed it to Dlahni.

The others crowded in, Da-hash-to almost falling from the stretcher. It was the most amazing tool they'd ever seen; it had cut through a log in a fraction of time they could have done with any other means at their disposal. They felt the material and rapped knuckles on it testing its hardness; Brun-dahni cut his finger on the razor-sharp edge.

Dlahni, who was usually steady, was visibly shaken.

"It's called a machete. The blade, the hard part, is a metal called steel." He took it from Dlahni and gave it back to Gary.

As he put it back, Gary said, "So you see we have a problem. We realized this from the beginning. If we showed everyone what we were carrying, we were afraid it would be disruptive. The items might be deemed more precious than anything else around. Everyone would want one."

They all nodded.

Nyaho, who to that point had hardly spoken, said, looking at Roland, "I don't know what you're hiding in that long cover you carry, but right now I don't want to know. One amazement at a time is about all I can handle. Besides, we've got enough problems right now and don't need any more."

"So what do we do?" Asked Dlahni, who seemed more deflated than amazed.

There was a lull for a few moments, but only a few. Da-hash-to started laughing, which not only caught everyone else by surprise, but himself as well. He tried to cover his face, but since he was on an elbow to take part in examining the machete, he lost balance and crashed back, losing it.

Finally the jag subsided and he exhaled and wiped tears and raised back up. Speaking *Atjahahni,* which was translated, he said ...

"Sorry ... If this isn't something; it's really more perplexing than funny. I'm an old man and expect to die soon. In fact I wanted to die a few days ago, but things have gotten too very, very interesting. John, Gary, Roland ... I want to hear more of this mission all of you are on. I want to see this place in the mountains you say you're from. I believe what you say. I also believe the Great Spirit is a part of it all, so I want to stay around as long as I can to help in any way. I just wish Ab Oh were still here ... he'd have loved it.

"As for tomorrow, there's a problem. John, you've been an object of interest ever since you came here. Now that you've fought like a demon and spoken to the Gods, you've become even more so. Coupled with the coming of your friends ... and a wife ... well," he shook his head.

"Discussions on the Gathering tomorrow will be enough to fill the day, and that's good, but I think it would be better if all of you stayed away. My suggestion is that you take a trip ... a long canoe trip around the lake for instance. We'll cover for you and make some kind of excuse. We just don't want to get into any of this until we have a way of telling it without causing more of a problem."

29

Affirmation

The hollow-log drums sounded for the second time that day, this time well after dark, and the village reassembled around the large fire by the Council House. As usual, many sat on the ground, particularly the younger, while others sat on logs that ringed in concentrics to form a rustic arena. John, who'd been staying out of the limelight as much as possible since returning, was on the farthest ring. With him were Annie and the rest of the Chosen, who he'd primed beforehand as to the program and its meanings. Naomi and Sara and the grooms, and the guests from other nations, sat in front of them.

Once the assembly was near to complete, Dlahni, who was representing Da-hash-to, called everyone to order and made some general comments; but like in all the years before, the night and its program belonged to the Medicine Man. Helping Nyaho was Mahsja, the precocious girl, now fifteen years old but still only four-and-a-half feet tall, who'd been so skilled in languages she'd been along at every one of the trips, including the Gathering. Nyaho had been impressed with her abilities and had taken her in since the first trip to the east, relying on her as an apprentice.

The crowd seemed to be more restive than usual, possibly because of what had happened recently, or because of the many special guests, or both. John certainly was, the same things being on his mind. He paid particular attention during the first parts of the ceremony—the opening remarks and the conveying of bones to the fire—as he was looking and listening for anything that might represent a subtle difference. But there wasn't anything he could detect, and since everything seemed to be flowing with expectations—the parade of tributes being ones he'd heard before—his mind wandered to recent happenings.

One was the Sunday service. Evidently it had gone well enough, with Da-hash-to masterfully handling it. When the socializing was drawing to a close, there'd been an undercurrent attuned to the absence of John and the visitors. At that point Da-hash-to said, "I know there are many interests here today … in fact too many. In my mind the day belongs to the *Atjahahni*, because great things have happened, and we need to hear them without distraction. Therefore I've asked the visitors, which is another story, to leave us to our day; we can meet with them later."

There were grumbles, but the statement was generally accepted, and the program moved on.

John's daughters filled him in on what happened after that. There'd been several dozen in the *Atjahahni* delegation, and even though each one had told his story many times since returning, almost every one stepped forward to repeat it, this time embellished with additional detail and emotional emphasis. By the time it was over every part of the experience—the storm, the battle, the recovery, the intermingling of nations, which had been the objective of the Gathering in the first place, and on and on—had been related frontwards, backwards and sideways. What made John cringe was the amount of telling centering on his part in the battle, where descriptions of fury and might had blood and brains spattering, and men flying and falling every which way, as he'd chopped and smashed through the mob. He preferred a low profile in the normal course of events, and had generally been out of sight since getting back, so this ran counter to what he wanted, and made things worse.

Then there had been the descriptions, or impressions of what was seen by a physically and emotionally strained people through the fabric of a driving rain, of what happened to John on the hilltop, with the combination of thunder and lightening and smoke and rainbow. In their eyes he'd spoken to the Gods, and may be one of them.

John didn't feel like a God, and didn't recall that one had spoken to him, so he didn't need any of this either.

On occasion Nyaho would say something that would bring him out of his thoughts and back to the history. At first he didn't attach any meaning to what was being said, although the presentation was good. Ab Oh had been a master with his combination of costuming and theatrics, so had been a hard act to follow. But Nyaho, the person once called Quiet Man, had not only done well from the start in taking Ab Oh's place, he'd also grown in the role and added his own dramatics to its effectiveness.

What were the somethings? The history was delivered in *Atjahahni*, which was natural and understood, but occasionally Nyaho would repeat a part, almost under his breath, in English. At first John thought this was for to the benefit of the visitors, only to cancel that thought out as it didn't make sense. If there was a message to him, why didn't Nyaho just tell him some other time? The names and circumstances that popped-out to catch his attention were Braga's wife, a quiet obscure woman John hardly recalled; another man he could barely remember; Dresh-na-togl; two more names that for some reason had no accompanying storyline; then another, who in the telling had married Braga's mother after his father died. These were not in a grouping but interspersed within the progression of people and events in the long, long narration. Muddled by his own thoughts, John didn't make a connection until much later.

What he became attuned to was nearer the ending. Both Nyaho and Dlahni seemed bothered by something, not necessarily the same thing, so he hoped Nyaho, being in the spotlight, would give him some clue to what it was for him. Since "giants" had always been a part of the conclusion, there is where he expected to find an answer, because he'd been told there was so much to the story, it would never be the same.

He wasn't disappointed.

In the conclusion the giants once more raised their heads. Nyaho related how they were large and strong and domineering; how they lived in great cities with buildings that disappeared into the clouds; how they had special powers and were like waterbugs on the water and birds in the air. He told how the giants dominated their ancestors until they tired of them, and then cast them into the wild to fend for themselves. Even when in need and appealed to for help, the giants chased them away without sharing what they had.

What the hell are you doing? John thought as the story ground to a halt. There were parts to the ending he'd never heard before, and he couldn't see how this was going to help relations with him and the other four, who many persisted in considering as giants.

"What's wrong," Annie whispered as Nyaho spread the ashes and started the assembly in the dance of remembrances.

John shook his head ... They didn't understand what was said, and this wasn't the time to explain. So they joined in the dance, John forcing the recent disturbances from his mind. He'd actually been looking forward to this part of the ceremony. In the past he had as well, but then he was hampered because of the question as to who were his ancestors—the memories being more like programming than reality. Now he knew they were real. So he danced and concentrated hour after hour, the images of his parents and Mark and Lawrence in particular being visualized. The connections he hoped for, however, never happened.

During all of this, he noticed the guests from the other nations were moving in a conservative manner, much like he had the first time he experienced the ceremony, as they tried to understand and appreciate what was happening. He also noticed that the rest of the Chosen were taking part in a respectful manner as well, which was good because he knew eyes would be on them, and anything callow or insincere would be noticed.

Judy was the most impressive. She wore a plain headband with tresses in a ponytail and a black feather tied to each side of the coil. John had been concerned that her moves would be too pronounced and out of character with *Atjahahni* expressions, but that wasn't the case. There was a feeling and rhythm to them that eventually was noticed, however, particularly by Ann and his daughters, who gravitated together to form a moving circle within the community body. The movements were easy to follow, and before the evening was over, many others had picked up on it.

Hours later there was the sunrise, more incantations, the serpentine spreading of ashes, final prayers, and it was over.

The Chosen met for a short time at John's stead, where Ruth and Brun-dahni had been, sitting out the ceremony while guarding packs and equipment. There was a hearty breakfast, then everyone drifted away to nap. Everyone, that is, except John. As soon as the group split, he headed out, stopping by the homes of Dlahni and Nyaho just long enough to signal them to follow.

Finding a private place wasn't difficult, as it was a time when the village was as quiet as it would ever get. After a short walk they settled in among the canoes stacked at the cove.

"So what is it?" John said, not wasting any time.

That didn't bring much of a reaction as Dlahni just shrugged and started fidgeting with some pebbles beside his crossed legs. Nyaho did about the same, but on switching his gaze to him, John caught him looking up and their eyes locked.

"What is it? Something's bothering both of you, isn't there?" You've been sending signals, but I'll be damned if I can read them.

"Nyaho? ...

"Dlahni? ..."

It took a little more prodding, but finally Nyaho opened up. "John ... yes, there is something, or rather things, because it's different for each of us. Maybe I should speak for Dlahni as I know it will be difficult for him to express how he feels.

"You weren't at the meeting Sunday morning to hear how you were exalted ... it was really something. We were at Pangaea, you know, and saw how you fought, and saw you talking to the Gods, so we know the stories weren't exaggerations. Then we come home to find your friends, and they're tall and from another world. You say you're not giants, and if that's what you say, it's good enough for us.

"But people are talking again.

"Then we see Gary's machete, another amazement beyond our understanding. It's intimidating.

"Dlahni is awed by it all. He feels inadequate when compared to you and your friends; he thinks you'll be leaving soon and we'll see little of you from that time on; he's afraid the *Atjahahni* will end up like ducklings in a pond following after you and your people.

"It's depressing."

"I see," John said, looking at Dlahni who continued shifting pebbles without looking up.

"So tell me, Nyaho, what's bothering you?"

It was easier speaking for someone else, so there were a few awkward moments, then ... "I love the *Denas Atjahahni*. I love how we touch and feel and live with the world around us. The Great Spirit has made a wonder-world of plants and animals and put us in it's midst. Ab Oh said each of them had spirits that spoke to him. I can't say they speak to me, but I feel them. To me it feels like the world is one living thing with many parts, and that if we consider them properly, we'll be in peace with the Great Spirit.

"I'm proud of our people. Though we are of two wolves, we work together well enough to make things work.

"But I'm disturbed by things that have happened recently. We've met three other nations; we've been part of the worst event in our history with madness and killing; we've heard the story of your other world and have met the Chosen. Any and all of these will have an impact.

"What then will happen to the *Atjahahni*? I don't want to lose what we've been and have become. When we danced last night I could feel the love that ties us together. Even your Judy had tears as she visited with the spirits she was discovering."

Now John was at a loss. He'd wanted to get to the bottom of what was bothering his friends, and got more than he expected. He'd wondered what all the emphasis had been about on the giants at the conclusion of the ceremony, and wondered what was meant by the mention of certain names in English, but those things could wait ... this was something else and the most important.

"Look ... I need your help," he finally said.

"You've heard about the mission we're on. Well, that mission isn't exactly a walk around the Commons. It's serious business to which we'll be dedicating the rest of our lives. In the *Atjahahni* culture you feel a strong attachment to the spirits of your ancestors. Well, we do too. We can't forget the fact that by living, we are unbelievably privileged, and with that privilege are obligated to multitudes the likes of which are hard to imagine. Among them, our parents and brothers speak.

"Whatever it is that we must try—to lay the foundation for a civilization that can not only live with itself, but also live in harmony with the rest of the Great Spirit's world—will not be easy. We'll need all the help we can get, and I can't think of two better people to add to the team than you two.

"You've said you feel overwhelmed and intimidated and depressed by being compared to my friends. In a way that's understandable, because my friends are all fine people. But no more than many I've met in this world.

"Remember now, you two saved my life soon after my coming here … I'll never forget that.

"And Dlahni, you said you saw me fight. Well, it just so happens I also saw *you* fight, and know from that there's no one I'd rather have by my side when the going gets tough.

"Nyaho, you're worried that the Chosen will impose a religion that will drive that of the *Atjahahni* out of existence. That may be the least of your worries. The Chosen are only fifteen in number, and come from almost as many religious backgrounds. This is, however, one of the areas we'll have to include in all that we do; and since what *you* do is much more considerate of the natural world, it well may be that we are the follower.

"Da-hash-to said he wants to go to where we come from. That's good, only I wish for you two to go as well … and as soon as it can be arranged so we're not caught up in snow. You'll see things that will astound you … the machete is nothing by comparison. Some of what you'll see may further intimidate you. If so, you'll just have to get over it.

"Let's join hands …

"In the world that died, I had a brother who was a fine man—a brother I loved very much.

"In this world I have two brothers, who I hold in equally high esteem.

"You *are* my brothers."

Dlahni blubbered …

30

Braga

The moon had completed another three-fourths of a cycle since Daj returned to the trail, and a lot of nothing had happened—a lot of nothing except recovering and surviving and introspecting and plotting.

Braga's mind was awhirl, with his fingers drumming and his knees pulsing, which he couldn't seem to control. He and Ah-ton-jacii had been fishing since dawn at the end of a long finger of the lake, and had done well; so well, that even after eating to ease their pangs, there were ample leftovers. Despite this, he directed Ah-ton to keep at it, adding for him at intervals to climb the vantage point looking east. This is what he'd finished doing for the third time before the sun reached full above, with only shimmering shades of water to be seen. He'd skipped stones for a bit each time he scanned, as if he was relaxed; but he was acting, and not too convincingly. The last one he threw so hard, it awakened all his hurts. And so he fidgeted, which bothered him for being so obvious. That's when he left, first giving Ah-ton his instructions.

He reached Pangaea and stopped, as always, making sure there was nothing moving before slipping into the clearing. There it was ghostly quiet, making it feel as if the spirits had moved in to hold the place in suspension. Then he noticed green sprigs peppering the landscape. Before the Gathering, the area had been solidly forested, requiring the concerted effort of several squads to get it cleared. Now the forest was fighting back, and spirits or no spirits, was beginning to recapture what had been lost.

Braga started to move on, then he turned to see if Ah-ton was in view. Since he wasn't, he broke into a trot, continuing to push himself. Ever since ripping out the arrows, he'd tried to move without limping or groaning, and the trot was the latest extension in this recovery. Although there was a chorus of internal screaming, he made it to the channel cut without noticeably breaking down.

He looked at the cut, and then at the black rubble jutting from each side, the way he'd done almost every day since first seeing it. Daj had said there was a mystery tied to it; but whatever it was, it continued to remain as plain, black rubble. He shook his head.

With nothing gained there, he back-tracked to the flats, dropping across the slope leading to it and stopping at a certain spot. *This is where we killed Matthew.*

Braga turned, slowly trying to picture all else that had happened. But this was also to no avail. At the time there had been wind and rain and fear and confusion and screaming and chaos, while now there was only silence with a whisper of a breeze.

Eerie. He shook his head again.

He looked up the slope to the summit crowned by a copse of trees … where Daj said John went after the killings. It was the only area he hadn't yet examined, so it had been on his mind. He tried to climb the ledge that framed one side of the flats, which was the shortest way to it, but that was more than he was ready for. So he retraced his steps on the slope and circled around. From there he picked his way to the top of the hill, and turned to take in the view. He could see everything—the flats, the channel cut, the quadrangle, and the places where each of the nations had camped. Most interesting, however, was the tree nearest to where he stood. It had a clear, ugly gash from top to bottom, ending in furrows radiating from the base. A few singed branches and lots of bark littered the area.

"This is the place," Braga muttered. "This must *be* the place the Great Spirit spoke to John." He sat on a rock, leaned back against another to get into a semblance of comfort, and nodded, "This *is* the place."

But did it really happen? Daj said the expression on John's face didn't look like someone who'd just spoken to the Great Spirit. On the other hand, Da-hash-to had remarked about John ... that the Great Spirit must be looking over him, the arrows always missed.

He groaned ... *while he had been skewered.*

Braga stood and paced in a tight circle, reviewing thoughts plaguing him since the latest failure. He'd failed in every attempt against John, even though every arrangement seemed to be perfect. Now he was banned, a man who could be hunted and killed on sight. He still had a few friends among the *Atjahahni*; certainly none with the *Anlyshendl* once the truth was out about the two he'd killed years before. He'd made inroads with the *Njegleshito,* who had a promising amount of discord among its factions, but the battle he'd instigated had scrambled that and strengthened their relations with the *Atjahahni.*

Even with the *Bjarla-shito,* where bonds had definitely been established, his welcome was doubtful as they'd suffered horribly. They were, however, still his best option ... really his only hope. A hope, that is, if he could find a reason for them to take him back into their trust.

He groaned again, realizing there really were no good options. He stopped, sighed as if with the last breath, his dreams had drifted away too. He turned to start down and made a step in that direction, when he saw something lying between the first set of stones. *What's this?* It was a spear point with a half-foot of shaft still tied to it. As he held it to the sky and turned it, the light sparkled off the chippings in scrambled sequence. His eyes widened. He returned to where he'd been pacing and began again, holding the point in the air. Sitting back down, he continued to turn it in his hands.

Is this an omen? Has all that has happened been a test? Did the Great Spirit have a plan for him as well? Or was he grasping at straws?

He sat and twirled.

It seemed his whole life had been a test.

He hardly remembered his father, as his father had died when he was young. But then his mother married again and the tests started. The stepfather was a bully who bounced his mother around, and slapped or booted him at the slightest provocation. This went on for several years, inadvertently teaching him the value of intimidation and perception.

One day he and the stepfather were fishing along a remote stretch. Following him through the bushes along a raised shore, he was only a few steps away when the edge crumbled and his stepfather fell. The fall turned into a slide that gained momentum, propelling him ten feet out into deep water. There was a frantic, gurgling, panicked cry to Braga, whose instinct was to get something quickly and reach out to him. He tried, but his pole wasn't long enough; so in a frenzy, he scurried about searching. He found a long branch that would have worked, but instead of rushing back to the edge, something else happened ... he hesitated. When his stepfather sank, he stayed back and watched; and when the ripples dissipated and the surface calmed ... he smiled. Then he ran screaming for help.

It was perfect, and he learned the merit of cunning.

Then there was the trip north and the first killings ... but that wasn't the test. The test was the retreat to safety. Inspired by fear, he'd led Dresh-na-togl and the two young captives on a return trip that exceeded in effort and stamina anything in *Atjahahni* experience. This taught there was a greater power within him than he had ever realized.

Later came a challenge by another whose ambition paralleled his own—an ambition for the next leadership position in the village. The contest was subtle ... hardly realized by his competitor and of little concern to everyone else. All of which was an opportunity for more development. The more was subterfuge.

Braga started by stealing a rolled panel of leather and hiding it inside the other's lodge. When the matter came to the attention of the Council, a whispered suggestion led to a search. Braga's home was the first on the list, which cleared him, while the third, to his subliminal competitor, resulted in an incredible, contested discovery. That was the beginning. More whispers which implied diabolical significance to ordinary conduct, added darkness to an already questionably reputation. It finally reached a pitch in a manner similar to Salem reasoning, where the man was deemed at odds with the spirits and a threat to the community. In a final judgment decreed by

Ab-Oh jsandata, a recently designated, fervent Spirit Man, he was terminated in accord with *Atjahahni* policy.

Braga never hinted of an involvement or showed emotion during any of this; he only nodded at one point when Ab-Oh seemed to waiver.

John's arrival presented a whole new list of challenges. After a series of setbacks, he adapted, as if in another series of tests, and survived, all his actions justified by his declared dedication to the *Atjahahni* against the tyranny of the giants. This premise was all he had left after the disaster at Pangaea.

But again, was all of this a trial to prove his metal? Did the Great Spirit leave this sparkling spear point for him to find? Was he, in reality, destined for greatness?

Braga hustled down, for the first time in weeks not caring about limping or expressing pain. He crossed the quadrangle and disappeared into the woods, ending beside the cave at a display assembled nearby. The display was on a level surface large enough to hold uniformly sized pebbles of various colors, in a replication of the *Atjahahni* Home Guard system John had presented years before.

Like he had done ever since assembling it, he studied it, trying to visualize a flaw or weakness in the strategy it represented. The strategy had eventually been successful, but it had been more of a joke at first. The truth was it worked, because year after year exercises had been held to make it work.

His original thought was that if he could get back into the good graces of the *Bjarla-shito*, he could show the system to them, making one similar but better, or at least larger because of the available manpower. In such an improved form, no nation he knew of would be able to stand against them.

Whenever his spirits rose with the excitement of the possibility, however, reality followed right behind. Standing in the way was the basic problem of how to be accepted to even begin organizing. He was banned and could be killed; he needed something drastic.

He thought of the *Bjarla-shito*. They were four different communities loosely tied by representative council. They were also larger in total than all the other nations combined, so there was every reason to look to them, even though the rapport he'd established during preparations for the Gathering had been with only two of the smaller communities within the nation.

He shook his head when he asked himself whether the other communities might still be ripe for him; but that wouldn't be the case ... because word gets around. He kept butting against the same problem.

But back to the array. The system it represented wouldn't work immediately for any nation. As with the *Atjahahni*, it would take time, maybe years, before arrangements would result in effective units. He didn't have years. And without years, any array would just be a mob.

So he stared.

He tried to define his own objectives, and determine what was important.

He didn't want to destroy the *Atjahahni* ... he just wanted to kill John and establish his leadership. Then he'd be in control. With that, and the awareness to other nations, the possibilities would be endless.

He stared. *What would work for such a kill?*

What if I had a small, highly trained unit—people like myself ... people who were strong, fast, brave, and able to withstand pain and hardship like he had during the retreat? Then an army needed to be no more than a mob, a distraction, while the special unit attacked from hiding.

Braga sat back. His hands shook; his mind racing to work out how this could come to pass. But the first problem remained—how to approach the *Bjarla-shito* without getting killed.

"Well this is a fine hello ..."

Braga jumped, scattering some of the pebbles.

"What?" Instinctively grabbing the spear leaning nearby and spinning, he came to face four smiling faces, with Ah-ton-jacii among them going bug-eyed at his reaction.

"You didn't hear us?

Braga stammered ...

Daj laughed, "I said this is a fine hello. We come a long way to see you ... and you just turn your back."

When the jolt from the surprise settled and joking ran its course, they made for the comforts of logs and boulders and squatted.

"You say you're part of an escort," Braga said, settling on a rocky, throne-like seat he'd fashioned near the mouth of the cave. It was a favorite place from where he could survey the stretch of woods before him, which while not far because of the profusion, was his realm. "Tell me more about that; I don't understand."

"It was because of John's daughters," Daj explained. "You may not have noticed, but Sara and Naomi were each being courted, one by a *Negleshito*, the other by an *Anlyshendl*."

Braga nodded, crunching his chin, "Not surprising, at least not for Naomi ... she'd spend a year up north. So?"

"Well, last Sunday there was a double wedding. It was supposed to be somewhat private, but with all else that had been going on, word got around and you can guess what happened.

"Anyway, the ceremonies were touching—part *Atjahahni* with Nyaho doing his thing, and part something else. It led to another festive occasion.

"The next morning the two couples boarded canoes and started out for their new homes ... new for the girls, that is. For this, it was intended there be escorts across the water portions of their trips, which although a fine idea, caused a problem because there weren't enough canoes to handle all who wanted to go along. I managed to get one, much to the chagrin of others, saying Shajsi-djuma and Ndjasa here deserved to go because they scored high during competitions prior to the Gathering, and yet hadn't been selected. I'd added that after the escort, I would take them to Pangaea, so at least they'd see the site where all the stories were based."

Braga laughed, "Very clever." Then speaking to the young men, said "I'm glad to see you again. As you know, I tried to get you both in on the expedition, but it wasn't mine to call. It was Dlahni's, and he did what he did.

"But something's missing here Daj, you've got that look on your face. What's with "all that had been going on", and "something else"."

"Oh, things you could expect. There was a lot to tell regarding the Gathering ... a whole Sunday was spent with people expanding on their experiences. And then the harvest ceremonies … stuff like that."

"Daj," Braga repeated, cocking his head and squinting. "You're toying with me. Ndjasa looks like he's about to explode. What is it?"

Daj settled back, his expression more serious than teasing. "The news is so startling, I'm having trouble forming words to describe it properly. There are parts I haven't been able to understand."

"Just tell it …"

"Okay. Two days before reaching home, a small party came out from the village to meet us. One was Dlahni, the other was an old friend of John's."

"An old friend?"

"Yes, no doubt about it. The way they circled and hugged and talked indicated so. I wasn't close to them, but I saw and heard enough to get me thoroughly confused. For one, the friend's clothes were unlike anything I've seen … and … he didn't seem any older than the boys here."

Braga leaned forward to question something that didn't make sense—the "old friend", if now the age of the boys, would have only been a tot when John came to the village. But Daj held up his hand. "There's more, a lot more. At the village there were three additional "friends", all big people. One of the women was the tallest I've every seen, and the same for one of the men, who was taller than John." Ndjasa tried to speak but Daj shook his head. "Word spread that the woman claimed to be John's wife … and," looking at Braga to make sure the words had the proper impact, "all of the other friends were also young."

Before Braga could respond, Ndjasa spurted, "They all smiled and were courteous, but they had secrets. They had weapons under cover and wouldn't show anyone what they were. The only exception was a bow—a weird contraption with criss-crossed strings and rounds called pulleys—that probably was too big to hide. It could outshoot anything our best could do."

Braga's jaw dropped at the barrage of unbelievables; then he stood and shuffled in a small circle with questions in mind coming in a torrent. *Friends? Tall people? Young people? Wife? Secrets? Exotic weapons?* All of which combined with the mystery of the drainage cut a short distance away.

"Did you say they were all young?"

"Yes … no doubt about it. It's almost magical."

"Did you say they had secrets?"

Daj nodded, "The whole village is whispering about what they could be carrying."

Braga walked over to the flat surface, where he'd been so engrossed earlier he hadn't heard the four approaching. Looking down at the array of pebbles, he fumbled at straightening out the part that had been messed, but his eyes were glazed, his movements robotic.

While the others looked on, eyes widening, he started to chuckle, the chuckle segueing to a laugh and then a twirling, leg-slapping, hysterical rant.

PART FOUR

31

Horses

Horses. John shook his head as he surveyed the sand-sculptures, whose faint outlines were barely visible. It was a bit before dawn and the sky was clear, but sprinkles from stars only sifted through the trees. He started a fire and bundled up.

Horses ... He'd been up to his ears with the harvest ceremonies, then two weddings, and finally with preparations for traveling to Olympia, as the cryogenic center was being called, when Gary complicated things further.

*   *   *

"Do you see what I see?" Gary said, pointing to Cherstabonashala, one of the *Bjarla-shito* dancing around in a game of kick-ball in the Commons.

"Yes ... handsome young man. He and his friends were a great help during that mess in Pangaea. So?"

"I don't mean the person, I mean what he's wearing. Some of his trimmings had to come from a horse."

"Oh yes, that. I noticed ... in fact Chjenohata, Sara's husband, shows some of the same, as do most of the *Njegleshito*."

"So both the *Bjarla-shito* and *Njegleshito* have horses."

"Well, I don't think they have them ... I mean under their control, but they hunt them. I asked Chjenohata about that during his visit a few years back, and he said the animals roamed in herds on the outer islands. They were skittish and fast and hard to get to, but they were highly prized for both meat and leather."

Gary nodded, but with an expression.

"What is it?"

"We need them ... horses, I mean. When you get to Olympia, you'll see why. There are so many things we need in order to live outside the mountain—lodging, work shops, plant nurseries, barns and sewer and water stuff. As you can imagine, the list goes on and on. Bruno keeps sketching designs to be considered for all of them; and when we left, he was working on a master plan tying them together ... fields and all.

Then there were the boats. He got us to build two of them a while back, just small flat-bottomed skiffs for the lake west of the farmstead; if we hadn't, we might never have found the messages you'd carved.

Another project on his hot button is a roadway connecting the lake to Olympia and beyond. The road, or a system of roads, makes sense; which leads us back to horses. To really use roads properly, we need them ... horses and wagons and all kinds of associated stuff. They'll make life a lot easier and much more efficient."

John leaned against a tree and looked back at the Commons where bantering in unrelated languages could be heard. "Do you hear that?" he said, pointing with his head.

"Yes, I hear. All of them seem to be getting along just fine, which is good because we need their help."

"To get horses."

"Exactly. So how do we get there from here?"

John shrugged and looked back again, "Actually, we may have been lucky if we get serious about horses."

"Lucky?"

"Yes ... in a strange way. Naomi and La-sa-sena are gone, which doesn't matter for what you're suggesting, because the *Anlyshendl* can't help you ... they don't have horses. What's good about their leaving is that Daj and some of his friends left with them. They're among the party escorting the newlyweds north. That's possibly good riddance. Daj is someone Dlahni doesn't trust ... thinks he's like a spy who's really tagging along to find Braga and fill him in on what's happened. The news about all of you being here, which has hit like extra-terrestrials would have in the good old days, should be enough by itself to make Braga spin."

"Daj ... he's that old, creepy, bandy-legged guy, right?"

John nodded. "I don't know why, but if your suggestion about horses moves forward, I feel it would be better to keep the fact from Braga. At least we should downplay any significance of it ... and that goes for anything we do. He's clever and will twist information if it works to his advantage."

"You worried about Braga? Why? I heard he was wounded ... and then banished by all the nations."

"I heard he walked away, which means he's out there somewhere."

"So you think he's a threat."

John grumbled, looking down and cursing to himself. "I could never believe he was as dangerous as Dlahni seemed to think. Now it's hard to relax as long as that bastard's still alive."

"Should we hunt him down and end the problem before he can do more harm?"

"It's tempting, but no. That's for someone else to do. Besides, there's a trip we need to be making ... and soon. Winter can come fast and furious here in the mountains."

"Okay, then back to the horses ... how do we start?"

John pushed away from the tree and squatted, picking up a pebble to massage. He shook his head thinking about the languages, the chatter from the Commons being a reminder.

When he first came to the village he'd been completely baffled by the *Atjahahni* tongue. It seemed impossible to decipher, yet over time the sounds segued to meanings that blended into understandings. Now there were three more, all unique and equally undecipherable, to such an extent that even if he'd had paper and pencil, he'd find it hard to represent any of them in terms of the modern European or English alphabet.

At the same time he noticed how quickly children adapted to the differences and learned. Mahsja, in particular, continued to amaze him; and Nyaho, too, showed a definite aptitude. Maybe it would be like in Europe where people were exposed to and learned four or five languages.

Whatever, for him, languages remained a puzzlement.

"Remember that totem we carved?" John finally answered.

"What? Yes, of course," Gary said, breaking into a broad grin. "What are you suggesting? Not a wooden horse, I hope."

"No, but you're close," plunking the pebble at a nearby rock. "The problem is communication. The first thing we have to do is make our friends understand what we want. The girls and Mahsja can help, but they might not be enough. I've used models in the past, because with all the confusion that can result, models have proven to be the best way to connect. So let's sculpt a horse, but not of wood. Let's use sand, like in those carving contests at the beach. Sand can be just as effective and not nearly as difficult. Once the *Bjarla-shito* and *Njegleshito* understand we're talking about horses, we can discuss their catching some for us"

"Sounds good. In fact, it sounds like fun. Where's the sand?"

"The best that comes to mind is in the sand bar at the swimming pond. It's getting late in the season, so there shouldn't be much traffic anymore."

He and Gary first started carving on the horizontal surface of one of the sand bars, which was the easiest way to work. But then they realized that since the sculpting would be viewed from the south bank, which had been cleared to serve as amphitheater seating for swimming events, it would be more effective to shape the carvings on the opposite bank in as much of a standing position as possible. The new approach was much more difficult, with sand collapsing time and time again, but they made it work. By wetting and packing and repairing and revising, an impressive rendition, with minor relief on the lower half and almost three-dimensions on the top, took shape.

But the work was more than impressive, it was also fragile, so much so that John became concerned about preserving it long enough to serve its purpose. With this weighing on his mind, he rose in the middle of the night and returned to the site.

*   *   *

John sat back on the bank and waited as the sky lightened. Soon he could see the sculptures—the horse, side view, with a man standing beside it to give the sculpting scale—much more clearly. This is where Gary and Roland found him when they arrived at sunup.

"So once everyone understands what this sculpture is," John said as soon as they'd dropped down to admire the work again, "you're going to ask for a few foals, male and female, from each of the nations."

"Right," Gary answered. "Getting a variety will be best. No telling what's happened to horses in eight thousand years. They may have drifted towards original strains and gotten smaller. Anyway, a variety will allow us to experiment, and over time bring the best of them back out."

"Makes sense. And who's going to show them how these horses can be caught."

"I guess that's my job," Roland said. "I practiced with the lasso most of yesterday."

"Okay, good. Now, if the people in each of the nations manage to catch a few of them, how do they get them here? And how do we get them to Olympia? I've been thinking of a few problems while here on guard duty."

Gary laughed, glancing at Roland as if he'd been waiting for this, then said, "Somewhat like the way Hannibal did."

Oh Christ, now what? "Hannibal crossed the Alps with a bunch of elephants. What's that got to do with this?"

"Well, it just so happened that before he got to the Alps, Hannibal had to cross the Rhone, which was a pretty big river. Now, elephants can swim, but not that far. Besides, there were a bunch of hostiles on the other side; and, since elephants are temperamental, he couldn't put them on simple rafts. So he had a massive pachyderm pier and ferryboat system made, complete with sod decking and bushes and stuff, to make the elephants feel at home. It worked. He was able to move his army, complete with elephants, across to the other side without a hitch. All of this was done in a short time, because time was of the essence for crossing the Alps."

"You've lost me. What has this got to do with moving horses?

We're talking about spindly horses a few months old, not five-ton elephants."

"You miss the point. The point is that we'll have to convey skittish animals a ways over water. For that we'll need a boat, maybe something like a barge, with special provisions. John, you *need* a larger boat anyway. Canoes are great, but to really trade with the nations, far flung as they are, something else is needed."

John snorted and shook his head, "You use a strange example to explain yourself … but I hear you. Actually, I've been thinking of a boat for some time. It's hard to consider, though, with what we have on hand here. We can't make planks with stone knives and wooden hammers."

"There are some pretty good tools back at Olympia for the time being … They should be of help."

"Time being?"

"Yes, time being. Huston and Reynolds stuffed an amazing number of things into the limited confines of the Storage Room, but most are single or limited copies. Once any of what's there is broken or worn out, it's gone, with no way to replace it for a long time, possibly hundreds of years. And that goes especially for tools, which are considered precious."

"Well, I agree with you about the boat and, oops … Here they come."

Any thought of secrecy vanished with the group that straggled down the trail and settled on the bank. Although the number intended was limited to the ones felt necessary, the group was still large. There were Cherstabonahala and his friends; Chjenohata and his; the daughters and the baby; Dlahni, Nyaho, Da-hash-to and Bran-dahni; and finally, Annie and Judy, and the others. The invited group assembled early and left quietly, but in a community like that of the *Atjahahni*, things are heard or seen and curiosities are aroused. Even at the early hour, a number of others tagged along to see what was happening.

The initial impact of the sculptures was more dramatic than expected. The *Atjahahni* were accustomed to artwork and creativity because of the Crafts Fairs, but this was something else; none of them had seen an animal so realistically shaped, whether in sand or any other medium. First one, then another, then the whole group dropped down and sloshed across the sand bars and shallows to get a closer look. This became a problem because water was deep on either side of a narrow stretch, a situation that could have led to dunking or even damage to the sculptures. Dlahni took control, fortunately, and directed traffic; but it was a while before everyone could be reassembled back on the bank.

When all had finally quieted, Gary started the discussion, explaining the shape on the far bank was a depiction of an animal that was of particular interest. "Do you recognize this animal?" He asked, quickly getting nods and affirming comments. But then during interpretations there was a hitch as to what it was called … the *Njegleshito* and *Bjarla-shito* having different names. This was resolved by an agreement to call it "horse", and with that the meeting moved on.

Dlahni was next. He stood and, speaking English in halting fashion with Nyaho, Mahsja and Sara filling the voids, explained with his comments directed to those of the visiting nations, "The *Atjahahni* don't have this animal in any of its hunting areas. Remember the things we learned from each other at the Gathering. One of them useful to all of us came from the *Anlyshendl*, who'd captured wild hogs, domesticated them, and therefore had them whenever needed. We think the same can be done with horses. Can you help us? We want to establish a herd here, so we can have availability to the things they have to offer without going on far-flung hunts. If we're able to succeed with what we think is possible, we will share what's been learned with you in return."

Chjenohata looked puzzled. He repeated what he'd said before with more detail. "The horses to the east are actually on several islands, with different herds taking on slightly different characteristics. They all move about quickly, though, making it difficult to get close.

"Do you want us to catch some for you? I don't know how we can do that."

Dlahni nodded, "It will be difficult, but we'd like both nations to try."

Cherstabonashala and his *Bjarla-shito* looked at each other, and after a flurry of comments among themselves, turned back to indicate they were eager to help as well, but how? He said "Horses, like those in the sand, were across the river from where their villages stretched. There they also moved in herds and ranged for great distances, often mingling with other animals." The other animals, as he described them, took on aspects of elk and deer and even buffalo. "All of the animals have been hunted, but none have ever been captured."

The concept of catching horses was difficult to convey. Roland attempted to explain by putting on a demonstration, casting a lasso at Gary and catching him, then getting the others to try until they managed to do so as well. But this alone wasn't enough.

Sensing this, Annie stepped forward. She'd been raised on a farm and had spent almost as much time in the stables as in the house in her early years. She said "It will be easiest to catch *young* horses ... they're really what are wanted anyway; and the best time to do that is in early spring, right after they drop and before they develop strength and speed. If you can capture the mother as well it would be good, otherwise you'll have to get into concocting foods and weaning."

This protracted the discussion as Annie tried to communicate all the nuances of keeping alive, caring for and transporting animals once the capturing had been accomplished. It was as confusing as three entangled languages deciphering complex concepts could be, but the interpreters, working together, kept at it patiently.

Finally a point was reached where both parties understood the challenges. With that they agreed to make their attempts in early spring, and if successful, bringing the animals to locations to be determined as soon afterwards as possible. For the *Bjarla-shito,* that meant the north end of the lake; but for the *Njegleshito,* it meant the end of the lake's finger opposite the *Atjahahni* village where Chjenohata and Sara first met.

Discussions ended with that, and didn't include how the animals would be corralled or pastured or moved beyond destination points. That would have been overload. Before an awkward lull had a chance to develop, the girls moved in, much to the delight of the young men, and expressed interest in the way parts of horses—particularly manes and tails—had been used to decorate their clothing.

John remained silent through all of this, as did the rest of the *Atjahahni,* the men only nodding from time to time as different points were being made. John especially didn't want to complicate the discussion by mentioning other uses horses could ultimately have—such as riding or pulling wagons or working in the fields. Like the details that hadn't been explained, anything more would have compromised what had been accomplished, and cluttered minds with already enough to think about.

32

Homecoming

"What do you think?" Gary asked, easing his paddle out to let the canoe glide.

"This is as good a place as any, "Roland replied, his eyes sweeping the inlet before them. "We're a good ways past that highest peak now. If we hike across that ridge in front of us, we should find home somewhere on the other side."

The four canoes strung out behind drifted in turn and soon were jumbled in a pack.

"We think this is the place, John. How do you see it?"

John guided his canoe alongside until the rails could be held. "I was going to suggest stopping here, and was trying to catch up. I'm not familiar with the lake this far south, because we passed where I came out twenty years ago a good ways back. Since this may be about as far you say you hiked to that peak back there, it makes sense to me."

With that they headed to shore, grounded and unloaded. Most didn't stay long. While three of them—young, strong men from the village—pulled the canoes on shore and began to set up camp, the others, with a half-day of sunlight still available, strapped on totes, gave last instructions, and cut into the forest.

Nyaho, who was still a little sore but otherwise fine, led the way, followed by Gary, then Judy and Ann, then Dlahni and John carrying

Da-hash-to on a stretcher, and finally Roland. This sequence would be jumbled from time to time to vary the loads, but generally Nyaho stayed near the front because of his unique skill in the woods.

There were no surprises. First impressions were that the ridge line was nearby and one steady climb. But as usual there were rises and falls and gullies and turns, with the ridge, when it could be seen, never seeming any nearer. Then on the second day, they came to realize a subtle change—they were past the mystical point that defined the ridge, and were moving more down than up. Later they came to a gully that was snaking principally westward, so they stayed close to it as if were a beacon.

At the campfire that night, Nyaho asked if there were any landmarks anyone could recall.

Roland and Ann shook their heads. "Some of the sights around here are pretty distinctive. If we'd have come this far east, I'm sure we'd remember them."

"Same here," Gary said. "I spent most of my time west of the mountain … Mount Olympus I mean, which is really more of a hill."

"You're only half right on that," Judy said. "From a distance it hardly stands out, with the forest masking most of it. But it's got more elevation than you might think. I climbed the damned thing and it wasn't easy. It's very steep on the north and west edges, by the way, forming a palisade. We probably can't see that part from this direction, though. There's also a river running right below it."

"The gully we've been beside has turned into a stream. Could it be the same river?"

"Don't know. There are rivers both north and south of Olympia. Could be either one, I suppose." She shrugged, "Don't know."

The next day a knob blocked their way forcing them to the south, which took them away from the stream, but still in a westerly direction. While negotiating their way later in the afternoon, Roland, who was leading, cut through a tangle of rhododendrons and assorted vines and stepped into a clearing. Only it wasn't a natural clearing.

"I think we're on to something!" He exclaimed. With those words everyone squeezed through and fanned out beside him.

Gary clapped and beamed, "This has got to be part of the farm."

"I agree," Roland said, lifting the blunderbuss above his head and dancing a light jig, while the girls hugged and twirled. The *Atjahahni* looked at John, who only returned a nervous smile.

When the bit of nonsense simmered down, they took stock. They'd punched through at right angles to what was obviously a controlled agricultural area, but not one in the usual form. There were still trees among the plantings—most likely ones which had been too large to remove during initial clearing. Below and between the trees were blended combinations of workings—first the clearing where they stood, which was like a buffer from the forest, then an assortment of low-growing crops, then grains and finally corn.

Portions of plantings had already been harvested.

"Sure is quiet," John said, looking at Gary after scanning what he could beyond the crops. "Where is everybody?"

"Now don't get excited. We're still a mile or more away from the homestead ... anyway that's my guess. There'll be people there."

"So why are we standing here? Let's go."

"Okay, but hold it ... not straight into the fields because Anton will have a fit. If we follow the clearing to the right, we'll hit the river, so let's go left. I think this will eventually curl around and bring us close to home."

"You don't know?"

"Not for sure ... a lot has changed since we left."

A quarter mile further the clearing turned as Gary had predicted, but then all hell broke loose.

"Get away you bastards!"

An apparition rose out from the base of the corn. When it snapped to vertical it was nine feet tall with a large head and wildly flaying arms. The head was capped with a black, crumpled, farmer's hat over stringy red hair; the face was bearded with large, rolling eyes complete with flapping lids; and a hideous mouth rapidly clapped, exposing spaced teeth and a flickering tongue. Along with the flaying arms, the body spun and dipped, but the head remained fixed towards the direction of the triggering sound, which was all of them. Obscenities poured out in concert with the movements.

They gasped … with Judy's "holy shit" audible.

Dlahni, who'd been on one end of the stretcher, dropped it and Da-hash-to and sprang into action. In microseconds he shed his tote, freed his spear and leapt forward. Fortunately he held back, because Roland recovered and started to laugh; the girls followed suit, shrieking and giggling; and Gary fell on the ground out of control. John recoiled at first as well, but then after watching the others, smiled and walked over to Dlahni, putting a hand on his shoulder.

"Easy … it's okay … it's some kind of joke."

Turning to Gary, he said, "What in hell *is* this?"

Gary rolled over and sat up wiping his eyes, but he was unable to speak, breaking down again when he tried.

"That's Homer, an animatronic scarecrow," Roland said, barely under control himself, "I'll explain later … but for now, let's get out of here. That damned thing will keep going as long as its sensors pick us up."

So they did, but with everyone, particularly the *Atjahahni*, continuing to revel at the monster until they were out of range, at which time Homer quieted down, folded up and bent over into the hiding place where it had been.

They didn't get much farther.

"*Hey! Hey!*" It was a call a stretch away from someone who'd stepped into the clearing and now jumped and waved.

"*They're back! They're back!*" The man shouted to someone farther back, then he turned and started to run. He was a large man, dirty and sweaty and shirtless in overalls, who proceeded to gobble up the distance in long, two-furrow strides. It was Anton.

He reached Roland first and jumped, almost knocking him down, the two men hugging and twirling around. Then he went to Annie and Judy and Gary with the same wild greeting.

There were more voices, Devon and Terry being the next. They'd been in the orchard working to extend the planting area, and when they heard Anton's cry, they dropped everything and ran.

Lisa had been returning to the cookhouse with a load of vegetables and greens when sounds reached her. She almost dumped the load right there, but then she stopped to listen and make sure she'd heard right. When other shouts, from voices she hadn't heard in months mingled with Anton's, she kept going, running to where Mona and Rebecca were beginning dinner preparations, yelling all the way.

"You sure?" Mona asked, bug-eyed and rising from the table. "Did you see Gary? Is he okay?"

Lisa shook her head, sputtering, "Don't know any details ... just heard voices ... *come on!*"

With that they bolted, all but Rebecca, that is, who had the presence to stop at the iron triangle hanging from the crossbeam outside and give it a lusty peal with another bar. The triangle had been improvised as a call to dinner or for any other reason to gather, and could be heard for almost a mile.

"What's happening?" Abram yelled, stepping out from the workshop farther back where Bruno, Benjamin and he had been working. They'd been noisily sawing logs into planks and had been oblivious to anything else around.

"They're back ... everybody's back," Rebecca spurted, waving for them to follow before sprinting to catch the other girls.

The men took only as much time to disconnect and put away as absolutely necessary, and then scurried after, except for Benjamin, who skidded to a halt when he remembered Rodney was in the library.

So singly and in bunches, the entire contingent made it to the clearing, where upon seeing the group ahead, dashed on, screaming like banshees.

Bruno was one of the worst. Bouncing off the first of the crew he came to, he worked his way to Judy, where he butted in and grabbed her by the shoulders.

"You okay?" His whole expression betraying something.

"Yes, I'm fine."

"You sure?"

"Yes, *yes!*"

With that he hugged and twirled and then broke back to arm's length with the realization he'd embarrassed himself.

Judy giggled, *"Bruno?"*

Gary was no better. As soon as Anton first yelled, he started to hop. He watched as each new person broke into view, and then when a certain dark-haired girl appeared, he ran to meet her. Like everyone else, she was a mess and bedraggled and absolutely radiant as he picked her up and spun around.

The reception finally ran its course, settling to a point where the greeters noticed there were strangers ... along with remembering the purpose of the trip. The strangers—blending together in earth-tones—had gotten separated and become inconspicuous because the others had moved forward to meet the greeters. To the greeters, there were four of them—four, small, older and weathered natives from another world, who were out of sync in this one. One was kneeling besides another grounded on a stretcher, while two others stood beside.

They weren't far from wrong. Dlahni and Nyaho, who stayed bundled in totes and equipment, felt like porters not knowing what to do. John was also ill at ease, becoming self-conscience of his own appearance, even though the greeters wore the results of hard work and were just as much a mess. What was worse was that in the blur of what was happening, combined with the years that had passed, he hardly recognized anyone. Then there was Da-hash-to, who insisted on getting out of the stretcher and standing despite the make-shift, lengthy splint he still was wearing. So John kneeled down to help him.

As John assisted the chieftain to his feet, and in so doing returned to full height, the celebration a few feet away dwindled to silence. He turned to see wide eyes and open mouths. The greeters, all ten of them, were looking at a tall man in leathers, rough weavings and fur trimmings ... a man scarred and tanned with white hair and a beard.

Ann, who'd been in tears with all the greetings, realized what was happening. She let go of Mona, with whom she'd been celebrating the baby bump, and went over to where John awkwardly stood, putting an arm around him.

"I'm sure you all know my husband.

"This ... is John."

33

Reunion

Murmurs, awkward shuffling ... Then Mona burst from the group with open arms, "John ... Thank God, they found you! You're back!" She scrunched in and gave John a big bearhug, squeezing and shaking and forcing a smile out of him.

Releasing to arms length, she looked up, saying, "John, we've been so worried about you ... We've prayed for your return each day." Then seeing the large red scar and vestiges of scabbing on his brow, raised her hands to his cheeks, "Oh my ... are you?"

"Yes, Mona ... I'm fine," beaming now, "and you look great ... a little different, but still great."

She stepped back and rubbed her stomach, pretending to blush. "Your good buddy Gary did this to me. Isn't this awful?"

John laughed. "I should have warned you about him. But I wasn't kidding ... you look *wonderful* ... better than ever."

The exchange broke the ice, with smiles cracking into the stony looks Annie's announcement had caused. The shuffling turned to movement, with Bruno being the next to come foreward. "John ... welcome back. You've been on our minds more than you can imagine." Then shaking his head, said "This is unbelievable."

"Unbelievable?"

"Yes, I mean, you *did* come back twenty years ago, didn't you? That was one of our speculations."

"You're telling me I look that bad?"

Bruno dropped his head back and hooted, "No, no ... that's not what I meant ... but you have looked better. Seriously, though, welcome back. We're all anxious to hear about what you've been doing."

And so it went, all others taking turns to greet and shake hands and hug and reacquaint, with the things that were John working their way out of the whiskers and wrinkles and scars.

"Look at him," Gary whispered to Mona ... the two of them had moved apart to make room. "He'd been worried about this, as you'd probably been able to see at first. But with all the kidding going on, he's come out of his shell. He's his old self."

"John," Gary interrupted as the line came to an end. "We have some distinguished guests who need introducing. I'd be happy to do that, but think you could do a better job."

John excused himself from Rodney, with whom he'd been having a lively discussion, complete with normally exaggerated animation, saying, "Yes of course ... my pleasure.

"Gary was referring to these three wrinkled, scrawny, miserable specimens of humanity ..."

Before he could finish, Nyaho blurted out in *Atjahahni*, *"We've been waiting for this, and somehow knew how it was going to go,"* with a sly grin as he spoke.

John snorted, his eyes flashing and in a wide grin. "I'm kidding of course. I couldn't say those things if I didn't consider the three among the finest people I've ever known.

"The man who just spoke is *Nyaho-se-de-uta-dena-ayoni*," pronouncing the name in indigenous fashion, which meant the sounds were hardly comprehensible. "He is the Spirit Man of the *Denas Atjahahni*, the nation that's been my home for the last twenty years. The Spirit Man is a very important person in his nation's leadership, as Ann, Judy, Gary and Roland, who saw him in ceremony, will surely agree.

"Nyaho was the first person I met in this world after months of searching ... We came together on the far side of that high mountain you can see to the north, and I might add, the meeting didn't start out well ... he shot an arrow at me."

"The big galoot ran into me and broke my shoulder," injected Nyaho in almost perfect English.

"Yes, that's true," John said, shaking his head, then "Anyway, Nyaho has an amazingly quick and perceptive mind, which you'll soon see. He's also unmatched as a tracker. We'd probably still be wandering around these hills if Gary had led the way.

"The man standing next him is *Dlahni-de-njsata-uta-slahama*, one of the chieftains of the nation, who at times shares in the top role of leadership. His steadfastness and bravery and strength are without equal in this world. With all these attributes, there's no one I'd rather have at my side in a tough spot … this I know from experience.

"There's so much to tell, as Gary will agree to because he's already heard much of it. But it's safe to say I wouldn't be here to relate any of it if it weren't for these two … and more than once.

"Finally, the man with the improvised crutch is *Da-hash-to-ma-se-danaga*. He's our Grand Chieftain. Yes, he's small and wrinkled and in sad shape with a broken hip; and, if appearances are the only means by which we are judged, then you might be wondering why we've gone to the trouble of bringing him along. We certainly could have made better time crossing the ridge without him.

"So why *did* we bring him? There were several reasons. One was that he wanted to come. Even though most *Atjahahni* were in awe of the few things Gary and Roland and Annie and Judy brought along, Da-hash-to was more fascinated than astounded, and wanted to learn more. Another is that he's an old man representing a rare opportunity. Life here in the forest," he said sweeping his arms for emphasis, "is very difficult. You may have an idea about that difficulty by now, but you have tools and provisions they have existed without, and you haven't seen your first winter. Life expectancy in the *Atjahahni* nation is such that death is a constant companion, and forty years is an achievement. We don't know how old Da-hash-to is, but suspect he's in his seventies … and that's amazing. Even more amazing is that he's managed the affairs of his nation for many years, maintaining peace and justice while contending with the same rotten human tendencies that have plagued every society. He's a wise man whose advice I value greatly. With the challenges we have to address, I feel his council will be of great help.

"I know that in your eyes we're a mess ... We're in ragged leathers and furs, and we're beaten and broken and scarred. The fact is we're this way because we've recently survived a harrowing experience. When the horrific storm hit about six weeks ago, we were not only camped in the open away from the comforts of home, we were also assaulted by a crazed mob who felt the *Atjahahni*, and particularly me, had angered the gods and caused the problem. Da-hash-to joined a thin line of brave men in an attempt to stop the mob and reason with them. The attempt didn't work, however; the mob trampled the line into the mud and broke his hip. The battle that followed was awful. Many were killed," John's eyes misted and his voice choked before he could continue. "And more were injured, including all of us.

"So please welcome them. In their eyes, *you* are giants. In my eyes, when I measure heart and mind and goodness, they are as well."

"Oh my! Oh my! *Bravo!*" Anton exclaimed, his meaty hands pounding in applause, a response joined immediately, in the same manner, by all the others in an explosion of sound. John swelled and broke into a grin from ear to ear.

Then the group lined up to shake hands, introduce themselves and extend a welcome.

34

Olympia

"Oops, did you hear that?" Anton said, stepping away and looking at the direction of sound. "Damn," as he saw the darkness taking shape over the ridge.

"Sorry, but I've gotta go. Those clouds could mean rain, which is a problem because I need to finish a few things before dark." With that he waved and started back.

"Same here," Devon said "The rest of you go on in, I'll catch up later."

"Oh Lordy, me too," Rebecca said, "If any of you expect to eat tonight, I'd better get crackin' … and now there are seven more to feed. Mona, you should stay with Gary, but can anyone else give a hand?"

And so it went, the greeters dispersing, as did some of the travelers, with Roland, Annie and Judy sensing that help was needed. Bruno, Mona and Rodney therefore became escorts for the rest of the way.

They didn't have to go much further. In less than half a mile, they passed the last of trees obscuring the view ahead, and saw they were near the base of Mount Olympus, as the hill was called.

"What's this?" Gary asked as they passed the first of structures he hadn't seen before, a log building of over-sized members situated on a rise a ways southeast of the hill.

"That's going to be a bunkhouse," Bruno answered. "It's not finished yet but it should be in a few more weeks."

"I'll bet this is Anton's idea."

"Yes. You remember the tents we were using when you left. Well they're still up and being used. The one nearest here was for Anton who wanted to guard his crops. This building will be a replacement for that, and will house bunks for as many as eight."

Farther along they passed excavations along the side of the hill, beginning about ten feet up the slope.

"And this?"

"That's one of the many future projects. We're trying as best we can to get out of the Incubator and live topside. The excavations are testing the site to locate bedrock and isolate foundation conditions with which we've got to work. We hope to build lodging units."

"Doesn't look like any of them will be ready for winter."

"Probably not. We're trimming logs for them right now, though; and design work is almost finished. We should be able to start soon, but don't know about the winter and how much we can accomplish then.

"John, what can we expect on that?"

John shook his head. "Hard to say. There'll be cold, that's for sure ... at times below freezing. As for snow, that varies. Sometimes there's hardly any, sometimes it's up to your ying-yang. Sorry, but that's not much help."

"Well, what you say is no surprise; we figured as much. We'll just have to roll with whatever happens."

They passed the cookhouse where the girls scurried about, then the workshop where men were doing the same ... a circular saw whining a tune. They passed the entrance corridor, which had been roofed over half-way to the shop to give the door more protection. John noted that the corridor was only ten feet wide so could have been roofed with a simple flat roof. But instead the extension was framed by trusses of oversized members with forty-five degree top chords ... the trusses tied together with timber purlins and supported by massive trunks. It was overkill, but sturdy and impressive, clearly the work of an architect on a mission.

Rodney left the group at that point and peeled off into the corridor.

"I was in the middle of something when I got the call," he said. "Left a mess," his hands reconstructing in the air what that meant.

Just past there an odd conglomeration came into view.

"What's this?"

Bruno laughed, "It's not exactly a spa at the Ritz, but it's the best we could do for the time being."

They were looking at a crude combination of utilitarian features. Most prominent among them was a round wooden tank about six feet in diameter and four feet high, supported on a framework of poles holding it ten feet off the ground. The tank was built of vertical boards that had been bevel cut, then joined and tied with multiple strands of rope tightened to force the sections together. As remarkable as this was, the jointwork still oozed water, with drippings visible in several places. An enclosure of logs and planks extended out from below the tank, giving a hint of privacy but mostly open to the air. There was a strange looking firepit, some wooden tubs, an assortment of pipes and covers in improvised assemblies, and clothes lines.

"Don't tell me ... It's an outdoor bathhouse and laundry," Gary said.

"That's right. It's brand new with still a few kinks to fix ... But it's working.

"Look, you remember how hard everyone was working before you left. At the end of the day, we'd be dirty and stinking, just like today. Then we'd go through those doors to a place that had been kept surgery scrub-room clean for ages. What we were doing wasn't good, but we kept doing it for awhile after you left. Finally we faced the fact that in addition to messing up the place, we were running out of soap and water. We needed this Rube Goldberg conglomeration.

"Once all this was built, which wasn't easy by the way, we started a practice of showering and laundering and changing clothes at the end of the day, then entering squeaky clean."

"All that with cold water?"

"There's an auxiliary tank on the side which is heated."

John cocked his head, "Wait a minute ... did you bring us here to clean up before letting us in?"

"I wouldn't put it quite that way, but yes ... that's part of the plan. All of us will be doing the same. The good part is that by going first, there'll be warm water. What we have probably won't last for everyone.

"Any problem? John, is this something you or your Indian friends will mind doing?"

"Indian friends?"

Bruno stuttered, then bounced his palm off his head, "I'm sorry … Dlahni, what are you called again?"

"*Atjahahni*," Dlahni answered, then looking at John with a puzzled look. "What are Indians?"

"They're the people who roamed these hills long before you roamed these hills. And it's not a bad thing. Judy claims to be part Indian and is proud of it."

"So are you asking if we'd be willing to clean up, including washing our clothes, before going into your lodge in the mountain?"

"I'm afraid so."

Dlahni smiled. "If you'd suggested this twenty years ago, we wouldn't understand at all. But through the years since John came to us, we've watched his every move. Many of the things he did we ended up adopting, after he answered our questions as to why. One of them was the time he spent at the end of the day washing and cleaning. So no, we don't mind, but," he shrugged, raising his hands. "We traveled light and don't have a change of clothes."

"No problem," Mona said. "John, you may not remember, but you have a locker with all the stuff you packed. None of it's been touched, except to find out what you packed. You do have several changes of clothes."

"Well I'll be darned. Yes, I'd forgotten."

Then half laughing, "That isn't going to help these three. The clothes won't fit."

"Still no problem," Mona added. "Between Lisa, Rebecca and me, we should be able to put some things together."

"I might have clothes to spare as well," Bruno said.

Clean clothes were collected and set to the side, and then the process began, all of which went surprisingly well. This was true even for Da-hash-to, who had to have his splint unwrapped before most of his clothes could be taken, and had to be supported and soaped and washed and wiped and dressed by others. Like all other experiences that might have been a shock, his reaction was more one of fascination, with an eagerness to move on to the next.

When the process was through, they would have been hard to recognize back home.

"Well, just look a you guys!" Gary said, clapping and snickering in a way that if any wasn't self-conscious before, would be now.

John had spent the last twenty years in organics, with the last combination a leather tunic with furred panels, tied at the waist by a fiber rope to which several storage packets had been attached. Under the tunic from the waist down were leather leggings, knee-high, woven-grass shin guards, and leather foot wraps. Now he wore a colorful, plaid, cotton shirt, light-weight cargo pants, and wool-lined, moccasin-like slippers.

The differences were even more so for each of the *Atjahahni*, who now wore poorly fitting garments of assorted fabrics, colors and designs. Nyaho and Dlahni looked at each other in a manner betraying a hint of embarrassment, but Da-hash-to smiled, fingering the new materials as if he were a child in a fairy-tale setting.

"Don't be silly, you lunk-head," Mona said, cuffing Gary on the arm. "You guys look fine. I'm sure it feels on the goofy side, just as it would if we slipped into your leathers; but you look fine. Just wait 'til you see how some of the others dress after they get off work.

"They can be pretty weird too. You'll see."

The first stop was just inside the door in the refuse collection area, which had been cleaned and converted to several other uses. A portion nearest the door was now a cloak room, with hanging spaces for changes of wear, and storage for things needed to bridge the gap between worlds. Beyond that to the door accessing the stairway down was a large area dedicated to a design center. It was the second stop, and the reason for stopping was Bruno's pride and joy—a large replication of Mount Olympus and its immediate environs—which was hard to ignore because it was where everyone passed at least twice a day. Besides its location, the model was large, expertly crafted, and invariably interesting, with representations of actual terrain by rocks and stones and seedlings and mosses and the like.

"It's as accurate as I know how to make it," Bruno explained. "I needed to be thinking in terms of overall planning, and had geological survey maps Reynolds left, which gave information that would have been difficult to come by. But the maps were only in two dimensions. I needed three."

John's experiences with civil engineering came to mind. "This has got to be great for all the designs you've got to consider."

"Oh my...The model has already been *incredibly* helpful. The blocks and miniatures you see on it are the bathhouse, the tanks, the workshop, the cookhouse and the bunkhouse we passed on the way here. I've also added hypothetical shapes for the lodging units in that area of excavations, but they're subject to change."

John nodded, but the *Atjahahni* remained generally expressionless, eyes darting from Bruno as he spoke to John or Gary to see their reactions. Only Nyaho displayed a grasp by subtly nodding.

"The projects we've taken on to date are intended, as I mentioned before, to get us out of here. But most of what's been done will be temporary."

Gary smiled, "He's got some pretty ambitious plans."

"Yes I have. You call them ambitious ... I call them realistic.

"Look, all of us collectively have a challenge to which we're pledged ... Don't you remember?"

"Of course."

"Well, in addition to that, we each have individual challenges in keeping with our training and skills. In my case it's architecture and planning. Up 'til now I've only gotten bits and pieces of your story, and am anxious to hear more, but I've gotten the impression there are only a few people in this part of the world, and they're scattered over a wide area. If that's so, then people are probably sparse all over the planet."

As he was speaking, Roland, Abram and Benjamin, having wound up what they'd been doing in the shop and now clean, came in. Realizing a serious discussion was underway, they stayed in the background to listen, except that Roland couldn't resist saying, "Hey, you guys ... nice digs!"

Bruno hardly noticed. He continued, "And if that's so, then we're unique, and more obligated than we may have realized. We don't know, for instance, whether there were other incubating complexes like the one we have. Did Huston share and coordinate his program with others? We don't know. But if he didn't, and there are no others, then we become even more of a rarity.

"I don't know how that makes you feel, but I feel humbled. Some have laughed at my naming this place Olympia, and have given names in sarcasm to some of the objectives I've hinted. But the fact is, if we're successful, then this place, which we hope will serve for many generations, is priceless.

"When I look at this model, I don't see a few log buildings to serve fifteen people for a few years. I see a grand complex, not exactly Emerald City, but impressive, of houses and schools and cultural facilities and so on for thousands of people for thousands of years. The more I think on it, the more expansive I see our objectives. I intend to make another model to place beside this one ... a model at a scale that will cover a larger area from the lake to the west, across the ridge to the lake to the east. The challenges and relationships are that large.

"It's boggling ... but it's no different for each of you. Rodney, for instance, feels he's obligated to a life in the laboratory. He'll be extracting things from the electronic files available to us, and putting the information into innumerable practical uses to help us not only survive, but also advance. The glop you used in the bathhouse is one of his first concoctions—soap. He's presently working out formulations and adaptable processes for concrete and masonry. And there's no end in sight.

"The same is true for Anton and the Noveyaks. They've done an amazing amount of work to get the fields and gardens going. There was a horrible setback with the storm, with so much swept away, but they had wisely contoured the plantings so the damage was minimized. Anyway their's will also be a work in progress ... and one without end.

"It's really like that for all of us ... just in different ways. And we've all come to realize and accept it.

"Whew," Bruno said, catching his breath. "As you can tell, I'm near to being obsessed with what I see before us. Thanks for letting me unload. But I didn't mean to hog all your time."

"Not at all," John said. "This is all more than interesting. I'm impressed."

"Me too," Gary added. "But when do we get to see your design for Emerald City?"

"When I get it all worked out, you'll be the first to know," Bruno said with a grin. "But for now, why don't you take John and his friends down and show them the place. I'll stay here, and when the girls clang for dinner, I'll come get you."

With that Gary led them out of the chamber into the stairwell, which led down to the real workings of the complex. There he guided them past the lounge, then the dormitory with its squeezed array of cots, the locker room, the library and so forth, adding comments about each, but moving along to provide only an overview.

"We can come back later, take a better look and answer any questions you might have; but for now, there are things in particular I want you to see."

When they passed the orientation chamber with its bordering area of casket-like cocoons, however, John said "Whoa ... Jim Wilson; he didn't make it. What did you do with him?"

"He's still here. We left him in his cocoon and reset the mechanism to freezing. The cocoon's in the back corner."

"Can we see him?"

"Sure."

Gary led them back to the one he'd pointed to, undid the series of catches, and then slowly opened the heavily insulated cover. A light fog puffed out as the seal cracked, dissipating as the door swung back. Pin-drop silence followed, for James Delaney Wilson appeared as if he were asleep ... the only hint to the contrary being the radiating coolness.

The *Atjahahni* crowded in to see all there was to see, one by one touching hair and skin and fabrics ... the jump suit being of special interest. When they'd taken in all they could, they turned to John with a questioning look. But John was deep in thought and didn't pick up on it. He was trying to recall the person without the benefit of a voice or an expression of personality or an action that would bring the person to life. Finally he returned the gazes. "The man you're looking at lived eight thousand years ago. I know the numbers mean little to you, but that time goes back to what you call "the time of the giants". I didn't know him very well, except that he was a good man, a man that would have worked hard for the benefit of everyone, just as those you've met today. You'll also notice that he's about the same age as Gary and the others, which was also my age at the time we first met."

"We didn't know how best to handle this," Gary said. "So we just sealed him back."

"What you've done is fine. You're all going to age now, just as I have. In the future, Jim, being preserved this way, will not only be a memorial, but also a reminder of what we used to be.

"By the way, I sense some of the other cocoons are operating. The vibrations? What's happening?"

"Oh that. Well, you probably noticed that some of the crop has been harvested. You may also have noticed we have very little refrigerator space. These cocoons were an opportunity we couldn't resist."

John walked back down the row, stopping at the two in the front corner nearest the orientation chamber. "These were ours, weren't they?"

"Yes. We were one and two."

He laid his hands on both covers. "Gary, yours is operating, but mine isn't?"

"Go ahead and open mine."

John did, undoing the few latches still engaged and swinging the cover over. The soft padding designed to cushion a body had been removed down to the first layer of insulation. The increased volume was packed full.

"Potatoes," he muttered.

"Is that okay?" Gary asked.

John closed the cover and reset the latches. "But you aren't using mine?"

"We may later. It's up to you."

John nodded and went over to his, putting his hands on top. After closing his eyes for a moment, he patted it, turned and walked away.

Walking through the orientation chamber, Gary said, "This is the part you missed. There isn't time now, but maybe tomorrow we can put on the program designed for you. That might finally tie everything together. But not now. Let's move on to the back door … there are things just outside it I want you to see."

Before they got there, however, there was a call relayed through the complex, "Chow's on," which brought the tour to an end.

It was a few hours after dark before everyone, squeaky clean and fed, were on hand to crowd into the lounge. The girls from the cookhouse were last, making for a real cozy group, because even in normal times the space would be filled, and now there were four more. And normally the hour would be late, because the day started early and included a day of hard labor. But tonight no one was tired enough to leave. Instead there was a buzz that seemed as if it would go on indefinitely. It didn't, however. Despite the excitement of a day that would always be remembered, conversations slowly dwindled, as if in anticipation …

Until Anton said, "Will someone please call this damned meeting to order?"

35

John

Nothing happened. Gary looked at John to lead ... he'd been chosen as the first to be brought back; but John shrugged, and by gesture, indicated for Gary to take charge. It was comical. Then in a move in keeping with the light-hearted nature of the group, someone started a chant ... "John, John, John" ... beginning to sway and clap. Others picked up the spirit and the chants got louder ... *"John! John! John!"* ... everyone wanting to hear more of what had to be a great adventure, increasing the volume until they were shouting ... **"John! John! John! John!"**

Annie was at John's side, grinning and clapping to the cadence along with the rest. She looked up at John and then at the others, but then snapped back. John wasn't enjoying this at all. His body had gone from relaxed to tense, his face had contorted into a snarl, his eyes were flashing and he looked like he was about to explode to his feet.

Not knowing what to do she grabbed him and held on.

Gary saw the transformation too, but didn't have a clue. Most others, however, never saw it ... absorbed as they were in their antics.

Suddenly Dlahni jumped to his feet and extended his arms ... **"Stop! ... Stop! ..."**

The group's momentum sputtered to a halt, followed by mumbles, wide eyes shifting about, shaking heads, whispers … "What the hell? *Jeez!* Did I miss something?"

When the room calmed down, John, who'd stiffened and was half way off the floor, deflated, his face rippling with conflicting emotions. His hands went to his head and he slumped back, while Annie struggled to hold back tears and soothe a hurt she didn't understand.

The silence lasted for more than a few moments … long, long uncomfortable moments. Then Dlahni, awkwardly in the spotlight and fumbling with his clothes, which was a way of collecting his thoughts, finally spoke.

"Let me tell you a story," he began, speaking away from what had just happened. "A story about a man who quieted a storm; a man who talked to the Great Spirit, and, in the doing was bathed in lightning before all the nations … bathed by the Great Spirit to prove he was the chosen one; the man chosen to lead all of them in peace and brotherhood.

"What I'm telling you really happened, and happened only a short time ago during the day of the great storm, which all of you remember. There's much more to be told about that event, but not right now, for the story really begins twenty years before. Nyaho can better tell you about that."

Being called without warning surprised Nyaho, who looked at Dlahni as he sat down with one of those thanks-a-lot expressions. But then after thinking about how the meeting had started off in such a bad way, he thought of how it should be started. So he stood and worked his way to the front from the corner where he'd settled. *Let's see now … in the beginning …*

"It was the middle of summer. I was mending a casting net by the shore when I heard hunters returning, which in this case was unusual because of the noise they were making. Listening from outside the Council House along with half the village, I heard the men explain they'd seen a large fire on a mountain top many days away. It was the same mountain John pointed to earlier today. In our society, fires like this, fires that can be seen, are not made … it's a brazen, threatening act. The fact of it caused a dilemma because the Council didn't know what to do. They could only conclude they needed more information. Because I was known as a good tracker, I was honored and sent to gather that information—find who was doing such a thing, and report back.

"Days later I found the answer—the fire was set by a single man, and the man was John. While moving to a nearby bush to get a better look, I made a noise which got his attention. Already in a bad mood, it seemed, and angered by the disturbance, he charged into that bush and knocked me flat, breaking my shoulder.

"We've been good friends ever since."

Even John looked up and smiled with that.

"When John introduced us a while back, he made reference to giants. You might have taken that as only a figure of speech. In our land, however, and in our culture, "giant" has a special meaning.

"We are a small people, small in size, that is. I don't know why for sure, but John tells me it's because of what we eat. We don't eat much, that's true, mainly because we frequently don't have much to eat. We hunt, we fish and we plant gardens. But often as not our meal for the day is what we find in the forest while hunting or fishing. This means winters can be difficult. And although we plan for this time and store as much food as we can, by late winter those stores often run out, resulting, particularly in the past, with starvations.

"John told you earlier today, that death in our society is a constant companion. That's also true, and because it is, the memory of the dead and their spirits are greatly honored. In a special yearly ceremony, we recycle bodies of the departed into the world about us, then address the spirits who have risen to the stars. We remember, never forgetting, who the people were and what they meant to us. We remember first those who died since the last ceremony, then those in the year before that, and before that year after year past the time of the great snows, to the time when we roamed the land, all the way to the giants who ruled. The four of you who came to visit were witness to this.

"Giants in our memory were not good people. They were large and strong; they had tall buildings; they had great machines that could fly; they had great powers and they ruled us. They ruled us for only a short time, then deserted us, making us fend for ourselves. They no longer shared food or gave us comfort; and if they saw us, they chased us away. They were bad. Since that time we've survived on our own and grown strong, but we've lived with the fear they would return again to rule and punish us.

"When I first saw John I was terrified. I was convinced he was a giant. He was the tallest man I'd ever seen and had the appearance of a monster. His hair and beard were long; his clothes were an unsightly combination of furs and skins poorly sewn together. He had the look of someone who would eat people.

"But he didn't eat me; and he wasn't a monster. Although his appearance was a mess, his voice was soft and his eyes were kind. He fixed my broken shoulder and fed me.

"I took him to where Dlahni was waiting and the three of us became friends. Then we took him to our nation, where first impressions were the same as ours had been—most thinking he was a giant and fearing him, even though he continued to be gentle and friendly.

"There were attempts on his life at first because of these fears, so we had to watch over him.

"Things were difficult then because we didn't understand each other. With what little understanding we could manage, mostly through hand signals and expressions, we soon realized that John was confused, not knowing where he'd come from or why he was here.

"Then a strange thing happened. John saw a thin sliver of a girl who reminded him of someone, a girl who brought back memories that, rather than helping, confused him more. We called the girl Nshwanji," pronouncing the name in the *Atjahahni* fashion which wasn't pleasant to English accustomed ears, "because she reminded us of the thin leaves of a spindly tree that tends to grow near the water. She wasn't *Atjahahni*, however, she was a girl from another nation far to the north who'd been captured a few years before. The man who captured her was Braga, a man later recognized as our greatest warrior and made a chieftain.

"John became fascinated with the girl and this led to a problem. He felt there was a certain significance to her, eventually coming to the conclusion that *his* god had ordained that they be together. That in itself wasn't the problem; but news in the village travels fast, and Braga, who claimed rights to the girl, heard of it. Sensing an opportunity to destroy John once and for all, because he continued to see John as a giant and a threat to his ambition, Braga arranged a situation that forced John into a fight—a fight whose outcome for John would be either disablement, disgrace or death.

"The fight was hard and brutal, a fight made more difficult because John didn't *like* to fight, and the person he was fighting was a fearless and cruel monster of a man. So it started poorly, with John taking a beating and almost losing. But somehow, after a frenzied time of kick and punch and grab and tumble with dust churning and blood flowing, he made a move that caught everyone by surprise ... and won. And, because he had won, he now had a wife—a wife he renamed Willow. The sound "Nshwanji" was unpleasant to him."

John had relaxed by now and nodded approvingly to the floor as Nyaho spoke, even though Nyaho told the story with illuminating details he wouldn't have mentioned. He looked at Annie and flashed the hint of a smile, which she returned with a sigh, bumping heads.

"If life hadn't been complicated and confusing and challenging enough to that point, it then became so, for John was not prepared. With winter already upon them, they were forced to move into a pitiful shelter, where they spent the first winter on the verge of freezing as well as starving. Then came four children in three years— first Sarah, then the twins Ruth and Naomi, and then Matthew."

There was a whisper in the corner that drew a few snickers. But then it went quiet, and Nyaho went on.

"None of you have children, so you don't know how impossible their situation was. I know. I have had children, and like with most families, have watched some of them die before they became adults.

"But this didn't happen in their lodge, which by the way, John had improved from the crude shelter to the largest in the village, using supports none of us had seen before. Their lodge and compound became like a beehive of activity as they struggled with surviving. Only it became more than that. It became of such interest that it drew in the friends of the children ... and others as well. John was always working on something which was new and unusual to the men. So for many of them, a day wouldn't be complete until they'd passed by to see what was happening.

"Without any intent to do so, this energy and activity introduced ideas that began to change our nation. One was language.

"John had made a rule to Willow that only his language be spoken in their compound, while *Atjahahni* would be spoken outside. This was so each of them could learn each other's language. With the children, he kept that rule for the same reason, but in so doing, with all the activity, *Atjahahni* children, whose minds like children's minds everywhere are quick to learn, were soon able to speak as well. Then there were the many adults who followed, not wanting to be left behind in something increasing numbers were doing."

When Nyaho hesitated to collect thoughts on where to go next, Da-hash-to leaned over and whispered, *"Tell about the Craft Fairs,"* in *Atjahahni*.

Nyaho nodded. then …

"When John, Dlahni, Da-hash-to and I came here, along with your four, we traveled most of the way by canoe. Twenty years ago that trip wouldn't have been possible. Twenty years ago, we feared the water and only went onto it in safe, slow, rounded, watercraft, staying close to shore for short distances.

"The *Atjahahni* feared many things back then. I've told you about giants, whom we'd never seen but which were a part of our thinking. In addition, we had a great fear of water. Even though the lake provided us with food and drink, we felt it was also lying in wait to drown anyone foolish enough to get careless.

"We feared the gods who sent thunder and lightning, and feared the spirits of the wind that rustled the trees and dropped its rains in summer and snows in winter and made sounds in the night all year round. We loved the forest and plants that formed a magical garden, but feared the bear that scavenged and lion that crept and wolves that hunted and snakes that bit.

"But then John came along and he's not afraid of these things, or at least considers them in a different way. Incredibly to us, he's not at all afraid of water and dives in it like a water eagle and swims like an otter. He makes a canoe so he can go out into it, even across the lake or to its islands or to distances in each direction. He scares us half to death with some of his antics, but somehow we survive.

"Then he teaches his Sarah, an infant at the time, to swim, and we are taught that while the water must be respected, it need not be feared. A year later, all of the children and most of the adults in the village know how to swim as well. The changes this made are hard to imagine."

Da-hash-to whispered again, "*The Crafts Fair*," Dlahni almost falling over suppressing a laugh.

"Da-hash-to keeps reminding me about an event that has become a yearly activity as anticipated and valued as our ceremony of remembrances. The idea for it came after a series of meeting in which the four of us were trying to understand each other and our relationship to the Great Spirit. As we were about to depart Da-hash-to asked John what could be done to help the nation advance itself. He'd noticed John was often doing things in a different way than the *Atjahahni*, and at times in a clearly better way. So he asked. John answered by suggesting an annual Crafts Fair. The concept and the details weren't understood at first, but having asked the question, and gotten an answer, we went ahead, with a bumbling first effort still having surprising results. The main achievements were in the excitement it created, and in the desire to make improvements to what had been done before.

"The event has been held every year since then, with significant advances being made in many skills, and in pottery in particular. In that regard ... Dlahni, this is as good a time as any."

With that, Dlahni got up and left, returning with a lumpy leather dufflebag that had been placed out of sight in the next room.

Nyaho continued, "Space was limited in our canoes, and there was much to carry through the woods, but we wanted at least to share a special gift for your ladies. It's something that's come to symbolize an offering of peace which we extend to all our friends."

With that he unwrapped six pieces—blue, ceramic bowls decorated with leaves and berries circling the bottom, and white sculpted doves around the top.

"*It's beautiful!*" Gasped Mona, who was closest, as Nyaho handed the first bowl to her. Then in turn similar expressions were made and the room was abuzz for a few minutes before settling down.

"I was describing improvements the Fair was making. But arts and crafts weren't the only changes taking place. When Gary and

Roland and Annie and Judy came to us, they saw several others. Most noticeable was the Home Guard, which is an organization to put the village into a structure for the purpose of defending itself if attacked. An attack has never happened, but the discovery of a small party from the nation to the east spying on us was disturbing, especially when we realized there wasn't a plan for responding to any kind of emergency. John solved our problem and organized what you saw."

"Oh yes ... do we ever remember that," Gary said. "When we came into the clear, we found ourselves face-to-face with a row of men, standing behind shields, and stretching as far as we could see in each direction. I left a good part of me on the trail that very moment."

"Well, it was pretty scary," Judy said as the reaction to Gary's comment died down. "But that wasn't all. We thought the village consisted of a bunch of primitive huts, but then we spotted a large building a ways off the trail, a building uniquely built into a piled-up jumble of oddly shaped boulders forming the west end. The building was a fairly sophisticated intersection of A-frames constructed of long, straight trunks. It and its well-crafted decorative panels and appointments, was very impressive. Bruno, you'd have loved it."

"This, I found out later, was John's doing," Gary added, then turning to John, "That must have been quite a project without tools like we have. How'd you manage it?"

John grumbled and shrugged, "There's been enough talk about what I've been doing. My guess is you're all getting pretty tired of it."

"Are you nuts?" Devon said, with everyone else on the verge of saying something similar. "We're anxious to hear it all ... every little itty bitty detail."

"Yes and amen," Rodney added. "We don't know squat about what's past that ridge you came over ... so keep talking, we're all ears."

"Hear, hear ..."

John sighed ... paused to think.

"A project like that doesn't just happen, there are things that invariably occur in advance that set the stage for it.

"Probably the first of them was the Crafts Fair, which became so popular, and promoted so many interests. It also introduced things that were new, like swimming and soccer, both of which came out of the first one.

"The Home Guard came next. As part of this there were games, contests and races ... things like that. With these activities, the *Atjahahni* began to think more as a nation then just individuals or families."

"There's something more," Nyaho interrupted to say. "The *Atjahahni*, at least before John, were very uncomplicated in certain ways. We recognized that there were days ... and that there were numbers of days called moons ... and, that there were seasons; but other than that, time wasn't measured. But John, with Willow and his family, were different. We noted that every so often, on certain days at seemingly regular intervals, he would take a break from the work schedule he maintained, and take a walk with his family. The walking led to relaxing in a certain common area and socializing with anyone who came along. Teas and treats were added, and before long more and more became drawn into the habit. Discussions naturally happened in addition to socializing."

"Sundays!" Gary said. "So *that's* how Sunday's got started. I'll be damned." Then laughing, "John, tell us how you figured out which day was Sunday."

When John hesitated and just smiled, looking a little sheepish, Gary went on with, "He shot an arrow in the air!"

More details about this followed and it was a while before the conversation got back on course.

"So that led to building the church," Bruno said more as a question than a statement.

"Not exactly," John answered, "but as the weekly impromptu sessions began to take form, there came a time, with the help of a few rains, that we realized the need for a shelter ... something big.

"However, we still weren't there.

"Then one day while a group of kids were playing kickball, a girl fell into a hole, really a fairly large depression—just one of the many defects in the largest area youngsters had as a playground. Anyway a strange thing happened. Without saying anything to anyone, she started picking up rocks and dropping them in as if to fill this hole.

Dlahni here had seen her fall and run over to see if she was all right; then he too started dropping rocks. With hardly a word spoken, and without an organization, people became drawn in, and, with every tool they could bring, were not only filling the hole, but also tackling every other feature that kept the site from being useful. Before it was over the whole village was involved, and in two days a large open area, which from that day on was called the Commons, came into being."

"Wow, that's not strange, that's spooky. So then you built the church?"

John waved him off. "Not yet; but yes it *is* spooky and it gets worse. You see, I'd been thinking about a large building and wrestling with several problems, like what to build and where to build and how to build. Well, for what to build, I'd been thinking. I'd been sketching with a stick in a level bed of sand ... We don't have computers or drawing boards or rolls of bumwad, you understand. Anyway, when ideas started to gel I collected sticks and began to experiment with models, much like you're doing with the master plan for Olympia.

"Then came the problem with where, and there it gets really spooky, so to speak. I'd looked all over the area and was at a loss. Then early one morning, bringing my fire back to life, I heard sounds from above in addition to the songbirds that usually chirped away at daybreak. Cooing sounds. I looked up to see two white doves that had never been *there* before. They were, however, the same ones I'd flushed while climbing that "piled-up jumble of oddly shaped boulders" as Judy called them."

"*Ohmygod*," Annie said. "That's why there are two carved white doves on the branch growing inside, isn't it?"

John nodded.

"By the way, that pile of rocks is called *Tschtaha-tata*, which means something like "spirits toy-box". Kids for generations grew up playing games around there.

"Anyway, now I had a design and a place, and the incident on the Commons gave me the how. That incident, which welded the spirit of the community to common causes, together with the organization created for the Home Guard, give me what was needed. The basic shell took two years, but since then, mostly from the women, decorations and panels have been added to make it what it is today."

"So now the spirits toy-box is a church," Bruno said.

"Well not exactly. It's some of that, but more of a community center.

"John, your father was a minister, a very well-known one ... Have you taken a call to convert the *Atjahahni?*"

"Religion's something we usually don't talk about, but there will come a time when we must. Now to answer your question, we have discussed our beliefs, but not in an evangelical manner.

"The *Atjahahni*, particularly Nyaho here, are concerned about all of us and how we might change them. As has been mentioned, there have been many changes in the last twenty years because of what I was doing. All of these have been for the good ... I think. But now Gary and Roland and Annie and Judy have visited, and although they made it a point to show very little, what they did show was shocking. It was more than that. They saw a much taller group, with clothes and weapons that, no matter how downplayed, made them feel inferior. They also found out there were more "giants" to the south and that there were more mysteries to be revealed.

"It's natural their old fears of "giants" were awakened.

"Unfortunately, in a way their feelings and fears are founded. In addition to being taller, we, the chosen representatives of the twenty-first century, have been privileged to receive an education, and with it the knowledge and accomplishment of thousands of years. They, on the other hand, have been exposed to and learned primarily those basic skills that allowed them to survive.

"That's an unfair comparison and denigrating, however, for this simple reason. As each of the *Atjahahni* came into this world through the miracle of birth, they came in with the same sensitivities and personalities and potential for good and evil and accomplishment as any of us.

"As you get to know them, you will find all of these as delightful as any you've encountered, and with the development of potential at surprisingly high levels in certain areas.

"And that brings us back to religion.

"The *Atjahahni* have a religion, partly shaped by superstition, but more rooted in the belief there is not only a Great Spirit to revere, there are also spirits of all living creatures with which they have a relationship. The Spirit Man when I first came to the *Atjahahni*, a man who died several years ago, maintained that the spirits talked to him. I happen to believe he was telling the truth. Anyway, with these beliefs they feel they must live in harmony with all creatures, and their spirits, as well as with each other.

"To do this they give thanks to the plants and animals as they are being used, then in return, when they die, return their bodies to nature … recycling, if you will. Remember what Dlahni said earlier?

"As you can tell, during the years spent with them, I've developed a deep respect for them both individually and as a culture. As we get into our mission, which is as big a challenge as ever faced, I think their example and input will be valuable. As a religion, when Nyaho expressed his concern for the future, I told him we were not of a common faith, so had no particular banner to force onto the *Atjahahni* or anyone else.

"Now, since religion is on the table, and if you don't mind, what religions are we? Let's go round the room and find out.

"I'm Lutheran … sorta."
"Methodist."
"Catholic."
"Catholic."
"Buddhist."
"Baptist."
"Jewish."
"Lutheran."
"Atheist."
"Deist."
"Muslim."
"Jewish."
"Mormon."
"Methodist."
"Baptist."

John laughed, "Damn, I was only making a guess about that, but obviously, there's more diversity here than I'd imagined.

"Okay, Nyaho … does that make you feel any better?"

Nyaho smiled back. "I really don't know what all those answers mean, but I get the point."

Da-hash-to spoke, this time loud enough to carry, *"Nyaho, this is very interesting, but most of these things we already know. The big questions for us are… Where did they come from? And, why are they here?"*

Nyaho nodded, then repeated the questions.

"John has explained some of this to me, so I have an idea. But there is still a void in understanding. That came to the surface when Gary and Roland and Annie and Judy came to visit. They were as friendly and nice as anyone could be, and yet I felt intimidated. Now we are here and there's the rest of you. And all of you walk around acting as if there's nothing out of the ordinary, yet everything we see is astounding.

"We pass along a field and a monster jumps up and threatens to destroy us. While we almost come out of our skins, you laugh and call it Homer, a toy. We have toys but nothing like this Homer.

"We pass a building and you say it's a simple, temporary shack. But it's sturdier than anything we've been able to build. Even *Tschtaha-tata* with its bold log framing is primarily enclosed by sticks and thatching.

"Then there's another building and in it some of you are at work. And there are sounds we've never heard before. We thought the machete was unbelievable, but now we see other tools that slice wood like it's soft mud. Can you imagine how long it would take us to split a log and smoothen its surfaces?

"We walk through huge doors, "steel" you say, into the mountain where even greater amazements greet us at every turn. You walk by without acknowledging them, while we bumble along wide-eyed and gaping. Do you have any idea how incredible to us a large, flat surface is? Some are of stone, some of wood, some of materials we can't begin to define, like the hard surfaces we could see through, or the hard surfaces where we see ourselves looking back.

"Gary takes us past wonder after wonder without comment, except to say there are more interesting things to see and tell about but not now, there isn't time. If we can't fathom what is ordinary, how can we possibly understand what is amazing to you.

"This room is an example. I've heard it described as stark or plain. Yet I see beautiful images on the wall. They are as if you've taken what has been seen by our eyes, frozen the images in the air, and somehow peeled them off to bring here. How do you do that?

"Then there are the cocoons and a man called James Delany Wilson. All of that, we are told, ties to a time long, long ago, and there's a thread of understanding with that. But where is or was that world? What was it like? If it was so amazing as has been hinted, why can't we see and touch it? And where are the people? We have been told they were as many as the stars.

"This leads to the larger question Da-hash-to asked. If you are the ones chosen from that time, what were you chosen to do? Why are you here?"

John nodded … "Good questions, but I'm not the one to answer, as there are parts I need to catch up with myself. Gary?"

"Yes, good questions," Gary repeated, returning to the front. "Let's see now … What was our world like?

"You've heard about tall buildings and flying machines and things like that, and they're all true … the world thousands of years ago was truly amazing. Now that we've been in this one for six months, that world in our memories has become even more so. You mentioned the pictures on the wall … there were also pictures where what was shown moved as if you were watching what was happening. There were small hand-held devices that could be used to talk to someone on the other side of that ridge we crossed, or even on the other side of the world. We could ask it questions and it would give us answers. Don't ask me how it was able to do this, because I don't know, much of this was astounding to us as well. The trip from your village to here took several days in a combination of canoeing and hiking. In our world, we would have gotten into a machine, driven on a road at speeds more than fifty times as fast as you can walk in the woods, and reached here in the time that passes from sun-up to noon. That may not be clear because you don't know what a machine is, what a road is, or what fifty times means."

"Isn't a road a wide, black pathway like what you found at Pangaea," Dlahni asked, directing the question at John.

John nodded.

"Okay, good," Gary said, "at least we have that much. But there's more that's hard to describe in terms you understand. Bruno, Rodney, have you or anyone else gotten a good grasp on what's in the library? Do we have any videos that would give a good, comprehensive picture of the world I'm trying to describe?"

"Without a doubt," Bruno said, "I've only scratched the surface with what I've been doing, but there's so much in there it's boggling. Give me an hour in the morning, and I think I can set up a power-point that'll blow their minds."

"Good, let's do that.

"Now, the next question ... where did the people go. That's an easy question to answer, but a hard one to accept. A short time before we were put into the cocoons you saw, there were over seven billion people on earth; and to say they were as many as the stars is an exaggeration, but it's a lot. And it may have been too many. There was a great deal being done that was good and impressive, like the things I've tried to describe, but there were also bad things. Plants and animals were being destroyed, many becoming extinct; the world's natural resources were being plundered; wastes and poisons were accumulating; the climate was being affected; and political and civil strife was putting nations on the verge of one calamity after another."

"It was a time of exhilarating promise and disturbing concern."

"Other living creatures were being destroyed?" Nyaho asked

"Yes, their numbers were being reduced at an increasing rate as the number of people increased."

Gary stopped with that, looking to see if there were more questions ... and there were.

"But the people disappeared."

"Well, yes in a way. A plague somehow developed on a remote tropical island. It was contained for a while, but then it broke out, spread around the world and killed everyone."

"Everyone?"

"Everyone ... everyone, that is, but very young children."

"So who are we … the *Atjahahni?* We were not killed."

"We don't know for sure, but we think you're descendants of the children who survived."

"But you survived too … All of you here were chosen, then put in the cocoons we saw so you could survive."

"Yes."

"And what were you chosen to do?"

"We were chosen to take the best of what mankind had accomplished by the twenty-first century, and use it to develop a civilization that integrated all of the living in a peaceful and sustaining way."

With that the Atjahahni looked at each other and mumbled in private conversation, eventually nodding in concert and turning back. But there were no more questions.

Gary sighed, then said, "Another question might have been "what has been accomplished on our mission to this point?" And to this, I'd have to answer, "not much", since we've been so busy just getting established. There's a great deal to be discussed about that mission, but I'd suggest not now. The hour is late, and as an emcee once said … *"There's one thing a speaker should remember for sure, is that the mind can absorb only what the seat can endure".*

"So let's call it a night. We've already made plans for tomorrow morning; we can continue after that."

"Before we split, there's some unfinished business," Rodney said.

"Rod, it's pretty late, can't this wait until tomorrow?'

"I'm just as tired as the rest of you; but something happened when we first got together. We started off having what we thought was fun, and instead stepped into something. Whatever the issue is, it's obviously sensitive, but I don't think I'm alone in wanting to understand."

Quiet, then nodding heads … "Me too,"

"Me too."

Gary blinked … He had an inkling about this but not enough to speak out. He looked at John, but he was no help, just looking down.

In the corner against the wall where the *Atjahahni* were seated, Da-hash-to looked at Dlahni and nodded.

A pin drop could be heard as Dlahni rose and walked the few steps to where Gary had vacated. He normally preferred for Nyaho to do the talking and had succeeded so far, but now it was his turn and one he couldn't avoid.

Now he had to collect his thoughts again … then …

"Nyaho told you earlier about the family and the children, but he only referred to the first few years. He told you that Sarah was the first to swim, and what happened after that in the village.

"But other children followed in quick order after Sarah, and the stories within the family only get more interesting. The twins, as soon as they could walk, became competitive to do the things Sarah was doing, starting a friendly but passionate rivalry that never stopped. It pushed them to better and better performances, and dragged friends from the village in as well. This involved everything children are prone to do, and extended from swimming into running and jumping and archery and anything that could be contested.

"Annie and Judy, you got to know the girls pretty well in the short time you spent, and from what I can gather, became friends. But I'm sure you recognized, besides being charming and friendly, how competitive they were.

"Well, poor Matthew was the youngest, and although he picked up the spirit of his sisters, he was pummeled and beaten on a regular basis. A regular basis, that is, until at roughly age twelve, he grew past them in every way. From there on he competed with boys, the older ones, and in doing so became a wonder. Faster and faster and farther and farther became the norm. I don't know by what means physical greatness is measured, and I don't know how fast he ran or swam; but in races he would win by so much that only the margin could be measured. But we do know how far he pitched the stone, and shot the arrow, and threw the lance. His performances were awesome, but that wasn't the best part. Monitored closely by John, he developed as a person so that he was humble with his accomplishments, considerate of his peers, and courteous to his elders. He excelled most at being a friend.

"I can say these things with certainty, because as families, we were very close. He was like a son to me.

"When the children reached maturity, the time coincided with efforts to organize the Gathering, the meeting of all the nations. This was one of John's objectives, something he felt he was ordained to do, in the way of insuring the nations would exist together in peace and brotherhood. All the children participated in this, which included substantial preparation and extensive travel and continual danger.

"The work, massive in its number of details, succeeded, and the four nations met on a carefully selected, centrally located ground which became known as Pangaea.

"The nations had no sooner arrived, however, when the storm hit. As you know, it was awful … and worse for us because we were in the open. That, however, would have been survived without incident, except for Braga. Braga had spent a year with the *Bjarla-shito*, the nation from the west. He was helping them in preparations for the Gathering, but as we have since come to know, he was also laying seeds of uncertainty against John, a man he accused of being a giant and capable of great harm.

"When the storm struck, the subtle influences, with expert prompting, turned a number of minds away from the rational into superstitious insanity. As we watched, hardly able to believe what was happening, emotions exploded in portions of all three other nations until an armed mob was formed. The mob felt the *Atjahahni*, particularly John, were responsible, and when emotions boiled over, they chanted "**John! John! John!**" Just like you did earlier, and attacked.

"You've heard the result—that Da-hash-to was trampled, Nyaho's ribs were broken, and many were killed and injured. What you haven't heard is that Matthew, with his magnificent promise of greatness, stepped forward to save his father, and was the first one killed."

36

Understandings

"Bruno, you awake?" Abram whispered.

"Yes, dammit ... can't sleep."

"Thought so. Could hear you tossing."

"You don't have to be quiet on my account," Rodney said, "I'm awake too. This day has been something else, hasn't it?"

Bruno threw back the cover a bit and rolled over on his elbow. He shook his head as a sign of agreement, then realized that no one could see. "Anyone bothered if I light the lantern?"

"Not at all," Abram said swinging out to sit, foot-feeling for his clogs. "I've got to step out anyway. Think I'll stoke the fire and heat some water. Tea anyone?"

"Sounds good.

"Me too."

A short time later they were each bundled in some manner, cradling cups and sipping.

"I'd rather have some schnapps to go with this."

"You're lucky the leaves aren't hemlock."

"Oops."

"John's back," Bruno said to start what was on everyone's mind, "It's so incredible I can't get over it. We all hoped he was alive, but I don't think we ever expected it ... or, if he was alive, to find him. It's like winning the lottery."

"I agree ... and after twenty years. You were right about that one," Abram added.

"It just made sense, that's all," Bruno said, shrugging it off. "Did you hear Gary's account of when he and John came together?"

"Yes ... "Mr. Anderson, I presume" ... unbelievable. I guess he thought he was like Owen Stanley on the hunt."

"He was pretty close."

Bruno got up and shuffled to the front, opening the flap, "I wonder if they're sleeping in the other tent."

"I hope so," Rodney said. "Anton works so damn hard. I know he was bushed tonight ... I mean he always is. He stayed to the end because like everyone else, he didn't want to miss anything; but when Gary said that's it for the night, he split."

Bruno returned, moved cushions and blankets around to form a comfortable spot on his cot and wiggled in, "It's just so incredible. I know, I know, I keep saying that ... but it is. Twenty years, and what we heard tonight is just the tip of it all. What an experience."

"Yes, but that "Gathering" back in August had to be awful," Abram said. "Imagine losing a son, and then running in to all of us. It's no wonder John's on an emotional roller coaster."

"It goes deeper than that."

"What do you mean?"

"Do any of you know what happened to Willow?"

"No ... not much was said about her after the kids were mentioned."

"Exactly. That seemed strange to me too, so I asked Judy about it."

"Is that while all that snuggling was going on?"

Bruno hesitated, trying to contain a smile, then, "Judy and Annie spent a lot of time with the daughters, and the lack of mention of Willow tonight gave the wrong impression ... as if she'd been insignificant. The truth is that while John was busy with all he was doing for years and years, Willow was the one doing most things with the kids. Willow was quite a runner ... that's what attracted John to her in the first place ... and she was also competitive. So when things got started in the village—swimming and Home Guard and stuff like that—she became heavily involved. As the kids grew, she brought them into whatever was going on. With the Home Guard, as it was being organized, John felt women could play a vital part, especially as archers. So guess who became the best of them, and eventually the leader."

"Obviously the answer is Willow."

"Yes ... was."

"Well, I figured that by all the omissions. What happened?"

"A bear. Seems about six years ago while berry picking, the daughters ran into a large one. They screamed and ran but Naomi fell and was about to be pounced on when Willow arrived in time to dive between them."

"Oh no!"

"Yes, killed her in an instant," Bruno said, rubbing scars that were still new enough to be red and sensitive, "As Daniel Boone once said ... *"the woods are so wild and horrid, that it's impossible to behold them without terror"*.

"Judy said the girls broke into tears when they told about it, especially Naomi."

"That couldn't have been easy on Annie either. How did she take it? Abram asked, "Any comment?"

"She handled it fine on the surface, but Judy said that deep down Annie was torn every which way. Before getting to the village she'd naturally been concerned about whether John was alive or not. Along with that, however, she couldn't ignore the fact that if he were alive, he probably had a wife and family? The possibility *had* to be great. If so then, what would be *her* place?

"Then on the day they came to the village, she finds he's alive, and that's exhilarating; but then she meets Ruth, his daughter, and learns of the family, and it's next to her worst fear come true. Then she hears of Matthew's death and she becomes wrapped in the anguish Ruth feels, and surely what John feels ... all of which awakens some of what she had experienced in her own life. Then upon getting to know Ruth better, Annie learns of Willow's death, which, although horrible and tragic adding to the sorrow, also brings on feelings of guilt. And I don't think I have to explain that one.

"Finally there was the wait for John with anxieties growing like "Would he remember?" "Would she only be a complication at a time when he didn't want it?" "Would he still have any affection for her after all this time?"

"All of this was far worse for Annie than the fear of death they contended with when they first approached the village. Remember Nyaho telling about the Home Guard, and then Gary saying he'd crapped when he first saw the squads lined up like they were?"

"Yes."

"Well, it was Annie who stepped out to stand before the squads and ask to speak to the leaders. I mean … she was a throw away from being skewered … that took guts."

Abram shook his head, "I'm not surprised. I worked with her a lot back at school and know her pretty well. She's taken some hard knocks in her day, but she hangs in there. She's tough. But talk about an emotional roller coaster. Both of them have been on one."

"That's for sure. Fortunately it's looking as good as could be hoped at this point."

"Yeh."

"To change the subject, what do you two think of John's *Atjahahni* friends?"

"*Ohmygod*," Bruno answered. "Can you believe I called them Indians?"

"Nice going."

"Well, it *was* stupid. Their clothes—leathers and furs and organic weavings and all—didn't really mask the fact their hair and eyes and facial features aren't Indian at all. I should have seen that … Dumb, dumb."

Abram chuckled, "No problem … they didn't know what you were talking about, and then thought it was funny when told. I asked the question because I was surprised at how well they spoke. Da-hash-to doesn't speak English, but he evidently understands everything."

"I was surprised too. They threw in a bunch of *Atjahahni* words along the way, but that didn't seem to affect the flow of thoughts."

"Well, let's talk about that. You'd think there'd be an accent of some kind. I mean, the languages are so different."

"I hear it was because of John again."

"How so?"

"Well, Gary told me that when John started to learn *Atjahahni*, he was determined to learn it correctly, so that he sounded just like them. He felt he'd always be an outsider unless he did. When it came to teaching Willow English, she insisted on the same standard; and so that passed on to the children and eventually everyone else."

"That's amazing ... and it sure worked."

Abram leaned forward, "I was fascinated by several things they said. That yearly ceremony must be something, going all night as it does. What was Judy's impression of that?"

"She said it was beautiful. They danced and danced; at times she felt close to something but never quite got there. Anyway she was touched."

"The whole spirit thing makes you wonder. Is it uncivilized, ignorant superstition, or remarkable sensitivity?"

Rodney snorted. "Oh boy, I can see it now. I'm going to be penned up in the lab working the real world, while all about are dances and incantations."

"You don't believe in much of anything, do you?"

"It's not that bad. I'm aware with what unbelievable performances spirit and belief have inspired; I just tend to approach facts from scientific points of view. I *am* impressed with the *Atjahahni*, however. I think they're reacting well to what has to be ... like you say, unbelievable."

"They mentioned how amazed they were at what they'd seen here."

"Those were only words, Bruno. Did you see the looks on their faces at the time they experienced each thing. Their expressions spoke volumes. I happened to be with the party as it went from room to room. We take for granted the lights automatically coming on when we enter a dark room, without thinking how technically advanced that is. Their faces told otherwise."

"And they haven't seen anything yet," Abram added. "But back to what I started with, the ceremony. There's another affair, which is for the harvest. I had a chance to talk to Nyaho and learned more.

"The harvest has a good bit of thanks in it, which seems similar to our Thanksgiving.

"It's interesting how many cultures arrive at similar things that not only bring them together, but also bring them closer to whatever being is most central to their beliefs.

"On that score the words spirits and harmony and recycling keep repeating in what they do. Isn't that somewhere near to the track we're supposed to be on?"

Heads nodded. "It may all boil down to that," Bruno said.

"By the way, Rod, I saw you corner Dlahni after the meeting broke up. I was helping get them settled for the night, but I couldn't help noticing what seemed like an interesting conversation."

"It was ... it certainly was. There was so much hinted at, or told without detail, that I couldn't stand it. All we'd been told, for instance, was that there was a fight, Matthew was killed first, then others were, and it was awful. That's not much to go on. Then there's that malarkey about the man who quieted the storm and talked to the Great Spirit. Weren't any of you curious about that?"

"O course we were. What did you find out?"

"The details ... the details. First there was this mob ... men who'd been spooked by the storm. From what I understand there were drums and a lot of jumping around yelling at the gods. Then someone started chanting and everyone—maybe three or four dozen, armed to the teeth with knives and clubs and spears and whatever they had—picked it up. Then they roared and came down the slope to the *Atjahahni* camp, screaming like banshees and blowing past the initial line of defense Da-hash-to had been in. Just picture what that must have been like when combined with the wind and rain and lightning and all. It had to have been like a wet, berserken hell with strobe lights.

"Dlahni heard them and knew they were coming, so he'd scrambled to set up defenses. He put his men, a squad he called Rovers, in the front, with Sarah and her archers in a line above and behind them. He was trying to get everyone behind those lines, but there was a lot of confusion and a bunch, including Nyaho and John and Matthew, got trapped in a lower area in front.

"The mob spots John, who is easy to see as he'd stand out almost anywhere, and heads for him with blood in their eyes. Well, Matthew jumps in front and blocks them, and might have stopped them too, but then this guy Braga pops out from behind and pins his arms.

Surprised and helpless, he's killed by a quick thrust and blood flows and all hell breaks loose. The mob then lunges at John, but John fights back. Dlahni and his men come to his aid and it *is* awful. In the most primitive way, men are stabbed and sliced and bludgeoned and eight more are killed, most by John who'd become like Samson after seeing what happened to Matthew. Dlahni's description of the scene when the fight comes to an end is pretty gruesome.

"Then, while the storm still rages, John climbs a hill beside where all this took place, and with spear in hand, screams at the heavens. No one down below can hear what he's saying but they can see.

"And then the damndest thing happens. He's hit by lightning, at least it looks that way, two or three bolts in quick succession. A tree nearby almost comes apart and there's smoke and debris raining down all around him. As the smoke drifts away, it just so happens the clouds do too—it's the last of the storm—and there John stands. He comes back down the hill to where everyone has now gathered.

"And get this …. his hair has turned white, and there's a bright rainbow behind him."

"I get a chill just trying to visualize what that was like … and certainly the same must have been true for all those who witnessed it. I'm not much into the supernatural as you know, but I can understand what happened next."

"Yes …"

"They, I mean *all* nations … bowed down before him."

37

Da-hash-to

"Anton, you care to start us off tonight?" Gary asked.

"Not really ... I mean, we got a lot done today, but there's so much more waiting tomorrow out there, and the day after, that I haven't *thought* about any kind of report. Thanks to everyone who's been helping, though. We've practically moved a mountain in six months, which couldn't have happened without all of you.

"When everything's in, hopefully before winter, I'll add it all up; then we can discuss it."

"Tell about the deer," Benjamin said.

"Oh yes, we got another one. The damned animals love our gardens, and they're getting smart. They've been chased away so many times by Homer and Jethro, they've learned where to go to be out of range. Anyway, I stepped out during the wee hours ..."

"You don't have to explain."

Anton snorted. "Like I was saying, there was this movement not too far away, so I grabbed the 'buss ... thanks by the way, Roland, for bringing it back in one piece ... and crept out for a better look ...

"Dropped it with one shot."

There was an immediate chorus ... "*Oooooo* ...."

"All right assholes, I hope you appreciate all the skins stacking up. Your clothes won't last forever ... you'll see. By spring you'll

311

be dressing like our *Atjahahni* friends. Some of mine already need replacement."

"Okay, we hear you," Gary said. "But nothing yet on the crops?"

"Well hell, we've been eating some of it already, haven't we? And there's more in store. We just need to wind it up, that's all."

Gary looked around the room. This wasn't the way the night was supposed to go. Yesterday had been as exciting as it could get with the return of the search party and John and all, and then the time afterwards getting acquainted. So he had expected this evening's gathering to be just as exciting, even if in a different way; but all he could tally so far was a difference. At first light that morning, with so much work to do before the winter closed them in, most had headed out. All, that is, except Bruno, who was preparing a program for the *Atjahahni*, and he and Annie, who were running the orientation for John.

Gary thought these two events would be good material for another assembly, with the guests expounding on what they'd learned. But apparently the day for them had been more shocking than enlightening … so much so that when asked for comments that could be shared with the group, he got nothing. Instead the *Atjahahni* returned clothes that had been borrowed, and switched back to their leathers which had been cleaned and mended. John also seemed in a funk, and he switched too.

"Bruno … anything of interest on construction?" Gary pleaded, groping for any topic of interest.

"Nope," he answered with an obviously uninspired response. "We're making a pile of sawdust, though. Glad to have you back, Roland. We've missed you for sure."

"Would you listen to that," someone whispered loud enough to carry, "as if he was the one being missed."

Rebecca nudged Judy, but Judy looked down as if not listening … She was betrayed, however, by a slight smirk punching her dimples.

So it went, with an elephant in the room and the meeting going nowhere. As it dwindled to awkward, Devon got up and zig-zagged off through the group, returning with his guitar.

There wasn't much doubt where this was going, but the change was welcomed. Heads turned and watched while he strummed and set stays and played a few warm-up chords, with a few starting to sway to the cadence being created. Then he gave a loud plunk, and went into another song from Walkin' Jim Stoltz …

If trees could talk
  what tales they'd tell,
when they'd get together
    their tongues would swell.
They'd chatter with the wind
    On each and every day,
a hundred years to go
    is a long, long way.

[If I were a tree
  Oh, I'd grow all gnarly,
    my roots would be nobby
      and my limbs all snarly;
  With moss on my back
    and squirrels on my knees,
  I'd grow old and wise,
If I were a tree.]

Several verses later, with everyone joining in with the chorus, the mood in the room lifted a bit. But then it settled back as Gary, who remained up front, looked from one to the other for somewhere to go.

Finally Da-hash-to fidgeted. He whispered to Nyaho and loosened some of the wrappings restraining his side. Then he struggled to his feet, with several helping hands, and stepped and dragged his way to the front. Gary hustled into the lab for stools.

Settling into position, more standing than sitting, Da-hash-to started, speaking slowly, with Nyaho interpreting after every few comments.

"Yesterday we were stunned by seeing the things that are a part of your world. Nyaho has already told you about how we felt … and we were up much of the night discussing what we had seen even further.

"Then there has been today. You told us of things to expect and we should have been prepared. But we were not ... Your words did not adequately describe what we have now seen.

"Bruno used a little "machine" that created moving images of the world you came from on the wall. The images were of buildings and cities in sizes and features beyond what all your words described; we saw machines that can carry a person from our home to here in only the morning hours; we saw machines that can carry a person into the sky and travel at speeds even faster, with views from the heavens that dip into valleys and soar over mountain tops; we saw machines and machines and more machines; we saw crowds so large, we came to understand what you meant by "as many as the stars".

"Then while we were still reeling from what had been shown, we were invited to watch what you called the orientation program John failed to receive twenty years ago. So we watched while people appeared out of nowhere to guide John along.

"The people, who I was told were your friends, moved and talked and laughed and clapped; and while they did, we were able to walk to them, and walk through them, and they were not there.

"You say they were not spirits, and that there was no magic ... and you expect us to understand.

"So if we are quiet, it is not because we are rude. We see these things and feel smaller and more insignificant than ever before. We think of all the wonders, then think of our village and how we live, and are ashamed. We feel stupid; we feel like animals. How can we go back after what we have seen, and accept what is waiting for us there?

"And John is quiet too. He feels responsible for the bad things that have happened ... all because he was impatient and didn't stay for the orientation. He had felt this way before when your team found him, but we told him then that there were reasons why it was better things had gone this way. What we said then wasn't enough.

"So we're quiet."

Da-hash-to limped back to where he'd been, and in a series of contorted movements, with more helping hands, settled back down. With that Gary returned to the front, with new hope that Da-hash-to's words would loosen things up; but when he looked at John, John was still saying, without saying, to leave him alone.

The only reaction was from Annie, who held up her hand …

"Gary, let's take a break. Give me ten minutes, okay?" Without waiting for an answer, she stood, indicated for John to follow, and side-stepping by and around the rest, left the room.

She didn't have a specific place in mind, just somewhere out of sight and sound. After a number of stop and goes, none of the places providing what she wanted, she continued to the far end and the cavern doors, John bumping along obediently with premonitions making him want to be somewhere else. But there was no else and she halted and turned.

"John," she said, her face rippling emotions, accompanied by disjointed movements of hands and feet and body parts.

"Look" … the words going nowhere at first.

"John … it's not your fault. The problems of the world, and all the bad things that have happened, are *not* your fault." She spun half way around while struggling to convert thoughts to words, and sprung back.

"Yes, some of what's happened *is* awful. But we've all been injured. When during our orientations we realized Reynolds and Huston were just figments of the past, it hit us. It hit us that our world was gone. For me, Mom and Dad and friends and relatives and farm and barn and chokecherry wine were all gone.

"They're gone … and each of our friends' loved ones is gone too.

"Please understand … your leaving early didn't hurt us one bit, except, of course, for giving me six months of anxieties. So instead of concentrating on the bad things, think of all the good you've been able to do in those twenty years. All right, Willow's dead, and that's sad. Just ask yourself, though, what would have happened to her if you hadn't come along? There wouldn't have been all those years with you … and there wouldn't have been those beautiful children. Instead she would have ended up with this Dresh-na-togl, a monster, who makes me shudder every time I think of him. And yes, there's Matthew, and that's awful too. But as bad as his death is, think of his life—a legendary one that never would have been.

"And finally, there's what Da-hash-to has been saying. According to him, you paved the way for all of us. He said that because of their fear of giants, the *Atjahahni* would have killed us had it not been for you. Think about that. He also said he feels the Great Spirit has been overseeing and influencing the way things have gone. I know they say God works in mysterious ways, but maybe in this case it's true. I'd like to think so.

"So what do *you* think?' She said, cupping his face in her hands. "Dammit, John, speak to me."

His eyes misted and his face quivered; he exhaled, flashed a nervous smile, then nodded, "I'm sorry."

"It's okay, honey ... it's okay."

"No, it's not ... I've been in a stew without thinking of others. You're right ... everybody's been hurt. And right now I've got friends who've been overwhelmed by what they've seen. So let's get back ... but first," he gathered her in, almost swallowing her in a giant hug. When he finally eased away, he cupped her head back and kissed her lightly ... "Thanks, I needed that."

They started back arm in arm; then as they entered the orientation arena, and without warning, he blurted, "By the way, I'd like you to spend the winter with me back at the village."

Still aglow from the tender moment a minute before, she stopped abruptly, spinning them around. "Back to the village ... to *that* ...?"

Her mind whirled. Six months ago she'd awakened to a world far removed from what had been her life, and to make matters worse, a world of uncertainty without John, who made life worth living. But she'd sucked up and worked along with everyone else. Worked hard. Then there'd been discovery and weeks hacking a way through a mountain morass—bushes and brambles and spiders and critters and rocks and gullies and bogs wrapped around trees of every kind; and there'd been people and danger and emotions tugged every which way. All of it. Until finally home, or at least what had become home, and clean clothes and clean bodies and a warm, clean bed, which were godsends. *Go back? No, no, no, never!*

She looked up at him as if he were crazy.

"Annie ... oops ... I should have approached you differently about this, but the thought of going back didn't occur to me until just now. I guess what Da-hash-to said has gotten to me and won't go away.

"You spoke of home and family and what has been lost … what all of us have lost, and it's true, we've lost them, and because of that we're pledged to do the right thing. Well, doing the right thing for me happens to be more complicated.

"You see, in the twenty years since wandering away, I've added families and friends and whole nations to that complication. For twenty years, with those people, I've hunted and fished and planted and scavenged; for twenty years, I've built shelters and canoes and traps and what-nots with the crudest of tools and materials; for twenty years, I've sat in groups, taking fibers from plants and weaving strings and nets and ropes and fabrics; for twenty years, I've stretched pelts and conditioned them to make leather … and then cut and sewn, making capes and tunics and belts and leggings and footwear; and for twenty years, I've relaxed by the fire and talked of the mysteries that men are prone to discuss … mysteries that confound and intrigue every aspect of our lives.

"Now, Da-hash-to said he felt stupid and ashamed. I can understand that. I was taken aback myself to be reminded of the tremendous gap between the different halves of my life. They, meaning not just the three here with us but all the *Atjahahni*, need our help now more than ever, and we need theirs.

"Remember the Pilgrims and Plymouth Rock and all that stuff back in the early seventeenth century. Well, the Pilgrims had a religion they felt was the only true belief; and while the Indians had several, which may have had as much validity as what the *Atjahahni* have, they were considered savages and heathens. There were other contrasts: leather versus cloth; bark canoes versus masted ships; stone knives versus steel swords; and arrows versus guns. With those contrasts, and forgetful of the fact the Indians helped them survive, there was a gradual expansion of settlements that eventually destroyed the helpers. And how sad … The Indians had characteristics that could have been assimilated to everyone's benefit.

"The situation today is similar to that at Plymouth Rock, with even greater contrasts in backgrounds. There is also another difference, which is major. The *Atjahahni* and the other nations collectively number from five to ten thousand people, which isn't very many. They are the blended survivors of whatever children made it into the shopping centers at the time of the plague, and somewhere among them hopefully are the strains of Bobby and Sissy. We, on the other hand, are only what we are ... We are fifteen in number and we won't be reinforced with a wave of immigrants. Therefore we need each other, and we need to start recognizing that now.

"That's why I asked."

Annie hesitated, thinking. Twenty years. Somewhere in her locker she had a picture of them together at an event after their wedding—a fun time with handsome smiling faces. Now, after only a few weeks, she hardly remembered that face. The one before her now was older and weathered and scarred, framed with a full head of white hair swept back and tied into a ponytail. His beard was white as well, and had been roughly cropped when she first saw him, but since last night had been trimmed, with cheeks shaved to leave a short mustache and goatee. Whatever ... the eyes and smile and voice and combination of mannerisms were the same, and altogether were still the man she loved.

She thought of that special night long ago—actually, however, only about nine months in real time. They had walked across the farmyard in the cold of winter with the wind driving snow seemingly through them. They stopped as a fence bordering the pasture, and there, with conditions as miserable as could be imagined, John proposed. Later that night they sat by the fireplace, bundled together, sipping chokecherry wine and talking of the future, and bumping heads in euphoria, and it was then she remembered those words of dedication she felt:

> ... *whither thou goest,*
> *I will go;*
> *and where thou will lodgest,*
> *I will lodge:*
> *Thy people shall be*
> *my people;*
> *and thy God*
> *my God.*

The recollection settled her down. Thinking for only a moment more, she smiled, saying, "Whither thou goest, I will go."

"What's happening now?" A commotion in the lounge broke up another giant hug … John had exhaled at Annie's answer and then encircled her again in his arms and crushed and swayed.

"Sounds like Becky."

It was. They parted and started walking again, bumping along arm in arm, and reaching the room just in time.

When they'd left earlier, the assembly sagged into recess, with only a few muted conversations taking place. Devon picked away softly in chords that drifted into the background, at the same time mumbling a tune as if composing. Gary, Bruno and Judy gathered by the *Atjahahni* and were in a quiet discussion, trying to allay the impressions that had been expressed. Several remained silent; most in some kind of reflection, like Rebecca. She looked at the pictures on the wall, the only décor in an otherwise Spartan setting … and wondered. *They're pretty, and interesting … but is there more than just pretty … Huston didn't do much of anything without a purpose.* Getting nowhere she tuned in to the conversations around her, and after a time with that returned to the wall.

"I've got it!" She exclaimed, jumping to her feet. By the time she got to the wall, she had everyone's attention, including John and Annie, who had just rounded the corner.

"Listen," she said. "I've been looking at these pictures for some time now, thinking there's more to them than decoration … and there is."

With that she began to sing, and with the first words, which were immediately recognizable, Devon struck a soft chord and accompanied her …

"Oh beautiful for spacious skies," with that line pointing to the shoreline scene with gnarled oaks and cabbage palms and a wide expanse of clear, blue sky… *"For amber waves of grain,"* … to the wheat field extending to the horizon with rippled affects of the wind invoking movement … *"For purple mountains majesty,"* and so on, each picture fitting into lines of the first verse of *"America"*. The first lines were delivered clearly, but softly and almost reverently. Then she

increased the volume until with *"Crown thy good with brotherhood"* the walls were ringing, and with *"From … sea … to … shining … sea,"* she stood, legs spread, arms swinging to targeted images, and voice belting at full volume, at which point Devon went nuts on the guitar, everyone else jumping up, whistling and clapping.

The room didn't settle until high-fives had been extended all around.

It was only then Gary noticed John and Annie had returned.

"Welcome back," he said. "You guys all right?"

Annie gave a subtle squeeze, waved to the room, and wound her way to where she'd been earlier, leaving John conspicuously alone.

John nodded, "I'm fine, and so is Annie, but the day *has* been something else, especially after that song … *Wow!"* He sidled along the edge of the group, taking a round-about way towards Gary.

As he passed the *Atjahahni,* Da-hash-to said, *"Isn't that the song you sang in Council several years ago?"*

"Yes …"

"She sings much better."

Dlahni rocked and almost rolled over laughing, as did the others when the words were translated. John faked a pained expression and nodded as truer words were never spoken, then he bonked Dlahni lightly on the head and continued to the front.

"All right, let's get serious, if we can." For the first time John felt like an elder statesman. It wasn't that he felt seriously past his prime, because even though forty-some years in the *Atjahahni* world was getting up there, he remembered how energetic and vital the forties were in his previous past … men were active, playing tennis for instance, into their eighties and beyond. It was just that the group before him was almost half his age, and in a way, with all their exuberance, acted it.

"I don't think any of you thought about how shocking what you had to show today would be," he said as he sensed having everyone's attention. "I'm referring to what Da-hash-to said a bit ago. If you don't mind, there are things that should be said that might help out."

"It's all yours," Gary said, sighing and retreating to the side.

"Okay, first, let me apologize. The orientation and then the trip into the cavern hit me pretty hard. I guess that's obvious. The two, however, did succeed in closing the loop on something I've been struggling with since day one."

"Do you remember all of it now?"

"Not completely. I'd been having nightmares about parts of it for years—you know, the falling, the helplessness of being lost in total darkness, the slime, things like that. Now it all makes sense."

"John," Rodney interrupted, "I think I know where you're going next, but before you start, there's something some of us have been curious about."

"Yes? ..."

"It's about what's left of the world we left eight thousand years ago. Most of us haven't been more than a few miles in any direction, so it's not surprising we haven't seen anything ... I mean, the country around here wasn't populated before. I've talked to Gary and Roland about this since they've gone a lot farther, but they hadn't noticed any ruins or remnants either. Have *you* seen anything? From what I've heard, you've been hundreds of miles in all directions. Even considering it's been a long time, things like concrete and brick and ceramics just don't disappear; there must be lots of stuff lying around."

John nodded, "You'd think so."

Rodney laughed, his head bobbing as if to say *"hello"*. "Weren't you even curious?"

"To tell you the truth, Rod, I wasn't. And that sounds strange, even to me now. But until a few weeks ago I didn't believe the world we're talking about ever existed. I don't know. Trees and forests have a way of covering most everything in time so that's part of it. Remember the ruins in Central America—great Mayan temples covered by the jungle weren't discovered until archaeologists dug them out. There most likely has been some of that around here, but again, I don't know. One reason is we haven't been looking; another is we haven't had the tools ... You don't do much digging with wooden sticks and hip-bone shovels.

"I didn't arrive at the truth of the twenty-first century until last month when a bunch of us dug, mostly with hands, a ditch to drain a flooded area formed during the storm. When the water gushed out, it sliced through a layer that proved to be an old roadway."

"Oh yes ... I heard about that."

"Now that the lack of ruins or the awareness of them has been brought up, you have to realize there's more to consider. And that is that except for geographical similarities to the old world, there are major differences. The main one I'm aware of is the lake we traveled to get here. The lake didn't exist before, and it's no small thing. The south end of it is just past the ridge to the east; from there it snakes its way hundreds of miles in a north-northeast direction."

"That generally follows the Appalachians."

"Generally yes, except that it wasn't there before. In the old days there were many lakes in these mountains, mostly formed by dam building, but there was nothing like this ... And, there's another long lake north of it."

"I've wondered about all of that," Roland said. "I felt something was odd when we boarded the canoes, but never brought it up. Now that we're on the topic, I remember something Nyaho said during the night of remembrances about great snows."

"Ah yes, I asked about that a few years ago," John said looking at Da-hash-to as he spoke. "It's possible there's been a glacier in the recent past."

"Hmmm, let's think about that," Rodney said. "For sure, glaciers can have a helluvan impact. Eons ago, there were some dandies which covered half the world. One report said ice accumulated to several miles in thickness, which meant a slowly moving, grinding force of over five hundred tons on every square foot below it. A pressure like that causes lots of things to happen, like obliteration and reshaping which can be far reaching. I read an article about the Great Lakes— you know Superior, Huron, Michigan, Erie and Ontario—saying the lakes were getting shallower. The article went on to explain that this wasn't because of a lack of water, it was because the lake bottoms were slowly decompressing and rising after the previous years of crushing by glaciers."

"That's interesting, but it was way back in time," Bruno said. "I doubt the same thing could have come and gone in the years we're talking about."

"I'd agree with you there, eight thousand years is just a blip in geological terms. But consider this ... the earth was going through some weird changes when the plague hit. It was called global warming caused by greenhouse gas emissions, which resulted in wide fluctuations in the weather—hot summers and cold winters and more frequent violent storms. Whatever was happening probably continued for a while after people and their effects came to a screeching halt, leading to the great snows that were mentioned ... and glaciers. Now even if these were only a tenth of what had accumulated during the last really big glacial period, there would still be fifty tons of pressure per square foot, which is certainly enough to reshape a few things.

"Anyway, if this scenario did happen, it's obvious it was momentary in geological terms, and that climates returned to where they had been before. With this return forests and trees and birds and bees also returned, so what we have now may be similar to what things were like at the time the industrial revolution began. Makes sense to me."

John laughed, "Okay, very interesting ... and even poetic. You may be right, though; at least it explains a few things. Now where were we?

"Oh yes ...

"About what *you* said, Da-hash-to. I watched the same movie all of you did, but have to admit my mind was wandering and didn't pick up on how it might be deflating. What was shown was fine ... the twenty-first century world was a marvelous place in many regards. The good part was the result of millions of people, with all sorts of business groups and industries, leap-frogging each other in accomplishments, not unlike what's happening with the Crafts Fair, through times like the industrial revolution, the atomic age, the post-war era, and finally computers and the global network of information and communication. Those expressions of ages and eras may confuse you even more, but what I mean to say is, the times *were* amazing.

"What the program didn't show ended up being misleading ... and Bruno, I realize showing everything would have taken days, not hours. It didn't show, for instance, the negative asides of mankind over the last few thousand years of recorded history. It didn't show the nationalities and cultures that led to war after war, with tremendous energies and resources devoted to better ways to kill one another. It didn't show the extent of horror war becomes. Yes, we had our horror at Pangaea, but that was with a few dozen people in a few minutes time. Try to imagine years of battles, and fields with fifty thousand bodies in every form of pain and agony and death. Imagine movies like *"All Quiet on the Western Front"* and *"Saving Private Ryan"*, classics which depicted war realistically.

"The program didn't show over those years of history the societies that rose to wonderful levels, only to crumble and fail. And it didn't show the dark side of the last few centuries. On that side, in addition to history's worst wars, there was an exploding population—over seven billion people, as many as the stars as you say. Of these billions, most were confined by limited opportunity, which was leading to unrest, poverty, starvation, and of course emigration, which mostly succeeded in transporting problems to another area. As a point of interest, during the time when the amazing things were accomplished in the past—the wonders of the ancient world, for instance—the population of the world was about one-thirtieth of what it eventually came to.

"And with that eventual population, the program didn't show what was happening to the rest of the world. Right now the lakes are teeming with fish, as are the forests with game and the sky with birds. Back then the number of people and their needs were slowly but relentlessly reducing all other life, as well as the planet's natural resources.

"Now I know I've been racing along and speaking in terms you may not be able to fully understand. But the gist of what I've been telling you is that the world of the twenty-first century was not all good ... all things taken together at the time presented problems of massive proportion.

"The people you saw during my orientation, as spooky as it may have been, *were* our friends. One was a successful business man; one was an environmentalist; and the other a medical scientist. They were part of a group working to counter the bad things that were happening here on earth. One of the programs they developed—a process for suspending life for resurrection at a future time—just happened to coincide with what happened. I mean the plague. That program therefore presented a rare opportunity, an opportunity to which all of us are pledged.

"Da-hash-to, you said you felt stupid. Well, intelligence comes in many forms, and a lack in one area can be balanced by an expertise in another. Fortunately for all of us, the human brain is absolutely amazing ... Its limits to learning are generally limited to what it has been exposed to. But even then, there are exceptions. For instance, little Mahsja, who amazingly interprets languages after only a little exposure; or Ab Oh jsandata, who said he spoke to the spirits, and I happen to believe he did; or Nyaho here, whose quickness on many things continues to amaze us.

"A wise old man, a friend of mine, explained what we know this way." He went to the chalkboard and drew a circle, filling it in. Then he drew another circle, a line, around the solid circle. "The solid circle," he said, "represents what we know; the space between that circle and the line around it represents what we know we don't know. As we grow older, and as we are exposed to more and learn more, the solid circle grows; but so does the line around it as we realize there's more we don't know. But the space beyond that line never changes. It represents what we don't know we don't know, and that's infinite. It might also represent the all encompassing knowledge of the Great Spirit, the creator of all things".

"So there's no need to feel stupid. You and your people know a great deal which you've taught me. Now it's our turn. In time my friends and I will teach the *Atjahahni* and all the nations what we've been exposed to.

"Da-hash-to, you also said you felt insignificant. You ... all of you ... couldn't be more wrong. Call it fate, call it the work of the Great Spirit, call it what you will, but we are linked together in this opportunity to which we're pledged. You can't improve your lives without the resources we have ... and we can't complete our pledges without your help."

Da-hash-to whispered to Nyaho, who spoke for him.

"John, you've spoken on this before, but would you describe again what it is all of you are pledged to do ... and why."

"Can I help?" It was Abram.

"Please do."

"John ... by the way, the circle of knowledge ... that's a great analogy. Never heard it before. Who was your friend?"

"His name was Lawrence. He was a structural engineer at the firm where I apprenticed. But he was more than your ordinary structural man; he went far beyond stilted calculations to incorporate aesthetics and originality into his designs ... Quite a guy."

Abram nodded, "Sounds like it ... Anyway you touched on a few things that maybe I can elaborate to give a better picture. You mentioned that throughout recorded history, time after time civilizations have risen to accomplish amazing things, only to crumble and fall.

"That's true, but before I go into detail, let me back up a bit. Civilizations and their governments have come in all sorts of forms, but the most commonly recognized ones are Monarchy, Dictatorship, Oligarchy and Democracy.

"In a Monarchy the power to rule is passed down through family ties, which means qualifications and fairness have nothing to do with leadership. It means that without anything rational to support the hierarchy, bloodlines take on a special privilege. It means Da-hash-to, if you had a son, the position of Grand Chieftain would automatically go to him when you died.

"History doesn't favor this form. There were times when the heir to the throne was cruel or incompetent or overly ambitious or cowardly, with horrible results usually following.

"A Dictatorship is formed when a person organizes a supporting group and takes control of the government. A dictator wants to dictate; he wants a nation to fall in line with what he wants, and secures the power to have his way. Although a benevolent dictatorship can be an efficient and fair form, it lasts only as long as the dictator lives, and more often than not is disastrously cruel and inhuman.

"From both of these types comes the saying, which is a warning ... "absolute power corrupts absolutely".

"The third—Oligarchy—is governance by a few, hopefully a few who have performed well and earned the respect of their peers, and thereby have been selected to represent them. This can be a good form, particularly on a small scale, and it appears to be what you, the *Atjahahni*, have.

"Which leads to a larger, more encompassing form called a Constitutional Republic or Democracy. In this form officers and representatives are elected to conduct the affairs of the nation for the betterment of all of its citizenry."

"Ahemmm ... Abram ..."

"Yes."

"This is all very interesting," John said, "but you're losing me with some of it, so I expect others are having the same problem. All Nyaho asked was "What are we pledged to do?"

"Okay, this has gotten a little winded, but it's really only government 101, so to speak. There are points tied to the concepts, however, that I'd like to get to. Nyaho, have I lost you?"

Nyaho looked at Dlahni and Da-hash-to, who both shrugged. "Yes, I have to admit you have. But it's no more new to us than most everything else we've been exposed to, and it *is* interesting. So continue. Maybe something along the way will tie it together for us."

"Good ... you okay with that?" Abram said looking at John.

John nodded with a look of resignation.

"All right. The last form of government I mentioned was a so-called Democracy, which was something an ingenious nation across the seas experimented with thousands of years before the twenty-first century. Well, in the beginning of our nation, an assembly of men, familiar with most forms of government societies had used, and being particularly sensitive to characteristics of them that were detrimental to the freedoms they wished for, sought to craft a system that would be the best men had ever devised. These men, who came to be known as our Founding Fathers, used democratic principles as a basis for what they did.

"The result was a nation, which includes the forests and mountains around us, that grew and prospered to be the greatest the world has ever known.

"I wish the story ended there, because if that were the case, all we'd have to do was copy what they did.

"But it didn't ... and it may have been predictable. A professor of history at a learned university had this to say about democratic attempts:

A democracy will continue to exist only until voters discover they can vote themselves gifts from the public treasury. From that moment, the majority votes for those who promise the most benefit, with the result that the democracy collapses for a bunch of reasons.

He added that from the beginning of recorded history, the average length of civilizations has only been about 200 years. During that time there has been a repeating sequence ...

> *From bondage to faith*
> *From faith to courage*
> *From courage to liberty*
> *From liberty to abundance*
> *From abundance to complacency*
> *From complacency to apathy*
> *From apathy to dependency*
> *From dependency back to bondage*

"Our nation, the great United States of America, was a little over two hundred years old at the time of the plague. At that time there were conditions too complex to explain now, that made us fearful we were past our prime and well into a spiral to our end.

"You ask what it is that we are pledged to do.

"Our challenge is to fully understand what the Founding Fathers were trying to do. And along with that understanding, also determine what they or their successors failed to do that allowed the government to follow the pattern of the failed attempts that preceded it.

"Ours is to craft a society that will be representative and beneficial to all people, that will be sustainable, that will mollify the good conscience that is within us, and that will be in harmony with all elements of the natural world."

The soft hum from the energy center was the only sound heard for the next few minutes.

John swallowed. "Wow ... Nyaho, Dlahni ... does that answer your question?"

Nyaho laughed. "I'm not sure if my circle of knowledge has gotten any large, because so much has been said about things which I have no familiarity; but, as I said before, all of it has been interesting.

"I ... we ... would like to come to a better understanding of these things. I do get the impression the mission you've pledged to will be difficult. With that being so, how do you propose to meet the challenge?"

John looked back at Abram. Abram had a degree in history and was continuing studies towards a masters when the plague emerged.

Abram smiled and shook his head. "It was easy to describe the problem. I think we all realize, like you do, that it will not be easy, maybe taking more than our lifetimes, to outline and refine a system that will do all that's needed. The Founding Fathers were hard working members of a largely agrarian society, that is, a society closely tied to farming ... like us. They were mature, intelligent, patriotic men who weren't diluted and swayed by the shallow influences of television and banal entertainments—things that complicated our society. Instead they were involved and dedicated, pledging all they had to get free from the yoke of tyranny and establish a new nation with perfect justice. In the final group there were fifty-seven men representing a few million people in thirteen scattered colonies; they were farmers and businessmen and attorneys and public servants; and their average ages at the time of their efforts was forty-four years.

"To give you an idea how difficult our challenge is, we're only what you see, fifteen people, mostly in our early twenties. And although we've enjoyed the benefit of excellent schooling, we were just getting into our chosen fields when the plague struck, and none of those fields were governmental. Frankly, I think all of us are awed by the pledge we've taken ... and at this point don't feel qualified to carry it out. Well, as a matter of fact, we're not. And we've been too busy to this point to do much about it. Hopefully, with more time on our hands this winter, we can get started. But as been said before, the challenge may take the rest of our lives or more."

Once again the room became nodding heads and shrugs and mumbles. Then Da-hash-to spoke, translated by Nyaho.

"The part I understand is that you are to craft a society that will benefit all people. That will not be easy. To do this you must remember that each man has two parts—a good wolf and a bad wolf.

"Your system must be for the benefit of the good wolf."

38

At The Cookhouse

"Do you have to be going tomorrow … so soon?" Lisa asked as she worked a bucket of potatoes, dumping the results into a second half-filled with water. All the girls were there at the cookhouse at one time or the other, mostly making do on the steps because inside was too small for all of them. Besides, it was just that kind of day that had to be enjoyed. There really wasn't work for all of them—the washing and peeling and sectioning and mixing wasn't that complicated—but they wanted to be together and wanted to talk.

"Yes," sighed Annie, who was beside her tending the next step in the jerry-rigged assembly line. "It'll take the better part of a week to get back, and John doesn't want to chance the weather too far."

Rebecca, who was at the end of the stoop mainly staying out of the way, said, "I suppose he knows best, but there doesn't seem to be much to worry about; the last few days have been absolutely beautiful."

"No doubt about that. But it's been a while since any of us have seen a winter …"

"Like about eight thousand years, give or take a few," Judy said making a face, "So what's the point?"

Annie nodded, "Ya, ya. The point is weather is weather, that part hasn't changed, and it can be unpredictable and bad. Remember how quickly that storm kicked up last month."

"*Oooo-weee.* Do we ever."

"Well, it's doubtful anything like it is going to happen again. Still there's a chance, and at this time of the year, with snow and ice as possibilities, John doesn't want to be in a canoe if it does. Besides, the leadership of the *Atjahahni* is in his care at what might be a sensitive time, given all that's happened. And … three men are waiting on the other side of the ridge. It's just time."

When the second bucket emptied, Terry eased up to stand, her bulk now well blossomed in its fifth month. "Pass them to me, I'll get another load."

"No, let me," Rebecca said. "I'm not doing anything right now, so was going to take scraps and feed the pigs; but that can wait. Besides, you should take it easy. I don't know all that lifting is good for you."

"Oh hell, I'm fine. Besides, I want to see how Devon and Anton are doing. They've been out there since dawn working their butts off."

"Everyone's working hard," Mona said as she watched the two disappear in the direction of the gardens. "So hard."

The saw cranked up again in the shop nearby to interrupt her chain of thought. "See what I mean? Roland, Abram and Benjamin have been at it just as long today. They'd been stockpiling lumber for a bunch of projects, like housing, hoping to get everything done before the cold settles in. They thought their list of objectives was long before, but then you guys get back," she said looking at Judy and Annie, "and while that's somewhere beyond wonderful, they now have more to do than ever."

"You mean because of the boat?"

"Yes, the boat for one. I guess that takes precedence over everything else."

"I don't know about that," Judy said, "but I do know Bruno hadn't been sleeping much even before the need for a boat came along. He'd learned a little bit about boat-building designing the skiffs, but the new one is something else. It's much bigger with not only multiple oarlocks, but also masts and jibs and stuff for sails. Remember now, bolts and lag screws and nails and metal brackets aren't available. So all pieces framing it need to be shaped to interlock, then fastened with wooden pegs. The process was almost fun for the skiffs because they were small, but this thing is almost ten yards long. Serious."

"Which means it can't be built here. All of the men combined couldn't move it to the lake; it's too heavy. And if they attempted to use rollers and pull it along like horses in harness, like the ancients supposedly did for this sort of thing, there are miles of primal forest between here and there, with a ridge to boot.

"No, no, you're wrong ... They'll *have* to build it here because tools and power are here. That's what makes it so complicated. After initial construction, they'll have to take the whole thing apart, carry the pieces to the lake and reassemble them on skids at the waters edge."

"Phew!"

"Yes, phew. What's more, it'll have to be finished and tested and adjusted and ready to cruise by early summer."

"All for a few horses?"

"Well, yes, that's the initial reason," Annie said, "but the boat will have a thousand uses after that. And don't belittle horses. John told the people back at the village the reason for horses was meat and leather, much like the *Anlyshendl* had done with wild pigs. This was something they could understand. He also indicated they would be pastured at the village; but he really intends to bring most of them here. If everything works out, they'll make travel between the lakes much quicker, and imagine what they'll do for work in the fields."

"I guess you'd be the one to know. Didn't you grow up on a farm?"

"Yes," Annie answered, settling back and letting her mind drift.

For a few moments she was back there ... back at the barn. She'd saddled "Missy", walked her out through the double doors, and lifted up and over into place. Missy wasn't just an ordinary horse, she was a member of the family. Twelve years before, Annie had been in the barn with her father and Doc McArgle the veterinarian, when a foal dropped, all messy and slimy, into the hay. Annie had been wide-eyed, biting her nails at first; but then she dived in to help with the cleaning, being playfully tolerated as she was really getting in the way. When doc said "We have a pretty little filly here", Annie had cupped the squirming head in her hands and said, "Oooh, a little girl ... Hello Missy", and the name stuck. Annie was in the barn every day after that, helping with feeding and cleaning and training, and growing up together. Two years later, she broke Missy in, riding at every opportunity after that.

On this particular day she was home from college, which should have been a joy, except that it wasn't. The memory of Karen, her best friend who'd been killed along with her mother in an accident a few months before, was still heavy on her. She needed somebody, another friend, and for the moment Missy was it.

The ride started at a walk, which seemed to fit the mood, but it still felt good. She loved the soothing rhythm that transferred the animal's movements into her with the effects of a deep-muscle massage. Even the trot, with its bouncing cadence, had its place; but it was the gallop, with its exciting oneness with the animal, the thrashing mane and flashing landscape, where it was really at. So at length, she gave the sign to which Missy responded, and soon the wind was in her face. They raced along the fence bordering the Hefta Pasture, not slowing until they reached Bentley's Creek. They forded the creek, which was solidly bottomed and less than two feet deep, then wound their way through the woods up to the knob called Brewer's Hill where they stopped. From there she could see in all directions the patchwork of fields, the farmhouse and barn ... even the First Methodist steeple jutting out above the trees miles away.

It was beautiful and lonely and unfair ... and she cried. Deep, shuddering sobs. And Missy didn't know what to say except to shake her head and snort. So Annie dismounted and held the sympathetic head of a friend and hugged and it was much better.

"Annie, are you okay?"

"Oh, sure; I was just thinking of something ... sorry," wiping a tear away. "Where were we?

"Horses ... they bring back memories. All I can say is that if we get some, I want to be involved. They're a majestic animal ... a pain in the ass sometimes, but not as much as people. I didn't only grow up on a farm, I grew up with planting and harvesting and yes ...

with horses. Here we are only a half year into our adventure and we're torn every which way by a world that confounds and threatens and challenges us. The situation binds us so completely, we haven't put form to the things that give us side interests and pleasure. The latter can come in many ways, but I can say as a girl born and raised on a farm, horses can be one of them. You'll see. You'll see if you ever saddle up and ride like the wind with your hair blowing and eyes squinting and frame synchronized with a magnificent animal. You'll see."

"Annie … Annie … come back down," Judy said laughing. "So you like horses … We get the picture."

"Okay, so I can get carried away. All I mean to say is that horses will change a lot of things, and if we train and manage them right, they'll make things better all around."

Everyone nodded with no reason to argue one way or the other, then Lisa sat up and dusted herself off. "The girls won't be back for a while yet … I think I'll step inside and see how Rodney's doing."

"Hasn't he been with Nyaho and the Grand Chieftain?"

"Ah huh. They're having a good time, now that they've gotten over being spooked like they were at first. Rodney's mostly working on the computer, taking them into all sorts of things, wherever their questions lead."

"It hasn't been all been fun and games, though."

"No, I didn't mean that. When John announced the other day that he'd be going back, it brought all sorts of topics to the surface. We thought we'd been focused before, but that announcement added a bunch more to consider. Anyway, I'm curious as to what they're into.

"Bye."

As they watched her leave, Mona, looking up from the pile of pods she'd been shelling, said "Yes, Annie, you and John caught us by surprise. No one wants the group broken up again, not so soon anyway. John's reasoning is easy to understand once he explained it all, but it hit Gary pretty hard."

"Why's that?"

"Well, they're best friends, for one, but that's not the main reason. Gary had been designated as being in charge simply because he was the first one back … and he was never comfortable with that. So when he found John, who he'd always looked up to, he was relieved thinking John, older and wiser now, would replace him. Besides, his interest is medicine, which is a responsibility he hardly feels qualified to handle. I mean, he felt this way before the trip and had been spending a lot of time in research, mostly diseases and things like poison and flu and dysentery and pneumonia—you know, the things that naturally surround us here. Then came the trip. When all of you almost got skewered at the *Atjahahni* village, it shook him up. Then he found John and saw his scars, and heard of Pangaea and its battle injuries … smashed bones and spilled guts and opened heads. Like what do you do for someone who's been clobbered with one of those primitive clubs you see the men carry, and has his skull dented? That kind of situation was serious, but solvable, in the old days with anesthetics and antiseptics and antibiotics on hand, and with neurologists and surgeons with scalpels and saws and intricate devices … all under operating room conditions. But how do you handle it now? So he's spending more time than ever in research, with much of it being in contrived solutions and medicinal plants. He can't learn enough fast enough … and he doesn't want to lead."

"It doesn't seem anyone wants to lead."

"That's strange."

"Yes it is … but think about it. Remember the group Huston assembled back at the French Broad?"

"I sure do," Annie said. "It turned out that it wasn't an accidental grouping at all. Everyone had been investigated thoroughly, and selected, with certain traits in common. I told John after the first two days that it felt like we were auditioning."

"Exactly … We were."

"So what did it take to make the final cut?"

"Well, the obvious traits were youth, health and conditioning. Gary said nobody would survive the Cryonologic process without those. Then, and I'm speculating here, there were things like work ethic and teamsmenship."

"But there were none of the type that have a desire, or need, to lead."

"You're right. We have a good mix of specialties, and certainly a lot of spirit, but there's a general reluctance to take charge. Why do you suppose that is?"

Judy nodded, thinking. "I've heard management consultants claim all personality traits have their place, so I'm guessing again. Some who want to lead have been good … there's nothing ironclad there. But consider this … egomaniacal, sociopathic types, which haven't been exactly rare among those hell-bent on leading, have been awful, pursuing agendas that included corruption and cruelty and greed. What was it Abram quoted the other night, "Absolute power corrupts absolutely". They've started wars, slaughtered populations and destroyed everything in their path."

"With that as a possibility, it may be that Huston didn't want to take chances, adding humility and character to the list instead."

"La-*dee*-dah … aren't we something though?" Mona said, her black eyes sparkling and highlighting an exaggerated grin.

"Could be," Judy said straightening up and extending her arms as if acknowledging ovation, then, "Since that's the case for all of us, Annie, why don't *you* take over … You did a great job with the *Easter Armageddon* conference. Now I'm serious with that," settling back.

"I can't … I'm leaving with John, remember? Why don't one of you?"

"I can't," Mona said, mimicking feminine frailty, "I'm in a motherly way."

Judy laughed again, "Just listen to that … Well, I'm not, and I don't believe in that immaculate stuff either."

"So no one wants to lead."

"Maybe we're an oligarchy."

"I'm not an oligarch, I'm Methodist."

"Give me a break."

Just then a loud crash resounded from the workshop, accompanied by exclamations and ingeniously creative cursing. The girls stopped to listen, only to hear after an unnerving lull, softer tones and finally relieved laughter.

"I guess it's not serious."

Getting back to the serious, Judy said, "We're not going to solve the leadership problem, so let's change the subject back to what we were talking about a while back. Stress. Mona, Gary's not the only one under a lot of stress. We all are, just in different ways. One topic we're aware o, but don't choose to talk about, is the complex we call home. What if it were to shut off?"

"I thought the system was good for thousands of years more."

"That was suggested as to its capability, but that was with little draw on it ... as if it were in hibernation mode. Since March that ended, with all systems firing under a much heavier load. Rodney's been concerned about it, but with all else tugging at him, he hasn't been able to get an understanding of the generators and how they're doing.

"Of course we hope the complex is usable a lot longer—years and years and even a few lifetimes—because the library and its data files are priceless; but what if? That's why so many are scrambling to get us out and independent ... all of which has been complicated by what John's return has added.

"But back to stress. Bruno is certainly another one that's there. He takes a lot of kidding about his grandiose ideas ... you know, "Tower of Babel", "Mount Olympus", and all of that; but the more you think about it, the more you see he may be on to something. He's spent hours and hours with the master plan model, for instance, trying to arrange the best way of doing things, and taking into consideration how important this place could ultimately be."

"And how important *is* that?"

"Well, when we were at the *Atjahahni* village, we became familiar with the community center called *Tschtaha-tata* ... you've already heard about that. Inside on one of the front tiers, I found on display a globe, almost two feet in diameter, that John made years ago to illustrate the fact the earth was round. The globe had continents, as he could remember them, depicted by fur cut-outs attached to a smooth, blue-stained, leather sphere. It was pretty cool.

"An idea came to mind at the time, so I grabbed some pine needles, sticking them into North America where I imagined the nations we know of to be—the *Atjahahni,* southwest of Asheville; the *Bjarla-shito,* across the mountains probably northeast of Chattanooga; the *Anlyshendl* in West Virginia; and the *Njegleshito* in eastern North Carolina or Virginia. Guess what? At the scale of the globe the needles aren't very far apart. Now it's reasonable to believe there

These Truths

are other communities scattered all across the continent, or even continents, at spacings that may be similar to what we know.

"The possibilities are astounding. The next question is ... are there any more complexes like ours? And the answer is "we don't know yet, but we don't think so". If that's the case, then this place—Olympus—is pretty important, or will be, to the entire world, and Bruno's thinking isn't grandiose after all."

The point struck home, momentarily stopping work as the girls looked at each other with impressed understanding. Then Annie asked, "Did you see what he'd like to do on the river north of here?"

"You mean on the shallows just past the palisades?"

"Yes."

"Sure did. Bruno sees a great long term opportunity there. Because of the lay of the land north of the river, a dam would create a lake a half mile across and several miles long ... right at our back door. A lake there would not only be part of defensive configurations, it would also be the source for irrigation water.

"Let's not forget fish."

"And of course fish."

"When I first saw the lake on his drawings, I didn't say anything. But then I came back when he was gone and wrote in "Lake Elroy"."

"Lake Elroy?"

"That's his real name," Judy explained, trying not to laugh.

"Okay, Lake Elroy, whatever," Annie said with a shrug. "Wouldn't all of that area—the area the water covered—need to be cleared first?"

"Yup ... Just another item on the to-do list."

"And wasn't the area on the other side, just west of here, going to be cleared for pasture land, just in case we get the horses the boat is being built for?"

"Oh yes ... still another item."

"Lordy ... When do we build the brewery?"

"The brewery."

"When I think about all that's got to be done, I need a drink."

"I heard that," Lisa said, returning from the interior. "I don't know what I've missed, but I know what all of you have."

"Oh no, what now?"

"Pigeons."

"Pigeon?"

"Yes, Pigeons … homing pigeons to be exact. It seems somewhere in discussions the other day the problem of communication had been mentioned. Annie, you and John will be over the mountains and through the woods and days and days away. The canoes and even a successful barge, whatever you want to call this new thing that's going to be built, won't allow us to communicate in any way that won't take a long time.

"Apparently Devon had mentioned "homing pigeons", and that's what got it started."

"So what did you learn?"

"A lot. You know Rodney and how excited he can be. Well, when I asked what they were discussing, I got a head-full.

"It seems homing pigeons, or carrier pigeons, same thing with a message attached, are nothing new. Apparently they were used by the Egyptians and Persians 3,000 years ago. I mean, that many before the twenty-first century, or 1,000 BCE … understand?

"Well, since then they've been used all kinds of ways: In the nineteenth century, Rueters Press used them to deliver news and stock prices in Europe; the outcome of the battle of Waterloo was first delivered to England by pigeon; during World War I, one pigeon, Cher Ami, was awarded the Croix de Guerre for heroic service; during World War II, thirty-two pigeons received the Dickin Medal, whatever that is, for gallantry and bravery; and birds played a vital role in the invasion of Normandy, as radios couldn't be used for fear vital information would be intercepted.

"Carrier pigeons were still employed in the twenty-first century in remote areas. In fact it was only because of expanded use of the internet, that a Police Pigeon Service in an area of India was retired … and that was in 2002."

"You've got to be kidding."

"No, Rodney can hardly contain himself, and the *Atjahahni* are wide-eyed and bubbling that this can be done."

"Which means yet another project."

"Projects. To do this special structures ... lofts ... need to be built both here and at the village. Then in the spring, young birds need to be captured and ..."

"Oh stop, that's enough," Mona said. "When you came up we'd just concluded the next need was for a brewery. Now I'm more convinced than ever."

"Why, what did I miss?"

"Oh not much ... just the boat, and a dam and its lake, and horses and their pasture ... all this on top of what was already on the list."

Lisa sat down on the stoop and thought about it, then looked up, "What does this do to the housing you marrieds were going to move into? We've all looked at the models and drooled. Two and a half story duplexes with shared fireplace walls; bedrooms on the upper level with indoor plumbing; half-basements for preservation and storage; passive heating and cooling with solar orientation, heat sinks and cross ventilation. Bruno really outdid himself on the designs."

"Well all that sounds good, but the reality is that initially the units will just be framed in."

"Why's that?"

"Mainly the plumbing—water supply and drainage, sewer systems, septic tanks, cisterns, pumps and all sorts of things. Bruno, Rodney and Roland have been bumping heads on these problems; but far as I know they're only into concepts. The materials for them, like piping or toilets or sinks or faucets weren't included in all that the Caretakers were able to squeeze into storage. So every bit of the systems need to be created ... or at least improvised.

"And then there's the matter of cooking. The cast-iron cook stove we have here is the only one that's been provided. There was nothing for individual homes except cast-iron pots with lids and ladles, and andiron sets, all for fireplaces. From that we've assumed that brick or stone fireplaces and ovens will be the order of the day in individual homes, with a lot of communal dining continuing with what we have here in the cookhouse."

"I suppose it's like with the boats. There's a need to concoct designs and methods of construction that haven't been used for hundreds of years ... I mean a long time before the twenty-first century."

"It's more than that. We'd all like to get back to lifestyles we're familiar with, but that may not be possible."

"We're resigned to that."

"So ... is the work on the units being put on hold because of all the other stuff?"

"That's not for me to decide. We'll just have to put everything on the table and see how much we can do and what comes first. The conveniences and comforts can wait, but some things can't ... We'll see."

"What was that?"

It was a sound they hadn't heard before.

Heads turned to the west where the sound seemed to be coming from. Further in that direction at the shop, the men stepped out for the same reason. Then it happened again, a flat, mournful bellow that hung on the air and died away.

"That's that damned horn Gary carved," Mona said, "Doesn't it sound pitiful?"

"That means they're returning from the lake ... I mean John, Gary, Bruno and Dlahni."

"Yes, John wanted to revisit the place where he'd spent the first few months after being revived. His account of that time is really amazing. Since he lost the only thing he had, the garment he'd worn in the cocoon, he started out naked. Can you imagine that?

"He eventually killed a bear, which probably saved his life."

"I can hardly wait to hear everyone's reaction. Dlahni won't have much to say, mostly grinning at how absurd the others can be; but for the rest ... *ohmygod* ... they'll make the most mundane bit of information hilarious. There's a lot of imagination loose between Gary and Bruno."

"No doubt about that. But they left with a bunch of tools. I though they were going to work on the trail, and then do some fishing, as well as take a tour with John."

"They were."

Good ... then maybe, besides the stories they'll tell, they'll bring back something for the table."

"Fresh fish would be good."

"*Mmm mmm!* It would wouldn't it? Whatever, it's time to stoke the stove and get ready."

39

At Pangaea

"Do you have to be going back tomorrow ... so soon?" Braga said with a sly grin as they sat around the fire, a scene as peaceful as could be imagined anywhere.

Daj smiled back, playing the silly game without revealing there was one. He broke eye contact, however, doing at least that much, and looked into the fire, trying to relax what was gnawing at his insides.

Scary.

He was at a crossroads, which was odd because he'd never been in a position like this before. He'd always been able to glide through whatever the circumstance, and choose the option that pleased him the most without much in the way of deliberation. It was easy when the good or bad of it wasn't a consideration.

This instance was no different in that regard; but the consequences of his choice were far different ... they were awesome. He could report to Da-hash-to and the Council when he returned and tell them everything. This would lead to capturing Braga, and bringing him to justice. Daj would be a hero in the *Atjahahni* world, which was a situation he'd never been in or wanted. But then what? What would be the next game, the kind that really gave him pleasure; the kind that had elements of intrigue and danger and exhilaration ... and that had such satisfaction when over? Braga had been a supplier of this kind of adventure like no one else he knew. He would be gone.

Then there was the option that sat across from him, the ribbons of flame shifting and snapping and creating innumerable variations in the features, but not in the eyes that bore into him ... wondering.

*   *   *

Braga had put all of them to work the day after the pleasantries of coming together. The work was hunting, and the focus was on deer. For this they worked like a pack of wolves, with Braga and Ah-ton-jacii, who still weren't moving very well, positioned in carefully selected stands, while the other three, Shajsi-djuma and Ndjasa in particular, moving in wide circling sweeps that encouraged game in the area to move past the stands. It worked; by the fourth day and several kills later they had more than enough to eat, and that was good. Except that it soon became apparent food wasn't the primary purpose of the hunt. The hunt was for hides, which were quickly skinned and framed and stretched, with working them immediately following.

Late afternoon on the last day of hunting, after gorging on venison, Braga asked Daj to join him in a walk, supposedly to work off the bloated feelings. Leaving the others at the cave, they backtracked into the Pangaea site, stopping once more to sit along the banks of the cut exposing the mysterious black rubble.

"Have you solved the riddle this represents?" Daj asked pointing down as he settled on the edge, his short legs dangling below.

"No, it's still a puzzle ... but the truth of it will come out in time."

"How? Braga, you have a look that says you have something in mind."

Braga smiled.

Daj cocked his head, squinting, trying to see into the mind that seemed to pulsate with mystery, "You can't return to the *Atjahahni*, Dlahni will kill you on sight if someone else doesn't get to you first."

"True ... I don't intend to go there, not at first anyway."

"What then? You can't stay here forever … but where *can* you go?"

Braga, still smiling, turned his head to indicate to the west.

"The *Bjarla-shito?*" Daj shuddered. "I don't understand. Because of you they went to war … and because of you many of them were killed. Because of you the wives and children who weren't here are now in mourning, probably just receiving the news. They'll all hate you."

"Perhaps … There's a chance of that."

"A chance! More than a chance … *What are you thinking?*"

Braga settled back, pausing as if to find the right words.

"Daj, do you remember years ago when John and Willow were preparing to travel north?"

"Yes."

"Well, in preparation for that trip, the wife of Da-hash-to made a robe which was to be given to the chief of the *Anlyshendl* as an offering of good will. Do you remember that?"

"Of course, the robe was beautiful. It went on to inspire the whole village as the quality level to be reached at the first Crafts Fair."

Braga nodded.

"So that's what you're going to do with the hides … make gifts?"

Braga shook his head. "No … that would be an insult."

He stood, began to pace on the shelf, scuffing the black rubble that was such a mystery as he did, saying "Yes, I'm going to find out what this is." Then he stopped and turned, reflecting an inner strength and resolve. "And I'm going to find out what the Great Spirit intends for me."

Daj sat stone-faced.

"Yes, I'm going to the *Bjarla-shito* … But look at me, Daj, I can't go this way. I look like a beggar; my clothes are worn and torn and stained and patched. That's what the skins are for. I'm going to make a complete new array … new tunic, new leggings and footwear, and new accessories. When the snows come I'll trap the weasels whose fur turns white, and use the furs to trim out certain points. I will have a decorated headband with eagle feathers; I will wear an amulet of special decoration. I will look the great chieftain that I am; my appearance will demand respect."

Daj gulped … *was he listening to a madman?* "Who's going to do this? You have no woman."

"My friend, before my wife died, she did all these things, keeping me in coverings that were well made. Since then, except for certain amounts of help, I've had to learn more than a few skills. We do what we have to do, and I have all winter."

Daj stared, nodding to himself while trying to picture what had been described. "What about Ah-ton-jacii?"

"The same for him … His clothes don't need all the embellishments, but they must be similar and new. For that matter, if you and you young friends will join me, you should match up with Ah-ton."

"You want us to join you?" Daj said, almost sliding off his perch.

"Of course. The more who accompany me, the more impressive my arrival will be."

"But …" Daj struggled to respond.

Braga sat back down, the smile returning, "Don't be so concerned about your safety … I'm the only one banished."

Daj shook his head, "I hear you, but I don't understand. You'll be walking to your own execution."

"You may be right, but I don't think so. I've given this a great deal of thought, and this is how I think it will go …

"When we walk into their territory, we will be recognized. Word will spread quickly; people will gather and follow us, many cursing and throwing things. But nothing more serious will happen because anything more is for their leaders to decide. At the Council house the chiefs and a surrounding crowd will be assembled. They will be furious and there will be more shouting and throwing. We must expect this to happen. When we get close to the chieftains, I will step apart from the rest of you and extend my arms. When the crowd quiets down I will say …

"Citizens of this great land, I come before you to do your bidding. I am sorry. I can not bring back the brave sons who died since the horror of last autumn.

"I am sorry. I did not understand the great power of the giant. I was wrong and there has been much suffering. If it is your wish that I be killed, I submit myself to you.

"But first hear me out …

"Like all of you, I have always had a fear of the giants who tormented our ancestors. So when one came into our midst years ago, I dedicated myself to watching him, hoping to counter anything he might do that would be harmful to my people.

"When the storm hit at the Gathering, it was something we had never seen before. This area was not hit nearly as hard, but those of you who were there know it was terrible. I was convinced this was a curse from the spirits against what the giant was doing. Many of you felt the same way and felt something must be done. I joined them. I tried to kill the giant but he was too mighty … I failed. Instead I was almost killed myself.

"The spirits were doing strange things that day. Besides the horrible winds and rain, they were throwing bolts of lightning and forming rainbows. They were also protecting me. Although I was hit with many arrows, I was able to pull them from deep within my body without being injured.

At this point Braga opened the top of his tunic to reveal the angry red scar in the center of his chest. He didn't mention this one was only superficial, having been protected by several layers of leather; but it was impressive. After the impact had been made, he repeated with a quick glimpse of others in his side, back and thigh, all of which had been much more significant, although hardly needed now.

"I do not fully understand these things. So it is confusing. I visited the hill where the lightning bolts were thrown and listened to the wind in hopes of a sign. But there was none I could read … I am a warrior, not a Spirit Man. Later in a dream, however, a voice called to me. It came from a shadowy figure I couldn't identify, who simply pointed west and said "Go, and do what you must".

"What did that mean?

"My intents today are the same as they have always been, and that is to protect my people and my friends. I believe that is what the spirit intended

for me to continue doing. Doing so, however, may be more difficult now than it has ever been.

"Because ... hear me ... there is something you should know. There are now more giants. Yes ... When my friends here returned from the Gathering, there were four more giants waiting for them at the Atjahahni village. Four more, including the tallest women they'd ever seen, and another man taller than John. And these giants' clothes and weapons were of designs and materials never seen before.

"There's more." His arms spread to the sky for emphasis.

"There are secrets. The giants were asked of things that were a marvel to everyone, but they wouldn't answer; they only smiled and were polite ... My friends managed to learn that there are even more giants farther south.

"What does all this mean?

"I don't know ... and that's why I'm here. To get help. For all of our sakes, I would like to find the truth. I don't wish for war; I don't wish for anyone to be harmed; I fully agree with what was agreed to at the Gathering ... that all nations live together in peace and harmony. All I want is for us to find the truth with regards to the giants. Then we can decide what to do. There should be no secrets. If it is their desire to live in peace and share with us, as we will share with them, then we will extend our arms in peace and brotherhood. But for the benefit of all our nations ... and our wives and children, we need to know.

"It is for this reason that I ask for your help."

Daj stared for several moments after Braga stopped talking, finally quivering to clear his mind. Braga's eyes were burning into him and there was that smile again. Daj stuttered, searching for words in response. *This man is mad. This man is mad ... but ... it might work!*

Braga had always been persuasive. With his combination of demeanor and forceful delivery confidently expressed, he'd always been formidable in debate. And what he had just expressed, even though expressed without the pressure of the trying conditions that could be expected, reminded him.

"Braga ... Braga, what you said was ... was good ... very good. But what if the leaders aren't impressed? People will be screaming ...

People will want you dead. What if they respond like the *Atjahahni* would … and reject your appeal, offering a cup of poison instead?"

Braga hesitated, his smile more one of resignation. "Then I would have to drink it."

Daj sat back, his own devious mind reeling.

Braga seemed to settle as well, the fire in him receding, "My friend, if you think about it … it's the only chance I have. Yes, it has its risk, but what else can I do? I don't want to live out my days as a rabbit shaking in hiding. The Great Spirit doesn't want this either … I feel he has great things in mind. He's already saved my life and given me direction. It's now up to me."

The conversation ended with that, the last question hanging without an answer. "Daj, it'll be dark soon and we don't want to be caught here when it happens," Braga said. "There *is* something else, though …"

Daj cocked his head as they picked their way through the debris around the cut and headed back in the fading light.

"You and your friends must leave. In fact, you should leave tomorrow. You've been a great help and there's more to do, but we can get by. You need to get back before the length of your absence raises questions.

"As I said before, I hope all of you will join me. I have a plan. It will be a *great* adventure. You'll see."

*   *   *

Daj continued to avoid the eyes, concentrating on the fire. *Thank the spirits for that,* he could relax, or at least look like he was mindlessly relaxing. Yes, tomorrow they would leave and be gone; but he would not forget the last conversation … or the final statement "I have a plan". His heart was racing so hard at the possibilities he thought his brain would burst.

PART FIVE

40

At the Village of the Denas Atjahahni

"You okay?"

John looked up, brow wrinkled, "Ah … sure. Why?"

"Oh nothing. It's just that you've been so quiet. Is there a problem?"

They were both sitting among cushions near to the fireplace where a small fire danced, giving more a suggestion of heat than the real thing. Even so the setting imparted a degree of comfort far beyond outside, where the gusts that made their domed homestead creak and groan, along with the sleet they carried, chilled to the bone.

Annie asked the question; but if there was a problem, it was her's not John's, and she knew it.

*　　*　　*

A week before they'd left Olympia. Leaving itself hadn't been the issue because of the busyness—with packing, then well wishes and goodbyes, and then accompaniments by many as they backtracked over the ridges and through the woods to the lake. For the three *Atjahahni* who'd been waiting, their arrival had been by far the most exiting event in almost two weeks, but that was short-lived. Rather than celebration, there was action—a quick placing of canoes in the water, a quick loading, a quick second round of good-byes and a quick casting off.

Since only eight were making the return trip, one of the canoes was left behind, which was a good thing because it would be Olympia's only waterway link. This also meant two to a canoe and as much as could be carried, which wasn't unusual, except that Da-hash-to was of little use in the one in which he was seated. Nyaho and Dlahni led the way, while Annie and John were last, doing so with gusto and brave smiles and that's when it hit her. She didn't turn around and wave until they were almost out of sight and the streams on her face hidden. Then it was onward with all the realities which she felt but didn't attempt to analyze except to the extent of thinking that *whither thou goest* bit was a bunch of crap. It didn't take a psychologist to understand. After finding John's etched message, she'd joined the search party and spent months on the trail, with all the discomforts and inconveniences trekking has to offer. Then she'd returned, and Olympia, her original home in the new world, was more appreciated than ever with its comparative abundance, cleanliness and camaraderie. Now she was heading back to the wilderness. Except for a few changes of clothing and as much food as the canoes could carry, there was nothing—neither tents nor machetes nor utensils nor twenty-first century conveniences. This was because John felt taking anything of the sort would cause problems back at the village.

So the return trip had been one of forced smiles and brave faces put to every situation, including the weather that continued to slide. Approaching home days later offered little to brighten this. With only a few miles to go they saw it coming. A generally overcast day anyway, it degenerated as soft clouds rolled over the ridges and swept down, turning the last leg into soupy visibility. Groping the rest of the way, they beached, unloaded and were stacking canoes before they were discovered, eliminating the rousing welcome that would have been of some encouragement.

But word travels fast. As the trudge up the slopes started, people began to materialize, Ruth and Brun-dahni and little Bobby among the first. The circumstances, even for those conditioned to the forest, weren't for any kind of celebration, so after the briefest of greetings, the party split into its parts and disappeared. It was more like horses returning to the barn.

For most, that is, except for Ruth. She'd been on the lookout and made what preparations she could, which was difficult because the estimated time of arrival extended over days. When the greetings were over, she raced back to the homestead and started the fireplace, lit candles, and scrambled to assemble the foodstuffs she'd set aside.

And that, with the family assembled, was the homecoming. After everyone had warmed and relaxed, however, it became as pleasant as conditions would allow, even with all the inevitable questions. Regarding these, Annie let John do the talking. The questions were about the same as were being asked in the houses of all the others in the returning party, and were ones to be repeated over and over around the community until everyone was informed and sated.

"What was the nation called again?
"Olympia."
"Oh yes, Olympia. *What's it like? How many live there?*

"We've seen the machete, what other tools did you see?

"It's rumored they have horrible weapons which they haven't been willing to show. Did you see them?

"What are their homes like?

"Did you see anything magical?"

But answers were only given to what was asked. Beyond that, nothing was volunteered, not yet anyway, which was something Annie didn't fully understand. When she'd asked John if that meant family too, he'd thought on it a moment and then said, "A secret is a secret until you tell one person." So she had listened as John danced among the probes, skillfully elaborating on what could be told, like the hard work of his friends in the fields which was similar to what the *Atjahahni* themselves did; and then the small water tower and showers and practices of cleanliness, which was of interest because of its scale, but was nothing surprising as they were familiar with John and his habits. Most astounding were the samples of grains, fruits and vegetables with which with they were not familiar, and the story of Homer the scarecrow that John presented with an enthusiasm that even had Annie laughing.

Nothing was mentioned about the mountain complex or the incubator and all of its wonders.

There'd been discussions about what could be revealed before the trip back started. All of the *Atjahahni*—Dlahni, Nyaho and Da-hash-to—were in awe of what they'd seen, and were bursting in anticipation of sharing them back home. John, however, who'd always been concerned about arms proliferation and other possibly detrimental bits of information, held doing so in question. The *Atjahahni* were puzzled ... and even disappointed that discretion needed to be considered. But as the matter was discussed, John continued to stress that the secrets the mountain held were not only priceless, needing every bit of protection, they were also so astounding they were beyond abilities to believe by simply hearing about them, particularly in a society far removed from those things. He felt the wonders of the twenty-first century to be extremely sensitive requiring a strategy and a process before being revealed.

The topic didn't move easily to consensus until Da-hash-to, surprisingly nodded, saying, *"What you say, John, is true. You have shared with us everything. These things you have shown are astounding, and they are precious. We will discuss them sometime in the future, but for now we will do as you say.*

"You have been touched by the Great Spirit. You are wise."

*   *   *

"No, Honey, there's no problem," John said, then snorted a laugh. "Actually, that's not true ... there are a bunch of them," leaning back against a cushion as he spoke.

"A bunch?"

"Yes, a bunch. A moment ago I was trying to figure where to start with them."

"I thought it was something like that. Any way I can help?"

John nodded. "One has to do with horses. Remember those

requests made to Cherstabonshala of the *Bjarla-shito* and Chjenohata of the *Njegleshito* regarding horses?"

"Yes."

"Well, if they succeed in bringing some in in the spring, we'll need pastures and corrals and shelters. That means clearing and fencing and gates and all kinds of stuff. You know better than I about these things. The same goes for pigeons. We need a shelter for them too. I was able to get plans for building one from computer files, but the plans are in terms of twenty-first century materials, which we don't happen to have.

"There's also the matter of the Sunday social a few days from now. I imagine Da-hash-to, Dlahni and Nyaho are meeting in council sometime today to report to all the Chieftains about what could be told of the recent trip, making plans at the same time for a bigger audience."

"You're not going to sit in on it?"

"No, I think it best to stay away so questions can be asked that otherwise wouldn't be. If they need me, I'm here.

"Honey, it may seem that we're stuck in an oversized tent of sticks one notch above a hole in the ground ... and while that's partly true, there's more. You've seen the rest of the village and experienced the rites of the harvest, so have a basic understanding of our culture. But what you can't understand by quick glimpses are the enormous changes that not only have already occurred, but are continuing to do so at an increasing pace. When I arrived twenty years ago the *Denas Atjahahni* were a culture hidden in the forest, a culture that hadn't changed for hundreds of years. Then the changes began, mostly influenced by observing and adopting what I did, even though I never intended to have an affect one way or the other.

"For instance, within their culture were many fears. They were afraid and respectful of spirits, spirits for almost every aspect of their world; they were afraid of nations they were aware of, even though they hadn't seen them in ages ... so long they were almost mythical; and, can you believe, they were afraid of water and couldn't swim, even though the lake was a life line.

"So there were gradual changes over those twenty years, but nothing compared to what's happening now. The last few months, with the Gathering of Nations at Pangaea, and more "giants", and the revelation of an Olympia farther south, has everybody off balance. I sense it.

"They're good people, Annie, and that part they did on their own before I came on the scene. One of the first things I noticed was that they've learned to live together with a reasonable degree of peace and justice and community. In fact community, the power of public opinion and culture are so strong they're exemplary.

"You must surely see that these things are ingrained in my family too, and that I care about them, not wanting something that's so good to be needlessly scrambled."

Annie nodded.

"And I'm concerned, because they're like people throughout the ages, including our great twenty-first century, and carry in their genes the same aptitudes for greed and ambition and malice we've had to contend with. I'm concerned that if we expose them to all we have too fast, the darker side of nature could be ignited in a mad scramble for new standards of living. Because of that it seems best to proceed at a pace they can handle."

"And that's why I've got to adapt to *their* way of living."

"I'm afraid so … at least for the time being. Look, those back at Olympia are in their own scramble to get to milestones, and I wish I were there to help … They could use a hand. But my place, our place, is here, and as for time, we have from here to eternity, and a whole world unknowingly doing its thing 'til we get there."

A few moments followed as Annie absorbed it all. She smiled, "Well, at least you answered my question."

"What question?"

"That you have a problem."

As they both laughed, Annie got to her knees and leaned over to give a quiet kiss, then sat back on her haunches. "Okay, so there are problems. If *you* have a problem … *I* have a problem. Let me know how I can help, and not just with the horses."

With that she stood and grabbed a jacket.

"Where are you going?"

"Just out … to look around."

"It's miserable outside…"

"But it *is* the world we live in, isn't it?"

He was right; it was miserable. She had taken only a few steps past the flaps before the foggy dampness did its thing, jacket or no jacket, and she shivered. Visibility was clear for ten feet or so, with the detail beyond that diminishing to form ghostly combinations of imagery ending in nothingness. Spooky. The spooky was enhanced by sound, which resonated even clearer than normally, or at least seemed so, which led to a game of trying to interpret what may be happening wherever the sounds came from.

She started in a direction leading to the bridge, intending to cross and make her way to the Commons, where subconscious sonar told her sounds were originating. She didn't get far. A few steps along, she detected movement.

"Who's there?"

When she heard giggles, she moved farther and soon the movements coalesced into shapes ... one, two ... seven in all ...

Children!

She recognized one of them ... "Bobby, is that you?"

More giggles.

"What are you doing here? What are all of you doing?"

That startled them and one retreated back into the gloom where a few others could be seen.

Annie laughed, "Is this some kind of a game?"

Bobby smiled, looked down, then to those on each side ... finally nodding.

"What's the game?"

He mumbled, not clear enough to understand, but his answer was clarified when the girl next to him blurted, "We wanted to see what you were doing."

"Why?"

More shrugs and kicking of pebbles.

Good God, Annie thought, *these kids have got to be bored out of their minds if I'm the best game in town.*

Oh my, then "Look, all of you, it's cold and nasty out here ... Why don't we go over to *Tschtaha-tata*. I'll tell you a story."

She knew she'd hit a note of accord because when they turned to follow, some of them skipped and twirled and ran about. That made her feel good, but the question now in mind was *What am I doing?*

This isn't my thing. She'd assisted with the young at church, but the stories told then all had a Christian message, and although that wasn't bad, she was mindful of the cautions John placed on things and didn't want to introduce what could be a problem. *So what was she going to do? Why wasn't Judy here? She was a teacher and probably had a thousand ideas for entertainment. Or Rebecca, she could get them to sing.*

Because of the visibility, the walk seemed longer than it really was, with apparitions for interpretation constantly popping out along the way. Then there was the large mass and she was lucky ... the building was empty. Once inside, however, she found conditions weren't a great deal better. The side panels had been dropped cutting off the breezes, but it was still cold, and the light through the winged skylights was the same gloomy grey engulfing the outside world. Adding to this, wisps of fog drifted through wherever lappings were loose.

Fortunately there were candles. It took a while to get the first one lit, but soon there were eight of them in varied dances depending on the drafts, half on the rocky west wall and the rest around the edge of the platform. When this had been done and the group, like restless cats, were seated in a semicircle crowding together to get warm, Annie plumped down to face them.

She started by saying, "My name is Annie Anderson. Please tell me your names."

While this went on, complete with giggles and elbowings and mumblings and such, Annie saw what she wanted. Among the group, now numbering twelve, of varying ages from just over toddler to about first grade, there was a girl with blond hair that fell in a tangle of curly ringlets.

"Mndana," She said, "I'm going to tell a story about a girl who looked a lot like you. She had beautiful hair similar to yours ... and her name was Goldilocks." With that she went on to tell the story of the three bears with all the theatrics she could muster. And in the telling the rapt attention, the flutter of expressions and body languages told her all she wanted to know. They loved it.

When it was over she asked "Did you like the story?" to which there were smiles and nods and a jumble of mumbled expressions.

"Okay, if you liked it, then clap your hands," which led to a game that made a lot of noise.

"Very good, very good, thank you," Annie said, extending her arms and patting the air to calm them down.

When she first entered *Tschtaha-tata*, she looked about in search of anything that could be used for entertainment. The candles had come first because there needed to be something to cut the gloom. Other things noted included the wall panels with their variety of artwork; hanging decorations whose meaning she didn't understand; large, circular but shallow ceramic bowls at the four crossings, each with ashy remnants, which meant they were primitive heaters; the globe John had crafted years ago on the upper tier; a collection of smooth flat stones arranged in another corner, and so on. Now as the children settled under her direction, another idea came to mind.

"Would you like to see some magic?"

The wild response she got with that required another calming. Then she told them of a magic way something could be told without saying anything. "Would you like to see how it's done?"

While the room rocked with the various ways of saying yes, Annie rose and went to the stones, picking the largest she could manage. Then she went to a bowl, and after digging, found a remnant near to a charcoal stick.

"I'm going to mark this stone with magic symbols … they're called letters. These letters are going to say something." When she'd finished she held the stone up for them all to see. "The letters say "Goldilocks"."

She only got blank looks.

"Now to prove this is magic, Bobby, you and Mndana take this to Mr. Anderson and ask him what it says. If he says "Goldilocks", it will prove what I've told you."

The two were gone in a flash, followed by a long period of restless waiting. Finally there was a noisy sound of approaching, a bursting through the flaps, and excited, babbling voices exploding "It's Magic!"

That evening the events of the day were repeated over and over, just like any unusual happening in a place generally starved for excitement. Ruth had come over with Bobby, laughing about what she had heard. Actually, the writing was a reminder of a lost art. Years before John had taught Willow and the children the alphabet and rudiments of writing. It had been fun for awhile, with being able to print their names and compose simple messages, but then the problem of writing materials, leather being too valuable to use, was such that it all faded away. Now it had surfaced again.

John said he had been in the woods, trying to visualize the lines that could be struck for a pasture when he heard the children calling for him. When they found him and showed the stone, his answer had them bubble and jump, then disappearing back the way they'd come.

He couldn't imagine what that was about.

Later, when they were alone, they settled in close to the fireplace similar to the way they'd started the day.

"How did you do with all of your problems?"

"Not very well. I tramped all around the woods south of here, and think I know what needs to be done for the horses, but I'd like to see it all again when it's not so foggy. It sounds like you did a lot better."

"Maybe, but it was weird. John, those kids are as bored as they can be. There's nothing for them to do."

"It seems that way. But you've got to realize it's been that way every winter for every generation going back forever. They get by because they have energy and minds and imagination. They'll find things to do … like seeing what the giant lady is doing. It sounds like everything worked well, but don't feel it's your responsibility to entertain them every day."

Annie sat up, "I wasn't thinking as much about responsibility or entertainment, as I was about opportunity. There's a need to be filled."

"You mean schooling?"

"Yes."

"Well, in a way you're right. The last night at Olympia, a few of us were talking about something similar."

"Who?"

"Mostly the men ... and Judy, who happened by, heard a bit and joined in. We were talking about all the work that's needed to be done and how good it would be to have help. That led to the fact that the source for that is from the villages we've gotten to know, which mainly means the *Atjahahni*. From there the conversation went every which way."

"Are all of you making the problem more than it is?"

John nodded, "Could be. But I'm not the only one concerned about security, and the best way to train a primitive culture."

"Come again?"

"That didn't sound right, did it? Well, let me explain. There was a concern about cultures and work ethic and things like that. But I reminded them about how the *Atjahahni* joined together to make community improvements, to build *Tschtaha-tata*, to make a fleet of canoes and to conduct two years worth of preparations for the Gathering of Nations.

"I told them I'd like as many as possible see the next Crafts Fair. I think they'll be surprised at the industry and ingenuity displayed there."

"Weren't we talking about schooling?"

"Schooling ... were we?" He laughed, "Oh yes, schooling. Well, Judy and Abram and Benjamin all jumped on that one. They felt that this had to be a part of the program ... an academy even. But they didn't get far with details.

"The problem right now is material. Reynolds and Huston jammed all kinds of things into storage, but the space was limited. We have computers and printers and lab equipment and a lot of handy things. And we have paper and pencils.

"Just guess what's becoming critical? It's paper and pencils. It looked like there were plenty, but soon everyone realized how precious they were and began rationing, using both sides, erasing, stuff like that ... because when the supplies are gone, then what? As we discussed this, Rodney had groaned. There are so many things in need, like brick and concrete and mortar and cement and ceramics and glass and on and on. He had solved the soap problem as one of the first, but the list of others keeps growing, and now with paper.

"And I certainly understood the last part. As Ruth mentioned, I started schooling of sorts years ago with the family, but could only go so far because of a lack of things to work with."

"What did the ancients do?"

"They learned how to make paper, for one. You know ... like papyrus. But that was in limited amounts for use by scribes."

"How did you design the things you built, like this home ... like *Tschtaha-tata*?"

"You do what you have to do. I used a sand-box and stick, and when I came up with something good, left the image until it was conveyed to memory. I also toyed with sticks and assorted materials to make models, like what Bruno is doing at Olympia. But none of these apply to teaching kids."

"Actually they might. There might be all sorts of things that can be used to stir imaginations and make a point. What about slate-boards and chalk. Weren't they used during colonial times?"

"Hmmm ... that's a thought."

"Any of that around?"

"Could be. There's most every kind of rock in these hills, and I have seen bits of slate. Maybe there's a place where it can be peeled away in sheets. I'll ask Nyaho, he knows these mountains better than anyone. If there's slate around, he'll know where."

Annie yawned, "This has been quite a day. One last thing."

"Promise it's the last."

"I promise ... It's about letters. You were handed a few when we returned to Olympia. Did you read them?"

John sucked air at the thought. "It's tough to read them."

"So you read them."

"All but the last one from dad."

"Same here with the last from mom. There's also a last letter copied to each of us from Huston, and one more to me from Reynolds. If the weather isn't better tomorrow, let's read them. They're a bridge to cross."

"Okay."

41

A Letter from Helen

Dear Annie,

The post office announced that in a few days they'll be closing service, so if anyone wants to mail anything, they'd better get with it.

I wasn't surprised. So that being the case, here goes.

You know how I liked to sit on the side porch and read or knit. Well, a long time ago I'd also made a habit of counting cars that went by. The number fluctuated, but generally fell within a certain range.

A few weeks ago, maybe a month, it dawned on me the number was on the low side. Then as each new count was made, I could not ignore why this was happening. A few days later, there were only a few.

So we began making plans.

One idea came to mind that was just too good to pass up. Remember that silly joke your daddy made about the barn John and he painted winning a blue ribbon? Well, I decided to make it happen. I took one of your awards, one with folds all around a center medallion with a large "one" in it and two ribbons hanging below, and drove into town. Stopped at Millies Millinery, you know that place that isn't much about hats at all but more of sewing stuff and rolls of material, and showed Millie your award. I told her I wanted one just like it only three feet in diameter.

There wasn't much going on there or anywhere else in town for that matter, but when I said what it was for, it sparked life back into the place and soon a half-dozen were cutting and sewing and laughing. When it was done, I took out my checkbook and asked "how much", to which Millie looked at me like I was crazy. She finally said, "I understand Fred makes great chokecherry wine. Get me a jug and we'll call it even."

Anyway when your daddy was out in the field, actually he was riding Missie, I think to keep his mind off things, I got out the ladder and hung the ribbon over the barn door.

When he returned I didn't say a word, just kept busy away from him because you know I can't keep a straight face and he'd know something was up.

Then I heard him laughing. He laughed so hard, that when I found him he had sagged down to sit on the front steps. He even called a few neighbors he knew to be still around, and soon we had a bunch in the yard, all laughing and sipping wine.

I thought you'd find that funny as we've sure had a good time over it. On a more serious side, you and John are on our minds every still moment. We know you are now on your journey, a journey like none other before. So we think of all the times of the past, and of the pride you'd made us feel. As to your challenge, we've tried to picture what it might be like. From what we understand, it's to start mankind all over again, and to do so in a way that prevents the mistakes of the past from happening again.

What a noble challenge. We are numbed at the very thought, because people can be so contrary sometimes, it's no surprise that things get muddled. Even at our Ladies Aid sessions at church, with the good lord looking over our shoulders, it's not unusual for someone to get in a snit and cause a problem. I've told you all about that before.

We wish we could pass on some helpful thought to consider, but it's far beyond our simple ability. The best we could come up with we gleaned from the bible, First Corinthians 13:13

And now these three remain: Faith, hope and love.
But the greatest of these is love.

Your dad has just come up from the cellar, and says the special batch of chokecherry wine is almost ready.
We are ready, and we send you our love,
Forever.

Mom and dad

42

A Letter from Reverend Anderson

Dear John,

I've been known as a person who never let an opportunity to speak at length go to waste, but I'm having trouble now. I guess a last chance to be profound is just too intimidating.

I know Mark has written to you as well, so there's no reason to repeat in detail, except to say how proud we are, and how proud you would be, if you were to see him in action. He spends most of his time either doing what he can for the children, or helping others. But it isn't just in the doing, it's the way his works are being done, always cheerfully and uplifting, even under the most dreadful of circumstance.

As mentioned before, attendance at church grew and grew until it was overflowing, even for multiple services. It has been wonderful, with a fervor in participation that's something we've waited a lifetime to see. And it hasn't been just here; from what I've heard it's been in churches all over the land.

Which leads me to a hope, and that is that there truly is a power of prayer, and with the voices that together resound, our great God in Heaven will hear and will look, not only on us with kindness, but also on you and your fellow travelers, with guidance and support.

We're now past the crescendo, and we know what that means. That point was reached a month ago, and since then the numbers have steadily dropped. I'm now working on the message for what is going to be my final service. That's because at the last one numbers were way down, and many, who were uncomfortable, took to the back rows in case a quick exit was necessary.

I'm having trouble with the message because you and Annie and your Chosen have been so much on my mind. Chosen ... what a wonderful word. In the past few years, books like in the "Left Behind" series have been popular with the theme of life on earth coming to an end, and there being an alternative. And now there are you two and the Chosen ... and there is an alternative.

I'm so proud I'm almost bursting, which doesn't make keeping the secret you promised me to make any easier. Anyway all of you will be having a challenge so much greater than my simple sermon that the latter pales by comparison. And I can't stop hoping that I would have some magnificent visionary idea to contribute to your deliberations.

I do, and here it is ... Of all the thoughts that have come to mind, the best of the lot have to do with training ... early training.

Why? Because the human mind is amazing beyond our ability to understand. That's why some compose musical concertos at four; that's why some remember events from every day of their lives; that's why some speak multiple languages; that's why some answer multi-numeral calculations in their heads in seconds.

Unfortunately the mind is also enigmatic.

Men have been brain-washed to follow tyrants. Men have been trained to maim and kill without conscience. Men have been swayed to dedicate themselves to fallacies. Men have been influenced by rumor and innuendo and flimsy rationale.

That's why we pick sports teams at an early age, and follow them the rest of our lives; that's why we choose a political party or a stance, not because of an understanding or conviction, but because of prejudice or emotion.

What I'm getting to, without belaboring the point, is that characteristics of the mind need to be addressed for the good that can come. That's important because I know all of you will be struggling to achieve a society that will be the best you can fashion, one that will be challenging, beneficial and sustainable. Church leaders have said, "Give me a child for five years and I'll have him forever," and what they say is true.

Therefore, if a society is shaped that meets your objectives, and its qualities are taught universally at an early age, I believe you will have the success you seek.

Putting these thoughts to words has given me an idea for Sunday. I'm going to say I've had a dream. And in that dream I was introduced to a group that was chosen to survive this pandemic, and although they were ordinary like you and me, they were also extraordinary. They were extraordinary because they not only believed in God and had goodness in their hearts, they also had the wisdom of the ages in their minds.

I'll also say that in that vision, I saw this group, a Chosen group, lead the remnants of mankind back from calamity, to the promise of glory that God the Father envisioned when he first fashioned all of creation, including man in his image.

Now, since we all believe in Christ, and with that believe we will meet again in heaven; I look forward to that time when once again, among friends, I can say ... "I told you so."

Our last thoughts will be of you,
With love

Mom and dad

43

A Letter from Huston

My Dear Friends:

It's been fifteen years and it's time to write. Yes, there's a log posted every day, but the postings are usually blah, which means digging through them for gems will be tedious. Besides, we're getting older, and while Bones and Reynolds are doing fine; I'm not and don't expect to be around much longer. So … if I've got things to say, which of course I do, it's now or never.

Passing on is not a problem. Actually all of us remaining here are bored as hell as each day, except for the weather, has taken on a sameness that truly tries the soul. We've listened to every tune and watched every movie to a point where they're memorized and without punch. The outdoors have more to offer, including work in the gardens or riding the trails, but even they have taken on a sameness.

As for the gardens, we assembled two animatronic scarecrows— Homer and Jethro—that really are something. I say "we", but as you can imagine I had nothing to do with them. You may have met some of the technically inclined and talented people who did, like Nadj Patanbuku, Mikal Bjorn and Benjamin Oki. Anyway they had a ball assembling the scarecrows and putting them to work—a success that would have delighted any Disney crowd, but which eventually led to a problem. It seems critters from the woods love our gardens, which means lots of movements setting them off, which means lots of programmed reactions, which means getting on our nerves. We'll try to preserve them for your use, however, because they really do a service. As for the problem ... you'll see.

All of this is not to say there haven't been things of interest. A year ago three of our group, not really needed anymore, set out on bicycles with bulging panniers. They intended to see the world, or at least what was left of it, by riding to the coast. There they hoped to find a boat—a sailboat large enough for accommodations but small enough for them to manage—in condition for the oceans. We heard from them for the first few hundred miles, but since then their attempts went from garbles to static to silence. We've only been able to hope they're doing well and having a great final adventure.

Another item was the hike Reynolds and some of the boys took a few weeks ago. They'd hiked and camped and in the process traveled fifty miles, when at one of the small towns in the valley they came upon a group of survivors. The survivors, a dozen of both sexes, were young, less than twenty in age, which meant they must have been one of those groups holed up in a food mart when the plague hit. Anyway they were a sad sight. They were small and undernourished and dressed in mismatching remnants ... They babbled on non-sensibly ...

They were a rat-pack.

Reynolds said when the pack spotted them, they shrieked and scattered. This was okay because, as you may not know, we'd agreed if survivors were seen, we'd stay away so as not to affect them one way or another.

Therefore our boys turned and skedaddled, or at least tried to, but lo and behold, the rat-pack reassembled and followed. Seeing no harm being done to them, the survivors closed in like begging urchins. Reynolds tried to shoo them, but they got nasty. So our group got nastier, screaming and yelling and cracking whips and throwing things and basically scaring the hell out of them. Reynolds said what they'd done bothered everyone, the youngsters being so pitiful and all, but they had to do it.

The main reason for writing is to share thoughts all of us have bandied about that might apply to the challenge for which you've been chosen. Please understand, we don't wish to dictate the course you should follow or the decisions you need to make. We can't do that because we can't possibly know the conditions existing eight thousand years in the future. *(Yes, we didn't tell you during our last time together, but eight thousand seemed a good time for the hibernation. Of course you know that by now).*

Anyway, with all the time on our hands, we've taken to studying the resources you have as reference. We had many ideas about society and governance before, but without question, the study, which has been considerable, has given much more to consider. *(Not to worry, I won't include all the ingenious conclusions arrived at during our late-night, wine-inspired symposiums)*

The following then are some of those thoughts, not necessarily in order of importance or chronology.

To summarize the Mission ... It is to start mankind over again, averting the mistakes of the past, to create a sustainable society in harmony with the natural world, a society which elevates mankind to the potential of his God-given genius.

(Wow! That's a tall order)

The challenge of the mission is composed of two basic parts—namely nature, which must be preserved; and mankind, which must be controlled.

First about nature. The creator assembled, previous to mankind, a world of plants and animals and birds and bees and fishes in seas amazingly in harmony. In every species, and in the combination of species, there was balance ... a balance characterized by interweavings of birth, death and regeneration. There has been ebb and flow regarding this, and there has been a rate of extinction as evolution in all things continued their processes; but generally things stayed on course, being biodegradable, recyclable and non-polluting.

Now comes man. He doesn't have claws or fangs and he doesn't run fast and he doesn't have great numbers, so you might think he doesn't have an impact. But that's not true. He has a thumb and he has a brain and along the way he has a spark. Anyway, he's different, and he's a formidable predator. Other predators hunt in packs and use strategies and so does man; but other predators generally stay in an area and are part of the natural balance of that area.

Not so man.

Studies agree that he initially took form in Africa millions of years ago, then migrated. From earliest times a movement, at roughly a quarter-mile per year, occurred from point of origin to the ends of the earth. This migration first crossed into nearest Asia, then Europe, then north across Siberia to the Americas, while extending south to the orient and the islands of the Pacific.

These migrations have been recorded globally with arrows and dates, and while they didn't reach a few areas until One CE *(previously known as the birth of Christ)*, most were inhabited 15,000 years before.

Why the migrations?

Reasons could be growing populations and lack of opportunity or dwindling food. Regardless, there was migration.

All this time the numbers of humans were small and shouldn't have been a factor in his surroundings, but it's been proven otherwise. You may remember what was said at the *Easter Armageddon* Conference ... "It has been discovered that man's migrations have coincided with animal extinctions. Man has, in fact, proven to be our foremost planetary killer".

This then becomes part of the challenge ... How mankind can become a part of nature and its balance without destroying it ... How mankind can manage its growth.

Making this difficult is the very animal we're dealing with. If we were trying to manage cattle or sheep or even lions, there would be simple answers and procedures. But we're considering human beings, us guys, who consist of complexities to which lifetimes of study haven't unraveled. While we've accomplished wonders of scintillating description, we've also exhibited depravities defying explanation, including a disregard for all of nature.

All of which has been exacerbated by population.

When you get settled after awakening, our guess is that you'll find the area within reach to be sparsely populated. So sparse, in fact, you'd have to go back tens of thousands of years before the plague to find a number as small. Now we know from that point the population grew slowly and didn't reach 300 million until about One CE.

What kept the population under control during all those years? And, is there a reason for the number to be controlled?

As mentioned before, in all of nature there was balance. That meant population control. This was affected in a number of ways, varying with the species, but generally consisting of innate life cycles, disease and predators. Without these controls, any specie can overpopulate and upset the balance.

A good example occurred along the northwest coast years ago. It seems during an unusually cold winter a channel froze, allowing a small herd of elk to cross to a remote island where lush arctic grasses and other edibles grew. In the spring the channel melted, stranding the herd. This wasn't a problem, however, because conditions were perfect—temperatures were moderate because of surrounding waters, food was abundant, and natural enemies were back on the mainland.

As a result the population grew and grew and grew.

A visitor to the island later described the scene that resulted. The ecology of the area was in ruin; the island was barren with only a few sprigs fighting to re-establish; and the area was layered with vast amounts of bleaching bones.

The lesson in this for all of life is obvious.

For mankind, it would seem that there have been more controls than has been the case for other species. There has been the life span, of course, and the diseases and maladies that assault all during that span. It's been estimated there are 20,000 diseases in the assault, the worst of which have been plagues, which time and again decimated populations, not to mention the last and worst. And there have been predators, especially in the early years. But predators have been minor compared to man himself. With mankind, there not only has been killing on an individual basis, there's also been warfare on a global basis. No other animal has been as prone to killing one another.

Our history, therefore, includes warfare and, incredibly, its art. Even when the world's population was at that level of 300 million and holding, history records the constancy of ambition and conquest and war and killing. At Cannae in Italy in 216 BCE, large Carthaginian and Roman armies took to the field, and with swords and spears and arrows slaughtered over 80,000 in one day. Later Genghis Khan in eastern Europe and Shaka Zulu in southern Africa compiled gruesome statistics while depopulating their areas. All of this and much, much more was exceeded by Hitler and Stalin and Mao Zedong in the twentieth century, when tens of millions were common statistics.

Then after World War II, with a substantial suppression of diseases and a marginalizing of conflicts, the world's population exploded. At the time of the plague it reached 7 billion, and projected to be 10 billion in another generation.

This begs the following.

If we don't have rampant diseases and raging wars, will planet earth go the way of that offshore island? Will our planet, an Eden-like island in the cold vastness of space, become a barren wasteland of bones because of unrestrained growth and consumption? That situation may be hard to imagine with the limitless expanse we expect you'll find, but remember the extent of teeming in the twenty-first century.

Interesting questions. At first, population won't be a problem, in fact, the opposite will probably be the case; but ultimately it will be if there isn't a plan. But must war be a part of this plan? If not, what then? Can culture and government include satisfactory controls?

Culture and government are closely linked, but let's consider culture first. We are of course, most familiar with conditions of the twenty-first century, but rather than comment on that, I'll return to the most basic of premises.

We are part of the animal kingdom, mammals to be exact. In this kingdom, the difficulty of existence in the balance nature has enacted can be expressed:

A lion awakens in the morning.
It knows it must run faster than the slowest gazelle
*   or it will starve;*
A gazelle awakens in the morning.
It knows it must run faster than the fastest lion
*   or it will be killed.*

Under these conditions, then, each creature must have a process, not only of surviving *during* maturity, but surviving *until* maturity. For that there must be a family of sorts.

The lion in the expression is a good example. As a cub it's nurtured. Like the delightful, innocent infants of most mammals, it's protected while it suckles and cuddles and plays; then as it gets older it follows along to see the dangers of the world; then it participates in the hunt; until finally it gets to a size and ability whereby it can survive on its own.

In contrast to this is the lion raised in a zoo where it lives in an environment without danger, and fed an optimum diet on a regular basis. This seems great for the captive lion, and in a way it is because most creatures, if given a choice, will select a life without fear or work or responsibility. The downside is that a natural culture is destroyed; and if the animal raised this way is released in the wild, it won't survive to perpetuate.

The parallel of this to the human animal is more real than you may realize. We've spent many a night discussing this very premise ... that there's a reason and a responsibility for each generation to train the next to be able to shoulder the responsibility of maturity and sustainability. There have been many examples where cultures did train for specific results. In some cases it was for obedience to a religion; in some cases it was to war, like the warriors of Sparta. In all of these there was a society that demanded obedience, or a family unit that provided guidance. If we return to the twenty-first century, however, we find conditions that are disturbing. We find political leadership overly partisan, we find governmental programs burgeoning and unsupportable, and we find families disintegrating.

All of them run counter to what's needed ... and I'll leave you with that.

Now on to governments.

There's plenty to study in this regard with thousands of years of history and scores of examples. The forms are as different as night and day, but they have one thing in common ... they and the societies they controlled ultimately failed.

And that's alarming, because now we know of even more essentials that must be met if the mission is to succeed. Now we know that a system must be sustainable, and, in harmony.

The earliest years of awareness to governance are of little concern because they were mainly of small communities with few effects on one another. If they were led by dictators in successive power struggles, or families, or oligarchies or selected leaders, it didn't matter.

But then populations grew and communities combined and nations took shape. The earliest for which we have record include Egypt, Mesopotamia, Persia, India and China. Each of these have unique histories, some extending over thousands of years. Although there were many variations within those histories, there was commonality ... a ruling order at the top, and a priesthood or religion that maintained control over all aspects of living. Together they made populations little more than slaves.

These societies did advance impressively, building great public works, temples and tombs including ones considered wonders of the ancient world. But war and conquest and ego and greed and intrigue were constant companions ... as was ultimate failure.

Then around the fifth century BCE, in Athens, among a group of semi-friendly city-states in Attica, a new concept came to light. Athenians were free thinkers, not beholden to the omnipotent rulers prevailing in the east who dominated most of the world at that time. Their great discovery was freedom, and with it self-government, which meant every farmer, shepherd, craftsman and businessman was a citizen taking part in government and the courts of justice. Freedom was something new and astounding, completely in contrast to the east where despots had ruled for ages, and was the first experience in a form that came to be known as democracy—government by the people.

They extended this discovery and their religion, which was for a pantheon of Gods, to the islands of the Aegean and the coast of nearby Asia Minor. Unfortunately, the proximity of this extension led to a conflict between Athens and Persia—a pygmy versus a giant—at the beginning of the fifth century BCE when Athenians came to the aid of a Greek colony on some issue, and in so doing burned the Persian city of Sardis. This irrational act led to war as Darius of

Persia assembled a huge force and invaded, intending to burn Athens in return.

What happened was Marathon, an impossible victory. Then a generation later, there were Thermopylae and Salamis, which have also been legendary battles ever since. These became part of the Golden Age of Greece led by Pericles, an age in which civilization sparkled with not only the torch of liberty, but also with levels of achievement in art and sculpture and architecture and writing and theater like no other time before.

The bright flame that was Greece in the fifth century, however, didn't sparkle long. There was a long, tragic war with Sparta, a neighbor within the Hellas that earlier had been an ally. When it ended near the beginning of the fourth century, Greece, as a nation, was only a shadow of its former self.

From the ashes, however, a number of concepts lived on to be studied. One was in cultural sustaining. During that Golden Age, Athens's young men were given several years of military training, and then in solemn ceremony took the following oath:

I will not bring dishonor upon my weapons nor desert the comrade by my side. I will strive to hand on my fatherland greater and better than I found it. I will not consent to anyone's disobeying or destroying the constitution, but will prevent him, whether I am with others or alone. I will honor the temples and the religions my forefathers established.

More of what had been survived through schools for which Greece maintained an academic prominence in the world. These were led by teachers and philosophers such as Socrates, Plato, Isocrates and Aristotle. From all of them, thoughts passed through the ages are timeless in their relevance. One of them that in my mind rings with an everlasting truth is the following:

The first purpose of government must be to train its citizens the right doing, since its strength was sapped and its existence threatened if they become corrupt.

The importance of nurturing and training keeps repeating (just as it had for the lion).

Nonetheless and sadly, these experiences with democracy in Greece failed, and the causes for that failure are similar to those that led to every other societal failure—power, greed, corruption, complacency and rejection of responsibility.

Forgive me for rambling on about Greece, but they were the first to recognize freedom and to attempt a form of government that would be the best for its people. Since then there have been many more forms, but rarely were they with the same objectives that gave democracy its exciting spin.

Our Founding Fathers, no doubt studied all of them in their attempts to form, as they called it, "a more perfect union". And there was no shortage of opinions as many attempted to outline considerations that would lead to that objective. Greece after Pericles had failed, but that didn't keep thoughts from being recorded. There was Plato and his *Republic;* then Rome, which rose to become the next major power of the planet, used the same word "Republic" to describe its representative form of government.

The Republic failed too.

Notable shortly after that failure was Marcus Aurelius, an emperor who, as a stoic philosopher, was a ray of hope within the madness that was imperial Rome. He lived a simple and admirable life when all about was the power and temptation to do otherwise, and wrote *Meditations* outlining his thoughts. His words and works came to naught, however, for when he died, his son, Commodus, rather than continue an enlightened path, reverted to the madness that preceded it.

And on and on and on.

In the seventeenth century John Locke wrote his *Two Treatises of Government*, which seemed to bring the best of thoughts to a topic that many had given their attention. The treatises may have influenced the Founding Fathers, as may have parts of the English Government with which they were at odds.

And finally the actions of the Founding Fathers. They debated and debated, which wasn't easy because the delegates came from colonies that were not only remote from one another, but also different in economics and interests. Along the way the following bubble of excellence was expressed:

We hold these truths to be self evident:—that all men are created equal, that they are endowed by their Creator with certain unalienable rights; that among these are life, liberty, and the pursuit of happiness.

This was a beautiful start to a document that inspired a nation to shine like a beacon for the world to follow for centuries afterwards. Unfortunately, even the best efforts can be imperfect, and can fail when imperfect isn't good enough. In one regard the fine message of the bubble wasn't followed. Half the colonies in the budding nation were slave states, with their delegates firmly dedicated to keeping it that way. This may be easy to understand since their way of life had been established for over a hundred years, with their economies securely wedded to the institution. But be that as it may, slavery was wrong, and the states in which it was a part ignored the reality that at some point it would have to be abandoned. There was no concession, however, leading to an eight-fold increase in the number of slaves eighty-five years later when the issue again came to fore, making the problem that much more difficult to resolve.

The Civil War resulted, 750,000 died, and problems continued 150 years later.

The issue of slavery hasn't been the only imperfection surfacing from the wonderful efforts of the Fathers. Most of them really belong to succeeding generations. The Fathers did not favor a large central government, and were therefore careful to preserve many rights of governance for the states. They felt representatives should be selected by their peers because of individual abilities and records of service rather than elections that could be influenced by contributions and special considerations. *(They would be disturbed by the continuous and incredibly expensive campaigning the process ultimately came to.)* In addition they felt strongly that an individual's fortunes in life should come from his own efforts, and not from favoritism, entitlements or welfare. In the years that followed these and other premises were revisited, challenged, diluted and whittled.

There was Thoreau and his *Walden Pond*, which espoused the simple life and suggested how it might influence society. But his were not the only thoughts at the time, as it was estimated every other person in New England had the perfect system tucked away in his back pocket. Near that same time came Karl Marx with his concepts that influenced so much of the world, despite its immorality and disregard of individual freedom. But the greatest eroding factor to the great work the Founding fathers began were the same as experienced before—power, greed, corruption and complacency.

All of which leads to where you are today, working on a mission of staggering difficulty. We know, being so familiar with the caliber of you, the Chosen, that it *will* finally be resolved.

With all our blessings, fare thee well,

Huston

P.S.

There's a reason I asked all of you to wait six months before opening your copies of this letter. By that time I felt you'd have worked together and gotten to know one another pretty well.

You probably noticed something else—that none of you is eager to lead. This isn't an accident. When we selected you, we were looking for specific qualities … certainly health and training and compatibility; we were also sensitive to work ethic and team skills and service orientation. On the wary side were profiles with strong aspirations to lead … not that such is damning because the general opinion of industrial psychologists is that organizations need all types. We felt, however, that there's a danger leading can turn to ruling … there are just too many historical examples to ignore that possibility. So we opted for leadership by service.

You'll work it out.

Cheers

44

A Letter from Reynolds

Dear Annie

 As I write I'm trying to visualize what it must be like to read this, since over eight thousand years will have passed … Talk about a voice from the past. Anyway here goes.

 This has been quite a day with a lot of things needing to be done. One of the last was to open the pens a final time. We've been working on that to get the animals accustomed to new freedoms, more independence, and hopefully survival.

 As part of this, I couldn't resist another ride. You'll recall that while all of you were going through your preps, you had a chance to see the menagerie of animals we were assembling, which included a good stable of horses. All of this, of course, was because we anticipated years with needing to care for things besides ourselves.

 That bit of planning saved our sanities … and being a farm girl, you may have similar recollections. Anyway, among the horses, the first colt born became my favorite and we became buddies, initially as "Peetey" and then later as "Ole Pete". So I saddled Ole Pete and rode … nothing fast you see as neither of us had bones for that anymore. We headed west along the dirt road; then a little past the spearhead we cut south along the well worn pathway, crossed a few shallows and wound up switchbacks to the bald a few miles south.

 Along the way it seemed every animal the forest had to offer crossed our path. Maybe they'd done that before and I just hadn't noticed. Anyway today I did.

From the bald so much came into view—the farm, the streams below and lake to the west, all imbedded in the multi-hued greens and shadows of the forested mountains. It was beautiful.

And all that I saw made me think.

I'd spent years with GreenPeace because of my concern for the forms of life that were being threatened. All of that came back amplified ... amplified because in the last twenty-six years, I've come to realize they're more than just low-level species. Much, much more. They're each part of amazing systems. They're creatures with senses: eyes that see and minds that think and cultures that unite and personalities that distinguish. You'll understand this—that all the animals on our farm eventually showed traits, were given names because of them, and responded to the attention given to them.

We tend to think we're unique and special and made in "His" image so the good book says. And that's easy to believe. For instance, we can look at our hand and as fingers move, we see veins and bones and tendons and joints move in unison on command, and so we marvel at how great we are with these and all our other parts, and how we are blessed to be so created. But if we think about it, every other creature, great and small, is just as amazing in its own way, and in like manner has been created ... created in an evolutionary process over gazillions of generations.

Forgetting Ole Pete for a moment, who was getting restless while my brain whirled me into such inaction that I had to lean forward and pat his neck, think of any bird. They're marvelous creatures. It will have oodles of feathers of many varieties, each with a different function and each somehow controlled so they act together to allow the bird to do the amazing things it does. Did you ever wonder how a bird can fly into a tree, banking and flitting and yawing while at full speed, and not hitting any of the leaves or twigs or branches that complicate its path, until it skids on air to a halt at a somehow selected perch?

Or a squirrel in what it does ... or any other animal?

Or a spider, with its tiny body and smaller brain, which exudes a thread—a thread of an incredible organic compound that's not only adhesive but also that's stronger than an equivalent weight of steel—lays out its exudation to somehow discerned supports, then returns to weave a web back to center and complete a pattern that any well-schooled architect would marvel?

How?

Yes, the world is a wonderful composite. I see it now as never before, and see that every living part deserves a voice as it spins. With all these thoughts, I felt like the Indian on Huston's bronze—a sculpture by Remington, I believe. He sits on his horse and looks at the heavens, arms splayed. And like him, I asked the question that's been asked by every person since climbing down from the tree—is there a God? Are you there? You must be because all these wonders just can't happen; they're so astounding I can't scratch the surface of how great they really are.

And another question, if you're listening … when I shed this mortal coil, is there more? Will my spirit remain and drift to a place where I can once more be among loved ones? Will I see Helen and Karen again? If so will I be watching you and cheering and helping any way I can, and then be waiting to greet you when your circle is complete?

I really want to know.

Well, I'm obviously back from the ride and have given Ole Pete a last hug. Now I must go …: there's a rendezvous …

One more thing, though … and it's hard to express. You became like part of the family back in those high school days when you and Karen began to hang out. Then you became all there was after the accident. That void was impossible to fill; but somehow you created something else, and gave new meaning and purpose to my life. As a result I've been as proud as any father.

Have you enjoyed the conversations we've had since you went to sleep? Maybe you didn't hear them. You see, I ask because every time I went down into the incubator, I stopped by your cocoon, set your picture on top—the one of you holding your gold metal from the Chimney Rock Relays with Helen and Karen clapping in the background—and talked. If you doubt this, the proof is scattered among the molecules of air down there.

I have that picture before me right now as I finish this ramble …

I go, loving you forever

45

Winter

It was early February and it should have been near to the coldest day of winter, but it wasn't. Instead the sky was clear, and although at daybreak it had been almost freezing, by midday temperatures had risen into the fifties, making the day surprisingly pleasant. It became a particularly good day for Ann.

Months before when the first make-shift class had been held, the concept of schooling had grown. Ruth and a few of her friends, young mothers all, took to the idea and were eager to help, learning in most cases along with the children. The biggest obstacle—materials to work with—had been alleviated by Nyaho just as John suggested. When a sample piece of slate was shown to him, with the question of where more of it could be found, he knew the answer. That led to an expedition to a ridge a day away to the southwest, where, by clearing a jumble of black rubble that was otherwise insignificant, a plane of slate came to the surface.

Then by meticulously cleaving and prying and breaking and trimming, a supply of semi-uniform tablets, enough for those who were interested and then some, was collected. With tablets in hand, a corner was turned allowing exercises and learning in a number of topics, most notably reading, but also numbers, crude art and whatever games could be contrived.

All of this was a great way to while away hours when winter

conditions discouraged anything else, adding skills and interests to what had been at times endless boredom. On this day, however, the outdoors like a siren song beckoned, so after a period of wandering attentions, class was dismissed, adults and children alike anxious to get away.

For Annie it was to give John, who could use all the help he could get, a hand. Still hampered by primitive tools, the things needing doing had piled up into an exhausting demand of time. Among them were preparations for receiving and caring for horses, which became top priority even though the chances of receiving them were remote.

Annie, whose experiences were invaluable, outlined those needs. They included a cleared and fenced-in pasture at least four acres in size, a corral within this area between fifty to seventy feet in diameter, and a stable of some sort to one side—the side nearest the homestead.

So with every hour the weather allowed, and quite a few when it didn't, John was at work. And he wasn't alone. Dlahni was usually at his side, as was Brun-dahni, and at times a surprising number of other young men, who through observations and the pride of previous involvements—like the Commons and *Tschtaha-tata* and Pangaea—had been affected with a work ethic.

When the location and extent of the pasture were determined, clearing began. Bushes and light vegetation were the first to go, being tugged and pulled out roots and all. Anything grassy or edible were left, however, and if plants had a use, such as berry bushes for food, or others for medicinal purposes, or bamboo for too many uses to mention, they were carefully replanted. Small caliper trees, which usually were straight trunked as they stretched skyward, were uprooted, trimmed and stacked for construction, for which there would be a big demand.

Then there were the trees … the big ones.

For these, John saw that areas on both sides of the outer fence should be cleared, leaving only those trees along the fence line for posts, with trees in roughly a third of the area nearest the village allowed to remain. This was because the openness created in the portion cleared would take away the hiding space panthers and wolves, who'd find horses, particularly colts, yummy, might use.

Annie arrived to find over two dozen at work, with John and Dlahni into fencing, a portion of which had already been completed. The fence consisted of small caliper trunk-rails spanning between trees retained as posts, where notches were cut and rails set-in, secured by pegs through reamed holes. With tree-posts at random locations, the fence zigged and zagged and wasn't, even with best efforts, a thing of beauty. Rails at the four to five foot height and half-way between, however, provided a barrier that should do the job of keeping horses in place, which was what it was all about.

The rest of the men were at the trees marked for removal, where they swarmed, digging and whittling in processes where progress was measured in chips.

Annie looked at that part of the work and shook her head. She was reminded of the same problem at Olympia when they'd first broken out. They'd compared the challenge then as the work of "ants that can't", and had sung the song and laughed. But at Olympia there were axes and shovels and saws of steel; while here there were imitations of those tools in wood and stone and bone. Even so, spirits were just as high … and … trees *were* coming down.

Hours later, in early afternoon, an interruption brought everything to a halt. Annie had been bouncing from one thing to another—trimming trunks, gouging holes, clearing and stacking trash—when calls came. They were from a few students who'd been by the lake, who now raced, weaving through the jumbled approaches with bugged eyes and babbling mouths.

"Annie … your friends are here!" They shouted repeatedly, words that couldn't be understood until they skidded to a halt, chests heaving.

"Friends? Who?"

They sputtered. "Two women in a canoe. One was here before."

"Judy?"

"Yes … yes, that's her name," bouncing now and catching breaths. "She said to get you and John … Hurry! They *have* things."

"Things?"

They answered with shrugs and shaking heads … but no more

needed to be said. There were visitors and there was a mystery and that was enough. Work stopped as this much was understood, and just as quickly tools dropped and everyone scrambled.

They weren't the first to get there. It didn't matter who the kids were racing to tell, word spread like ripples arcing out in water, resulting in an echo of people in return. Which meant when Annie and John arrived, they had to thread their way through a crowd to the water, where what the youngsters had garbled was confirmed ... Drifting thirty feet offshore was an odd combination—a heavily laden canoe pulling a Rube-Goldberg-like mini-barge, also heavily laden. Despite its size, the barge bulged with several times more in mysterious wrappings than the canoe.

Rebecca, in the forward seat of the canoe, sparkled when John and Annie parted the crowd and exclaimed *"ta daah,"* throwing out her arms.

"Ohmygod! Rebecca! Judy! What are you *doing* here?" Annie said.

"What are we doing here," Judy repeated. "Now that's a warm greeting if I ever heard one. I assumed we'd be welcome."

"Of course you're welcome," Annie laughed. "Come on in. Why are you treading anyway?"

"Just being careful," Judy said. "The stuff we have here is for the whole village, so we didn't want to fend off anybody trying to get at it. We thought it better to hand it over to the Chiefs and let them decide how it would be used."

Annie only managed "Stuff?" She looked at John, who nodded as if he knew something.

"Must be food," he said.

He'd hardly spoken when Dlahni and another chief broke through to stand beside them, at which time Rebecca and Judy dug in and paddled ashore.

With things under control the girls, who enjoyed a bit of a reunion with high fives and hugs, left and meandered up the slope to the homestead, where they soon came to relax beside the fireplace. Ruth, who'd joined the girls at the shore, left them on the way back, but joined them again soon after they'd settled. Detouring by her home,

Page 388

she had chopped, watered and churned a pot of *Atjahahni* stew, which meant anything edible on hand had been tossed in, correctly guessing the travelers were not only cold and tired, but also starving.

"*Ooo wee!*" Judy said. "You must have heard my stomach growl."

Annie placed the pot on a stone platter over the pit, and soon an aroma, a head-turning, lip-licking aroma, drifted in all directions. Before it got to a bubble, however, Annie got back to the questions she'd been asking, without satisfaction, ever since the canoe reached shore.

"Okay now, let's start over ... *Are you two crazy?* How did all this happen? You must have been traveling at least a week in the dead of winter."

"A week?" Judy said with a grin, shifting her focus to Rebecca. "It wasn't that long, was it?"

Rebecca, who'd settled into cushions and sighed as tired muscles began to unwind, cocked an eye back at the question, "Wasn't that long? According to my calculations it was six days, fourteen hours, twenty-seven minutes and twelve seconds ... give or take. Yes it was long ... damn long."

Ann shuddered. "But why? I mean, everyone's flipping over what you brought—seeds of vegetables the villagers had never seen before, and all that food. We weren't exactly starving but it was getting close for some. So back to why? You didn't know any of that."

"A good guess," Judy answered.

"No it wasn't," Rebecca said, groaning as she sat up and crossed her legs to get into the conversation. "We'd been doing fine with our food, so much so it became clear we were going to have some left over. We naturally wondered how you were doing. You happen to be on our minds a lot ... and in our prayers.

Annie nodded and smiled thanks.

"It was Roland who brought it up. One night he mentioned how amazed he was at the effort the *Atjahahni* had made for the Gathering. He figured a third of the village had been wrapped up in it for the better part of the summer. Then he wondered what the effort had done to planting and harvesting which he understood were critical to them.

"That's when the idea came to send some of our surplus in case any of you were running low."

"But why *you* two? Why not men?"

"Annie, you wouldn't believe how busy they've been with that damned boat. They had a lot to do before, but this thing is gobbling up almost every hour they've got. Bruno's researching and designing and detailing, and the rest are sawing and fitting and drilling. They're in a mad scramble to finish and be here by early spring.

"I mean, everyone's excited about getting horses ... and if it *is* possible, they want to do their part. The big question is whether the others will do theirs. Trapping and roping horses can't be the easiest thing to do, especially when the whole concept of even trying is new to them."

"Don't underestimate our neighbors," Ruth said. "My sisters rave about the peoples they've married into at every opportunity. All you know is that John asked that several colts be captured and they agreed to try. You may not realize the power behind that request. I wasn't at Pangaea so didn't see what happened during the storm ... the lightning and rainbow and all. But I've heard about it over and over again from those that were. They're all convinced John spoke with the Great Spirit then, and therefore, what he does is blessed ... and what he asks for is ... well, you can imagine."

Annie thought about it for a moment, her face reflecting the thought, "John hasn't said much about it, but maybe it's so. Whatever. In this case it sure wouldn't hurt. Getting back to my questions, though ... what about the little barge you were towing? How'd that come about?"

"That was another one of Bruno's ideas. He figured it didn't make sense to expect a canoe, the only one we have by the way, to do the job ... It just wouldn't carry enough to make the effort worth while. So he designed that thing using the thinnest boards millable and *voila!* ... it worked."

"Wasn't towing it hard? Paddling a canoe by itself for days isn't the easiest thing going."

Rebecca groaned. "Hard doesn't cover it. If Brunhilda here hadn't been at power stroke we'd never have made it. Hell, she can stand up to any of the men. But me ... my arms and back were so tired I came close to cutting that monstrosity loose."

"Oh bosh ... listen to her," Judy said. "It was hard, and it hurt; but she damn well did her share. And we had plan "B"; we'd agreed that if the going got too tough, we'd tie the barge somewhere on shore and have the *Atjahahni* retrieve it. One way or another, we were going to get here and find out how you were doing. Fortunately we had a few helping winds.

"Now that we're here, how *is* everything going?"

"We're busy too," Annie replied, "and there's lots to tell both ways, but before we get started, the pot's about to boil over."

Hours later, after stomachs had been filled and almost every topic exhausted, the flames still danced, creating a kaleidoscope of shifting patterns on the walls. Except for a few candles above the fireplace, this was all the light there was because outside had taken the darkness of a forest at night. Most of the world had therefore gone to bed, including John, who'd earlier returned and told of the decisions regarding the cargo: The seeds, of which the *Atjahahni* were in awe after a description of what they represented, were to be stored for planting in a special communal garden. The food, mostly potatoes but also turnips and carrots and radishes and beans and peas and the like, were to be shared as soon as it could be arranged. The best thought for that was for an *Atjahahni* version of a soup kitchen at next Sunday's gathering. They reasoned that at *Tschtaha-tata,* the preparation and ladling could be controlled as fairly as possible, which was essential with everyone watching. So most were asleep, except for the girls.

"Tell me again about what you've been doing with the kids ... Some singing?" Rebecca asked.

Annie chuckled. "Well, *I* might call it that, but you might not. I found some of those old ditties useful in getting points across, that's all, like "A B C D E F... ", and so on, singing our way through the alphabet. We also did that one on musical scales, you know, "do ray me fa sol la tee do", but I didn't know where else to go with that ... it turned out to be just a game.

"Golly, I'm *so* glad you two are here because I *really* need more material. I need help. How long can you stay?"

"Not long, I'm afraid," Judy answered. "This trip has been on a short tether from the start. In fact there'll be people waiting at the landing in a few more days."

"*Shoosh*, short tether's an understatement. Bruno's been having a fit ever since one of the persons tagged to go was his precious Judy."

"Aha!" Annie said, flashing a look ...

Judy snorted, but couldn't help smiling, "Well, he wasn't the only one concerned," winking back at Rebecca.

"Now as for the trip, we've been very careful. The weather's been a factor, of course ... If it hadn't been favorable, we'd never have started. We can't assume the good graces of "Ole Man Winter" much longer, however; so when we start back, which has to be soon, it'll be a mad dash without the barge. Don't you agree?"

"Yes, of course," Rebecca said. "But let's see now, Sunday is only the day after tomorrow ... right?"

"That's right."

"And according to John the food is going to be served at something like a soup kitchen ...

"And ... you've been teaching the kids the basic "do ray me" ditty."

"Where are you heading?" Annie asked.

"Well, I think we should stay through Sunday. After all, we did bring food representing Olympia, and should be here to take a bow. We'll then head back the next day, weather permitting.

"Now, in preparation for Sunday, can you get all the kids together for a few hours tomorrow?"

"Sure ... Why?"

"I have an idea that should be fun."

It would be one of the best Sundays ever. Word spread about the meal, and that's all it took to insure the entire village would be on hand. There'd also been mention of foods different from anything they'd ever eaten, but that part didn't matter much as some had been eating bark and weeds and anything with a smidgen of nourishment, so mud pie would have sounded good.

Da-hash-to saw as soon as preparations began that *Tschtaha-tata* would be overloaded, and there'd be a lot of work; so he did the only thing that made sense, he turned the matter over to the *Atjahahni* equivalent of the ladies auxiliary. They gladly responded, and although they were excited about the new foods, saw that the amount on hand wasn't enough to make a complete meal for everyone.

They solved this problem by preparing a porridge of what was on hand, enough to fill half a bowl for everyone, then filling the rest with a mixture of new foods. This put the exotics on top where they would be identified and specifically tasted.

The Sunday crowd, as expected, was more then could be sheltered under roof, so the decorative side panels, usually tied down for the winter, were rolled up, opening the interior to the yards. As it happened, there were almost as many on the deck and yard to the east as under the roof.

While food was being prepared on a dozen fires, Nyaho brought the assembly to order, giving a simple prayer; then Da-hash-to made a few announcements, the most notable of which was about a Crafts Fair. "We couldn't have one last year because of all else that was happening. But we wish to renew the fair in the fall before the Ceremony of Remembrances." Smiles and corresponding sounds swept through the crowd on hearing this.

Then he thanked Rebecca and Judy and all their friends for their generous gifts. With that, and in orderly fashion, the assembly formed lines and passed by the servers.

It was near to noon when the last had eaten, the crowd then doing what crowds do, settling into scattered, low-level conversations, and filling the air with a pleasant hum. But there was definitely a sense more was to come; so when Da-hash-to climbed back to the first tier serving as a stage on the rocky west end, the murmurs drifted away. When reasonably quiet, he announced that a number of children had been meeting during the winter and had prepared a program for their entertainment. He then returned to the floor, shoving away helping hands as he limped his way down. At the same time the youngsters, all twenty of them, snaked out from the opening in the rocks that tied to the cave-like room below and behind the stage, and formed a semi-circle facing the audience. The last to emerge was Rebecca, who went up front to the open end of the arc.

Using hand signals, she first directed the chorus into a soft "do ra me" exercise up and down the scale; then the same a bit louder. Next she directed them through a soft rendition of the song by Julie Andrews as sung in *The Sound of Music*, which set the stage for the finale. The finale was another repeat of that song, choreographed with the youngsters, but different, even to them. During practice, they'd only gone through the song enough to know when to respond. Now it was different. Rebecca sang the same words, only this time she belted them, dancing and twirling in a performance of sounds and moves never before experienced. When the finale notes ended in crescendo, the beautiful notes hung in the air and dissipated to silence. This result had nothing to do with acoustics, which were surprisingly good because of the rock background and the highly absorbing ceiling. The performance was therefore heard clearly to the farthest reaches, including the lawn. It was a silence of awe … and it was awkward, lingering until John's clapping, joined immediately by Ann and Dlahni and Da-hash-to, began an applause which grew into thunder. When it began to wane, Rebecca pointed to the youngsters, who stepped forward and bowed, causing the clapping to ramp back up.

That night the girls settled once more around the fire, reliving the day with the glow for what had gone so well. There might not have been much in the way of social graces in the *Atjahahni* world, at least as might be recognized in a developed society, but on this day it hadn't been obvious. Almost everyone in the crowd had stopped by with compliments and expressions of gratitude. More important than the thanks was the fact that a bond was forming to replace the apprehension that had lingered about the giants—Americans or Olympians or whatever they were called—since last fall.

Annie relaxed, smiling and shaking her head as she did.

"What is it?" Rebecca asked.

"Oh nothing. Well no, that's wrong … There are things. This morning you did a version of a musical that thrilled the world and won every award. Now I may be somewhat prejudiced, but I think what you and the kids did today was just as good. It was sensational!

Rebecca, you never cease to amaze me … and I mean amaze. There must be a way of using your talent and your music to help with what we're trying to do."

"Maybe so," Rebecca said, as if to change the subject.

But Judy said, "Oh definitely!"

This went on and on, and as it did John once more eased away from the group and settled into a pad at the farthest wall away.

His eyes had drooped when Ruth said something. It didn't matter what, but the sound of her voice unknowingly took him deeper, back in months to a similar scene. Four young people—Ruth and Sarah and Naomi and Matthew, his family—were talking with an interest and enthusiasm much like what his mind had just left.

Only they weren't talking about schooling and singing, and how things like that could build bridges to other peoples. They were talking about other peoples, all right, but in a different way. They'd all been a part of preparing for the Gathering of Nations, for which bags were packed and canoes loaded for a launch the next morning. Ruth was the only one not going, which disturbed her; but she was married with a young son and understood. Besides, someone had to stay behind and she and Brun-dahni were it.

But the others were bubbling.

Naomi was looking forward to a reunion with the friends she'd made during the year she'd spent north, friends that included relatives and a special young man whose name kept popping up.

Sara was excited for several reasons. For one she was leader of the archers, an emissary squad among those Dlahni had picked to train in secret and be prepared in the event things went wrong. The main reason, however, was a young *Njegleshito* chieftain named Chjenohata. He's the one that retrieved her hair band from a branch in the water a few years before. Soon after that the two began to sparkle whenever they were in each others company, a fact which also overflowed into conversations.

John wasn't much into the giddy actions of girls in love, but he couldn't help but sympathetically smile as he drifted farther away.

And then there was Matthew, whose newly acquired man-voice still crackled at times, but who had grown into a well-chiseled specimen that had every young female's heart aflutter. In the confines of the home, he'd only recently grown to the stature that could withstand the competitive and taunting nature of his sisters. And while the taunts would never end, it was now laced with a respect for what he'd become. Matthew's enthusiasm was different. He's been on all the expeditions, and had worked as hard as anyone on the incredible number of details needed doing, surely being an influence on his peers who had also pitched in.

Matthew looked forward to the games. Although an outstanding athlete, he primarily saw the games as a way to meet the young men from other nations, whether it fitted in to any of the other long range objectives or not. It would just be fun.

John was so proud as he relived the chatter, his cup runneth over. And he was asleep.

But then there was a strange voice. It was a nice feminine voice other than one of his daughters. She was speaking about something different altogether from the Gathering, and it jolted him back from his drift.

"There was a man in the crowd today who really gave me the willies," Rebecca said. "It seemed that every time I looked up, he was nearby listening in and looking us over. Who was this guy?"

Ann mumbled "I don't know ..."

But Ruth said "I saw him, and you're right ... he *is* creepy. His name is Daj."

46

Spring

Nshtanja and Tadjahni felt lucky. The day before, with the easing in weather, they'd felt it was time ... tomorrow had to be one of those days when fish would be jumping. So they planned to get an early start, grab a canoe, then cross the lake where certain inlets always had a good catch waiting. Only there'd been a problem. During the night, which had been complete with heavy gusts and rain, a branch broke loose and crashed through the domed roof that framed Tadjahni's home. As a result, repairs were needed and that came first, making it late-morning before they could break away.

And that's when their luck changed. They'd feared all canoes would be long gone ... but there one was, ready and waiting. And it didn't matter that it was the oldest of the fleet, and had a recent accident, coming apart at the seams and almost sinking, because it supposedly had been repaired and was good to go. A stigma must have remained, however, explaining why it was still there. For the two, at this time and place, none of this mattered ... the canoe was just fine. So with time wasting, it was quickly untied and lifted off its stand, eased in, loaded and launched. As they paddled, Nshtanja, sitting in back, surveyed the condition of the relic they'd been lucky enough to find, slowly coming around to feeling they weren't so fortunate after all.

"They still haven't returned, have they?" He said.

"What?" said Tadjahni, who was looking north not liking what he was seeing.

"Daj and his cronies ... they haven't returned."

"Not that I know of."

"Those bastards. They leave early one morning without telling anyone, take the biggest and best canoe, and are gone ... who knows where? That was weeks ago."

Tadjahni didn't turn to answer but kept looking north. "Don't ask Chief Dlahni about it. He's *seething*. My guess is that he suspects a tie to Braga, who may still be alive and holed out somewhere up north. If true, that they're helping him, I mean, the fact would be very serious; but other than expressions, Dlahni hasn't said anything, so it's just a guess."

"Well, something smells and most of the village has been whispering, with comments like "they're acting strange" and "what's with the new clothes?""

"By the way, what *are* you looking at?"

"See for yourself."

Nshtanja did, the sight causing him to lift his paddle and coast, while groaning *"Oh no ..."*

It was fog—a wall a hundred feet high like a huge tidal wave, wide as far as could be seen—moving in. As they coasted to a stop and waited, it swept past with a moist, cool sensation. That, and the fact they could now only see ten yards, generated a few choice words in *Atjahahni*.

They drifted without much else to say, until Tadjahni spoke, "Let's not cross. I'd rather stay close to this side and head south. If this crap ever clears, then we can give it a try."

So they did, easing along in a surreal world that twenty years ago, if they'd been alive, would have had them screaming. But now it was just surreal ... and somewhat interesting. Besides being mysterious with grey nothingness, it was also quiet, with sounds, even from perceptively remote distances, being amplified.

Uncertain of any direction, they drifted, casting lines along the way to give fishing at least a try. They also made a game at guessing what the sounds might be, never failing to put a spin on them they wouldn't repeat in public, giggling and outright laughing at their brilliance.

But drifting as they were, they eventually distanced themselves from shore, enveloping themselves in not only nothingness, but also silence.

They shivered.

It seemed to stay that way—sameness in nothingness—until there *was* somethingness and Tadjahni whispered "What was that?"

"What was what?"

"Shhh ... listen ..."

It was a sound new to them, a slight slurping sound ... like something in the water, but far away. As they listened, the sound became sounds and became clearer. When they realized the whatever was getting closer, coming their way, throats went dry. There were many sounds now, creaks and thuds like wood on wood, and sloshing like oars in water, and voices, quiet voices, like in people sneaking.

"That's John's tongue," Tadjahni mouthed, hardly audible.

They couldn't move ... spellbound ... not knowing which way to turn.

Then it was there, a huge silhouette forming out of nothingness, at least three strides wide and almost two high, with another behind it almost blotting out the sky.

In seconds the apparition turned real. They saw lapped boards with rows of pegs, much like what they'd seen on the small barge the girls pulled months before, a rail capping the top, and a monster head lunging towards them ... all this in the last moment before the behemoth cut their canoe in half. And as they screamed while in the air heading for the water, they also heard ...

"What the hell?"

The collision was immediately followed by frantic strokes to the surface, gulps of air, then helping hands pulling them up and over the rail. And that's how Nshtanja and Tadjahni met Devon and Abram and Bruno and Benjamin.

John couldn't stop shaking his head, sometimes snorting a laugh. He'd been far back in the pasture, working on one of the last sections of fencing, when word reached him, so a throng had already gathered at the shore before he'd gotten as far as the Commons. There he met the haggard crew following Annie. After a quick reunion and overview of what had happened, he continued down, Bruno in tow, diverting to the heights instead of heading into the crowd. He now paced back and forth above the landing, with Bruno standing by, looking down at a scene that electrified most of the community. There were the pitiful remains of the canoe, that had been retrieved and now lay stacked; there were Nshtanja and Tadjahni in the spotlight and loving it, telling and retelling what had happened; and there were the curious, young and old alike, who were taking turns walking the gangplank to touch and feel parts of the most amazing watercraft they'd ever seen.

Finally he turned to Bruno, "I'm sorry, but that's got to be the ugliest thing ever put to water. It's what you architects call "form follows function" isn't it? I mean, an extreme case."

Bruno smiled ... a weak smile.

John reached around and grabbed him by the shoulder, giving a good squeeze. To an observer, if there'd been one, they were themselves quite a scene. For one thing, they were both a mess. John, very much taller, and, with his white hair and beard, looking like a cross between Moses and Daniel Boone, was in his customary leathers—a sleeveless tunic to his hips but untied in front; an apron lapped at the side; and leggings to his knees; all stained and dirty because he'd been on his knees and literally in the dirt while at work. And Bruno, who had started the trip as if out of the L.L. Bean catalog, was disheveled, his shirt open, his pants rolled up, and his tee-shirt, marine green with a "Save the Whales" logo, torn and bloodied where it had snagged on the rail when he pulled in one of the canoers. "I'm kidding, Bruno ... just kidding. The boat's quite a piece of work. The girls told us last winter how hard all of you were working, but we didn't know what to expect."

Bruno relaxed, the smile now more genuine. "Yes, it *was* a lot of work ... and everyone became involved one way or another.

"What's it called ... I mean, does this kind of boat have a name?"

"Well, it's basically a barge, a flat-bottomed barge that can be used for hauling horses ... anyway, that's the premise."

"So form and function was a good guess."

"It was … but even that part's complicated. None of us had any experience with boats outside of Ski Nautiques and Sunfish, so we were at a loss. Rodney, who's pretty much glued to the lab and all the files, came to the rescue, rolling out reams of stuff for us to go by.

"We tried to keep it simple, because even though we had saws and drills and electricity in the shop, we didn't have rivets or bolts or any the metal accessories that would have been nice to have. Even the ancients had those, so our situation was unique … actually unique in more ways than one. Because we didn't have umpteen miles of extension cord, we had to assemble the barge at the shop. Then after everything had been worked out and fitted, we had to label each part, disassemble, lug the parts across the ridge, then put them back together on a slide at the water's edge.

"The hardest part was installing the planks forming the bottom and sides. After lapping each board over caulking-like gunk, another Rodney creation, we inserted pre-cut wooden pegs through pre-drilled holes, and then hammered them from both sides simultaneously to create rivet-like connections. Most everything is fitted together--interlocked or pegged in some way—because there was so little metal to work with.

"And finally, after launching, we had to figure out how to move the damned thing around."

"Besides the sail, I see that you have seats for three oars on each side."

"That may be overkill, but we had no way of knowing what it was going to take to move it when loaded. Only four of us could break away to make this trip, which had us worried because we didn't know if four would be enough. Fortunately, it was; but we may need help from here on."

"No problem, there'll be plenty of volunteers for that. By the way, how'd the sail work out?"

Bruno laughed, shaking his head. "I've already told you we didn't know squat, so that was part of the research. We focused on primitive vessels—those of Egypt and the Mediterranean and even the Vikings, who had shallow-draft long-ships with square sails. The simplest system we could copy turned out to be a single mast with top spar and square rigging. It's much more complicated than that as you can see from what we did. We tried to envision all sorts of situations and work in provisions to address them, like ropes and pulleys and cleats and stuff."

"And?"

"It worked ... In the end, with all the assumptions and guesses, the conglomeration worked. After launching, the four of us loaded up, pushed off, turned and started north. There *was* no trial run, instead we gambled that, one way or another, we'd move it along. It wasn't until well underway that we fiddled with the sail, and after a few hiccups ... *voila!* The first night we picked up a breeze from the southeast which was too good to resist; and since the sky was clear and visibility good, we kept going. We made pretty good time too."

"Wow ... like I said ... amazing!"

They turned and looked down. The scene below, despite the number of people, was well behaved. Dlahni, who hadn't seen John previously, had in his absence taken control from the start, gathering hands and seeing that the barge was treated properly. He looked up and waved as they watched, quickly returning to oversee what was happening.

"You two go back a long way, don't you?' Bruno said.

"All the way to the beginning ... I owe him everything." Then he added, "Don't ever underestimate him or any of these people. They may be behind us in certain ways, but believe me, they're ahead in others."

"You don't have to remind us," Bruno said. "We saw that last fall with Dlahni and Da-hash-to ... They're not dumb Indians."

"Bruno," John said, his voice rising, "there you go again ... They're *not* Indians. Not that it matters, but Indians weren't dumb either."

"Oops ... I know, I know ... It was just an expression."

They both laughed, exchanging elbow punches.

Settling down, John said, "Tell me more about your creation. There are parts I don't understand."

"Well, let's see. To keep it moving, there were times when all four of us had to row. When that happened, someone still had to steer, so we put in a tiller extension from one of the seats to the rudder. That's what that diagonal bar is. Then there's those box-like features you see tied beside the seats, they're feed troughs for the horses. We don't know how well that'll work, but it's the best we could come up with.

"The wood deck ... won't that spook horses that are already rattled?"

When Bruno puffed, John knew he'd asked about something special.

"You just hit on one of the main concerns." Bruno said. "Here again we don't know how well what we've planned for is going to work, but we got some ideas from history ... it's amazing where you find answers. Remember what I told you about Hannibal? He had his men put sod and grass over the planking, which seemed to calm his elephants by putting them on a familiar surface.

"Well, we're going to do the same thing for our horses."

Impressed, John nodded, then gasped as a previously hidden feature swung into view, "That awful dragonhead! What's that about?"

Bruno doubled-up, spinning away. "I expected you to notice that *first*. We needed a bowsprit anyway, so we figured what better way to decorate it than with a dragonhead. After all, you're part Viking aren't you?"

John could only shake his head and grin, "You guys are too much." Then turning to guide Bruno away, "Let's join the rest of your crew back at the homestead and get cleaned up. Annie's fixing something warm that should taste pretty good after what you've been through. Here, let me give you a hand," picking up one of the bundles that had been set aside earlier.

As they walked away, Bruno asked, "What's the schedule going forward?"

John shrugged, "Don't know. We didn't know if and when you folks were going to show up, so now that's one thing out of the way. But we haven't heard from either of the other parties—the *Njegleshito* and the *Bjarla-shito*. I'm guessing you're in a hurry ... right?"

"Actually, yes. There's so much waiting for us back at Olympia, that we hate being gone any more than necessary. Besides, Devon is now a proud parent with a baby girl. So you can imagine."

"Is everything all right?"

"Oh yes. Terry and the baby are doing fine. I imagine Anne is getting all the details as we speak."

They entered the Commons, with traffic both ways now as late arrivals hurriedly past those who were returning. Stopping there, John looked back. "Bruno, let's be proactive."

"Proactive?"

"Yes, proactive. We don't know if and when our friends will contact us … hopefully soon, but we just don't know. So let's do this: All of you get a good night's rest, and then tomorrow head out with a few canoes in escort. There are two possible pickup points, the closest being the *Njegleshito* less than a day away. The second is a few days beyond that at the north end of the lake. Once you reach the first, the canoes can head to the other. This way we can find out what's happening a lot faster than by sitting around."

The next day, when the barge and canoes accompanying it were about at mid-point, they were met by another canoe approaching from the opposite direction. Aboard were Sara and Chjenohata, who were on their way to tell John what they now related after a brief reunion with Annie, who'd insisted on being part of the first excursion, and introductions to the rest of the crew. They reported that the *Njegleshito*, as usual, had been in winter quarters near the outer islands. With the winter there cool but its weather less of a factor, they'd put the roving herds of horses in their vicinity under observation from the time they settled in. From what they learned— migrating habits and all—they were able to devise a strategy for entrapment, which they successfully put into action in early spring soon after a number of foals were seen. The results of all of this were now waiting for pickup.

With that they parted, each resuming directions, Sara still longing for a visit home.

At the *Njegleshito* stop, which they reached in late afternoon, Annie's greatest fears were realized. The people who'd captured the animals, and then driven, or rather pulled them for weeks to the landing, had done the best they could. But animals had died along the way and another at the landing. The remainder, three fillies and a colt, were in sad shape. Anticipating this, Annie had loaded as assortment of vegetables as well as clay pots, planning to do what had been done for the piglets captured at Olympia.

As before with the pigs, the thin, soup-like concoction of vegetables, crushed to a pulp, mixed with water, stirred and warmed, wasn't close to mother's milk, but is was nourishing, and the starving animals quickly went through all that Ann had been able to bring. While this was going on, the barge was prepared for the return trip: sods were stripped and placed over the deck planks; and the area around the landing was scoured for hay and edibles to fill the troughs. When everything that could be done had been done, the foals were brought aboard and tied beside the troughs. A quick farewell later, the barge shoved off, the last operation being completed under torch-light as the sun had set an hour before..

When the *Atjahahni* village was reached, which happened to be before sunrise the next day, no one in the crew had had more than a few hours sleep. They didn't stop, however, but continued until the horses were in their quarters at the new stable, fed another batch of concoction, and guided into place before freshly filled troughs.

A days rest later, the barge again launched, this time without Annie, who needed to stay with the new arrivals and make sure they survived. This wasn't a problem because the others in the crew, particularly Devon, had assisted her at the first landing, and were now knowledgeable enough to carry on.

The second trip was much longer, a week passing before word arrived that an approaching flotilla was sighted. Like before, the trip was successful, with not only three young animals aboard, but also a mare, the mother of one of them. A full grown horse, with as many fears and anxieties as the colts, presented another set of problems, which included almost having one of the sides of the boat kicked out, in addition to the jeopardy it subjected each of the crew who were in unavoidable close quarters.

That evening, after the animals had been introduced to not only new quarters but also new companions, and matters had settled to a reasonable calm, the group gathered to eat and relax. The gathering became larger and larger because Sara and Chjenohata were still visiting, and Dlahni, Nyaho and Da-hash-to stopped by, as did Ruth and Brun-dahni and Bobby.

With so many gathering about, more than the house itself could hold, a thought was considered to move to *Tschtaha-tata* where there was more room. But the weather was pleasant, and the setting exotically appealing after a few posted torch-lights had been placed, so everyone settled outside the homestead around the firepit, relaxing on logs and crude benches and whatever way improvised. There were sore muscles and tired minds, but a lot had been accomplished, and the aches and pains were trumped by not only the pride of accomplishment, but also the warmth of family and friends. It was nice.

"Frankly, I thought we were nuts to go so hard," Benjamin said. "But now that it's over, I'm glad that we're not still out there somewhere."

"I thought we were nuts putting you on the tiller in the middle of the night," Abram added, at which everyone howled.

"So I ran aground, it could have happened to anyone ..."

And so it went. In this relaxed setting, the adventures of the voyages were narrated in detail, with versions of the same incident being told in different ways by the viewpoints involved. One of the more puzzling had to do with impressions at the northern landing.

"You knew the men who gathered the horses pretty well, didn't you?" Asked Abram.

"Yes," John said. "The only name I remember is Cherstabonshala, but he and several of his friends had been on our side during the mess at Pangaea. They also hiked back with us afterwards and stayed for a while last fall ... and I thought, enjoyed themselves here."

"I don't doubt that, because for Nshtanja and Tadjahni, who were in one of the canoes, it was like old home week with broad smiles and manly greetings."

"You're hinting at a problem, though."

"No, we didn't have any problems to speak of, because everyone pitched in at what needed doing. But there was an edge we could feel."

"How so?"

"It's hard to explain. Certain hurriedness, whispers, nervous glances, things like that. They were all anxious to get the horses off their hands and get back."

"Didn't you ask?"

"Actually we tried. But outside of signs and gestures on basic stuff, we didn't understand each other. I asked Nshtanja about it. All he could say was that he had the same impression."

"Strange."

47

These Truths

When a mile away, they blew a horn, their latest ridiculously ingenious gimmick. It wasn't the one carved earlier with only a blatant blare, this one was new and improved. Rodney had researched and Bruno had designed and Gary had carved a thin but lengthy contraption with a truncated, heavily decorated stem ending with a slightly flared bell. Its sound was basically monosyllable, like a fog-horn, with only a slight ability to vary, and carried an impressive distance over water. All things considered, it was a hoot.

Since it threw a sound new to this world, although more mournful than threatening, it still succeeded in scaring hell out of a few. Scaring, that is, until those along the shore hearing it, also saw John who was pacing on the heights. He'd stopped by several times that day to scan the lake to the south, and on this occasion, when he heard the sound before anything came into view, wrinkled with puzzlement for a few moments, then broke down laughing.

He was still smiling when the "Svenska", the name given to the six-oar, single-masted barge—a poor imitation of a Viking ship— pulled up to shore. It was jammed with duffles and bundles and rumpled waving bodies and tired smiling faces.

"Well I'll be damned," John said as the barge was tied in and the gangplank set. "I was beginning to wonder if any of you were going to get here."

"You mean we made it in time?" Bruno said as he jumped off, securing the plank and assisting as others began to disembark.

"You are perfect," Annie shouted. She'd also been scouring the lake and upon hearing the sound raced down. She ran up to Bruno and gave a big, crunching hug, repeating the same to each as the rest stepped down.

"We haven't missed anything?" Bruno asked again. "We stayed on the water from the start, rotating on the oars; but since we were timing everything by moon cycles and gnomons, which aren't exactly our thing, we weren't really sure how close we were. To us, schedule wise, it was like pinning the tail on the donkey."

"You did fine." John said. "The Fair, which is something you all should enjoy, doesn't start tomorrow until noon, so there's time to spare. The Harvest Festival and the Celebration of Remembrances will follow in the days after that. All of these together will give you a good idea of what the *Atjahahni* are all about.

"Let's see now," he added as he took stock looking over the group, "Rebecca and Lisa will stay at our home, while the rest of you go to the community center, *Tschtaha-tata*. That's you Bruno, and Devon, Abram, Anton and Benjamin … right? Five guys, seven in all. Wow! Svenska was pretty well loaded, wasn't she?"

"She was."

"Actually, we had a better time with horses," Devon said. "They were nicer and didn't give me nearly as much crap. But we had to take all those nagging to come along, so we had no choice."

"Would you listen to him," someone said as most were still bouncing and stretching and working out kinks, as well as trash talking with the lifted spirits of being on dry land. As this was winding down, Ann grabbed Lisa and Rebecca and said, "Come on you two, this togetherness thing is way over-rated. The fires on in the house and its nice and warm."

And so it went, the girls splitting away.

The *Atjahahni*, who stood to the side watching, looked at each other shaking their heads—a way of saying the antics of these people weren't always easy to explain.

"Is there any schedule for what's going to happen?" Bruno asked as they grabbed bags and began the trudge up the slope.

"Not really," John answered. "As before, we didn't know for sure when you'd get here, so we've just been standing by. But I imagine the first thing all of you want to do is clean up and get some rest. We figured that much and have set things up as best we can, which is a way of saying we're not the Ritz either. Then we'll have something to eat, and by then it'll be dark … after that, whatever."

"What's for dinner?" Anton said. "I'm so hungry I could eat the ass-end of a bear. We cleaned out the bottom of food sacks hours ago."

"I hope it's more than *Atjahahni* stew," Benjamin added.

"What's that?"

"That's anything half-edible thrown in a pot of water and boiled."

John laughed. "Hey, in a pinch that can be pretty good. But we're not in a pinch and you're in luck. Dlahni and I were out fishing early this morning and came back with a pretty good string. And there's venison."

"You've got deer?"

`"Yes. Two nights ago I heard something messing in our garden. A lot of that goes on this time of the year, so I'd taken to sleeping on a cot under flaps outside the house. Anyway, there were three of them and I got one. It was a lucky shot in the dark; because to be honest, I'm not that good in broad daylight. Anyway, most of it's left."

"Oh Lordy. Now I don't know if I can rest … I'm salivating already … the dried meat we had aboard was like shoe leather."

A few turns and *Tschtaha-tata* loomed into view beyond the last of the trees in between.

"Damn," Anton, the only one who hadn't been here before, said. "So this is the "toy-box" I've been hearing about.

"Big!"

"Wait 'til you see inside," Bruno added. "It's quite a place."

They entered then and began setting up in an area around the western rocks, which was the part that could come closest to being cordoned off. Side panels had already been dropped for that purpose; and clay wash basins were on hand, as were water urns already filled. Fire-boxes had been placed to semi-enclose that wing of the building and stacked for burning, all of which looked good, but in reality their ability to warm the place was more psychological than real. As for sleeping, cushioned mats were rolled and stacked on the stage tier for use when the time came. When everything that could be done had been, John turned to go, but Bruno stopped him, "If there isn't anything planned after eating, I have a suggestion."

"There's nothing I know of … unless the girls are cooking up more than dinner."

"I don't think they are, because this isn't just my idea, it was discussed on the boat."

"And?"

"It's mainly to talk."

"To talk." More a question than a statement.

"Yes. Remember last fall when we were all together at Olympia? We had good meetings on those nights and a number of things were said that needed saying. Since then we've been busy and there hasn't been a chance for all of us to get together again."

John nodded.

"But there *have* been talks. Winter was long, with days when we couldn't do much outside. During those times it was only natural to reflect on what'd been said and what could be added. Anyway, we'd like to meet again with as many of the original group as are here … and pick up where we left off."

The meal was great, probably the best since the plague finished its work some millennia before, and the fact of it was mostly an accident. There was fish—mountain trout—and venison, as expected, but there was also wild turkey from a kill that afternoon. All that added to an *Atjahahni* stew enhanced by potatoes and vegetables that hadn't been planted here before, with a special bread on the side, the result of better grains, sweetened with honey. The only thing missing was a cordial, which when mentioned, started a small chorus of comments. It made Annie think of chokecherry wine. "Many of the berry bushes in and about here are now doing their thing," she said. "I'll work on it."

It was dark by the time the meal was over and the area cleared. Everyone was groaning for all the right reasons, and if given a choice would have flopped, but then they revived to get busy. Torches and candles had been lit during dinner as the light faded from the gable panels, so all that needed doing was to rearrange cushions, seats and benches to something more appropriate for a group discussion. Since there were only a dozen to contend with, it being decided to hold to only those who'd met before, this was easy to do. John and Annie moved to a bench against the stone rise forming the stage, while Da-hash-to, Dlahni and Nyaho sat on cushions nearby. Everyone else scattered in no particular order.

As the last were settling in, Bruno stepped to the front.

"I'm standing in for Gary, who, with the others holding the fort back at Olympia, would like to be here, but can only send their regards. As I mentioned to John earlier, the mission we are on is one that can't be forgotten ... and isn't being forgotten. Although we're all busy with a list of things to do, a list seeming without end, there are times when we've been in limbo, and when that happens, we've talked.

"Now those discussions haven't solved the problem ... I want to make that clear. If we've even scratched the surface, that would be as much as we could claim. Frankly, we don't feel qualified *to* solve it, most of us being in our early twenties and novices at our crafts."

John couldn't resist reacting in some way to that. He stood, or rather staggered, to his feet, and then stooped and pretending to be using a cane, shuffled in a circle, disrupting Bruno's well-composed preamble. If that weren't enough, first Dlahni and then Nyaho struggled to their feet and did the same, while Da-hash-to rolled on his side laughing.

Oh give me a break, Bruno thought as the rest picked up on it, with moans and groans and assorted insults before settling down.

"Okay, some of us *are* more mature," he said, almost starting over. "What I was getting at is, that while we may have the benefit of a fine education, none of us have created or run a business; none of us, with the exception of you, the *Atjahahni*, have managed people in any part of government.

"Furthermore, we're trying to devise a system that will guide a multitude of people, millions and billions even, when that systems initial application will only apply to hundreds.

"So, recognizing these limitations, we're suggesting that what we should do is to establish basic premises, seeds really, from which can grow the systems that need to develop as the societies to which they apply grow.

"In order to do that, to create the seeds, we've started by posting on a wall, a wall in the lounge where we met before, truths that can be the building blocks for those seeds. We call the wall "These Truths"."

John pursed and nodded, uttering, "Hmmm" Then he smiled, "And let me guess the first truth …

We hold these truths to be self-evident, that all men are created equal, that they are endowed by their Creator with certain unalienable rights; that among these are life, liberty and the pursuit of happiness."

"Yes, we thought the eloquent words of the Founding Fathers were a good place to start. Actually we were reminded of them by Huston in his letter. This phrase in particular is beautifully composed and embodies the ultimate in human objective."

"It's hard to argue with that, "John said. "But we've got to remember that as beautiful and objective as it sounds, its application was layered over mistakes whose haunting has never ended. Anyway, that's for another time. Is that all you've posted so far?"

"There's one more. Remember what Da-hash-to said last year?

That each man has two parts—a good wolf and a bad wolf. A system must be for the benefit of the good wolf. "

John looked about at the faces of the other Chosen. They were all glowing as if in agreement with the selection, and proud they'd made it. John smiled too, then reached down and squeezed Da-hash-to's shoulder. Da-hash-to's only reaction was to look up, but Dlahni and Nyaho, who'd settled from the foolery they'd uncharacteristically taken part in, beamed.

"Sounds good," John said, "Sounds good. We collect a number of irrefutable truths, and use them as building blocks or genes or whatever, to form policies that will achieve the objective of our mission. Sounds good.

"What else? If you've been doing all that talking, there must be more."

"There is," Bruno continued. "That's what this is about, but those are the only ones posted. By the way, have you read all your letters?"

"Yes, several times. There were thoughts in all of ours that shine like beacons. It's clear that Huston and his crew had lots of talks … many years worth. So keep going."

"Okay. The two truths posted have had to do with governance, which Huston hit hard on, but there are others. There's the environment, of course, that's basic and already being worked on back at Olympia."

"How so?" John asked. "We don't have a problem here at this time because everything's biodegradable, and there's no waste. So what are *you* doing?"

"It's really Rodney who's doing the doing. He's leading the way in developing a lot of things, like soap and lotion and glue and caulking and concrete and brick and terra cotta, and even metals, which he doesn't see we can avoid. In each thing he gets into, he follows a hard line rule that toxins, if created in any of the processes, will be neutralized, and whatever wastes generated recycled. There will be no garbage dumps.

"There's population control, which Huston also highlighted, and which gives me chills considering.

"We haven't gotten far with this part of the challenge because, frankly, we need people right now. When we think about it, though, we have to conclude that man is a very sexy animal. It may be for the same reason other creatures are. Most, if not all, whether plant or animal or fish or fowl, reproduce in numbers that exceed, sometimes by far, the number that can be expected to survive to maturity and reproductive age. The rest fall by the wayside one way or the other, usually ending somewhere in someone else's food chain.

"In man's case, beginning with the early homo sapiens, this had to be touch and go because they were without sexy clothes and cosmetics, and were under conditions of heat and cold and exposure and hunger and sabre-tooths. However, they still managed to get aroused and fornicate and impregnate and populate in sufficient numbers that the survival rate equaled or bettered the death rate.

"Huston had a lot to say about this as he rambled through from origins in Africa to the Twentieth century explosion. Along the way he snuck in a subliminal message that each time a horrific event occurred that killed tens of thousands and even millions, the population sprung back.

"It's horny homo again.

"And he asks "Is war an important part of population control?".

"John, I know how you feel about that, and all of us agree. But here's what others have said:

"That when a population overgrows the resources available in its area, it either expands or migrates to another area; engages in a civil war thinning out the population; or invades a neighboring country with the intent of killing off its population and taking its resources".

"Now this isn't conjecture because all three happened time and time again in the centuries before the plague. The questions for us are … How do we determine an appropriate population level? And, how do we control it to fit in that number?

"We all remember the *Easter Armageddon* Conference and the story of Easter Island. This taken together with everything else, would lead us to believe the problem has never been solved, just like political sustainability. But that's not true.

"There was another island in the Pacific much like Easter, only smaller. And those who came to colonize it became marooned just like the Rapa Nui, facing the same problem. The only difference is they adapted and survived. Rather than cutting trees and destroying nature, they worked with their resources, selecting and planting and nurturing until all needs were being supplied by what was retained. As for the population, that part was grim. They recognized that overpopulation would tip the scales and destroy them, like with those elk on the northern island. We don't exactly know what they did in this regard, except that it wasn't unusual for groups or families who were obvious overages and causing a problem, to peddle out to sea, never to seen again.

"Yuk! That's enough of that for the time being, because there are more issues.

"There's the assimilation of cultures that needs to come about, and there's education. These are biggies too. They're part of the questions Huston listed ... "Can man become part of nature without destroying it?"... "Can man manage himself?" If we do succeed in putting an ideal government together, how do we maintain it? His comment relating to that was ... *The first purpose of government is to train its citizens the right doing* ...

"That comment can probably be added to the wall back home. And there's another, by of all people, Ronald Reagan, who said something like *In a Democratic form of government, it cannot last unless each generation reinvents the principles on which it is founded.* I don't think he meant to change everything like man is prone to do, but rather to reinstall the reasoning and dedication that comes with the concept."

"Actually, the seeds, and we're talking about seeds," John added, "should start early in life. We're not talking of brainwashing as in a cult; we're talking about setting a person's gyroscope for a life that suits what our Creator would endorse. My father underscores the importance of this in his letter."

"Good," Bruno agreed. "Huston gave further examples of education and nurturing and how they are vital to many others in nature. And since it is, we could focus on it and use up the night, but since we've started with governance and have listed truths regarding it, let's return to that.

"Abram, you had comments."

Abram was on a bench against the drop panel to the south. Next to him was Rebecca, the two of them a little closer than normal, but to this point not doing anything telling. He did seem to be brought back from somewhere else, however, when he heard his name.

"Abram, you had comments about governance?" Bruno repeated.

"Oh yes ... ahh ... One of the objectives we have to solve is sustainability, and I don't mean the environment, that's another issue as you mentioned. I mean the politic.

"The historical record of political systems isn't good at all. Some lasted only a few years, as long as the tyrants behind them lived. The Thousand-year Reich went for only a dozen or so years, and rather than enlightening the world with its brilliance, caused the deaths of forty million and immeasurable horror and hardship for many more.

"Remember what was said a year ago, that the average length of civilizations was only about 200 years, listing the reasons why. We'll want to revisit those reasons at some point.

"So here we are, faced with the challenge of bucking the trend, and possibly all odds, and creating something that lasts.

"Now some of where I'm going next was also mentioned in Huston's letter. But they're important and can't be emphasized enough.

"When the Founding fathers did what they did, laboring over all the arguments, they finally arrived at a system that was admittedly imperfect, but which had aspects in it that have proven to be timelessly profound. For instance, they didn't consider that individual welfare was a governmental responsibility; instead they mentioned *general* welfare ... and the concept of entitlements didn't exist. They generally held that each man was the captain of his own destiny, wanting only the opportunity to succeed. With this philosophy the nation grew to be the greatest on earth with the highest standard of living ever experienced. This philosophy doesn't appear to have survived.

"The Founding Fathers were also big on limited government. And look what happened to that.

"The Founding Fathers didn't vigorously campaign for office, if they campaigned at all. There were instances where someone being considered for office made it a point to stay away from the deliberations, letting his stature and record of accomplishment speak for him. Contrast that with the twenty-first century when campaigning became a full-time job, with winners heavily compromised to those providing the funding. In addition, politicians carved out generous salary and benefit packages for themselves.

"The Fathers would be appalled at these things. George Washington, for instance, served as Commanding General full time for eight years, under the abominable conditions of the Revolutionary

War, for nothing. The only thing he received were reimbursable expenses, for which he kept meticulous records.

"Those who signed the Declaration of Independence did so pledging their lives, their fortunes and their sacred honor. Most are familiar with those words, but few are familiar with the extent to which those pledges were collected. Five signers were captured, tortured and killed. Nine more died in the fighting. Twelve had their homes ransacked and burned. Most were successful and with means before the war, but ended in poverty. Some were hounded and driven from their homes and families, having to constantly move about, often living in forests and caves. Yet they stuck to their pledges, in some cases, like George, serving without pay.

"Unfortunately, in the years that followed, this wonderful nation they created changed, the principles the Founders so carefully struck being eroded. During the Great Depression, when economic conditions were bad for almost a third of the population, a liberal philosophy to improve the lot of the citizenry gained a foothold. Although not to be faulted as an objective, it had the effect of opening Pandora's Box.

"Let me explain it this way. There was a great man in the twentieth century named Winston Churchill, who during World War II was Prime Minister of England. Your grandfathers are very familiar with the name if you're not. Anyway, in addition to being a renowned leader, he was a prolific writer, philosopher and a wit. He supposedly said regarding the liberal/conservative debate that:

If you are twenty-five or younger, and are not a liberal,
you have no heart;
If you are thirty-five or older, and are not a conservative,
you have no brain.

"This sounds like a joke and is fun to repeat. But in reality it isn't, and in a way it's right for both sides. Think about it. It's natural for the young to be idealistic and hope that the lot of their fellow man can be improved in a constantly progressing manner. That's quite an ideal, and if it can be done, it's wonderful.

"But there's a reality.

"One of the most notable scammers in the investment world was so successfully bad he gave a name to the concept. The concept became known as a Ponzi Scheme. A Ponzi is basically a promise of an impressively profitable return, based on supposedly unique and exemplary strategies. In reality its returns are based on future investors and investment success or both. In other words the system is a fraud—it's without funding and ultimately guaranteed to fail—with catastrophic losses for the investor.

"What does this have to do with governance?

"Well, during the Great Depression, social programs were initiated to provide at least some guaranteed income for retirement, based on withholdings not tied directly to the eventual obligation, but supposedly on a rational actuarial basis. In time the program was increased several ways, in instances adding recipients who were not contributing to withholdings. Several other programs were added, most notably to provide health coverage, following similar rationale.

"Guess what? There were no funds for these programs, and all of the promises were based on future investments called taxes.

"And how were these programs working?

"They were working fine except for the fact the nation was having to borrow to meet its promises, and was going into debt at a rate that wasn't sustainable. The country was following a number of other nations that had initiated similar highly beneficial socialistic programs, and were leading the way to economic ruin. Are they Ponzis, as some have asked? Well, if it walks like a duck, and quacks like a duck …"

"Do you have answers for these problems?" John asked.

"Not hardly," Abram said, "other than to have a conservative leaning. There's nothing wrong with a benefit as long as it's funded by the here and now.

"Huston had something to say about that … which we got from his notes. Anyway, early in his career he wanted to set up some sort of benefit for his employees in their retirements. In the process of doing so consultants explained two tax-deferred systems recently made available. One was called a profit-share plan, whereby funds were set aside in the employees name, added to each year in accord with business success and invested. Upon retirement the fund was what it was and the retiree owned it to use as he saw fit. The other was a pension plan in which the employee was guaranteed a certain amount per year upon retirement, depending upon years of service. This amount was not directly tied to funding during the time of employment, so depended largely on future company profits.

"When explained the provisions of the pension plan, Huston said, "Are you nuts? There's no way to guarantee future income or the fact that the company will survive. This is not only unfair to the company and its employees who are continuing to work and funding someone who isn't, it's also unfair to the retiree, who may see something promised and depended upon vanish if the company fails".

"Yet by far the largest business in the country—a unionized, self-regulating, multi-departmental corporation called the United States Government—used this system. Salaries and benefits including pensions were unfunded and predominately paid for by the private sector who did not share in or determine those benefits."

"Ahem ... Abram, this is interesting, but I don't see where this is leading in this time and place. Dlahni, Nyaho, Da-hash-to ... are you following any of this?"

All three shook their heads.

"Okay," Abram said chuckling. "Let's get off this then."

"Not so fast," Benjamin interrupted.

"Now what?"

"Well, governance is a big topic. But it doesn't just start at the top with the leaders; governance also considers its basic ingredient, and that's people and their characteristics. And I think that needs to be said.

"Now ... we've come to agree that people consist of both good wolves and bad wolves. That goes beyond politics and works its way into every aspect of human endeavor. I don't want to go on into anything all encompassing or highly technical, but there are points about all of this that are worthy of considering.

"One point is that man is a wanting creature. If he is in a community where everyone around him has little or nothing, then most will accept their lot. But if someone else gets something desirable, then he will want one too. In fact in a developing society characterized by advances all around, the wants become needs and leap-frog on and on.

"Another is that man naturally looks at issues in which way is in his best interest. An example that comes to mind had to do with an experience my uncle had. As the project leader for a team working out of town, one of the matters to be managed were expenses. Being somewhat loosely generous with employee policy, his bosses told him to pay whatever the expense. Well, the team worked hard so that wasn't a problem. But then when the day was over, the evening meal started with drinks, then an appetizer, then the most expensive meal on the menu, followed by dessert and a cordial. When the bill came, management said "whoops". They then instituted a reasonable per diem allowance for each worker, letting them pay their own bills. My uncle noticed that from that day on, evening meals became more on the order of a soft drink and a hamburger, the employee pocketing the difference.

"You're going to ask what this has to do with our problem, and all I can answer is "I don't know". But these characteristics are very human and need to be kept in consideration. Fortunately, these aspects can be mollified. By developing a strong sense of family and community and country, people can get to looking beyond themselves to serving a higher purpose."

"Good points, Benjamin. It sounds to me like you've looped right back to education. Thanks …."

"I'm not done yet."

Bruno laughed, "Ooookay …"

"Well, I wasn't happy with what our government came to and I don't want to just drop it. I wasn't happy with the election process. I think the Founders had it right.

"I wasn't happy with what happens once our legislators get elected. I feel most of those elected are honest and dedicated and go into their first term with enthusiasm and good intentions. But I think in many cases it's like the new employee who comes to work all bright-eyed and bushy-tailed, working hard to do the best he can for the company. Then he notices the others aren't working hard, so he slacks off, soon taking 45 minute coffee breaks if that's what they do. In other words there's often a slowing down or dumbing down that doesn't have to be and shouldn't be.

"So I wasn't happy. I wasn't happy that our elected officials got locked up in partisan politics, seeming to work for a party and their re-election rather than for the public at large. To me the concept of service has been diluted.

"In contrast to this were many in the private sector. My dad was a long-time member of a service organization. In that organization the members met each week, and often more, devoting countless hours to serve needs throughout the community and worldwide. An outstanding example is the fact that polio was eradicated throughout the world through the efforts of a service organization. Things like this were done not only without pay, but also with considerable expense.

"Now I don't expect elected officials to go without reward, but I do think emphasis has been placed on the wrong sy-LA-ble, as the saying goes.

"If no one has an objection, I'd like to add the motto of that service organization to our board …

Service above Self

"That's a noble thought," Bruno said. "I have no objection. Does anyone?

"There being none … fine.

"Are you done yet?"

Benjamin smiled and settled back. But then Devon jumped in. "I think we're ignoring other experiences that may be as important as anything else."

"And that is?"

"Well, I'd been thinking about the problem that's been mentioned several times, the problem of developing a society that's sustainable. Then I remembered something. I'd been on a trip with my folks a few years ago …"

"A few years ago, Devon, you were a slab of ice," Anton said.

"Huh? Oh yes … the rest of you know what I mean … Someone explain it to him.

"Anyway, dad likes to see Civil War sites, and on this occasion we'd gone to Chattanooga. We drove to the top of Lookout Mountain, from where we could get a good view of the entire area. The Battle Above the Clouds was on this mountain, and we could see over to Missionary Ridge where another had been fought. What we could also see was the Tennessee River which formed a loop below as it worked its way west. And that's the part I'm getting to. The loop formed a peninsula called Moccasin Point. On a map outlining the area we were looking at, it stated that Indians had a village at Moccasin Point for thousands of years. I forget how many.

"Now, we don't have to research them to find out how they managed to do this, we have the *Atjahahni* right here, who may have existed even longer. So John, what have you observed about them that might be a factor in why they've been so successful."

John didn't say anything, looking like he'd never thought about it, which wasn't exactly the case. He looked at the three beside him, who just looked back, Dlahni snorting and giving a reflective shrug. Then he looked back at Devon, "That's a good question. I've never tried to dissect their lengthy survival and apply it to our mission."

"Well, it's a good question. This is my second trip here and I've wondered about a couple things. I see the building we're in and the Council House and a bunch of homes scattered through the woods. But I don't see any special purpose structures, like a jail for instance.

"How does it all work?"

John looked down at the three again and asked, "Any of you care to answer?"

Dlahni shook his head, but Nyaho said, "This is something we don't think about either. I'd have to say that what we do is largely done because of all the things we tried that didn't work. We'd be interested how you might answer though."

John stood and rocked, there being no place to go. "Let's see now … the *Atjahahni* are a simple society, but a good one. They're not ruled in that sense of the word, but rather led by six or seven chiefs. They meet semi-regularly … I say semi because the meeting are usually called because of specific needs to address."

"How did the chiefs come into being?" Anton asked.

"From what I've seen it's a seamless process, with the existing chiefs usually picking someone to join them … someone who has distinguished themselves by qualities or deeds or both. Sometimes a person is recommended by others in the community, but there are no elections outside of what happens inside Council.

"Now remember, death is no stranger in this world, so turnover is fairly frequent. To my knowledge the transitions have always been well considered and smooth. The nation has also been blessed to have had Da-hash-to as its Grand Chieftain for so long a time, because he has been a wise leader and a stabilizing force."

"But there are no jails as Devon said. Is there no crime? Can that be possible?"

"Well no. The people here are like people everywhere, and they're not perfect. But there's a strong morality, a sense of goodness, and a strong sense of community. And there's more … something special, something I don't know how to name, but which you'll see in the Night of Remembrances."

"Oh yes … Judy told me about that," Bruno said. "She thought it was awesome."

Devon nodded, "I've heard of it too from Gary and Roland who saw it when they came last year. I'm anxious to witness it along with everyone else here.

"Back to what I was getting at … If people aren't perfect, which I didn't expect them to be, then there's crime. How is that handled?"

"This isn't easy to answer," John said, "and you may not like what you hear. Let me back track a bit.

"You know life is difficult here and always has been. The physical size of individuals is the result of getting by on meager amounts day after day and generation after generation, so don't compare their meals to what *you've* just eaten. That was a feast the likes of which has never happened before in my experience here.

"Now, that being said, providing for food is every family's responsibility, and it isn't unusual for a family to get into straights. There *is* a lot of working together among family and friends, but that doesn't change the ultimate responsibility, or the rationing in tight times. So it can get tough and people die.

"Rebecca, I hope you told everyone how much the food you

brought last winter was appreciated. You guessed right because times *were* tough then. The soup kitchen held as a result was the first decent meal many had eaten in a while, and while some died anyway, I know there were lives saved.

"And of course there are deaths for all kinds of other reasons, like diseases that always linger about, and accidents. For those our Spirit Man, Nyaho here, is a savior. There is literally a medicine cabinet of plants in the woods about us that hold relief or remedy for many of those things. He's become a master of them. I know he and Gary want to spend more time together and exchange information. We'll all benefit by that.

"I've mentioned these things to get to this point ... that life is precious. And since it is, in the confines of the community as we relate to one another, it carries an obligation of acceptable behavior to justify itself. So now I'll ask you a question. You see there isn't either a jail or the ability to provide for anyone who would be retained in it if there was one? Under those circumstances, what would *you* do to someone who committed a serious crime, or was found guilty of protracted unacceptable behavior?"

Devon swallowed, stroked his chin, then looked round to a chorus of shrugs and avoiding eyes, finally saying, "I suppose banish the bastard."

"That's been tried and didn't work, "John said.

"Why?"

"Because it put the whole village at risk one way or another. Remember now, the person was in that fix because of something bad. So putting him out would give him a chance at revenge or other mischief. Every pathway out could have him lurking in the shadows."

Devon remained silent, thinking, until he turned his head sideways looking at John. "What then ... execution?"

John nodded, "In a way."

"Sweet Jesus! What do you mean, "In a way"? Dead is dead. Is he killed or not?"

"He's given a chance to redeem himself."

"Redeem himself?"

"Yes, by drinking a cup of hemlock that's offered."

"So he kills himself, or he's killed if he doesn't. My ... that's quite a choice."

"Actually it *is* quite a choice, and when you come to understand the culture and the reasoning, you'll see."

"Well, I sure as hell don't understand now," Devon said, murmurs growing around the room as he did.

"Let me explain," John said.

"This whole topic came about in answer to the question as to how the *Atjahahni* managed to survive for thousands of years, in fact solving a problem we have to solve. Well, to do what they've done, they had to learn to live in harmony with the natural world, it boils down to that. Until they did, they were like every other naked ape, so to speak ... killing all the animals they could find and digging up all the plants. When an area became barren and unable to support them, they'd move on. In that way they were no better than the homo sapiens who came out of Africa and migrated, killing off whatever animal they found wherever they went. Because of this they had to keep moving and they did, eventually populating the globe.

"Did you know that North America once had mammoths, tapirs, lions, cheetahs, saber-toothed cats, anteaters, camels and several species of horses, cattle and goats. Those that migrated over from Siberia roughly 30,000 years ago managed to kill all of them. Which proves that the ability of mankind, with its brains and analytical skill, has often been its own undoing.

"You might say the Indians weren't like that even though they were descended from the original migrators, and you're partly right. Along the long line that transpired, some did change their ways.

Fortunately in *Atjahahni* history, someone, or someones, also figured out what they were doing wasn't working. With a brilliance of perception that never came to most of our enlightened world through to the twenty-first century, they deduced that it wasn't and wouldn't until peace was made with nature. They came to realize that every plant and animal, great and small, was a creation of the Great Spirit, and like themselves, had a spirit and a culture and a right to live. Annie has a letter from Reynolds that says the same thing. Anyway they settled down and changed their ways. They took some plants, but not all, from the forest and planted gardens, leaving the rest for the other animals;

they hunted and fished, but were careful to allow the replenishment of numbers rather than drive them to extinction. And they did more. When they themselves died, they gave their bodies back to nature, as if in an exchange. When their bodies were so returned, their bones were collected and burned at the Celebration of Remembrances. Their ashes are then scattered about the community.

"By doing these things, they believe their bodies are recirculated to live again in others, while their spirits stay in the community and survive to share with their loved ones who live on.

"These are powerful beliefs, and ones you need to understand. Because with these beliefs and deeds, the *Atjahahni* have developed a love for family and friends and community unlike anything I've ever witnessed.

"You ask "Why would a condemned man drink the hemlock?" He will because by redemption, he will be forgiven, and then returned to the living and to the community in the same way as any honored citizen is returned. If he doesn't drink … well, you can guess. The difference *is* important … and because of it, crime is very low.

"Now, I don't know if or to what extent this fits into population control. That's a huge problem needing hard decisions to put us in sync with the world around us. Forgetting that for now, let me say only this … that I look forward to this year's Celebration for a special reason—my son, my only son, will be among those who'll be returned.

"That's important because he loved this world and it loved him.

"And someday, I will join him."

It was late, and the last topic was probably going to take years of experimentation and debate to resolve, so it was a good time to stop. This was doubly understandable as most hadn't had time to rest before dinner, and all had been for days with only intermittent breaks. Part of the obvious was that Devon started strumming after John sat, the sound slowly building. It came to a point when all was quiet except for that strumming, which rose to full volume.

Devon then backed off and said, "This has been a good meeting, a meeting characterized by attitudes reflected in this song. It's called *Harmony,* and yes, it's by "Walking Jim". Please join with me …"

Harmony's a wonder,
    it makes things agree,
        and makes all fit together,
      so very easily;
    like the winds and the seas
        and the flowers and the bees,
    nature itself
      is the best of harmony.

[It's a song for the hills,
It's a song for the trees,
It's a song for the sky,
It's a song for the seas,
It's a song for you,
It's a song for me,
It's a whole world harmony.]

The world that we live in,
    it suits me just fine,
        if we treat it with kindness,
      it'll last a long time;
    so we must be gentle,
      no push and no shove,
    but sing to our planet,
      it needs all our love.

48

A Run

The morning broke with a gloomy cover not unusual this time of year. A light rain had fallen during the night, so the world also had a dampness that spattered from the leaves with every pulse of air. It didn't appear to be the kind of day they'd hoped for the Fair, but then it was what it was and was part of the outdoor world with which they were all accustomed.

Despite the gloom, sounds began to filter in early from the Commons, where preparations were already underway. Among the sounds were occasional squeals and laughter ... as obviously fun was too.

At the homestead, everyone was also up early. There was a quick breakfast, and then a split, with John heading to *Tschtaha-tata* to see how the men were doing. The girls—Annie, Rebecca and Lisa—responded by doing what women do getting ready for what the day required. Part of this was to tend to the horses.

The mare and her filly remained well out in the pasture, silently perking to watch as the three came into view. The others, however, grazing nearby, began to edge towards the stables, heads bobbing, eyes shifting.

"Just look at them," Annie said. "They're like children, slowly developing a trust. It's working, but don't make any sudden moves ... They're still skittish."

She opened the gate into the area where the stalls were formed, then after closing picked up a crude wooden shovel and began cleaning.

"Anything we can do to help?" Lisa asked, the two resting their elbows on the top rail and looking in.

"Actually, yes," Annie said, walking to the end with a shovel-full and pitching it wide to the start of a manure pile. Returning and before digging in again, she added, "See that pile of green over there?"

"Yes."

"Well, that pronged thing hanging next to you is our version of a pitchfork. If you could gather the greens and spread them in the feeding trough ... that would help."

As the chores were being completed, the colts, which had stopped short outside, renewed their advance, edging in all the way to the trough, while continuing to eye Ann who concentrated on ignoring them.

"Everything seems to be going well," Rebecca said. "They look healthy enough to me, but Devon said they were scrawny and panicky and a real mess when he first saw them."

"Devon was right," Annie replied, "and for good reasons. Imagine the trauma of being chased as if your life depended on it, then roped in a way that almost strangles you, then separated from the herd and in most cases your mother, and then pulled ... for days. When I first saw them, I cried. They were so pitiful."

"And some died?"

"Yes, a few died along the way, and another died after arriving here. Most of them hadn't been weaned yet, which was a problem because the friends who'd caught them didn't have a clue about feeding. Therefore the colts almost starved ... It's a miracle any of them made it."

"They're looking pretty good now."

Annie nodded, "It's still touch and go. They've grown a lot and have filled in, but keeping them fed is a real chore. Do you have any idea how much they eat?"

The girls shook their heads.

"When fully grown, which will be within another year, they'll each need over twenty pounds of hay or pasture grass a day. That's going to be tough for us to provide."

"Isn't that hay growing over there?" Lisa asked, pointing her head in the direction of a plot of tall strands waving in the breeze. "The patch looks ready."

"It is and it is," Ann answered, leaning against her shovel like a road superintendent. It's just a start, though. We'll soon gather the heads for next season's seed, and then cut the hay for feed. As you can imagine, what that amounts to won't go far. To help we've also planted grasses in the pasture to go along with what looked edible when the area was cleared. The grass is also just a start."

"Whew!"

"You said it."

"Devon says a pasture and stables and all should be ready back at Olympia by spring," Rebecca said, "Isn't the plan to transfer some of these our way?"

"Yes, eventually most of the horses will be there; but there's some training I'd like to give them here first. For that we need to improvise harnesses and reins and stuff. We also need to get ready for another batch of horses … if we can ask our friends for another roundup, that is.

"By the way, have you noticed how the horses have calmed down as we've been talking?"

"Sure have … I guess that's a sign of progress," Lisa said.

"It is. I've actually been able to touch a couple of them, but didn't think it wise to try right now with you two looking on."

"Any names yet?"

Ann smirked, "But of course; they've been showing traits for some time."

"And?"

"Well, I haven't named them all yet … just a few. The third one over is Gladys Rose …"

"*Gladys Rose?*"

"Yes," Ann said, giggling now. "It's her walk … her canter is more of a swagger."

"And the one closest to you?"

"Why do you ask?"

"It looked to me like she made it a point to be next to you."

"My goodness, you're observant. Yes, she has a way about her that reminds me of someone ... I call her "Missie," her voice almost cracking.

"Whatever, I'm impressed," Rebecca said, quickly changing the subject. "I do have a question, though. This with the horses has taken a lot of work, both here and at Olympia. From what I understand, the *Atjahahni* have been told it's being done for meat and hides ... *only*. Now, since they're no dummies, sooner or later they're going to figure you're not being straight with them. What then?"

Annie, who'd been watching the colt still in the pasture with the mare, turned back, her face screwing up as if caught at something. "You're right ... We have a problem."

"And it's because of John. He tends to be cautious and play things close to the vest. Sometimes too close, I think. But then he's been through so much it's hard for me to judge. It may be he just doesn't want to say things that will get people excited before everything's accomplished and under control.

"Speak of the devil, there he is with the whole gang. It looks like they're heading to the pigeon loft. That's another project that has us excited."

"You're not the only ones excited," Rebecca said. "Just think, if we can make those birds work, we'll be able to communicate in a matter of hours rather than weeks."

"So how's it going on your end?"

"We've put up a loft too, and have a half a dozen young doves in training. We're following the manuals as closely as we can, but it's still too early to see if we're going to make it work."

"Aren't we done here?" Lisa asked, sweeping her hand back at the horses.

"Yes."

"Then let's join the men. Maybe we can pick up some pointers."

By late morning about all there was to see had been seen and all that could be talked about had been discussed. Attention turned to the Commons where more people and activity could be sensed, even though the area was well hidden by the bushes and trees in between.

The awareness, however, didn't matter as the Fair wasn't going to start for another few hours, putting them in a limbo of sorts.

So everyone plunked one way or another and bided time, which Annie found a little awkward. She finally stood and announced, "I'm going for a run. Who'd like to join me?"

The invitation didn't have any takers; instead there were shaking heads and looks that said "count me out", including John, who usually would be in favor. Instead he waved off, looking back skewed.

"I'm not going far … just wanted a little workout," Ann explained.

"But there have been wolves about lately," John said. "Those horses may be the cause of that. If you're going to go out any ways at all, at least take the whip."

"Okay, okay," she said, darting into the house, then quickly out again and on her way. There was no use arguing … the whip wasn't big and lethal like a bullwhip, it was smaller and coiled into a shape easy to carry. But it made a loud crack when snapped that could scare hell out of most anything … and, according to John, once landed on the nose of a bear, probably saving his hide.

She'd crossed the bridge and was approaching the pathway leading south when she heard … "Annie, where are you going?" It was Ruth, who was heading in the same direction with Bobby skipping out in front.

"Oh hi … I was going to jog a ways." Ann said, then laughed, "We were running out of things to talk about back there."

Ruth, like John, screwed up her face.

"Just needed to get away." Ann said. "So where are *you* going … and why are you carrying a bow?"

"When the sun broke out a while ago, Bobby got antsy and wanted to swim. I thought I'd take him to the pool so he could work off some of that energy before the Fair starts."

"For that you need a bow?" Annie asked again.

"Just being cautious. Some kids ran by as we were starting, all bug-eyed and blabbering. It seems they'd been down the trail and something had spooked them. It's not the first time that's happened, but you never know."

With her plan really to get away for a while, Ann, rather than running, walked along with the two. She followed as they turned off towards the swimming hole, where several others had gathered to take advantage of the turn in the weather.

"There won't be many more days like this," Ruth said as they settled down along the bank, Bobby already in the water before they did.

"Don't say that. I don't want to even think about winter so soon again. Last year is still fresh in mind.

"By the way ... aren't you preparing an entry for the Fair?"

Ruth hid behind her hands.

"What happened?"

Ruth pointed to the bank on the far side of the pool, "That happened."

"What? Oh, you mean the sculpture of the horse? I'm surprised there's anything left of it."

Ruth nodded. "We tried to preserve it. Everyone was so amazed by the sculpturing, three-dimensional I've heard it described, that a cover was made to protect it. Anyway, it was only sand, so eventually it crumbled. Before it did, however, it inspired quite a few to try a hand at it.

"Including me."

"And?"

"Months ago when the horses were brought in, I was so taken by them I decided to sculpt a head, but in clay, not sand. Well, things went along fairly well ... the sculpting part, I mean. But then the clay dried and parts fell off. After many tries to make it work, I finally gave up."

They were still talking about working with clay when John walked up. "Heard you were here. I thought you were going for a run."

"Oops ... got sidetracked." Ann said. "We've just been gabbing away."

"You still going to go?"

Ann grunted while straining to get to her feet, then shook off the stiffness from sitting. "I guess so. These bones need to do more than sit around all day."

"You'd better get going then. It won't be much longer before the drums start sounding. I'd run with you, but I really need to go to the Council House. The chiefs usually want me to help in some way."

With that he turned and left.

"I'll go with you," Ruth said, standing and dusting off. "Bobby will be fine here. He can swim, and with so many kids around, he'll be safe, especially with the other mothers looking on. Besides, if you go slow enough, we can keep talking."

"It's a deal," Annie said beaming. "Who's in a hurry anyway?"

They jogged southward, weaving in and out and up and down and through creeks and past switchbacks as the path meandered its way following least resistance. On the way they talked and bumped and giggled like the girlfriends they'd become. Twenty minutes or so later, which meant they hadn't broken any speed records, they came to Lookout Point where they stopped, coming to rest against the tall rocks anchoring its side.

"Just look at the view," Ruth said, shielding her eyes as the sun hadn't topped the arc. "The lake, the mountains and all. I love this place."

"So does John. It's the first landmark he remembered seeing the day Nyaho and Dlahni brought him in. He said he often came here after that to meditate.

"And it seems so much happened here, like an attempt on his life. He told me how he'd seen Willow run past him back at the village, and how she'd reminded him about a bunch of things, including me. So he'd come here and sat against this rock attempting to sort things out. Anyway, that's when it happened … an arrow right by his head."

Ruth gritted, emitting a low growl. "That was ordered by Braga. He was behind a lot of things … and he killed Matthew."

Damn! Ann thought, not knowing what to say, *I didn't mean to get into that.*

But then Ruth broke into a smile, a clenched teeth smile. "Both Sara and Naomi stuck arrows in him though … at least that's something. I only wish I'd been there to add mine."

Ann put her arm around Ruth's shoulders and gave a light squeeze, smiling back. "I suppose we should be returning. Things might be about to start."

Ruth nodded, then asked, "Have you ever walked to the edge of this clearing? The rocks drop away opening up the woods ... that's what gives the view."

"No, but let's do. Shouldn't take but a minute."

They threaded their way through the clearing, which was surfaced with smooth flat rocks mingled with moss and grass, and almost reached the edge when Ruth stopped ... suddenly stopped ... grabbing Ann's arm and sucking air.

49

The Plan

John didn't like it. He'd lost Willow to a bear years ago, and the fact of it had never gone away. Now Annie was going to run alone, which wasn't the first time ... but he just wasn't comfortable. He hadn't moved down the trail far before he stopped and turned, intending to do something about it, when he saw two people fading the other way. Ruth, who had a bow threaded diagonally across her back, had joined Ann and the two were bouncing along and laughing. *Would you look at that.* He remembered the first time he'd seen Annie run ... it was at a "Run for Life" event in another world; and then there'd been Willow, a smaller version of her with the same stride. Now Ruth ran, somewhere in between in height but otherwise alike, and she and Annie had pigtails swinging in unison. He turned back, snorting a grin and relaxing. Another memory flashed about the first meeting with Chief Mahacanta a few years before, when Sara had been by his side. He'd explained then that Sara "could take out your eye at 100 paces".

Well, so could Ruth.

No problem.

He entered the Commons soon afterwards where finishing touches were nearing completion, with displays that profused from the Council House along irregular juxtaposed lanes almost to the water. As he threaded through the maze guarded by all the happy faces, he couldn't help but swell. He remembered the first Fair and the surprises in ingenuity it had shown; but surprises hadn't ended with that. The years since had proven that human ingenuity and creativity were almost boundless, and that if allowed to develop, will do so. Examples now abounded in many mediums. Pottery was the most outstanding, with artwork and technology combining to advance to where other nations were astounded by them, as evidenced by the trading that had gone on at Pangaea. There were also basket weaving and leatherworks and woodcarving and fabrics and clothing, all noteworthy. And there was another entry he couldn't remember seeing before, sculpting—sculpting in three dimensions rather than just relief—which made him wonder what had prompted it. Then there were the displays themselves, which were long past being scattered on the ground, as had been the case in the beginning. Now presentations were developed as well, with several booths assembled, some with bamboo-framed cubes allowing hangings on three inner surfaces, like in the art festivals he remembered thousands of years before. There were other exhibits that in the quick walk-by he didn't fully understand, which only underscored creativities reaching out. Except that he didn't get a good look at much of it. When he entered the area and passed the first exhibit, the artist looked up flashing a smile, then remembering that the signal hadn't been given, suddenly changed with a smirk and wagging finger, covering her work and chasing him away. The rest picked up on this, playfully ushering John out the rest of the way.

He arrived at the Council House, almost in a giggle, where the chieftains were assembled, Da-hash-to and Dlahni among them. They were monitoring preparations and coordinating them with a gnomon whose shadow inched its way towards a point of predetermined significance.

"Well, look at you!" John said.

Da-hash-to looked up and smiled with a hint of embarrassment. Usually dressed on the dull side of conservative, he was now anything but. Besides his usual scepter, and the necklace of canary feathers surrounding a gemstone amulet, he was bedecked. The scepter was no longer a plain staff with a gnarly head; it had a decorated leather wrapping below the gnarl, holding in place a surround of hanging eagle feathers. All of which was nothing compared to Da-hash-to's clothing. Several women, knowing that special guests were expected for the fall festivities, had decided the Grand Chieftain needed to look the part. His hair had been combed back and braided, a decorative band around his head holding hair in place as well as a feather each side. His tunic was new and a piece of artwork; it had ermine trim bordering decorative panels at the shoulders, around the collar, and along the pocketed sides.

"May I be of service?" John said, trying not to smile once the impression of the look-over had receded. Da-hash-to was obviously uncomfortable.

"Do you really want to be involved?" The old chieftain answered with faked gruffness. "I've had a look at entries as they've passed by, and don't know that I want to be among the ones to decide the winners."

They looked at the shadow, which continued inching, being relieved the formality of monitoring time was being a distraction. Everyone was ready, the exhibitors standing by, the rest of the population respectfully staying back as if the waiting was part of a game.

With only moments remaining, Da-hash-to nodded to the drummers to make ready, then raised his staff in preparation for the special moment.

That moment never arrived.

Instead there was a sound from the west, from somewhere just beyond the last of the homes. A sound of men suddenly exploding in a yell—a threatening, challenging yell—accompanied by the banging of weapons on shields, whose dull sounds like sinister drum-beats could *not* be mistaken. Before the impact of this could be understood for what it was, it was joined by a similar commotion to the north, then another in between and another and another blending until a wave of sound descended from almost half the perimeter outside the village.

What in hell is that?

Wherever people were assembled, including all the exhibitors, smiles vanished, jaws dropped and heads turned to one another. It was as if hundreds of warriors, possibly thousands and more than the entire *Atjahahni* village, had somehow come close and were threatening. It also seemed that birds quieted and breezes disappeared.

Bewildered, Dlahni approached Da-hash-to, and after a quick conference and nods of agreement, went to the drummers and directed a response—a hectic, chilling beat of imminent danger and mobilization. With that the Fair dissolved, exhibitors and spectators alike bolting to retrieve the equipment and weapons needed for Home Guard assignments. While this was happening in pandemonium, Dlahni called to the officers for a quick meeting—a war council—to determine strategy: squads needed to be formed, then aligned, as did the archers, who were without their leader; auxiliaries—the women who would be in the rear, and the slingers, who were boys too young for assignment to the squads—also needed direction.

John couldn't help. The best he could do was stay out of the way, which he did by threading through the current of people to where the visitors, the Chosen of Olympia, had gathered to wait on the Fair.

"What's happening?" Anton asked, his eyes as bugged as any of the *Atjahahni* rushing past. "Are we under attack?"

"Don't know," John said. "This is the first time anything like this has happened."

"So what do we do?"

As they talked the woods continued to thunder.

John shrugged, a worried shrug as he turned looking south. *This is a fine time for Ann and Ruth to be away.* "My first choice is to stay out of it," he answered, "but we may not have a choice. The *Atjahahni* may need all the help they can get.

"By the way, did any of you bring weapons?"

"You told us not to … remember?"

"Damn … Yes, of course."

"Well, I forgot," Anton said. "I've stashed a pistol in one of my cargo pockets … you know, just in case."

"And I have the bow," Lisa said. "Will that be of help?"

"At this point, anything is good to have. The rest of you might scrounge around for staffs, spears, shields … whatever. But we should stick together until we see what happens."

"What is it?" Annie said.

"Something's wrong! The woods ... *they're moving!*

And they were.

As Ann and Ruth stood unable to believe what they were seeing, the woods on both sides transformed with branches and leaves slowly turning into something else—things separate from the trees—and moved towards them. Then there were heads and arms and legs in bigfoot-like shapes; and as they get closer, eyes glaring out of blackened faces inside the moss and leaves.

Ruth screamed as hands grew from the moving vegetation and grabbed her. She lashed and spun away, yelling *"Run! ... Run Annie, run!"*

But Ann couldn't. Couldn't, that is, until hands reached for her as well, at which time she fought free, backing across the rocks they'd just crossed. For brief moments this zombie-like scene continued with slow, uncertain moves, until one apparition in particular, not as heavily camouflaged, stepped forward and shouted in a language the girls didn't understand, but whose meaning became clear.

Ruth backed and dodged to avoid the branches turned hands, when upon seeing that apparition, an apparition with familiar scars and a familiar voice, she sputtered a message beginning with disbelief building to panic ... *"Braga! Annie, it's Braga ... Run!* **Run! ... Warn John!** At which time the man-bush nearest her swatted, hitting her in the head and knocking her over the edge out of sight.

Ann gasped ... Her impulse was to rush to Ruth's aid, but an advancing thicket blocked the way. With that and Braga's chillingly toned shouts, she could only dance going nowhere, not even able to remember the coil at her side. When the nearest man-bush raised an axe, however, lunging forward with eyes wild with intent, she reacted, ducking to the side just as the axe smashed against the rock behind her. Turning to another transformation, she pushed off and broke free, spinning and eluding groping hands, finally sprinting through an opening to the pathway they'd traveled minutes before.

She was now in a race, but not one she'd ever run before, because in every other she could pace herself and save for the final push. This was different. She had to accelerate like a sprinter, hit maximum speed fast and then maintain it as if her life depended on it. It did ...

and the footfalls stomping behind her and missiles ricocheting in front of her made it clear.

Braga was livid. He jumped around, waving his hands, directing his forces to chase, then following and screaming orders, *"Don't let her get away ... **Kill her!"***

Once again he was on the verge of a triumph. He'd persuaded two of the tribes of the *Bjarla-shito* to support him in his plan—a plan to extract the secrets of the giants who'd come into their world—so all could live in peace without fear. At least that's what he told them.

He ran, trying to keep up with the rest who were all half his age, his mind reeling ... *mustn't lag ... this is my last chance ... it's now or never.*

The men he followed were the best from those villages. They were the strongest, the fastest, and after months of severe training in which large numbers were eliminated, the best trained, the most savage and most dedicated. They bounded after Annie like a pack of wolves, staying mostly on the pathway, but also billowing out to test every option and opening along the way that might give an advantage.

He cursed. The plan had been working perfectly. From spies he'd learned of not only the day of the Fair, but also the time it was going to start, all of which gave him what he needed to complete the details. Ah-ton-jacii and Daj and his clique would orchestrate the legions in their noisemaking, which with the complication of the Fair would create chaos, while he would lead the strike force in ambush. But then things began to unravel. He'd sent two men forward to make sure conditions were as he'd assumed, and even though they were heavily camouflaged and moved as trained, they'd startled some boys, mistakenly made eye contact, and left them screaming and running.

So they'd retreated all the way back to Lookout Point and waited.

Then, just as it was time to move out, came the women ... foolish, curious women ... and now one was escaping!

"Kill her!

"Kill them all!"

Ann ran and ran and ran and ran, keeping to the contorted pathway like in a cross-country from hell. She hurtled a log, catching a toe and tumbling, then righting and spinning back on path as the lead pursuer, who tried to follow, dove face first into the dirt behind her. She crashed through a bush on another shortcut, bouncing off a tree, continuing by every means to stretch out the sounds that kept following.

All of that should have been enough to exhort every effort, but there was more. With still a mile to go, and with lungs and every muscle screaming, she heard drums ... and not the pleasing sound of a call to assemble. It was the rapid, urgent peal of crisis and mobilization, the same she'd heard the year before. *What was happening?*

She somehow accelerated beyond what was possible, hurtling the last creek and streaking past the pool and *Tschtaha-tata* towards the Commons. There she could see chaotic movements as the community scrambled to convert from Crafts Fair to Home Guard.

She shouted for attention between gasps as she ran, but no one noticed in all else that was happening. Then she saw John where the group from Olympia had gathered. Turning, dodging and threading her way in his direction, she shrieked, *"John! It's Braga ... Braga's coming!"*

John looked up ... froze. Ann was sprinting—wild-eyed, dirty and torn and bleeding—and yelling the word that fomented instant rage. But there was more. Bounding behind her like a string of attack dogs were men, black-faced men with multi-colored leathers, shrieking like the fabled berserkers.

When Annie reached him, skidding to a stop and blurting an attempt at explaining, John, seeing the threat immediately behind her, grabbed and jerked her behind him ... and that was the last thing he remembered.

The lead dog at full speed threw a chipped-stone tomahawk at John's head. John flexed just enough that the missile, instead of burying into his brain, hit above the ear, ripping the scalp and sending blood and flesh and hair spattering back onto Devon who'd turned to help.

Then came the second dog ... and the third, and fourth and on and on in quick succession, like demons, attacking and chopping and stabbing in a frenzy. Anton brought out his pistol, but when he raised it to fire, a tomahawk smash broke both weapons as well as fingers. Lisa tried to bring her bow into action but was tackled, the bow flying.

All this, out of sight and sound of Dlahni and the Home Guard who were desperately trying to mobilize in an area several hundred yards to the north of the Council House, was a fight of highly trained, armed attackers in greater numbers against a stunned, unarmed group of non-combatants.

The ambush should have been over quickly, but the Olympians who confronted them had dervishes of their own. Abram reacted immediately, crashing into the second attacker, and then with kicks and chops and jumps and spins, created his own form of havoc, so much so that bones cracked and men growled and grunted and screamed and died. And Bruno too. He tackled the one that downed John before he could do further damage, and in the frenzied dirt-churning wrestle that ensued, dislocated the man's arm, then broke his neck, before turning to another. Devon, recovering from the shock of the spatter and seeing John crash, wielded a staff like a grim reaper, slashing and clubbing and stabbing. And there were more ...

All of this in less than a minute.

Then the main body of the attackers arrived, and should have finished the fight; but they came to a stop because of confusion—a whirlwind of action was before them with people running about and dust in the air and bodies screaming and crawling and worse. Snarling with blood up and ready to attack, they shuffled waiting for the word from Braga who was only moments behind.

Braga, likewise uncertain upon catching up, and with his chest heaving, jumped onto a rock beside them and after a quick look, caught enough of a breath to smile. It was perfect. He could see that the Home Guard, and that meant Dlahni and the officers, were away to the north and west, mostly out of sight, and most likely setting defenses around homes along the perimeter. *The noisemaking trick had worked!* While before him, the defenders, mostly giants, seemed to be at their limit with several down. Most importantly, none of those still standing was John, who could be the one being dragged away.

This wasn't exactly how he'd intended everything to go, but what happened had happened and now it was time to finish. So he puffed and extended his arms, like Benito Mussolini of another time, to yell orders to the forces below him who were revving in anticipation.

The words didn't come. In his excited concentration he hadn't felt anything, but his lips moved without making a sound except for the gurgling in his throat. Then he noticed an arrowhead sticking from his chest.

Strange.

He felt the next thump, though, and then there were two. He turned, staggering now, energy seeming to drain, and looked at a young woman, slender like Willow but taller, with a grim, focused look contorting her features.

He heard her say, "This one's for Matthew."

… Just before the third arrow went through his eye.

50

Terrible Swift Sword

Braga folded and fell, thudding in a billowing heap, and it was as if a whistle blew. The first wave of attack dogs still standing, broke off the fight and stepped back to where the later arrivals bunched. Leaderless, the fearsomely camouflaged cast deflated to nervous glances amongst themselves, then regressed further to dropping mouths. It wasn't because of the remaining defenders, even though they stood bristling just beyond the field of crumpled; it was because of confusion turning to chaos in the form of a mob swarming around both sides of the Council House. And it didn't matter that the mob was mostly women and children, and that most of the mostly were unarmed and panicked, the effect was the same.

Prior to the attack, Dlahni, at the northern outskirts, worked to get his forces aligned. Squad after squad shuffled into place, shields held to eyeballs, spears in hand, nervously twitching while the woods in front of them continued to sound. While wrestling with this, Dlahni was interrupted by someone calling attention to several *Bjarla-shito*, the same ones who'd stayed last fall after returning with the baggage train, and the same ones who'd captured the horses, who were crossing the stepping stones above the cascade. They were waving arms and yelling as if they had something important to say.

They did. But with the din and all else, their gesturing and

445

sputtering only added to the confusion. So Nyaho was summoned …
or at least sought. He had left the Council House and was finally
found among the auxiliaries who were trying for their own semblance
of organization behind the lines. When he heard the problem, he
brought Mahsja.

"The people making noises are *Bjarla-shito*," Nyaho said after
a brief exchange. "But Cherstabonshala says they're not from his
tribe."

"Okay, okay," Dlahni said, walking to the edge of the creek and
looking across into nothing. "So what tribes *are* they? And why
isn't this making sense? There's a large number of men out there …
a number that could have swarmed all over us. But they haven't
moved?"

There were more gestures and expressions and pointing …

"They're not going to attack, Dlahni … It's just a trick."

"A trick? Why?"

More expressions …

"To take your attention away from something else that's going
to happen," Nyaho said, his face wrinkled at a puzzle that wasn't
unraveling.

Before another question could be asked, Cherstabonshala
exploded with a look on his face as if he'd just figured something
out, yelling "Braga!" And pointing south in the direction of the
Council House.

"*Braga!*" Dlahni spewed, adding choice *Atjahahni* words. He
spun, grabbed a spear from the nearest warrior and started in that
direction.

Da-hash-to, John, the Olympians … they're all there!

"*Follow me!*" He shouted to the squads closest by, shouted with
the sickening feeling they might be too late as other sounds, sounds
that had hardly been noticed moments before because of the thunder
from the forest, could now be heard—sounds like those at Pangaea
that would be forever linked to horror.

"*Follow me! Hurry!*"

He ran, only to catch up the last of the auxiliaries who were
stampeding in the same direction. *How ridiculous, that with all our*

planning, our men are away facing an enemy who isn't attacking, while women and children are facing one who is.

Being as close as they were, and suddenly hearing sounds that trumped those from the perimeter, the auxiliaries reacted, moving like moths to the fire past the Council House to the origins of the sounds, arriving as Braga tumbled. Most were stunned at what they saw, many becoming hysterical; but others, like the archers who had veterans from Pangaea in their ranks, maintained order and fell into line to the side facing the attackers. A few slingers also got a grip, broke free, and although in limited confines, began to make throws.

While this was unraveling, there was Ruth, and Ruth wasn't finished. Still heaving to catch her breath, she circled the attackers who were bunching, and came around to where the archers had assembled. Like a goddess of war, torn and bleeding but still contorted with rage, she barked orders. Bows lifted, arrows flew, and after a few volleys, the attackers, with only thin trappings and paint for protection, settled into a quivering mound.

All this took place before Dlahni could reach the scene. He slanted to the right to pass around a crowd too packed to penetrate. That brought him to the first of the Olympians, Devon—Devon the forester, the guitar playing troubadour, the gentle man horrified at the thought of killing—who was bloodied and bent and with a staff in hand, heaving to catch his breath, but still pumped. Then he saw Devon relax and seem to shrink like a red-hot iron that cools and loses its glow. Dlahni started in Devon's direction, but before he could get to him, Devon turned and moved to where Abram lay. Abram was on his back partly on Rebecca's lap, who'd also just moved to settle in. Abram was a mess, his color a waxy grey in contrast to the blood draining from several places. From somewhere to the left, Benjamin, in a condition similar to Devon, joined them, dropping to his knees.

Dlahni looked past them to the scene that was still fluid but settling into place. There were bodies littered about, bodies mostly in camouflaged colors with ensembles of sprigs and mosses. Those nearest were bludgeoned and in gruesome contortions, while beyond was a porcupined mass, the many altogether moving and groaning in assorted agonies.

While cringing at what he could see, a feeling boosted by the hysterics of the auxiliaries that continued to rise and fall in emotional pitches, Cherstabonshala and his friends elbowed past, adding to the din with their cries. Once they'd realized what could be happening, they'd followed behind hoping to stop it, and saw they were too late. As would be learned later, some of the duped attackers were their friends.

Dlahni looked back to the Olympians—Devon and Benjamin and Rebecca—who were now trying to comfort Abram. But Abram was barely conscious, his eyes rolling and out of focus.

He heard Devon say, "You crazy bastard, what were you trying to do?"

"You saved our asses." Benjamin added. "How did you learn to fight like that?"

Abram's eyes swung to a stop and he sputtered, bubbling blood over his chin. He briefly focused, and then smiled, settling back as if on some gentle cloud. He whispered, "Dachau," and winked, after which his features collapsed and eyes glazed.

Rebecca, her face a mask of disbelief, began to sob.

Dlahni gawked, feeling a lump form, but turned knowing he couldn't stay. *Where were the rest?* He worked through another tangle to a shrieking, out-of-control, hair-tearing group that parted as he approached.

Two of his men were helping Chief Djada-sato to his feet. The chief was shaken and bloody, his ear almost torn off and his arm cradled, but the outpourings didn't stop once he was able to stand … and then Dlahni saw why.

Oh no!

The helping hands had uncovered another body face down with dirt and blood and crumple and more, the more being feathers and ermine and tailored leathers … and a hand holding a gnarly scepter.

Dlahni collapsed to his knees, his hands waving over the body as if afraid to touch and hurt it more …

"Aaaeeeeeooooooeeeee! Oh no! Oh no! Da-hash-to, Da-hash-to! Why? Why?"

After moments of uncontrollable anguish, he settled. Then he eased the body over, carefully cleaning what he could, and picked it up. Standing, Dlahni cradled the body, burying his face in its chest in a hug. *Da-hash-to, Da-hash-to.* He heard others talk about how the Grand Chieftain had been at the Council House when the attack started, and, seeing it first hand, had led other chiefs and whoever else was nearby in an attempt to help. *So light, so frail… with the heart of a lion.*

Dlahni thought of the night before, when there'd been the lengthy conversation about the mission the Olympians were on, and the "Truths", as they'd described their initial findings. After it was over Da-hash-to, Nyaho and he had returned to their homes, but before parting, had a long talk about their impressions of the night, just as they had after the meeting in Olympia. Da-hash-to's eyes had been sparkling. He hadn't spoken during the meeting, but he'd followed all that had been said. When they were finally about to part, he said "Ab Oh spoke to the spirits." They had only nodded, not knowing what this had to do. But they listened as he added, "And the Great Spirit has been talking to me."

"Oh," they had remarked, surprised but eager to hear more. "And what is he saying?"

Da-hash-to had shaken his head, "He doesn't speak in words, so I can't tell you in words. It is with feelings, and now I see."

"What do you see?" We asked.

"Everything is going to work fine," he answered. "You two were worried that John and his friends were going to rule over all of us, make us second-rate, so to speak. But that's not going to happen. The friends are all good people, and the Great Spirit is tying us all together. I wasn't able to understand before, but now I see." He had patted us then and repeated, "It's going to work fine."

They had said, "Of course it will … with your leadership, it's sure to."

But he had smiled and said, "No, I'm an old man. You two get some rest now ... tomorrow will be a big day."

Tomorrow will be a big day, Dlahni repeated in his mind. Then, knowing this wasn't a time to mourn, he gently transferred the body to those crowding in and asked them to take it to the Council House. As they moved away and were swallowed by the throng, he lost it.

"Braga ... Braga did this! Where is the miserable son-of-a-bitch?"

Someone pointed and he bounded away, hurdling bodies as he went, his left hand fisted and his right clenching a war club.

"Braga ... where are you!"

Cherstabonshala, who along with his friends, were sorting through the refuse, untangling bodies and trying to give comfort to those still with senses, looked up ... realizing what this was about. Another pointing and Dlahni came to a stop over a quivering clump at the base of a boulder. He grabbed its shoulder and rolled the body on its side, seeing at first an unrecognizable mess of paint and moss intermixed with sweat and blood and dust. But then there were the familiar scars and features. Growling like an animal from deep within and raising his club, his impulse was to strike hard, brutal, obliterating smashes; but he held back, the sight of an arrow pushing the eye-ball half out, and the bloody froth stringing from a sagging mouth and draining life away, having its affect. After a long last look, and breaths that gradually slowed, he straightened, letting the body flop back Then he turned and retraced his steps.

When Dlahni got clear of the wreckage, he was met by one of his officers who stood holding Da-hash-to's scepter. The officer handed it to him without saying a word, just looking, like others were who'd gathered behind. Dlahni hesitated, reluctant to take it. He saw that its eagle feathers were splayed and the staff seriously gouged, but it still carried a deep meaning. The situation reminded him of years before when Nyaho first realized his new station. In like manner, he now was in the spotlight ... He was the Grand Chieftain. And somehow, despite the conflicting feelings, he had to pull himself together.

He did, slowly ... somewhat in keeping with the situation around him, as emotions were subsiding. So he took the scepter, held it firmly and looked back at those gathered and nodded.

The situation was still confusing, however. Even after asking those nearest questions, the first impressions were that no one really knew what happened, other than that a brief but horrible battle had been fought in the small area where bodies were being tended. Nearby a group of women, red-eyed and sniffling, were in the process of settling, so he walked over and asked "What did you see? How did it start?"

At first he got twisted faces and shivers that said it was too horrible to describe, but then one blurted, "They were monsters. It was awful. The visitors from Olympia held their own for the most part, but Da-hash-to and his men … they were just chopped down," and started crying again.

Still seeking answers, Dlahni turned away, then stopped as he thought he noticed a change. He asked the officer who'd handed him the scepter and was still nearby, "Does it seem like the sounds from the woods are dying down?"

After likewise giving it his attention, the man nodded "Yes, I think you're right."

And they were. Dlahni held up his hands for silence, which only worked for those close by, but it was enough to catch the fact that one by one, sections of the perimeter outside the village from which sounds had been coming, were dwindling and going silent.

"Good … good," Dlahni said as the last section sputtered out. Then to the officer, "I don't know what's next, but Cherstabonshala said they weren't going to attack and maybe that's so. In any case we need to have another officer's meeting. Only a few have returned, so send runners to the lines and have the squads pull back. I want to see the leaders at the Council House as soon as possible."

While watching him turn away, he saw Devon carrying Abram, Benjamin and Rebecca following behind. He wanted to call out to them for what information they could give, but he hesitated. It was another part of a sad scene with Benjamin holding the girl, who stumbled along almost collapsed with grief. His own emotions rising again at the sight, he realized they were heading for John's home, which reminded him … *Where were the rest of the Olympians? Where was John? He could use his help.*

Circling the ground where the attackers were clumped, the

Olympians passed a group Dlahni hadn't noticed—the archers. Mostly young women, the archers formed a major component of the Home Guard, and as such, from comments circulating through the crowd, had saved the day. They were still in the formation in which they'd fought, but were starting to unravel, some dropping weapons and sobbing in each other's arms. So he went to them to give words of praise and understanding, but not yet knowing exactly what had happened, he was at a loss. The most he could do was give hugs and consoling pats and ask questions, which led to another …

Since he was told Ruth had directed the action … *Where was she?*

He looked over at Cherstabonshala and his friends again, who continued to try salvage lives, and the sight triggered a thought. If the demonstration in the woods was only a trick, then someone should go to whoever was in charge and tell them what had happened. The whole episode was so bizarre, they may be just as confused. In the meantime, the bodies of the attackers could be collected and laid out across the river for them to recover. But he needed Nyaho or Mahsja.

And where were they?

He paced going nowhere, his mind reeling. And he wasn't happy with himself. He was the leader of the defenses, and should have been in the middle of the action; but he wasn't. And all the chest-thumping and stomping didn't change the fact he didn't have a scratch. Had he missed clues that should have warned him? Some kids had been spooked a while before; but everyone, including himself, had ignored it. Was that a sign?

How many attackers were there? Looking back at the area where the fighting had taken place, and where now only the bodies of attackers remained, he could count about twenty. *Where had they come from? What, besides creating chaos and mayhem, were they trying to do? Why were they costumed as they were?*

The costuming reminded him of something Nyaho had done years ago when they were children. In a game similar to hide-and-seek, Nyaho had disappeared and no amount of searching could ferret him out. Then while a group of them were discussing what more could be done, a bush, or what they thought was a bush, in their midst, growled and almost scared them out of their skins. Nyaho had painted his face and hands, and with the use of leaves and twigs and moss had virtually vanished.

Had these attackers popped out of nowhere like that?

All of what had just happened, didn't just happen. There had to be extensive planning and preparation and training. And to coincide so well with what was happening in the village—the Crafts Fair, for instance, the exhibits for which a years worth of work had been invested, and which now lay scattered nearby where it had been abandoned only an hour before—meant an Atjahahni had been involved. This was treachery at it worst. Many died because of it. Da-hash-to, probably the greatest chief in the history of the nation, was among the dead.. Could Daj be the traitor? There had been so many peculiar circumstances. Daj and Shajsi-djuma and Ndjasa?

Dlahni was going over these things, when he noticed across the crowd, which had quieted but was still milling about, the rest of the Olympians—Bruno, Anton and Lisa—who being a head taller, were easy to spot. Even so, he could see they were also bloodied and torn, but were giving their attention to someone else.

Whomp!

Dlahni started towards them, once more having to elbow through. As he approached he could see they were standing as if overseeing others. They were. The others were hunkered down and rocking and bobbing and moaning. *Ann and Ruth.* Obscured beneath them was someone with long legs covered by familiar leggings and foot-wraps. And the legs of that someone were not moving and the soles of the wraps were worn through.

He groaned.

But John wasn't there. He was in a fog-like swirl that reached everywhere and nowhere, with eddies that defined then dissipated back to indeterminates. He seemed to be rising, but really couldn't tell as he was in a state of weightlessness; then it got brighter and subtle colorings became discernable. Colors then shapes. Were those faces? *Dad … is that you? For years I've tried to reach you … Then it's true!* The face was smiling as if communicating and was except there were no words, only a warm feeling of knowing. He wanted to move closer but he couldn't as he continued being swept along. There were other smiling faces, somehow transmitting with outreaching sensations. Mark ... *Mark! Wait! There's so much to tell ... Oh, you know.* The movement gentle but unrelenting ... More and more faces ... *I know them!* Then another ... Lawrence, dear Lawrence. *What is it you once said? "If there is a heaven, I hope I make the cut ... and that I get to work in God's workshop ... to work with God ... to be his servant." Is that where you are? Is that where I'm going? Lawrence ... Lawrence?* Then the faces, or what he thought were faces, faces and people, receded and the light intensified. Only it was light in colors that turned and curled and brightened and joined with sounds ... *Were those sounds?* He didn't understand, but there seemed to be others, somethings now ushering and welcoming and guiding towards an opening far in the distance that even with speeds that seemed to increase and distances that seemed to pass with a blur yet stayed far, far away until suddenly he was through. And there was a realm, not of form and color and sound, but of understanding. *Was this beyond the circle around the circle?* Yes ... it was and it was beautiful ... It was simple and complex and indescribable yet comprehendible and amazing... so amazing. And there were voices ...

Ann rocked as she held his head, "John, John, don't leave me." She tried but didn't succeed in holding back tears, feeling so helpless ... as did Ruth at her side, who gritted and held back from screaming but couldn't stay the tears either. Ann thought of the ridiculous irony, that Gary, John's best friend, who'd been studying to help in situations like this, was a world away when desperately needed.

So ironic ... so awful.

She was in this hell of hopelessness when she felt someone settle beside her. It was Nyaho, who said in almost a whisper, "Let me see what I can do."

She looked up. *Oh please, please help, please do.* Then before she backed off to make room, she leaned forward again and kissed John's cheek and whispered "John, John, you can't leave me ... We're going to have a baby."

EPILOGUE

They walked up the steps, single-filed through the heavy automatic sliders that hissed as the air-locks released, passed the decontamination area with its still active paraphernalia, and into a larger space that appeared to have been an improvised design studio, with aging exhibits in glass cases on tables and walls. An elongated room, it led to a large, thick, vault-like steel door leading out. Out, however, meant another landing, then more steps upward, leading from what had seemed the bowels of the earth. These steps tied to still another level and more doors, and another station where friendly guides were on hand to assist and control the traffic, a necessity as a similar number were assembled and waiting to start down. Leaving from there the group came to a wide interior concourse that arced its way along the fringe of the hill called Mount Olympus, from which a variety of rooms, stairs, elevators and escalators could be accessed. The south side of the arc was mainly glass punctuated by sculptured alcoves and ancillary facilities, including exits opening to a wide veranda overlooking the broad, heavily landscaped expanse called the Commons.

The proctor for this experience, one near the end of the weeks schedule, stopped the class at the central exitway, made final comments, and dismissed them. With that, the assemblage, only twenty in number, threaded out the doors, and, after brief hesitations, slowly disintegrated as individuals, pairs and smaller groups split away and drifted down the steps.

"Dinner isn't for a few hours, so what are you going to do 'til then?" Thad said to Johan, who had stopped at a pilaster at the top of the steps and was surveying the space spreading out below.

Johan, deep in thought, mumbled an answer, "I don't know. It's a beautiful day … maybe just find a spot out there and plunk …"

"Sounds good to me. Let's do."

As they started down they were joined by Mohiud, Potuca and Stefan, who were also at odds. The five who trudged were in appearances an odd clique whose paths had crossed a number of times during the week, leading to a mutual accord. The odd had little to do with diversity, as that had pretty well been blended out since the plague. But there were differences, mostly caused by centuries and then millenniums of peoples confined to small populations in isolated sites. The last few hundred years had seen the beginnings of reblending, but the differences were still noticeable. For whatever it mattered, Johan was the tallest at six feet two, with dishwater blond hair and blue eyes; Thad was the shortest and stockiest; Mahuid was the darkest with black, curly hair and eyes to match; Potuca was slender and wiry with sharp facial features and a mop of reddish hair; and Stefan was the most muscular, and also the quietest. Like all inductees, they were young and impressionable, averaging seventeen years, coming from all parts of the nation—a conglomerate extension of territory from Olympia to portions of mainly North America; this meant the comingling that invariably resulted was an education in itself.

The Commons was an adventure. It was wide and long and included generous landscaping, with fountains, arbors, babbling brooks, ponds and lawns, and monuments in an amorphic combination of rustic, historic, classically artful and contemporary. The area was bordered by a university complex, public buildings, housing and an outdoor arena with complementary entertainments which completed three sides, and the huge Potala-like mountain complex on the north, from which they had exited. These were in a combination of intimate to soaring in vibrant colors and shapes, giving Olympia its nickname "Emerald City". Beyond the structured enclosures, and virtually hidden by shrubs and vines, were ramparts that dropped precipitously to surrounding lakes and streams, from where fields and gardens and orchards and pastures extended for miles, ending at forested hills in the distance.

It was a busy place. It became so on a day as this, a day not only clear and balmy, but also near the end of an intense week of inductee orientation, of which the twenty were a small part. The twenty was a typical division because of the limited capacity of some of the instructional areas, and in particular the sanctum—the incubator complex—which was the highlight of the orientation. Because of the busyness, there was a lot of casual movement and a lot of gaming and a lot of lounging, all of which led to a lot of meandering for the five before an area could be found on which to plunk. The space finally reached was small, but it had visibility in most directions and shade from an ancient oak towering overhead.

After jostling and settling like a dog in high grass, Thad, seeming to burst with things on his mind, said, "That was really something, wasn't it?"

No one directly answered, contributing only grunting and nodding in a sort of distracted agreement. It didn't help when there was a noise a bit away that caught their attention, causing necks to strain to see what was happening. It appeared to be no more than a bunch clowning and picture-taking around a tall monument that was the centerpiece of a garden of boulders. The monument seemed to balance a setting that had at its opposite end a jagged rock that shot from the maze like the head of a spear.

Seeing nothing of consequence, they settled back, but the interruption did raise questions. "What *is* that thing anyway?" Potuca asked.

"Not sure," Stefan answered. "I meant to take a better look at it the other day, but didn't. All I know is that it's a stack of sculptured stones, each one with a meaning ..."

"Everything around here seems to have a meaning ..."

"Yeh, but I didn't get to what it or they were ..."

"I think it's called a Totem ..."

"Whatever ... at the time I was more taken by the other carvings."

"You mean the hearts?"

"Yes ... They go all the way back. Can you believe that?"

Thad fidgeted while all this was going on, not willing to give up when his mind was locked on to something. At the first opening he asked again, "What part of the last few hours impressed you the most?"

Johan, whose plunk had put him between some large roots at the base of the tree where he sat cross-legged and slouching, stirred, shaking his head as if to sort out the options, finally mumbled, "It's hard to say. The last hours? The whole week has been ..." He shook again at a loss, "I don't know. From what dad told me I'd been looking forward to all of this. That old building over there, or rather shack, is really something. It supposedly was the first one built ... a bunkhouse. It's hard to imagine wrestling those huge trunks into place without any equipment. But I guess tops for the week is what we just finished, the trip into the sanctum. It was beyond what I could have ever expected."

The others, who lay and sat and sprawled every which way in almost a circle, nodded as if to say "same for me".

"What hit me as much as anything was the man in the cocoon. He was so natural. It seemed like he could wake up and rise at any moment ... *He was eight thousand, four hundred and twenty-two years old!*"

"Jim Wilson?"

"Was that his name?"

"Yes."

"Okay, whatever ... his being there was something else."

"What about that bit with Huston Burner and Reynolds Bascomb?"

"The holographic greeting?"

"Yes. They were the ones who created the incubator and the systems that linked us to the old world. You hear talk about voices from the past ... but when you're exposed to it this way, it's ... it's so amazing."

"For sure. And if I understand everything correctly, Jim Wilson, the talk, and the carving of the hearts on that rock over there, all date back to the same time."

"More or less ..."

"All of those were astounding. But I was particularly struck by the movies of the twentieth and twenty-first centuries. I'd heard about that time, but seeing it with its wars and technology and killing ... and population explosion and pollution and all ... *wow!*"

Just then a few girls walked by, naturally interrupting the chains of thought. When they'd passed, Thad, at his irrepressible best said, "Speaking of wow, did all of you see the smile the attractive one laid on Johan here?

"What's going on buddy?"

Johan snorted, a smile breaking his attempt to be cool, "That's Nshswanji. We sat together at one of the classes yesterday."

"Nshswanji ... What a pretty name."

"That's what I told her, but she laughed. Evidently the original native sound as it was pronounced way back was something else, "like a pig eating slop", she said."

That went nowhere, so after a lull, Mohiud said, "Basic training starts next week." It was a simple statement, but in reality a question.

Thad cursed. "Why do we have to go through all of this? I mean really, really, hard training ... and two whole years of service in all. *Why?* There's never been a war since that god-forsaken twenty-first century, so what's the problem. There are better things to do. Dad has a booming medical practice and I could be on my way to joining him."

"What has your dad had to say about all of this?" Mohiud asked. "Has he tried to get an exception for you?"

Thad growled and looked away, "No ... he wouldn't help. When I bitched about it he quoted something which, I guess, came from ancient Greece. He said, "Son, you're going to go and when you return, you will do so with your shield, or on it"."

"What's that supposed to mean?"

"*Duh!*"

"You sound scared."

"Well, yes ... honestly now, aren't all of you?"

Reluctantly, but eventually, everyone nodded.

"From what I hear, it's pure hell. There are months of not only military training, but training under extreme conditions with freezing, sleep deprivation, exhaustion, and on and on with most extended beyond their limits ... *Why? Some have died!*"

It was the kind of question every inductee asked, but only in whispers if expressed at all.

"Sure, some have died," Mohiud said, "and I'm as scared as any can be. But think of this … those girls who walked by, they'll be in on it too. If that's not enough to spur you on, I don't know what is. As for my dad, he didn't say much about it, but I could tell the call wasn't debatable. What was it your dad said, Thad, "Return with your shield or on it?" I guess that's what mine would have said, and what I'm expected to do as well."

"I'm surprised," Potuca said, "Isn't he the Governor of your state?"

"No, he's just Governor-select. He won't take office for another six months, about the time our basic training will be over. Right now he's sort of shadowing the current administration to understand the issues and actions before taking over."

"He still sounds pretty important, though. Couldn't he pull strings?"

"You crazy? He wouldn't do that. I've already explained how he feels. And as for the office, he didn't run for it, you know … his involvement was requested. Furthermore, like so many others, he doesn't intend to make the position a career; he just wants to get in and do the best job he can, then pass matters on to someone else."

"Someone said people used to compete for political offices … I mean, spend lots of money and campaign all over the place … way back in the old days, that twenty-first century again. I got the impression that once in office, they were constantly campaigning to stay there … with lots of benefits stacking up."

"Don't know about that. Doesn't make sense though … Why should someone get into office just because he or she wants it? Anyone can want. There's a difference between want and deserve."

"There's a lot about all of that I don't have a handle on. In the past there were words like entitlements and welfare and stuff like that that we don't hear about now … yet we seem to be doing fine. Just strange, that's all.

As this bit of conversation ran its course, Thad settled down, but not out. "What did all of you request for duty assignments? How about that … Stefan? Johan?"

Being the last targeted, Johan spoke first. "My top choice was Foreign Service, but I guess my chances there depend a lot on how I do in basic training."

"Why that? Foreign Service can be dangerous."

"True. There have been incidents and people have been hurt. But if I understand our policy correctly, it's about mutual respect, and if anything, gradual assimilation; it's never about taking the offensive or attempting to conquer. Therefore training and the tour of duty will be ambassadorial with defensive strategies our only resort if things go wrong."

"Yes, but those defenses are still with shields and spears and bows and arrows. I know we have the capability of making much more advanced weapons, guns for instance. Guns would make us invincible like in those old war movies."

"Oh sure, but Dad says doing so would lead to arms proliferation, and once that starts, there's no end in sight. We'd be back on the path that was leading to oblivion before."

"Well, I'm not bothered by the weapons, what makes a defensive position workable is the training and discipline that should work in our favor. Anyway I'm not concerned. It's exciting because there are so many places that haven't been reached, or have for some reason been by-passed. They've all got to be interesting. The people and cultures, from what I hear, are pretty much like what the Chosen encountered when they came out of that incubator. I mean four hundred years doesn't change what's been going on for the eight thousand years before it, if there haven't been any outside influences."

"Potuca?"

"Who doesn't like Foreign Service? But I'd be just as happy with Archaeology. The possibilities here seem endless. All that was built in the old world collapsed, was over-grown and buried, and then subjected to all sorts of workings like glaciers and floods and rising seas in addition to chemical reactions and critters. Even with all the scrambling and blending, diggers have come up with treasures of every kind—rich iron-oxides for instance, residues of other metals, and gold and ceramics … a bunch of things. Anyway, the world up to the twenty–first century was amazing. Archaeology is a lot of work, but every now and then, there's excitement too."

"Mohiud?"

"Maritime services appeal to me. I know there's adventure to be had on the continent even though expansion has been slow. But just think for a moment about oceans. You talk about wow! Trips have been completed around the world many times. In the process they've found places, particularly islands, that aren't habited, and others, where there are people, they're so savage our ships keep a distance."

"Sounds like there's just as much of the military in this as in Foreign Service."

Stefan snorted.

"What did I say?"

"Oh nothing … It's just that all of you seem to think that the military is an isolated assignment. It isn't. All of us will be a part of it and forever more … like those "Minutemen" we heard about in Colonial America.

"My older brother went through all of this ten years ago … and guess where he was assigned?"

Everyone shrugged.

"Right here. He was one of the guides, or guards if you will, in the museum.

"What you probably haven't caught on to, because it's so well concealed, is that this whole city, I mean Olympia, as grand as it is, is also a citadel … an ingeniously and heavily defended citadel.

"It had to be.

"It had to be and has to be because of the sanctum and the treasures it contains. That treasure is knowledge … the knowledge that billions of people had assembled up until that twenty-first century.

"Now much of that has since been brought out and used and disseminated to everyone's benefit, and even exceeded in many cases; but there is still much there that must be protected. From the Chosen until the here and now, there's been the realization that if all that information were destroyed, or if it fell to the wrong hands, the mission many have dedicated their lives to could be lost."

After an awkward silence with eyes darting about, Mohiud stood and slowly turned. Johan did too, leaning against the tree.

"Doesn't look like a citadel to me," Mohiud said, scratching the side of his head.

"Come to think about it, though," Potuca added, "When we climbed to the top of Olympus the other day and looked around, it kind of looked that way. Now I see..."

Thad nodded too, then said, "Stefan, what makes you so damn smart?"

He laughed ... "Like I said, I have a brother."

"Okay, but I still have a question ...Why have explorations and assimilations taken so long? You'd think more would have been done in four hundred years. There are instances where primitives are still only a stones throw away from mainstream ... Seems strange."

"Well, maybe not so strange," Johan answered. "Remember that review of ancient history?"

"Which part?"

"The discovery of the new world by Columbus, and then the expansion into and subjugation of the territories in it by the leading European nations. That was all over in a hundred years or so, and in that time native populations and their civilizations virtually disappeared And bad things didn't stop there. A few hundred years more, like in those movies, seven billion people were on the planet, still squabbling over this and that, with all other life heading into oblivion."

"So we all understand. But what happened next was worse."

"You mean the atomic war?"

"Well that was awful, but I meant the plague, which almost wiped mankind away."

"We've been hearing that story since the first grade," Thad said, "I was just questioning why everything's moving so slowly."

"I'd say it was because of the Chosen," Mohiud volunteered.

Johan smiled, "You just stole my thunder ... but go ahead."

"Okay ... Well, they made up all those rules ... They called them "Truths", that were the building blocks by which all peoples must agree to live," and then he laughed, his face exploding in a grin reaching from ear to ear.

"What now?"

"Oh, I was just thinking about one of the so-called truths, the one on religion. It seems some old codger had said ... "I don't care if you eat shit, chase butterflies or bark at the moon, if you don't hurt anyone or mother earth, it's okay with me". They didn't adopt policy in exactly those words, but it seems to be the gist of what did go down."

"Mother earth," Johan repeated, "that would be another one of the truths, and another reason things have moved so slowly."

"You mean the environment."

"Yes. The Chosen made it a requirement that nothing be done that was harmful to other life. That meant hunting was so regulated it was almost eliminated. That meant mining and manufacturing and product development were forced to conduct operations in such a way that no poisonous or harmful by-products resulted, and that everything, as in nature, was recyclable.

"And then there's the matter of politics. Politics in the old days came in many forms, with most of them easily corrupted and contorted to favor special interests. It was completely revised in hopes of preventing that. Mohiud, your dad is a perfect example of the system that resulted … qualification and sacrifice and service… those were the bywords."

"Yes, yes, I understand all that. But the part I don't is how you get a primitive society to accept all the constraints and regulations."

"It's not easy, and apparently it takes time. Maybe that's why basic training is so tough … because in a few years it's going to be our turn to make sure the system of truths works."

"Yeh."

Later, when the group got up to get ready for dinner, which was a concluding affair for the week, Johan excused himself, saying he'd catch up with them later.

He wanted to be alone.

He retraced his way back to the mountain complex and into the concourse, then to another hallway. With the lateness of the day traffic was thinning, and as he walked, the PA system announced that because of the special evenings activities, the building would be closing soon.

After passing sections exhibiting notables through generation after generation, he was there, and like before, he felt a chill. The chamber was the most sanctified of all with a high glass dome casting its glow to accentuate the exhibits surrounding the room. As he stepped in, the guards he passed were cordial as always and smiled, but they also looked at their watches. There wasn't much time.

He was in the hall of The Chosen. They were sculptured as they looked when they emerged from incubation, and were in poses and settings reflecting the specialties they later shouldered. The sculptures, in white marble with tints expertly applied, were so well crafted that with concentration and a little imagination, a viewer could expect to see the person depicted return to life.

It was hallowed. At plaques beside each statue, an outline was made of the person and the incredible role he or she had played in shaping the future. There was Roland, tall and muscular with his blunderbuss—the Builder; Anton, gangly and shirtless in overalls—the Father of Agriculture; Rodney, his wild hair and gleam hinting of the next exciting thought—the Father of Chemistry; Bruno, the smallest in stature but greatest in vision—the Architect; Judy—the Teacher; Gary, with his irrepressible sparkle of personality—the Father of Medicine; Mona—the Nurse; Abram—the Hero; Rebecca—the Nightingale; Devon, tall and ruddy with his guitar—the Forester; Lisa—the Archer; Annie—the Ecologist; Terry—the Gardener; and on and on like gods of the more ancient Olympus, but no less revered in any lifetime. Most lived to a ripe old age; some never married, but all dedicated themselves to a mission that transcended any other interest.

Johan passed by one after another until he stood before John, the reason for his return. John was depicted as he looked to the other Chosen upon his return to Olympia with Annie. He was therefore bearded and dressed in frontier leathers, and older and scarred, but with the look of determination that characterized his life. Like most others he lived into his eighties, with the plaque recording an almost impossible list of accomplishments, including eight children with Annie, all of whom went on to carry the torch. John received the ultimate of honors, being recognized as the Father of the Country.

Johan looked on in reverence and pride. With the generations that had passed, the family trees for those living today reached out and crossed lives that extended to the times these people had graced, and he knew from studies kept by his own family, his history had started here.

"We're closing in a few minutes," the guard reminded. "We must ask you to leave now."

Johan nodded and turned, but then he noticed another preparing to leave in the next chamber, which was dedicated to the luminaries in the nation that had been nearest Olympia in the beginning.

It was Nshswanji, who was turning and wiping a tear when their eyes met.

Johan beamed and said "Hi."

AFTERWORD

Writing is, among other things, a learning experience. That's been true in many ways, the most startling of which has been the realization that in fiction, the story can take you where you didn't think you intended to go.

And that has happened.

As explained in the Afterword for EASTER ARMAGEDDON, the driving reason to become involved in writing at all was the environment, which had been a concern reflected in aspects of my architectural practice for forty-five years.

During the later part of that practice, there'd been a yearning to return to interests of early years, such as art, for which there'd been a good start, or woodworking, for which a fine shop had been assembled and lay waiting. Writing wasn't showing on the radar at that time, except for the fact the environment kept nagging and wouldn't go away. Then while looking over the rail at my "tree-house" in the mountains, looking down into the woods to the river sparkling by—a setting a friend described this way, "I wake each morning and pinch real hard to make sure this isn't a dream"—the course became set and writing won out.

After several years and my best shot, I had to accept that the story started wasn't finished, and that there was a pulling from where I hadn't intended to go. The environment never lessened in importance, so that wasn't it; it was just that there'd been a bombardment of other events on the world's stage that also make us question the future ... like the stupid, lengthy war and its numbing cost, the Arab Spring and its specter, the continuing development of arms and its alarming atomic aspects. Then at home there'd been the financial scandals, the longest recession in memory, the rise of partisan politics to new disgusting levels, and the matching, lengthy election year that made you wonder if the 200-year average life of governments was about to have another applicant.

So the story became extended rather than intended.

One of its characters, who was supposedly intelligent and successful, explained that the mission was …

To start mankind over again, averting mistakes of the past and creating a sustaining society in harmony with the natural world, a society which elevates mankind to the potential of his God-given genius.

Wow (as explained), that's a tall order, one that it's possible the Founding Fathers considered when they did their works. But although opinionated and swayed by the reading listed herein, I didn't presume to have the answer, and don't have, unlike the many in Thoreau's time who had the perfect system folded in their back packet. This has been reflected by the Chosen, as exemplary as they were, who were humbled by the challenge and didn't feel adequate in its pursuit.

By writing about these things at all, however, I hope the book raises questions, and makes you ask what you would do if you were put in the position, a position of rare challenge, to make the world a better place, a place that fulfills the mission listed hereinbefore.

Above all, enjoy …

Attention is called to the following:

Chapter 12: The song *Come Walk with Me*, and others in the book like *If I Were a Tree* and *Whole World Harmony*, are from an album *Come Walk with Me* by Walkin' Jim Stoltz, a wilderness songster and long-distance hiker, as produced by Earthtalk Studios, A product of Wild Wind Records, Big Sky, MT.

Chapter 23: The story of the blacksmith, his hard work and fortitude, was too relevant to ignore. And it's true … He was my father.

Chapter 37: The two-wolf theory ... how profound, supposedly by a wise old Indian. Yet the person who mentioned it before an assembly, couldn't remember what he's said later when I asked more about it.

Chapter 47: The characteristics of people in the workplace are not speculation; they are neither good nor bad but actual as experienced, and represent realities that confound dealing with people.

The same goes for benefit programs, which although not mentioned, are further complicated by governmental intrusions that continually change requirements. This means that a program designed for a particular situation in the beginning, and approved, might be something else several years later, something that never would have been adopted.

Recommended reading, in addition to what might be referenced in the book, include:

God is Not One, The Eight Rival Religions that Run the World and Why Their Differences Matter, by Stephen Prothero, HarperOne 2010.

The God Species, Saving the Planet in the Age of Humans, by Mark Lynas, National Geographic 2011.

The Eagle and the Bible, Lessons in Liberty from Holy Writ, by Dr. Kenneth Hanson, New England Revue Press 2012.

The Answer, Grow Any Business, Achieve Financial Freedom, and Live an Extraordinary Life, by John Assaraf & Murray Smith, Atria Books, 2008.

Outliers, The Story of Success, by Malcolm Gladwell, Little, Brown & Co.2008.

The Tipping Point, How Little Things Can Make a Big Difference, by Malcolm Gladwell, Little Brown & Co. 2000.

Cradle to Cradle, Remaking the Way We Make Things, by William McDonough I & Michael Braungart, North Point Press 2002.

Walden, by Henry Thoreau 1854.

The Sociopath Next Door, Who is the Devil You Know, by Martin Stout, Broadway Books 2005.

Confessions of an Economic Hit Man, by John Perkins, Penquin Group 2004,

The Republic, by Plato
The Greek Way, by Edith Hamilton, W.W.Norton & Co. 1930.
The Echo of Greece, by Edith Hamilton, W.W.Norton & Co. 1957.
Greece and Rome, Builders of Our World, by National Geographic society 1968.
The Rule of Empires, Those Who Built Them, Those Who endured Them, and Why They Always Fail, by Timothy Parsons, Oxford University Press 2010.
The Decline and Fall of the Roman Empire, by Edward Gibbon, the Modern Library 2003.
Two Treatises of Government, by John Locke 1690.
Lives of the Signers of the Declaration of Independence, by Rev. Charles Goodrich, Hartford 1841.
The Founding Fathers, The Politically Incorrect Guide, by Brion McClanahan, Regnery Publishing 2009.
Washington, A Life, by Ron Chenow, The Penquin Press 2010.
American Creation, Triumphs and Tragedies at the Founding of the Republic, by Joseph Ellis, Alfred Knopf 2007.
Signing Their Lives Away, The fame and Misfortune of the Men Who Signed the Declaration of Independence, by Denise Kurnan & Joseph D'Agnese, Quirk Books, 2009.
To The Finland Station, by Edmund Wilson, New York Review books 1940.
Patriotic Gore, by Edmund Wilson, Farrar, Straus and Giroux 1962

Biomimicry, Innovation Inspired by Nature, by Janine Benyus, HarperPerennial 1997.
Secrets of Native American Herbal Remedies, by Dr. Anthony Cichoke, Avery 2001.
Grassland, The History, Biology, Politics, and Promise of the American Prairie, by Richard Manning, Penquin Books 1995.
Eating Animals by Johnathan Safran Foer, Little, Brown & Company 2009.

ACKNOWLEDGEMENTS

In any undertaking, unsolicited words of encouragement are an immeasurable boost to your efforts. With writing, it is especially so since even the most acclaimed of books have divided opinions as to their enjoyment. Therefore you know that in the judgment given to what you've done, some will remain silent or look away. It is with the others that becomes the treasure—those who debate with you important messages woven into the fabric of the story, or share comments as "couldn't put it down", or "loved it", or "wow! in relation to a particular passage, or as one said "I found myself speed-reading to get to the next part".

Special thanks go to Dr. Cabot Jaffee, Wade Edwards and Leslie Fugleberg Lynch, who again read the manuscript with the objective of not only spelling and grammar, but also logic and flow and impression, providing a blueprint to follow in the editing process. The same goes for Chief Critic in Charge, my best friend Charley, with whom we're now to 56 years and counting.

Another thanks to Joe Lynch, Bob Werrbach and Doug Fugleberg, who assisted in guiding me through the many issues encountered with operating in the computer age.